S0-AEW-107

SIMON & SCHUSTER

A Comforting LIE

a novel

Linda Phillips Ashour

SIMON & SCHUSTER
Rockefeller Center
1230 Avenue of the Americas
New York, NY 10020

This book is a work of fiction. Names, characters, places, and incidents either are products of the author's imagination or are used fictitiously. Any resemblance to actual events or locales or persons, living or dead, is entirely coincidental.

Designed by Barbara M. Bachman
Manufactured in the United States of America

10 9 8 7 6 5 4 3 2 1

Library of Congress Cataloging-in-Publication Data
Ashour, Linda.
A comforting lie / Linda Phillips Ashour.
p. cm.
I. Title.
PS3551.S416C66 1999
813.54—dc21 99-18369 CIP
ISBN 0-684-81834-5

Acknowledgments

I owe much to Linda Upton, Susan Taylor Chehak, and Colleen Craig, faithful friends who have read various drafts of this book. Their comments and generosity have been invaluable.

Thanks to my longtime friend and gifted interior designer, Catherine Bailly Dunne, for decoding elements of her professional world.

I am grateful for my friends in the Lunch Group: Jo Giese, Yasmin Kafai, Dale Pring MacSweeney, Jo Ann Matyas, Luchita Mullican, Virginia Mullin, Maria Munroe, Doreen Nelson, Amanda Pope, Judith Searle, Carolyn See, Janet Sternburg, and Susan Suntree. Their stories have provided the real nourishment.

I thank Sarah Pinckney Whitmire for the early guidance and Marysue Rucci, my editor at Simon & Schuster, who guided this book through to completion. And thanks to my agent, B. J. Robbins, for the enthusiasm and persistence.

Finally, thanks to my children, Savannah and Chris, for the laughter and love.

For Bob

"It is love in your pursuit," he replied,

"but it does not know with whom it is dealing. . . .

Soon this music will be nothing but noise."

—Jean-François de Bastide, *La Petite Maison*

A *Comforting* LIE

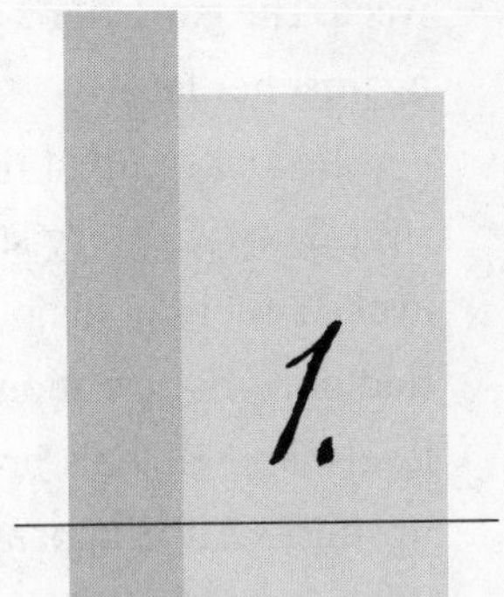

1.

The week had been nicked by gray mornings and a nasty, uncommon wind. It began teasingly, tossing a straw hat straight into the ocean, leaving a redheaded divorcée from Atlanta unhappily clutching the guardrail on a narrow dirt path. Hours later, an unsecured parasol flew up from a beach table, knocking over a heat lamp and a low picket fence.

The wind didn't stop there. A Chihuahua, slipping out the doggy door early the next morning, was sucked from the edge of its own yard to the beach below just before the wind began to die down. Puzzled gulls circled the fallen dog as the owner scrambled down the hillside, grabbing a heavy rock to clip a bird that was taking the first hesitant peck.

But Helen Patterson wasn't thinking of those things as she stood at the end of the narrow path. She watched the water skid in and out of the dark blue cove below and resented the rough invitation of the tide, the way it pulled at her wrists and arms. Her true home was here, on a high, protected cliff that no wave could disturb.

Helen had almost filled a large plastic sack with garden debris collected from the elaborate grounds behind her. She turned to cross the lawn, then dropped the heavy sack and cleared away a patch of thistle at the base of a stone fountain. Her cheeks reddened at the sight of the weed. The gardener's carelessness stung more than the slap of cold wind against her face.

She looked up at the gray stone building that housed Alice Nash Design. The two-story structure was a memory in miniature, designed to evoke sweet details of the French château where Alice and Jack Nash had once honeymooned. High, narrow windows looked out from both levels, and Helen's breathing slowed as she watched a light switch on upstairs. Alice appeared in a second-story window. From where she knelt in the grass, Helen could just see the bright scarf at her neck. Alice settled a client into a plump down chair, offered tea. Another light flipped on at the opposite end of the store.

The new girl was upstairs. The plastic sack bumped heavily against Helen's leg as she trudged up the middle of the walk. She frowned as something sharp poked her. The wind split her hair from the back and she imagined a stiff finger running down the crooked white line of scalp. So much had changed since Alice had taken the new girl on. Before the girl had been hired, Helen could slip away to the pleasing hidden room on the second floor, to the ceiling pitched and perfect with beige and white striped paper, a real fireplace just across from the footed tub. Since Patricia's arrival, the glossy door to that room was likely to be locked.

Helen sighed and pressed the garbage sack into the bin by the side of the building. She walked around to the front, checking the two tightly tended green squares that introduced the shop to the beach community that lay beyond. Lemon trees lined the path that led to the sidewalk. They were planted in plain clay pots that sometimes burst from the pressure of the roots.

Helen felt a thump of excitement inside her chest as she closed her hand over the brass knob at the entrance to the store. She stood for a moment imagining Jack and Alice, the way they must have looked on their approach to the country château where they would spend their first night together. A first night that would last the rest of their lives. Alice! Clever enough to want things early, right from the beginning of the marriage. Helen peered through the tall window, her breath smoking a round O of delight and desire onto the glass as she guessed how she might have sounded. Jack, I want that so much. Oh, would you? I wonder if we should take this, too. Alice sweeping through shop after Paris shop, making a purchase here, a purchase there with Jack only too happy to oblige.

Helen knew this version of things was imaginary, a comforting lie. She didn't like to think of how things really were. The zoning battles and the outraged cry that, for once, united commercial and residential interests in the sequestered coastal town. This isn't France. If that Nash woman is bound and determined to copy something, she ought to choose something that fits in. Helen knew how Alice toiled, hunting down elusive, one-of-a-kind items, scouted out remote resources, badgered and begged for names and addresses of suppliers. Helen knew Jack had borrowed on everything they owned to launch Alice's business venture and even that wasn't enough. He accepted a partnership in a bigger investment firm when he'd been all too content where he was. The store had succeeded wildly thanks to Alice's hard work and Jack's capital. Even so, Helen clung fast to part of her vision: Alice Nash Design was a honeymoon come true—a honeymoon of luxury and harmony that had never really ended.

She pushed through the front door into the greenhouse Alice filled with rustic dining tables set formally for ten or twelve. Fruit trees shivered near the windows as Helen firmly closed the door. Candles burned at a wide side table loaded with plants and herbs, racks of vintage wine subtly supporting the whole display. Helen breathed in the sharp, stinging smell of citrus and perfume, then tied a fallen strand of ivy back into place. Ivy wound through the candelabras. Ivy had even twisted its way toward the spiral staircase, startling customers who supposed it was plastic. The waxy green introduction to Alice Nash Design was all too real, slipping and slithering its way to the second floor. Helen nearly tripped over Poor, the sheepdog who snored at the bottom of the stairs. After Alice bought him, the clumsy, indolent dog was stepped on so often that his registered name soon vanished. He became Poor.

Helen made her way upstairs and felt her spirits rise as she climbed.

The polished wooden steps led straight into the master bedroom, and she paused there for a moment. How many times had she felt just this way, happy and jarred by the sudden intimacy? An ornate Italian bed stood in its center, claiming most of the space. Aubusson pillows were heaped at the head of the bed, and a satin comforter strewn with worn embroidered flowers lay in the center. The room was flirtatious and gay. A price tag dangled easily from the edge of a gilded mirror. It fluttered slightly in the breeze as Helen glanced at the small writing table with spindly wooden legs. Two ivory-colored chairs with needlepoint cushions stood to either side of the window facing the front garden. Even paying bills would be pretty and painless in a room like this. Helen paused over a heap of antique silk tassels that lay in a basket. She ran one lightly over her cheeks, then carefully returned it to the pile.

A greenhouse on the first floor and seven small rooms clustered directly above . . . which story told the true tale? Helen knew the impediments had been carefully designed. The tight, narrow climb to the second floor was meant to protect the real treasures from the merely curious. Though there were always exceptions, most serious clients stepped straight over Poor and tackled the steps without hesitation.

Helen moved down the hall. Her desk was tucked at one end of the long corridor. On her right two narrow sitting rooms faced the street; a formal dining room and a child's bedroom opened on the opposite side of the hall. There was even a small kitchen here. A bottle of Jack's favorite whiskey stood in the center of a handsome tray set for two with biscuits and cheeses. Jack and Alice. Alice and Jack. Their names filled Helen's mouth like a dense, complicated flavor.

Symmetry prevailed in these small, crowded rooms. Lovely pairs of lamps and chairs triumphed over clutter. Sunlight settled on rich fabric and bubbled hand-blown glass. Sounds were muted and hushed here, absorbed by beautiful things. Alice thickened the long hallway with heavy cushions and sofas. She set deep chairs that were good for resting before ottomans that were good for trays and teacups. Alice's polished desk sat inside a deep niche in the center of the hall. Helen and Alice often worked at their desks simultaneously, protecting their clients' privacy with ornate Chinese screens. A fire always burned in one of the sitting rooms during the winter months, and the sweet, drowsy smell of almond wood filled the upper floor.

"There you are!" Alice sounded happy. She sat with a slight, pale woman who jumped at the words.

"I got the mess up," Helen said.

"Which one?"

Alice could be so oblivious sometimes. Helen's lips lifted in a smile.

"The wind knocked over all the new plants I potted last week. None of the lacquered pots cracked."

"A miracle." Alice took the woman's hand in both of hers. "Helen, come meet Charlotte Ruskin. We're just getting to know each other."

When asked about design services, Alice cocked her head in genuine curiosity. A few good things are all you need. What about a little of this tea while we chat? She would lift the round of linen cloth from the top of an enormous glass jug, its crinkled edges weighted down with seashells, and drop a dipper into the spicy blend. Client interviews became interrogations about personal history, loves and hates. Memories from childhood that could be expanded into cheerful, soothing rooms. When there were no warm recollections, people sometimes broke down and wept. Helen wondered how Charlotte Ruskin would hold up under questioning.

Helen turned toward the little girl's bedroom. A telescope stood at attention by the window. A row of neat, child-sized garden tools lay side by side on a narrow bench, each end of which was weighted down by pots of red geraniums. Busy children were always (in Alice's mind) dirty children. Galoshes, red and yellow, lay heaped in an antique wooden wagon in one corner of the room. Helen pressed out a wrinkle in the area rug with the flat of her hand. Patricia came flying into the room and Helen winced, thinking of Poor, the sad, dumb obstacle he represented. What if Poor had been lying in the doorway?

"I'm going to lunch," Patricia said, pulling at the strap of her backpack.

Helen put one hand on her hip.

"*Can* I go to lunch?"

Helen nodded. "We'll talk about the late shipment when you get back."

Patricia was young, not that much older than Helen's own son, and a stray on top of it. She'd turned up last week with a pink patch of skin on her nose and Alice had said yes. The pink patch was toughening now, going the way of the rest of her skin. A thousand details must have distracted Alice Nash the day she hired Patricia.

The phone rang and Helen moved down the hall to answer. She smiled, hearing Elizabeth Adams Perkins introduce herself with a voice that trembled slightly. They had been doing business for a year, but Elizabeth never remembered. What she did remember was a set of silver dessert spoons she had seen on an oak sideboard. Her grandson was coming.

"I would need them by Friday. Neddy's birthday, you see."

Usually her secretary called. Or the nurse who pushed her into the store, setting her in the center of the greenhouse, the wheels of the chair crunching over the gravel. Elizabeth Adams Perkins sat erect, her back barely touched the wicker imported all the way from Indonesia. Hardly a wheelchair, it seemed a portable throne for a paper-thin princess. She waited quietly while Helen or Alice, if she was free, carted accessories to where she sat fingering the edge of a table or chair. Helen wondered what dessert Elizabeth would serve Neddy, what delicacy she could pull from her memory of meals.

Elizabeth mourned mealtimes, the array of things that one was obliged to eat, for they made her think of Arthur Adams Perkins, dead. Lying unfed and untroubled by meals in a family plot overlooking the San Diego harbor. She much preferred watching exotic birds. They swarmed her aviary, scaled the inside of the wire mesh walls with their curved beaks and claws. One of them had taken careful sidelong steps up Helen's arm on a visit to deliver throw pillows for Neddy, who was on his way down from "the university," as Elizabeth put it. "The university" was at Santa Barbara and Neddy barely noticed the throw pillows Elizabeth provided. Academic probation had gotten his attention instead.

Now when he retreated to La Jolla, to Grammy Liz, he shut himself away from all fun and trouble, arriving every other weekend with books and papers littering the inside of his trunk. Helen would sometimes see him in town, drinking mournfully and longing for shouts and beer, the rowdy joy of a keg party. There were no keggers in La Jolla, but there were dessert spoons.

"Wonderful news!" Elizabeth's voice was cheery, but fading. The energy it took for Neddy, for dessert. "Perhaps you should speak with my secretary now."

Helen and Elizabeth's secretary chatted for a moment, then Helen began to write up the order. Alice and Charlotte murmured behind the dark screen.

The store sat perched at the end of a busy street. Traffic snaked around the edge of Alice's property, then dropped down to the ocean boulevard below. The tall windows along the back wall upstairs carried the view inside, the dark pines that wound down to the cove, the smash of waves on rocks. From her desk, Helen could just see the top of Patricia's head as it plunged under water again. Helen watched her progress, the way her arms cut through the waves. The water was still choppy—Patricia shouldn't have gone out on a day like this. Helen might have spoken up, though that would have spoiled the secret for both of them. Patricia's daily swims were a delicious insult. Helen could taste it; salt rushed into her mouth as she watched.

Patricia couldn't think she knew, for who would brave the water in January? Her short hair, gelled in the morning, always returned gelled after lunch, and she never mentioned the current or the absence of swimmers in the rough water. She swam beyond protected areas. There was no one to call on for help where she swam. Helen looked down at her watch, then back out to Patricia. There, she cut in, made the turn that would bring her back just on time. She hadn't been late yet.

Helen heard a light cough and turned her head slowly. She preferred watching Patricia swim all the way in. She swam faster on the return, cutting along the top of the water with fast, messy chops.

A man stood over a club chair. He ran his hand down one side of the smooth brown leather and Helen felt something hot pass quickly over the surface of her skin. The corners of the man's eyes turned down slightly, and their color made her think of the small amber stone she had pried from her mother's favorite brooch when she was a little girl. She would rub the pretty stone against her cheek before falling asleep. Where was it now? The wind had raked through his hair. He sat down, the seat cushion sighing softly as he did, and stretched his legs out in front, planting both hands on his thighs. He smiled at Helen and leaned back in the chair, letting his hands open over the rounded arms.

"Pretty good fit."

His toddler ran up and down the long hall, darting into the bedroom and emerging with a pair of mismatched galoshes. The child was excited, staggering toward the brightest brass tray or Poor, who had successfully lumbered up the stairs. The picture pleased Helen. The two of them made the upstairs look whole and complete. A real story in a real home. But then the baby seemed to run off course after a moment, losing sight of bookshelves to ransack, baskets to upset, and tassels to pull. He began to waddle too fast for his fat legs, guidance system all awry. Helen saw he was falling forward as his mother stood with her back turned, lost in fabric samples. His father moved toward the baby whose plump hands waggled in the air, reaching out to hug a table leg. He was almost there, quick enough to brace his child from a bad fall.

He arrived an instant too late, the baby shrieking as the edge of the table struck him above the eye. The man bent down on one knee, his back still straight, and drew him close. He kissed him softly where it hurt. Eyes, ears. There you go. Better? He rocked back and forth on his heels, whispering to the boy as he curled up in his lap.

Helen ran to get ice, padded it inside a velvet swatch. The baby wailed, but the cries were wearing down into wet little gasps. His chin was turned into his father's chest by the time Helen got back. The mother watched the scene, then took the ice quickly from Helen.

"May I?" She asked with a faint smile. The man passed her their son, tucking the end of his shirt back down into his pants. Sniffs, then the ice Helen offered was shoved away decidedly.

"Good thing it didn't break the skin," the man said, pushing his hair out of his eyes. Thick, rowdy hair teased the straight angles of his face.

Helen heard the door open below. It was Patricia, back from the water.

"My son's certainly taken a shine to you," the mother said, her baby squirming in her arms, stretching out his pudgy hands again. The search for the table leg had been abandoned; the baby reached out for something else now. They weren't a family? Helen's smile faded. The ice was beginning to drip through her fingers. Humiliation pushed color up into the mother's cheeks and over the tops of her arms.

"Quick question for you," the mother said to Helen. "How soon can I have a special order on this?" The baby's struggles were genuine, he wanted freedom. He pulled the collar of her dress, stretching it down beyond a comfortable point until Helen could see the white cup of her bra.

"Zachary!"

They discussed slipcovers as Helen struggled to straighten the picture in her mind. The man was not the father, and yet the baby cried on and on, wanting him. Patricia had skipped up the stairs and was heading for the bathroom, the back of her calf showing a strand of seaweed. Colorfast, yes. Yardage, price . . . the woman had to speak louder and louder. Her baby sobbed as the man made his way back down the steps. Helen watched him through the front bedroom window as he turned down the corner of the street. He would probably disappear into one of the small shops that spread out below Alice Nash Design. The shops sold starfish and wind chimes, books on air and the movement of light. Tourists ambled about in the shady passages connecting the shops and restaurants. They rooted about for treasures to take home as if they were snuffling the floor of a forest that bloomed with truffles.

"Down!"

The baby wiggled free from his mother's arms and swayed at the top of the steps. Blind to danger, he insisted on making his wobbly way to the first floor without help. Helen led the way through the fragrant greenhouse, then held the front door open for the woman and her unhappy child. The woman strode to the street with his hand squeezed inside hers. She strapped the little boy into a car seat and jammed a cookie into his clenched fist.

"Want!" The baby complained.

"All gone," his mother answered. "No more man."

The wind still blew, but it lacked conviction. The tops of trees shifted heavily and bushes trembled now and then. Papers rustled in a wire trash can and a plastic cup toppled from the curb to the street. Whitecaps near the shore were disappearing, as if plucked from the water by a strong, sure hand.

2.

The hem of Patricia's dress was scalloped, creamy and smooth as potatoes in a pan. When she bent over to look for a file, its short edge looked demure.

"Your son called," Patricia said, looking up quickly.

"When?" Helen realized she still held the velvet patch in her hand. It was sopping.

"Must have been around ten."

"He called from school?" Helen's voice was panicky. Maybe he was sick. Or in trouble. Maybe there was a bus strike and he couldn't get to work.

"He said it wasn't important, though."

"I'd like to have my messages on time," Helen said.

Patricia shifted papers, sighed. "Helen, how about if I clean up these files? That would be good, wouldn't it?"

Patricia's things were inside a painted wood cupboard. If Helen opened the doors, she knew what she would find. Her red canvas backpack, the ends of the straps flipping with age, the suede worn down on the bottom. It must have carried schoolbooks at one time, now it held whatever cheap novels or cheap food Patricia consumed, brought into the store from the apartment she shared in Pacific Beach with three other girls. She claimed to have been a vegetarian in high school. When she began living on her own, she discovered the high price of fresh fruit and vegetables. She returned to pork chops and poultry grudgingly, buying cellophaned value packages of each when it was her turn to shop. My roommates want me to eat *hash,* she hissed once to Helen. Do you believe that?

"As long as you call Andrea Rhodes before three," Helen answered.

"I left her a message." Patricia shrugged as she said it.

"Then try her again," Helen said. She didn't want to call Andrea Rhodes, either. She didn't want to hear the excuses for delayed textile shipments, the brisk, clipped British accent that implied order and failed to produce it.

"How old is he, again?" Patricia stood up straight. She rubbed a shoulder and moved it in slow circles, the curved hem of her dress sliding up and down as she did.

"Who?"

"Your son."

"Fifteen." Helen lightly touched the top of her hand. She'd skinned the knuckles picking up trash.

"He sounds so mature on the phone. Guess he'll be driving soon." Patricia's eyes wandered up the side of Helen's bare arm. Helen felt them as they inched forward, sharp as claws, every movement as measurable as those of Elizabeth Adams Perkins's birds.

"Scared?"

"No," Helen answered too fast and thought of Lang, how he would soon be opening up a can of tuna fish or finding a piece of ham to slide inside a hamburger bun. He used to oversleep, slamming his hand over the clock he had next to his bed. She'd settled that when she bought a different sort of clock at a trade fair. Standing in the middle of the convention center in Los Angeles, without Alice, without a clear view of the ocean or the rooms that caught every draft of clean wind that rose from the water, Helen had lost her balance for a moment. She had settled on the clock quickly, talked the vendor into accepting cash. A raunchy recorded message guaranteed that even the heaviest sleeper would eventually wake up. Lang's pleasure at the inappropriate gift embarrassed Helen as much as her own decision to buy it had.

Helen heard the crunch of gravel downstairs and smirked as Patricia dashed off to greet the customers. Patricia wasn't that different from Lang, putting off all the unpleasant chores. Procrastinating. Helen reached for her pen, comforted by the feel of her own engraved initials. It was a burgundy Montblanc, the first gift Alice had ever given her. She tilted her head slightly and began to write out a note to Elizabeth Adams Perkins. Personal notes to their best clients . . . Alice had thought it was a wonderful idea. She was appalled at not having thought of it first. The voices behind the screen lifted slightly.

"Before we begin even thinking about that room, I've got to know what it is you love."

"Love? Well, I'm not sure I could say exactly. But there is this funny shade of green . . ."

"Good. That's a start."

"Actually, if I could just bring in these petit point cushions my mother made for my sister and me—"

"Now we're on to something, Charlotte."

Alice's tastes were classic and simple. She believed in horses and sunlight. She held that certain places on earth lent their grace to the people inhabiting them and the objects they made. Some of her ideas were inviolable, beyond discussion. Beds should be dressed up as beautifully as men and women, and children should have telescopes instead of telephones. Women ought to destroy the tyranny of mirrors and dressing rooms with lengths of fabric that could be raised and lowered over their own reflections like iridescent curtains. Alice Nash Design furnished these notions and others, stocked them with proper lamps and comfortable sofas. German storybooks for sleepers of all ages lay open on night tables for the sake of their illustrations. English riding boots stood erect and empty by the front door. Alice Nash Design carried one pair in every size.

Patricia laughed. Her voice rang on the steps and Helen felt relief. Probably tourists, the kind Helen had less and less patience with. Patricia seemed to consider it a game, feigning interest in their hometowns, the drought or the rainfall, the monotony that had driven them to La Jolla in the first place. She sat them down in a creaky wicker chair near the supply room while they wrote out checks for scarves and shawls they would never wear back home or packages of paper napkins so expensive they would press wrinkles out under phone books and use the same one more than once, hoping friends wouldn't notice. Patricia pressed mint and lemon pastilles on them as she led them to the front door, making them promise to return on their next visit. She probably had six or seven women from Omaha nibbling out of the palm of her hand right now, content as Elizabeth's birds. Helen turned her head to say hello.

"Voilà, mesdames." Patricia spoke to the women, then motioned to a low chair by the window. "Faites comme chez vous."

Two tall, slim women entered the bedroom. The first woman, who wore her hair in a low ponytail held in place with a bow, was dressed in a dark knit suit and stockings. She accepted the seat by the window and sat waiting for her friend, apparently uninterested in the store or Helen, who gave her a bright smile that went unreturned. The other woman hurried through the rooms in jeans and a trim, gold-buttoned cardigan. She exclaimed over the view of the ocean and the vision of Poor, who was limping to her side. His tail knocked at the branches of a fern and he wagged his wet, loose jowls to her continued delight. Patricia flailed her arms in the air as she spoke, her words like high, tinkling musical notes played in an impossible key. Helen blinked at this version of Patricia. It didn't make sense—but it did bring the first woman to life. She rose to follow Patricia, whose voice fluttered and fell over familiar surfaces like shiny new fabric. Helen slid her tongue quickly over the edge of the envelope and slapped on a stamp. The angel was crooked, but it didn't matter. Elizabeth Adams Perkins didn't open her own mail.

"Whew. Parisians." Patricia leaned into her desk once the two women were gone. She scratched some rough skin on her elbow.

"You should put some cream on that before it gets worse. Did you sell them one of those candles?" Helen asked. They were expensive. Alice had grabbed up the licensing before anyone else. A family-owned business in the Antilles had found an unusual way of weaving shapes of leaves and flowers along the sides of fragrant wax blocks. They continued to look and smell real even as the garden burned.

"Uh-huh. They want them shipped."

"How many?"

"A couple dozen. Cool, huh?"

They were two hundred dollars each.

"Yes. Cool," Helen's voice was level.

"Guess I'll box them up now?"

It was an apology for being abrupt about lunch. Turning a statement into a question meant deference. Lang did that, too.

"Fine." Helen looked for an address book that must have slid to the back of the drawer. "Why do you think they were from Paris?"

"Oh, you know."

She didn't. Helen didn't know at all. She was getting hungry, even though she didn't know what it was exactly she wanted to eat.

"Their accents. Their attitude. It's fun to speak French, though. I miss it."

Helen stared at the top of her desk. She tried to imagine missing a language and cleared her throat loudly. She would eat a Japanese pear apple for her lunch. They were in season now. Expensive, but worth it. Then a big slice of ripe, runny cheese and crisp bread. She'd drive all the way over to Feydus to get it. Patricia suddenly pointed her toe.

"I can't wait to go back."

"Go back where?"

Patricia giggled and Helen thought of Lang's smile. She hadn't seen it for so long and it was probably all because of that chipped tooth. A chipped tooth was nothing when you thought of it. Even so, she would figure out a way to take care of it soon.

"To France. French was my major. I studied in Provence."

Helen thought of the bleak community college she had attended, the business and accounting courses with endless columns of figures. She remembered the girl with a thin, pointy face who had tried to be her friend.

"Have you eaten?" Patricia asked.

Helen shook her head no and looked at the hem on Patricia's skirt. It seemed shorter than before. Patricia's nipples poked rudely at her dress, rose like goose bumps. Helen thought of Patricia's wet bathing suit, pictured it wrapped up inside a towel at the bottom of that red backpack. She must have worn her bathing suit under her clothing in the morning. She must have slipped out of the suit in a public bathroom. Peeled it off fast, rolled it up, and hidden it away along with what she supposed was the secret of her swim. Didn't she feel embarrassment standing there like that? Helen wondered. What on earth had happened to modesty?

"You work too hard, Helen," Patricia said flatly.

Helen thought of her out in the water, well beyond the caves, past all the careful, competent swimmers who measured their strokes and diminishing strength. It was Patricia who was working hard, making each and every movement count.

"Keep an eye on things while I'm gone."

Helen caught herself just in time. She'd almost added a question mark of her own.

3.

The smell of fresh bread saturated one end of town, but Helen drove past Feydus without stopping, turning instead down Spindrift Drive to The Beach Club. She thought of the menu in the formal dining room with a mixture of dread and envy.

The club, occupying what was once a cow pasture prone to flooding at high tide, lay along a prized length of La Jolla shoreline. The low, red-brick buildings housed swimming pools and tennis courts, as well as apartments and dining facilities, for members. History of the pond lying just beyond the parking lot was taken casually, as were most things there. The area had been dredged in the 1920s, and ducks now paddled quietly over the dreams of the original investors. A thousand-foot sea-wall shielded members from floods and misfortunes of any kind.

Helen sat with her ankles hidden under the long, white tablecloth. Legs locked together and hooked under the rung of her chair, she sat straight-backed at the center of the dining room, lifting bites of lobster thermidor from a thin pastry cup. Food in The Grill had continued unchanged since the death of the old chef, even though his passing had caused a flurry of hope among younger club members. There were enough fans of hard sauce and lurid, flavored gelées to keep the dead chef's menu intact well after he ceased to be. Though the food was heavy, conversation in The Grill could still be frothy and light.

"Would you care to know my secret?" the woman at the next table asked. "I simply dabble until I get to the voilà moment."

Helen looked over her shoulder and saw no one. It was late for lunch.

"I'm speaking to you and I'm speaking of painting, but it's the same thing with men, dear. You dabble until you hit the right one."

Helen found it hard to swallow her food as she thought of the man in the store. It had happened so fast. What had she said? She couldn't remember. She cut a sliver of pâté, using too much force, and set it on a butter plate. It would go untouched for the rest of the meal, as so much of the food in The Grill did. The older woman had brilliant red hair. It was cut severely, then weighted down with glossy spray. Her face barely moved as words tumbled over words. She had no frown lines. Helen wondered if dabbling chased them all away. She wiped at the corner of her mouth and smiled.

"I've had the advantage of living long and living well. I am seventy-five years old today."

"I would never guess that." Helen thought of ordering champagne. A birthday toast—why not? Alice wouldn't mind.

"Then you're not a terribly good observer." She gestured with her left hand, waving each statement to a close with a twist of three metals, sprinkled with sapphires. "Working girl?"

She had spotted the briefcase. It was stuffed with design magazines. Helen loved to leaf through them over meals.

"Yes."

"Are you a new member here?" The woman's voice shook slightly. "Or just visiting over the summer?"

"Neither. I'm a guest of—"

"You're my guest now. I like to drink from a full glass and I like to boss people on my birthday. You'll indulge me, won't you?"

The woman took tiny bites, then chewed furiously. She must have chewed until there was nothing left in her mouth. Helen tried not to stare as she waited for the invitation to join the old woman. The invitation was not forthcoming.

"What a lovely woman you are. Terribly serious, I would guess. Does that bear results?" The woman had lips that kissed without a partner. She held them tightly pressed together.

"Sometimes."

Helen sipped from her water glass and wondered why she didn't feel offended. She didn't. She wanted to know about a life probably more tangled than the golden bands on the woman's left hand.

"May I ask what you meant about dabbling?"

"I meant a stroke here, a stroke there, put down without the horrible earnestness I see today. That is art. That is also living. Young people refuse to understand how this can be."

Helen thought of Alice, exceptional Alice.

"And the voilà moment?"

Helen folded her hands in her lap.

"My goodness, I hope you don't have to do a *great* deal of observation in your work. Why, it's the moment of completion. The moment of full and perfect understanding."

The waiter winked at Helen and rolled a serving cart to the table taking care not to disturb the small cake and burning candles, then spoke with the old woman in a low voice. The woman leaned forward with a tremulous smile and turned the kissing lips to the matter of the moment. She didn't stop until every candle was extinguished. The waiter (what was his name?) brought Helen her slice of chalky chocolate cake and a glass of champagne. She lifted her glass to her hostess, who studied her face in a golden compact mirror.

"To many more," Helen said.

"And if I don't want them? What then, my dear?"

She offered Helen the last vacant kiss as she left the dining room on the arm of her driver. Helen watched him help her into a burgundy Town Car that smoked as it pulled away from the club. She rinsed the taste of the cake away with the last of her glass of champagne and pushed her plate to the other edge of the table. She got a pen from her bag and started on her stack of magazines. She liked to bring in new ideas for the store. She bent over the magazine to look at something more closely, and smiled at the photograph. A staunch, round weaver from Oklahoma stood beside her loom with rough, red arms folded across her chest. The lush textiles contrasted her homeliness. Helen marked the page just as the waiter reappeared. She wrote Hollis Ryan's name out in bold block letters, adding notes she would go over with Alice.

"Would you care for anything else, Helen? More coffee?"

"Please."

He could have been a young forty or an old twenty-eight. He smelled stale; it must have been the food wearing off on his jacket. She didn't remember him ever calling her Helen before. He slipped the check under her salad plate.

"It was nice of you to treat old Mrs. Talley to a birthday lunch. She's awful lonely. It was nice of Mrs. Nash, I should say."

Helen's smile spread as slowly as her own understanding. She put her chin in her hands. The voilà moment came to over seventy-five dollars with the tip. Mrs. Talley's taste in champagne was impeccable.

"That must be so great."

"What?" She watched his hand as he poured her coffee. It wasn't as clean as it should have been and she thought of that notice posted in cheap restaurants. ALL EMPLOYEES MUST WASH THEIR HANDS BEFORE LEAVING.

"Eating for free."

A little of the coffee splattered onto the cloth. She covered it with her napkin when he apologized and stared straight ahead. He asked if there was anything else she wanted and she shook her head no.

Coffee cooled in Helen's cup. The sun settled on her shoulders and the top of her head, but she still felt chilled as she lingered in the room. She could see him through the kitchen door. He horsed around with the cook, slapping at him with a towel. He was vulgar. He'd talked himself into believing he was a member here, that he could chat it up with whoever he pleased. She could imagine his apartment house, the loud music, the girls. Girls like Patricia, who wandered in without knocking.

The pace picked up inside the dining room and inside Helen. The Grill bustled with an unexpected second seating. Fathers and sons, grandfathers. The dining room became a meeting room, a boardroom for the business of family life. Trinity uniforms appeared. The prep school required dark red ties, gray jackets. The room filled with drab tones suited to the unsmiling tier of boys who ordered lemonades and Orangina, peered at their fathers through the bottom of a dirty glass as they their tongues swabbed out the very last drop. Four o'clock. The boys brushed away cookie crumbs, yawned, and frowned at their book bags. The grown men swallowed scotch, wound up phone conversations or strained explanations of the Pythagorean theorem. What would Mrs. Talley make of their seriousness? Or Helen's own?

Helen took the long way back to the parking lot, walking past the apartment where she and Lang had lived two years ago when she left Boyd. Alice and Jack leased it year-round, keeping it open for friends and relatives. When Jack had heard of her troubles, he insisted they live there. You'll stay at the club. He'd said it so easily, as if she and Lang had just dropped in for a visit themselves. He'd made them promise to stay for at least a month, until she found an apartment. Alice is just sick over this, he kept saying, making his priorities clear. Helen's predicament became one more problem for Alice, and much of Jack's energy was spent eliminating those problems. Thinking back now, Helen was glad for his clumsiness, his failure to recognize that it was her own life that had fallen to pieces. It would have been too easy to confuse kindness with something else back then. Jack had made perfect sense when nothing else did.

Helen rubbed her hand along her neck and stood beside the palm tree that framed the wide bay window above. No one was there to admire or enjoy the empty rooms. The fabric was fading in the sunlight, all the color bleeding away, because Alice didn't like lowering the blinds. Helen peeked through the window, the muscles in her calves stretched long and hard. There, they were still there. The row of shells above the fireplace seemed like glossy, listening ears. They listened as closely as she did to the drag of the waves as they ran up over the sand, the children's cries down by the water's edge. Helen felt her worries peel away one by one.

It had been that way then, every morning a gift of sea and sound and smell. Helen had chosen Alice and Jack's bedroom. Their wide bed dominated the room with fat, firm pillows and Sea Island sheets made from cotton grown in the West Indies. The air in the Indies must have been so gentle . . . she had felt the softness of the bedding coat her legs like lotion. She would wake before Lang, who took the guest room down the hall. He talked incessantly when he slept and, rather than try to decipher the stream of fuzzy words, she would curl into a warm ball and listen to the seals barking outside her window. She had often thought about Alice and Jack, letting her hand slip between her knees as she did.

A blue rosette lay on a night table at the edge of the bed. An equestrian award, it was a reminder of another time, a childhood that Alice dismissed with a wave of her long, narrow hand. Helen understood what the prize implied. Alice, with her steady gray eyes and strong back, was a thoroughbred herself. Helen had touched her face with the ends of the show ribbon, wondering what else there was to do with such an important memento. She lifted her arms in a stretch. She lay the award above her breast like a corsage.

Alice had eventually lost interest in winning first prizes. When she did, she then pressed forward in a great hurry toward contests of a different sort. She won merit scholarships and design awards, brought them home for her aging parents to praise. Later, Alice met Jack, another handsome trophy to present to her hopeful mother and the gruff Scotsman who cherished the two women in his life.

Photographs of champion tennis players lined one long wall of the apartment. Helen would wander about in the early morning before work, bathrobe cinched tight, to study every player and wipe off a smudge that clouded the glass. The pictures recorded every singles champion at the Beach Club since the forties. Jack's father and grandfather were both featured, though Helen's favorite was an unnamed champion who had won for six straight years. She liked the rogue she saw in him, the nonchalant tip of the trophy on his knee, as if winning was beside the point. She couldn't read his name on the faded photo, but the blurry figure reminded her of Lang, the way he posed for wrestling photographs. He never lined up like the others. He always had his eyes off center, his hands open and relaxed while other boys held theirs in nervous fists.

Helen relived those mornings as she stood below the window. The sun was burning off the fog, but it was a slow task. There were few people on the beach, just parents of children impervious to the chilly air. Helen stepped quickly out of her shoes to stand on the low concrete wall in front of the apartment. She felt secured by the scrape of sand under her bare feet. She wouldn't slip. Nothing could make her fall. She could look all the way through the apartment, tunneling through the living room to the kitchen that looked onto Spindrift.

Alice and Helen had sat by the pool before the painful move to the plain little house on Feldspar. They had stayed well out of the way of splashers and lifeguards and young beauties flipping themselves for even tans. Alice watched them for a moment, then turned her head to appraise Helen.

"You're as pretty as they are, you know." Alice's eyes rested on Helen's face as if it were a piece of fine art.

Helen laughed. She had soft, full cheeks that seemed to hide stores of chewy candy, large brown eyes, and a lavish mouth. A deeply clefted chin that her mother had always found handy, laying a finger in the deep space and saying, Look at me, honey, bringing Helen's attention back to where it should have been all along.

"Don't laugh. You'll have to put your good looks to good use."

"What do you mean?"

"*You* know." Alice's hand lay on the table. It flipped over as suddenly as a tanning girl. "I mean you're going to have to track down some interesting men."

Lang was fourteen then. His wrestling had received serious attention, and Helen's appearance at matches was important. The coach had phoned and said so. The men at the matches were excessive. They raged at their sons. They sometimes cried or hugged them too hard when they came off the mat. Boyd did neither. He had managed to miss every match that year. Helen took a moment to collect her thoughts.

"Sounds pretty complicated." She paused.

"It doesn't have to be. You could start here." Alice raised her hand to wave at a client. "This place is packed with men."

Alice's face looked rosy and moist, as if she'd just stepped from the shower. Her thick blond hair was tied back. It swung from side to side as she talked. Helen had known girls like Alice in high school. They'd been her best friends; they'd grazed on the same field of popular boys until she'd gone to live with the aunts. The girls in that place seemed dull. Their talk was as flat and colorless as the land where they lived. Meeting Alice for the first time had been like finding her best friends again.

"Jack grew up on these courts, you know. The first time they handed him a racket, he fell down just trying to hold it steady. Or so the legend goes."

He hadn't fallen down since, Helen thought. And neither had Alice. Helen kept her eyes on the deep end of the pool, watching as a man bubbled to the surface. He sputtered, then latched on to the side of the pool with his elbows. He said something to one of the suntanned girls. Helen looked at Alice and raised her eyebrows.

"I've got an idea!" Alice's voice was loud. "You'll come lunch here once a week on me. You can eat here or at The Grill. It doesn't matter."

"Alice!" Helen sounded surprised.

"Promise to pay attention, though." Alice's expression darkened. "Some of them are summer people."

Just mentioning summer renters and out-of-state owners made Alice's mouth twist with condescension.

"That's awfully generous." Helen forced herself to say it. They both understood that she was underpaid. Alice thought unconventional compensation was more "fun" than a dull salary increase. The I.R.S. would pounce on a paycheck. But not on a month's residence at the Club. And not (apparently) on lunches at The Grill.

"Pooh. I couldn't run my store or my life without you. Now that that's settled, I can relax." Alice sipped her drink eagerly. "Has Boyd stopped by at all?"

"Sometimes. To pick Lang up," Helen answered. He came by more than sometimes, and mostly at night.

"Why do you ask?" Helen sounded rude, but she didn't like thinking about the big gash in his car, the one on the driver's side, and the way his surfboard was always strapped to the top of the roof.

"Helen, I've been good for a whole month! Even *Jack* says so." Alice lifted a cocktail napkin and peered underneath, as if something were hiding below the sharp green edge. "But now I have to know or I'll die."

"Oh, don't die!" Helen mimicked her silly tone, trying to push away the terror she felt.

"Tell me why you left such a fun, handsome man and I won't have to."

For a moment she had weighed caving in once and for all. Helen imagined the sharp thrill of sharing secrets with Alice. What if she let down her guard and treated Alice as if she were a true friend? But then Alice began to twitch and the familiar impatience restored reality. She gave Alice too much credit sometimes. Fun. Handsome. What did either of those things have to do with a good life, a life you could count on?

"Because he still *surfs*. Because he's a big, overgrown kid."

Alice didn't look pleased at hearing this.

"He gave you a child." She still didn't look pleased. Or puzzled. Alice looked angry.

"Gave me a child?" Helen's face burned. She thought of Lang's night sweats when he was a baby and her own, the doctor's promise that he would grow out of them. She thought of his broken hand and his sobs as he tried to lift it, and how he had stopped sobbing, stopped crying altogether, so that it seemed to her . . . she rubbed the top of her arm. Had Alice gotten children mixed up with presents? "We had a child together, Alice. I stayed home for seven years to raise Lang, who's managed to grow up quite nicely."

"And Boyd didn't."

Now Alice finally understood what Helen had been up against for nearly twenty years. His failed business schemes and real estate deals, her office jobs and bank jobs, none of it coming together. Boyd's residuals had thrilled them when they were young and living at the beach. But, more than ten years later, Boyd still lived at the beach while Helen had moved on.

"Once a child actor, always a child actor."

"I know you'll hate me for saying this, but I adore those old reruns," Alice said. "Ask Jack."

The Langleys at Sea was a sitcom that still haunted Boyd Patterson. As actor Boy Patterson, he had played the youngest member of a seafaring family. Baby overboard! The frightened Langleys would rush to a corner of the deck to find the baby gaily bobbing on the surface of the water at the end of each show. Baby overboard! He got fewer crank calls every year . . . his audience was dying off.

"All right. Boy never quite became Boyd. Now, what about you?" Alice pulled her shawl over her shoulders. Her eyes flattened . . . she looked like a silky cat who was used to being stroked.

"But you already know," Helen said.

"Tell me again."

"When Lang got older I went back to work in offices. Things like that." She slid an olive into her mouth and chewed slowly, making it last. "Then I got tired of being an assistant manager in a bank."

"It took you a *long* time to get tired of that." Alice tilted her head and smirked.

Helen thought of her old time card, announcements of structured pay increases and the doughnut that always followed. She remembered the manager's bald spot, the way it grew larger every year.

"Then I took a design course that got me the best job I've ever had."

"I love you, Helen. I love that you think that."

Alice smiled. She was playful again. She covered the lower half of her face with the shawl. The disguise was their shorthand for the Saudi princess who came to the store at least once a week, whose young sons took turns stoning each other in Alice's garden.

"I didn't hire you because of that silly course. I hired you despite it." She used the princess's accent.

"What do you mean?"

"I hired you because you understand beauty." Alice's accent deepened. Helen could barely understand what she said. "And because you *crave* beautiful things for yourself. I plan to capitalize on that appetite of yours, Helen."

"Hey, lady. You're going to fall."

Helen had nearly slipped on memory. She snapped back to the present, to the small boy below her with a metal toy truck in his hand. Something brown was smeared all over his mouth.

"You're not supposed to be up there." He said it with an authority she hated. She felt like pinching his freckled face.

"Oh, yes I am. This is *exactly* where I'm supposed to be."

His parents were making their way down the sidewalk, walking arm in arm. She couldn't hear the slap of their sandals yet, but she would. The little boy ran toward them to tell.

Helen stepped back into her shoes. She thought of the design course she had taken at home, the listen-and-learn tapes, homework on color planning and wall and window treatment that she mailed to a post-office box in New York. And the ad, a photo of a woman a bit older than

Helen. *Me a decorator? I love it!* Helen sniffed loudly as she passed the parents who were as spotty as their little boy. Helen was no intruder here—she was an invited guest in a world almost too lovely to bear. Other worlds waited for her, too, worlds she could barely envision.

"Provence." She said it once, inside her car. Just whispering the word felt wonderful.

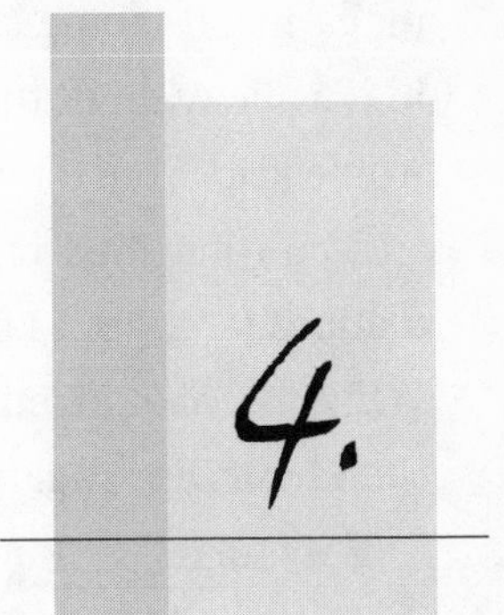

Helen opened a cupboard and thought again of the man in the store, the easy way he had slipped into that leather club chair. She threw a dish towel at a moth that flew out from behind the neat row of containers. The house was infested with them. Even though she was fastidious about crackers and cereals, moving everything into glass canisters as soon as the boxes were opened, the colony of moths managed to prosper. She complained endlessly to the landlord, who would send out an exterminator, never the same man, never from the same company, but each one evasive about the moths. What did they live on? What were these men spraying her cabinets and cupboards with, exactly? Why did the moths always come back? The bug men settled masks over their faces and bent over nooks and crannies, bumping the metal canisters along each time they sprayed another spot. Their vague, muttered answers made her think of the aunts, the way they would never answer her questions. Helen would get angry at the bug men, her big eyes blinking back tears in a kitchen slowly filling with dangerous fumes.

She trapped the moth inside a bit of paper towel and with one motion wiped up the dust it left on the floor. She squeezed the wadded towel quickly, made a note to call the landlord again and took a last look around the kitchen. No crumbs, no spills. The bugs weren't her fault.

Lang, under headsets, was oblivious to her. He was leafing through a magazine, listening to music, and turning on the television every once in a while without the sound. He'd been picking at his skin again. If he would keep from touching his face, everything would be fine.

The room had one plump chair that stood beside one crookneck reading lamp and Lang wasn't reading—he was looking at pictures. While listening to music. And glancing at the television. She slapped *Architectural Digest* against the side of her leg.

"My turn."

He glared at her and looked down at his magazine.

"Up."

He heaved himself to a stand, dropping his headsets in the middle of the chair so she would have to move them. He turned off the television and tossed the magazine into a basket on the floor.

"When I have a kid . . ."

"Tell me, Lang."

Helen sat and stretched her long, tired legs. Alice always accused her of protecting Lang too much, but she was dead wrong. Helen thought of the man in the store, the way he had nuzzled the little boy, protected *him,* she thought defensively. Sometimes Lang told her what he was going to do when he grew up. Not work, not that yet. But who he was going to be. What stories he would make up for his children, the games he would play. She would sometimes drift off as he described those peaceful games, the way he would one day teach his son to roll a rubber ball between two paper plates set way, way apart. Lang would gradually narrow the distance between the plates until he could remove one and have his son roll a ball directly over the round white disc. A ball and two paper plates. I WON'T EVEN HAVE TO BE RICH TO BE A GOOD DAD! That would wake Helen up, bring her back from plush dreams.

"Changed my mind. I'm not having kids."

He started to stomp off to his room.

"Honey, wait. I'm sorry. Let me help you."

She didn't need to be more specific. Lang lay down on the campaign bed in the living room and she went to get a washcloth. The bed was a find. The delicacy in the slender wrought iron curves was deceiving. The narrow bed could have supported her weight along with his, though she didn't test its capacity now. She sat on a low ottoman, pressing a terry cloth square over the cyst on his face.

"Ow."

"Serves you right. Remember what I told you? You were supposed to ice this right away."

"That never works. This doesn't, either."

She leaned over to kiss him.

"This does."

He was going to allow the kiss this time. She let her lips linger on his cheek, surprised and happy. His skin was soft here. There was no acne to disturb the smooth white surface. She thought of what a lucky boy he was. Once she imagined her mother's lips softly striking her own cheek in a kiss, but the firm, velvet knock had been a monarch butterfly that bounced from Helen to the top of a hedge.

Her parents had died when she was fifteen, the same age as Lang was now. Great walkers, examiners in every sort of weather, they yearned to see the desert in the moonlight. They had died in Arizona, on a vacation their teenage daughter had declined to take. Their bodies were brought up together from the bottom of a box canyon. The canyon was dry by then, the stones shining and reassembled by a flash flood. A burro was found languourously propped against a boulder, as if it had been scratching its hide. Helen's parents had made it to the limb of a tamarisk bush when the water came at them. They had wandered through that stony place several times, had the chance to study the look of things, their hands clasped while they wandered deeper and deeper into the narrow, rocky cut that finally claimed them. A letter mailed home said so. Oh, Helen, why be so obstinate? Think of all you could sketch. A long list followed, filled with the flora and fauna that cost them their lives.

Helen went to live with the yellowish aunts in the Midwest. They fed her, gave up narrow upstairs bedrooms or garage apartments during college and were kind. Both women spoke of the accident rarely and what they said was uttered softly, with their backs turned or their faces averted, so Helen missed the meaning of her parents' death, if her aunts had ever mentioned it. That their romance ended so brutally suggested that all romance did the same. But these conclusions were decidedly reversed by Alice and Jack Nash. It had been Alice and Jack, not Boyd, who introduced her to the sort of love that could retrieve lost beauty and pleasure. The sort of love that could triumph over death.

The living room mollified the California sun with its putty-colored walls and painted wooden floors. Helen's chairs stood around the long window seat that had been built to follow the same jutting angle as the three drafty panes of glass. The chairs were all different styles and the way they looked made Helen think of introducing them to one another as if they were shy, singular guests at a party. These chairs, and everything else in the room, were upholstered in a shade of white. Dark-brown wooden legs, a green bud about to unfurl into fern under streaming sun, any point of color, in fact, became remarkable in this room smooth and polished as an egg.

The edge of Lang's T-shirt was stained red and Helen thought of how she would wash it. Blood was easy enough if you caught it right away, but you had to be fast. She looked at the rest of his T-shirt, the way Lang's belly moved. Helen watched with alarm as it blew up into a big round swell and settled down again.

"Lang?" She lifted the edge of the washcloth, ready to run hot water over it again. He didn't move his head. Maybe he was asleep.

"Mmmm?"

"Did you make yourself something good for lunch?"

"Mmmm."

"What? Tuna, like yesterday?" Packed in water, no mayonnaise, she prayed.

"I guess."

She kept lifting the washcloth and as she did, he kept his eyes closed.

"Don't you know?"

She winced as she pulled the terry cloth down lower and was glad he didn't see her look at the cyst between his eyebrows. Oh, they were so vain at this age. The furious swelling seemed better, though it was far from pretty.

"Mom. Stop."

"Well?"

"Jello with fruit in it and—"

"Was there whipped cream, too?"

"Tuna, I guess, with whole-wheat bread and some of those yogurt dealies."

"Flavored? Did you take that bag full of raw vegetables I washed?"

"Uh-huh."

She took a good look at her son's face and figured it would take two weeks to heal, with a visit to the dermatologist. Lang would have to go back on tetracycline, and that meant another fight with Boyd and a second fight with the insurance company. She wasn't about to pay forty dollars for a prescription just because Boyd had forgotten to mail in a payment on the drug-discount card. She took the cloth from Lang's face.

"Hang on."

He acted as if he hadn't heard her. She walked to the kitchen and opened the refrigerator door. The vegetables were on the second shelf, drying out inside the sack. She'd stir-fry them tonight for dinner.

"What's the point, Lang?"

He lifted the crook of his arm over the top of his head and burrowed inside, turning his face to the wall. The cloth slipped a bit and she reached over to straighten it.

"Of me cutting up vegetables and you lying about eating them. Do you want to drop the whole thing?"

"No!"

"Do you want to make weight?"

"Yes. Yes, Mom."

"Do you want to go to college?"

He opened his mouth in a silent scream.

"Then pay attention."

She took the cloth from his face. She stood up and looked at the length of her son, stretched from one end of the campaign bed to another. It was Helen, not Lang, who was doing battle. She should be stretched out, closing her eyes for a few precious minutes.

Helen closed her bedroom door and took off her clothes, one piece at a time, until she stood in bra and pants in front of the bed. She liked the feel of lace as she ran her finger over the top of the bra. She prepared a cradle for herself, a cozy cradle of cushions and pillows and the silk comforter Alice had given her for Christmas. Laying inside her cradle, eager for the cool surface to warm, Helen closed her eyes, listening to Lang move on the other side of the door. She ran her hand over her abdomen and pressed as she heard him begin his crunches. With each grunt, each low outburst as he completed his set, Helen felt her shoulders ease, all the tension melting away inside the soft, tight cocoon. They both pretended she didn't hear what he said at the end. She didn't understand why he had to say those things, but she knew the harder he worked, the worse the words became. He knew lots of awful words. She heard the squeak of vinyl, saw the padded black slant board through her closed eyelids and the closed door. Then she saw her son's muscled back. She thought of how intricate Lang's back was, how it changed as he pulled and stretched, his raw face knocking at his knees. She thought of the V, the sudden outline of the letter that narrowed to his spine. Seeing it for the first time had frightened her.

She could rest. She could think of him going off to college. Not like Neddy, not like the boys in La Jolla Cove, but going away all the same. If he kept after it, his coach said, if he kept working up to his potential, he'd bag a scholarship. Helen thought of college as a bag, too, but a Halloween bag full of tricks or full of treats. Lang's bag would be full of treats only if he worked, sculpting and polishing his gift of physical strength until it gleamed.

She thought of his baby body with a sudden stab of pleasure, how happy it had made her to just hold him. How happy it had made both of them. A colicky baby, Lang had been soothed by movement and touch. She'd supplied him with both back then. Helen rolled onto her side under the layer of silk, caught it between the tender skin inside her bare thighs. She slowly moved her legs back and forth, enjoying the slippery heat.

The boys who lived near the cove. She loved the look of them, their bright, untroubled surfaces, the way they took off in aged vans and Volkswagen Bugs. This year Vassar had been very popular. The stickers had showed up in several back windows. One boy, her favorite, stood in the middle of his cul-de-sac, all the neighbors out to wish him off, the men in shorts and the women in flowered, sacky sundresses firmly cinched at the back of the neck. He accepted kisses on the cheek from adoring women or stern, slapping handshakes from the men. His mother, a heavy, good-looking woman with piles of white hair, pushed at his chest and blew him his final kiss. He heaved his leather suitcase into the backseat of a dumpy blue car and was gone. Helen had been walking down that way. She'd come close enough to them to see the stitching on the suitcase, the piece of luggage that had been handed down to the boy without ceremony, the way those things were. What belonged to him belonged to him. No fuss. A push on the chest and then he was gone. Harvard, his sticker had read.

No, it wouldn't be like that with Lang. But he could go off to college just the same. A scholarship was a thing to be proud of, not so different from that handsome suitcase. His education paid for (room and board, too, the coach had insinuated), and maybe she and Boyd could give him enough spending money so that he could join a fraternity. Why not? Because afterward . . .

Helen fingered the rolled edge of the comforter, catching more and more of it inside her fists. She was so afraid sometimes. Boyd, what are we going to *do?* She'd asked the question so many times. He would look at her, his face hard and white as a stick of chalk. The best we can! He would punch up simple-headed statements about their overdrafts, the collection agency, and the repo brothers, as they came to call the men who stood in the yard demanding the one lovely thing they owned, a white sports car. They kept its hardtop in the living room of the apartment and sometimes ate TV dinners on the lustery surface.

Helen heard the heavy thud of a weight. She imagined the curl of Lang's arms, the way the veins stood out in his neck as he worked slowly, carefully. He was proud of his arms.

Helen pulled the pale silk over her own face and turned over on her back to play Dead Woman, even though it made her think of Boyd. His playful side was the side she'd run to after aunts who served dry soda crackers for treats and turned the lights out in the middle of a card game just because it was ten o'clock. Play? The concept was remote. No wonder she had found Boyd so attractive . . . she lay still. She lay dead, trying not to smile, trying not to think of Boyd, who wanted her to laugh more than anything in the world. Boyd, who designed games just to see her careful smile break into coughing, choking laughter, who called her in the middle of the day or night, with a joke that ended in a crazy, unexpected twist.

Dead Woman has pretty toes. (He would pull them.)

Dead Woman has pretty knees. (He would rub them.)

Dead Woman has pretty legs. (He would stroke them.)

Hmmm. Dead Woman not so dead after all.

She would be laughing by then, and laughter would topple over into something else. Something that felt like love for years. She didn't know what it was, really, because every bit of that had gone away. And what was left was Lang and a future that flickered on and off like a lantern battered by a storm.

Lang knocked on her door. "Wait!" she cried, then crawled into a flowered dress that bared one shoulder completely and knotted above the other. She could never get it to look quite right.

"OK."

"Wow." Lang had dried off, but new drops of sweat appeared on his lips and the tops of his arms. She could look at his face now. Maybe it would only take a week to heal.

"Wow, wipe the floor with that thing or wow . . ."

"I don't know. It's different."

With Lang positioned at the door, she asked her question brightly, as if asking it couldn't possibly offend either of the pair she saw in her mind, the dark-haired woman in a springy cotton dress or the panting, red-faced boy several feet beyond.

"Lang."

His breathing steadied. She waited until it evened out completely.

"Why do you keep tearing at your face?"

The boy struggled with his answer and the woman struggled with her dress. The knot that held the whole thing together had begun to come undone.

5.

Helen watched the light go out of the sky. The red-orange line of fire thinned; she could watch it efface from where she sat. Alice and Jack no doubt shared the same scene. Perhaps they were outside now, on the wide terrace that wrapped snugly around a home far from this one. A day was being summed up over drinks. Alice would be pressing her leg to her chest, tugging lightly on a strand of black pearls, to tell Jack about a near miss. Three sofas about to be shipped to Telluride, all of them two inches off. If she hadn't been there to see for herself, if she hadn't heckled Stan until he got it right, had him open the cotton and shave down the base, everything would have gone haywire. Her voice would rise, and so would Jack to fetch another drink. But the sunset no longer drew exclamations—it probably hadn't for years. It was only one strand in a life woven with beauty so rich and complete that single elements in the composition (sunsets, hummingbirds that hovered and fussed when the feeder was dry, punctual, precious tides) no longer drew even the softest sigh. Instead, it was Helen who sighed and soaked up the last bit of red sky.

She took the clasp from her hair, shaking it out over her shoulders. Maybe the man would be back for the chair. Everything had happened too quickly; he had left before he had seen all of what they had to offer. The leather chair had been the only temptation.

She thought about her mother's brooch again, the flash of that amber stone. His eyes had that same golden glare as they flickered over the room, finding little to light on. The baby seemed to see more than he had. If he returned, would it be the same? Would his attention skitter over everything a second time? Helen dropped her head to the back of the chair. The dark circle the light cast on the ceiling seemed to shift and expand. It was getting late.

Helen loved her old Bakelite phone. Its grumpy blackness and the rotary dial turned the most mundane calls into an event.

"Alice, it's me. Sorry to bother you."

"Never a bother. What's the trouble?" There was a bit of cell phone static. They were on the terrace, just like she thought.

"Jack? Refill, please. It's Patricia carrying on, isn't it."

Helen looked hard at the telephone. She worked her little finger into the coils of the cord. Patricia carrying on about what?

"No. I want to bring a few things over from the warehouse tomorrow."

"What things exactly?" Alice's voice turned a corner. Ice cubes tinkled.

"The three-seat sofa, the one from the Linz fiasco, and the second club chair."

"Oh, Helen, I *am* pleased."

The Linz business had put them all out of sorts. Janice Linz had purchased the sofa to surprise her husband in the first early weeks of their marriage, but this honeymoon period came to an abrupt end one week after the sofa was delivered. Janice cried real tears in the upstairs office. She hadn't known she would have to consider the tastes of her husband's ex-wife. Cerulean blue was her favorite color. How was I supposed to know? Janice Linz had sobbed, tipping over her glass of tea.

"Did you settle on a price?"

"We didn't talk about price at all." Helen cleared her throat. "You taught me that, Alice. Remember? Wait until they can't live without it. Then tell them what it will cost."

Jack's voice was running in the background. Thursday was golf day and he probably wanted to show Alice the way he stroked the ball, beating out Harris for the third straight Thursday or, the other player with ruthless orange pants. It was always hard for Jack to win when he wore those pants.

"We'll have to do quite a bit of shifting around."

"The rung on the banquette is loose. Stan can repair it while we use that space. We'll put the second chair by the front window."

"Great. Now, Helen . . ."

"Yes?"

"Who are we doing all this for?"

"I left his card at the shop, but he went wild over the club chair." She paused for a moment. He *had* liked the chair. And if he hadn't reached for his business card, it was because things had escalated and there hadn't been time. "Then there was this terrible scene with a child who crashed into a table. We missed a lawsuit by an inch, Alice."

"Where was I?"

"Behind the screen with Charlotte Ruskin."

"Now that I think of it, I *did* hear something this morning."

The things Alice could ignore. Toddlers, for one. Helen continued. "This man wasn't even his father, but he got him settled down anyway. Then he had to speed off for an appointment."

She could hear Alice take a sip of her drink, the metal tap of her wedding ring against the glass.

"For this we're rearranging the whole front room?"

"He's interested. I was also thinking about those English andirons They've been sitting around out at the warehouse forever. This feels just like the Sadler business."

Patricia's language skills were impressive, but Helen had something much more important. She had good hunches. Mrs. Sadler had popped into the store one day and disappeared. But Helen had remembered her, and when she returned, Helen welcomed her, careful not to stare at the shredded scarf she had wrapped around her throat. Helen led her to a French farm table that Stan had just restored, watching as the little woman ran her finger down the ridges in the dark wood. Mrs. Sadler started pointing. Because of her laryngitis, she just pointed at whatever she wanted in the store. She forced her voice at the end, when the store was full of SOLD tags. You've been very patient, she had croaked to Helen, one hand over her throat. An article ran later in the *La Jolla Light.* A photograph showed Mrs. Sadler Sitting Pretty, with a mention of Helen Patterson's expertise in arranging the furniture. Helen put *life* into these rooms, a fully recovered Mrs. Sadler exclaimed.

"You're manipulating me. Why do I allow this? Jack doesn't know, he's shaking his head. I'm the one who's supposed to manipulate you!" The phone line crackled and spit. "All right, bring over the andirons. I won't be in before eleven, so you'll have to deal with Stan. His back's out again."

Helen ignored the dig and remembered how the man's big hand had covered the top of the baby's head, tight and secure as a second skull. Her heart raced after she hung up the phone, even though her skin was chilled and damp. Helen looked out at the dark sky. She had forgotten all about the finale. Every last bit of red was gone.

Alice's warehouse occupied one section of a vast hangar by the San Diego airport. An ultralight airplane–manufacturing firm had gone out of business ten years earlier and leased sections of space to body shops and body builders before Alice finally muscled her way in. She filled the long, narrow structure with lathes and buzz saws, pallets and packing quilts, then won the complete confidence of the other occupants by hiring big, hairless Stan Converse, recognized as the real thing by both muscle men and tired executives who trained in the building. He had nothing but disdain for his body. Its strength was slack and painful, beaten into place by a lifetime of lessons. Lessons cost him a little finger and a scar shaped like a scythe or a single cap sleeve, and he wouldn't talk about them to anyone but Alice. Stan had respect for his upholsterers and woodworkers, even for the delivery boys who never seemed to last. Since he didn't want to talk down to them, he talked over their heads, staring at a space several feet above baseball caps and dreadlocks. Better have that sewn up by four o'clock if you want a paycheck. Ralph, if you don't find the Hollister house by noon, you're off the team, benched for good. Sometimes he had to shout, so tough had communication on India Street become. The low tin roof of the building seemed to shudder and crouch under the sheer weight of all the noise. Freeway traffic and the steady drone of aircraft landing pressed hard on every side. It all pressed harder still on Stan Converse's back, pushing it out of whack every few months. He blamed the noise for his troubles.

Helen waited until a plane passed overhead, its sound bearing down on the top of the building then fading. She stood at the entrance to the warehouse, pleased as always to see the wrought iron initials A.N.D. Stan had once told her just what he thought of the squat wooden door, which Alice had hauled back from a trip to Morocco. It was Stan who had rebuilt the entrance, lowering it to fit the door's odd angles, Stan who had to crouch to get inside the building from that day forth.

Helen heard a radio blare and unlocked the door. A sharp, edgy wolf whistle went up once she was inside and Helen rolled her eyes.

"Someone's got admirers."

She had a bag of his favorite doughnuts, the caky kind with the glaze. He liked having three of them with his first cup of coffee.

"Somebody's also got something to ask me."

Stan didn't like rain or noise or last-minute changes. Helen settled the doughnuts on a table. She'd eaten two herself on the way over, and a little sugar stuck to her lip. She licked it off as she scanned the room for her sofa. His sofa. She sucked the inside of her mouth and saw it behind a pine chest. Helen frowned. Alice couldn't stand pine.

Stan ate the first doughnut in three bites, but slowed down to savor the second. He wiped the tips of his fingers on his work coat.

"I want you to send the blue sofa over on the truck."

"No room. Truck's full."

"And the second club chair. Where *is* the second club chair?"

"You speak with Alice?" Stan stared at the top of her head.

The chair was beside his desk, for some reason. He wasn't using it, it was carefully covered in plastic. But it was pulled in tight next to his swivel chair.

"Last night. Why is it there?"

He didn't want to tell her. He stuffed his mouth full of the third doughnut, slurped coffee. Put his hand to the small of his back and winced.

"How's the back, Stan?"

"Back's very bad, very bad."

The shop was already humming. Arturo raised his hand and smiled at Helen. He was beginning to load the truck, wrapping a quilt over a fruitwood chest of drawers. That sale was a big coup for Patricia. She'd suggested changing the hardware for a hesitant customer, casually lifting an antique pull from a basket on her desk as if it were the sort of suggestion she made every day.

"We might be able to make room for the sofa." He burped and didn't excuse himself, then ran a sugary hand over his bald head.

"I need that chair this morning, Stan."

Stan turned his hands over, looked at first one, then the other. Then he squeezed them closed and stuck them inside the pockets of his work coat.

"I need it, too."

He looked at the club chair and took a few steps toward his desk. Helen studied his back for a moment. He talked about surgery every six months or so. She'd never given much thought to Stan actually having a home, let alone wanting nice things for it. She wondered if he had a girlfriend, someone who slipped over to pick and choose from the warehouse after everyone had gone home. Maybe the girlfriend was furnishing her own place. Maybe Stan was storing her pine chest until she could move in.

"You're buying it, Stan?"

"Bought it yesterday. The line's discontinued, so I figured . . ."

He wouldn't even look over her head. He seemed embarrassed, as if his own desire exposed him. Helen thought of how he'd look, this hulking, unattractive man, in an apartment indirectly appointed by Alice.

"Good people should have good things. Things they love. You've earned that beautiful chair, Stan."

But Helen said it too feverishly. Now they were both embarrassed. Stan ran his hand over his head again before searching for the andirons. Helen would have to take them over to the store herself.

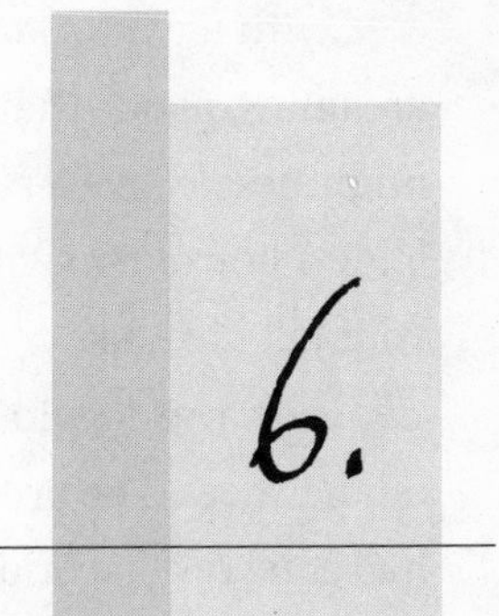

Patricia was wearing new glasses. The heavy dark frames suited her, tempered her flippant good looks. She was developing gestures to complement the glasses. She plucked them from her face with a single, emphatic movement and settled them on top of her head. Sun glinted off the glass lenses and tippled down over her hair.

"When did you get those?"

Patricia was wrapping a wedding gift, a box full of pale Pratesi sheets and pillowcases.

"The other day. They're not prescription or anything. I bought them to help hold me down."

Helen watched her smooth out a crease. The paper they used was tricky. Mistakes showed up easily. Patricia's hands moved quickly over the package, cutting and folding with precision. She was good with her hands, putting unexpected twists into the most simple, straightforward things. Patricia floating away? Was that what she meant?

"People don't take me seriously. And I want them to. I really, really do."

She finished the last touches on the bow, prodding one of the satin loops into place, then attached a cluster of silver beads to the inside of the bow, with just the right amount of pressure. They wouldn't tumble off in the trunk of a car. They wouldn't be missing on a long table covered with a white damask cloth and hundreds of other gifts. Helen liked dreaming about that table and the sea of silver polished to a blinding brightness. She even composed the thank you notes in her mind, scribbling a line or two with her favorite pen. You have no idea what pleasure your gift gives us.

Helen was logging in numbers for the month, staring at the figures on the sheet. The profit was extraordinary because of her own sale. She had gone to get a bridal registry for an elderly friend of the bride's family, and when she returned he was sitting at the immense gray table in the center of the greenhouse. Helen had slipped into one of the graceful iron chairs and watched as he opened his checkbook for the deposit on a forty-thousand-dollar wedding gift. She'd excused herself to run cold water over her red face, then returned calmly to write up the sale for the table and chairs. Alice's imports from France had come to represent excess, what with shipping charges, taxes, and the floor space consumed by the enormous pieces she bought routinely. But not since Helen's sale. Now the thick slab of stone mined outside of Saint-Rémy years ago would lock a marriage into place. Weigh it down with ceremony and appropriate seriousness, Alice said as she hugged Helen. She hinted about a grand Christmas bonus.

Patricia looked at Helen again. She took the glasses off the top of her head and bit down gently on one thick black stem.

"Weddings! God! You go to bed the first night, you wake up, and all of a sudden it's the *rest* of your life. What will they talk about?"

"Plenty of things," Helen answered in a sharp voice. The couple had come in days before and huddled on the sofa with Alice about the design for the main entryway into their home. He wanted stately, she wanted cheer. They hunched together over Alice's fluffy head. She promised both, sketching out a design they cheered by the end. That chandelier, Alice pointed, hung low. And a bench Stan will build. I own the very same one, you must both come see. What if Patricia was right? What if they didn't talk after the trip to Portofino, lay silent on sheets now wrapped up in paper too pretty to tear? No. They would talk, Helen decided, her fear finding another target.

"They'll plan the rest of their lives."

"They will?"

"Probably. They'll stay up all night and make terrible promises."

"Why terrible?"

"Because they really believe that they'll keep them."

Patricia put on her glasses and peered out the window to the spot where she swam. Maybe that daily swim kept her weighted down, tethered to secrets in the middle of the day.

"Someone's downstairs."

Helen listened as all the promises returned, one by one, filling her head as she left the computer and walked down the hall to the child's bedroom looking out over Alice's garden and the ocean beyond. Two Japanese maples crawled toward each other at the bottom of the path. The trunk of one of the trees lay so low that Alice had it supported with a metal prong. Birds argued among the branches; Helen heard their angry chirping even with the windows closed. Boyd had promised her nightmares would stop because their life had begun, and their new life would cancel out others begun long before. That's what beginnings are, Helen. He swore to things that had sounded ordinary even at the time, the same things that now sounded extravagant. Lasting love, protection. He stood up in bed, bumping his head on the water-stained ceiling in their apartment, and beat his chest. His promises made her thick and silly. They had named their unborn baby that same night, extracting Lang from Langley. The name signified something fine back then.

Why hadn't she learned? Why had she believed so ardently in promises *again?* That they came from another man, a married man, made those assurances more plausible, not less. The things he would have to do for her, the old life he would have to abandon for the new one only made the future appear more certain. Sacrifice and hardship seemed to secure what lay ahead. Helen would soften his tough, strong exterior. Or so she'd thought then. These feelings scare me, Helen. I don't think I've really loved before. Helen slammed both hands over her ears and pressed hard. In the end, she had borne the sacrifice and the hardship alone, while his life went on much as before.

She straightened a picture frame, checked the drawer full of lace gloves. They would have been so easy to slip into a shopping bag or the pocket of a raincoat. And yet no one did. A dozen pairs lay side by side, price tags neatly tucked under lace tatted in a hot Italian courtyard. No one had ever disturbed this room. It cast a spell on people, just as Alice implied. A good room creates good behavior. Helen opened a window and turned her back on the view, then wrapped her hair in a tight coil on top of her head. Stiff, salty wind beat the back of her neck and she let her eyes close for a second.

"Hi there."

His voice made her jump and she caught her hip on the edge of a dressing table.

"It seems like every time I come here, somebody gets banged up." He smiled as he said it. His eyes moved up Helen's face toward the messy twist of hair at the top of her head.

Alice's iridescent curtains were down today, lowered over an oval mirror. She hoped she didn't look the way she felt—embarrassed, as if she'd worn the wrong socks on the first day of school.

"This looks like a room in a real home. May I see what you've got in here?"

"Oh, yes! Come in. I was just straightening up."

He traveled over the room with his hands, opening drawers, turning pages in the storybooks and photo albums, examining everything he could, thoroughly, at a new pace. Not like the other rushed day. He studied the curves of the "lit bateau," the single bed that seemed to float along the side of the room. He watched the hands on the narrow grandfather clock jerk forward and rattled the red pencils in their silver cup. He seemed to forget that Helen stood in the room with him. She cleared her throat after a moment, but he still didn't seem conscious of her. He scratched the back of his head and didn't smooth the hair down again, crossed to stroke the top of the telescope and tilt it at the water. He knelt at the base of the long cylinder, then extended it for a better view, sucking in his breath.

"Swimmers and sharks. Now there's a bad combination."

She was kneeling beside him before she realized it was a joke. Her hair was beginning to come undone and he laughed at her as she fussed with it. What had all those years with Boyd meant, anyway? She still didn't know when the most obvious joke was headed straight at her.

"I made your heart beat for a minute, didn't I?"

"You sure did."

He wore work boots that she wanted to think about. The tan dye was completely worn from the heels and the stitching had given way on one instep. His fingernails were meticulous. Something had bitten the back of his arm and he scratched the same spot mindlessly, his short, square nails not doing much good.

He sat down on the edge of the bed, his heels knocking the trundle tucked away underneath. He switched a lamp up to its highest setting, then carefully reached inside the shade with his hand.

"Why the pink inside?"

"We line all our lamps with that fabric. It creates a nice, soft light."

He stretched his fingers open inside the shade, right next to the bare bulb. Helen watched the outline of his hand, the light that spread through his fingers. "Someone's really crazy about kids."

Helen smiled and didn't reply. Alice liked handsome, well-made children with passions as intense as her own. Less-attractive children barely crossed her consciousness.

"Has anyone ever come in and bought a whole room just the way it is?"

"Twice."

His hand slipped down from the lamp shade and closed over the top of the stand, then slid over the slim legs of the lamp. Helen fidgeted in her long, narrow skirt.

"Down to the things in the drawers?"

"Twice."

He cocked his head and sat still for a moment. "So somewhere there's a little girl and she's just waiting for this room to be delivered."

Helen's chest rose and fell conspicuously with a sigh, strands of hair swept against the side of her face. He didn't turn his head to look at her, yet she felt herself filling the whole room, becoming the paperweight in his hand, the pillow sinking underneath his elbow.

"She's a lucky little girl," he said.

She wanted to tell him about another little girl, the one she knew, and an amber stone that she should have been given. It was the first beautiful thing the girl had known, and now it was lost. Helen wanted to tell this stranger how she had found the stone again in his eyes. A pleasant pressure struck her chest. She felt it thudding against the bone beneath her skin.

Patricia leaned into the room on one leg. She looked silly with one leg bent and out of sight. The glasses failed—she would always float and flutter.

"I have some bad news. The other chair is sold."

"All right. I'll just take the one then."

"You mean you still want it?"

"I'll take it off your hands today. I've got a truck parked out front."

"Well, great! I'll go write you up."

There were loud hellos on the stair, a returning customer she knew. For once, the girl didn't respond, bounding toward them like Poor. She lingered in the doorway.

"Is there anything else I can help you with?"

"I'll handle it, Patricia." Helen's voice was too loud.

"I just—" She squeezed the handle of the door. There would be greasy prints all over the brass.

"Patricia, take care of the order, please."

She made a smacking sound with her lips and turned to go. She stomped down the stairs for extra emphasis.

"You've got yourself a hard worker there." His speech had an easy slowness to it, as if he were reluctant to let his words go.

"Oh, yes. She's quite a prize." Something rolled over inside her. She ignored it and reached out to shake his hand. "I'm Helen Patterson."

He didn't speak for a moment. His hand rested quietly in hers and she squeezed it gently. His skin was rough and she felt stupidly hopeful. Boyd's hands were always baby soft.

"I'm the new kid on the block. My name is Ray Richards."

Helen wondered if he knew of Peaches, the place where everyone new or newly eligible went to drink and dance. Helen had gone there once and it had frightened her into months of quiet weekends. Alice objected to the place on other grounds. The building was rude and its interior just as bellicose. The tacky club made her furious.

"Welcome." Helen let go of his hand. Alice was fervent about other things, too. Dating clients was forbidden. "Do you live close by?"

"Gatley Point."

"It's so beautiful out there." Helen had once sloshed through the caves under the lush promontory at low tide, slipping on the lichen that turned the rocks into glass.

"That's exactly my argument. It *is* beautiful and I want to see as much of it as I can."

"Is something in your way?"

He laughed and looked out the window. Helen started to fill in the silence, but then he spoke. "You might say that. I'm trying to open a section of the house for a real ocean view."

"Sounds terrific."

"You think so?"

"Why live on the Point if you can't enjoy the view?"

He stood up and walked to the window, drumming on a pane of glass with his fingers. The noise was irritating.

"It's the city that's holding me up. At least now I'll have something comfortable to sit on while they're fooling around with the permit. I tell them this is no way to welcome a newcomer, but they're not exactly paying attention."

"They're fools."

There were only five houses on the point, and she'd never known one to come on the market. The houses were passed down to family members, together with a disdain for real estate brokers. Boyd had cold-called one property years ago, and to his surprise, his telephone queries had been promptly addressed. And as conversations with the owner continued, he had managed to confuse dreams and reality until Boyd's Big Deal was the talk of the town. Afterward, the polite, firm refusal to sell carried with it not only disappointment but humiliation.

"If you need any help pulling things together, Alice does have a design service."

"Is she any good?"

"She's more than good. Alice is wonderful."

Ray tipped his head slightly, as if he heard a new sound in the room.

"You sound pretty devoted."

"I am. If you're interested—"

"I'm very interested."

Ray Richards wasn't looking at the room or the view or the pretty pink inside a lampshade. He was looking at Helen and she thought of Alice's albums, stuffed with drawings and photographs. The haphazard collection couldn't have been more clear, declaring her talent, her impeccable eye.

"I've got a wonderful sofa coming over this morning. Cerulean blue."

"Cerulean blue. My favorite."

A seagull shrieked outside the open window. A turf war had begun, but Helen didn't turn her head to see.

"May I call you, Helen?"

She pulled a card from a scalloped dish on a table by the side of the bed. Next to the dish, old yellow roses were crowded into a glass bowl. They seemed to wrap the two of them in a scented cloud. Helen slowly wrote her telephone number on the back of the card.

"That's my number at home. In case you can't find me at the store."

She thought of Lang as she slapped at the side of her skirt. Lang as he looked on the wrestling mat, wearing that perfect, furious scowl he'd developed last year. All sweetness gone, the expression had startled her until she understood its usefulness, its ability to trouble an opponent.

"So we'll talk. At this number, right?"

He grinned and slid the card into his back pocket. Helen straightened her shoulders as he turned to leave. The store was filling up with people. They were loud, probably exuberant at their release from a tour bus. What if she were preoccupied with people just like that, in town for a day with no real intention of buying anything, and she missed a call from a real customer because of it? Patricia would only bungle it. Too eager. Too young. Alice would have agreed that giving out her home phone number was the right thing to do. Helen took one more good look at those boots, the easy way Ray Richards swung down the steps. She would like thinking about them, wondering what kind of work or play had caused all those scuffs and scars. A woman from Middleview, Louisiana, was shouting at her friend to come look and see what all she'd found inside the chest. Blankets! *You've just got to touch this, Edie. It's perfect for the bitter cold nights back home.*

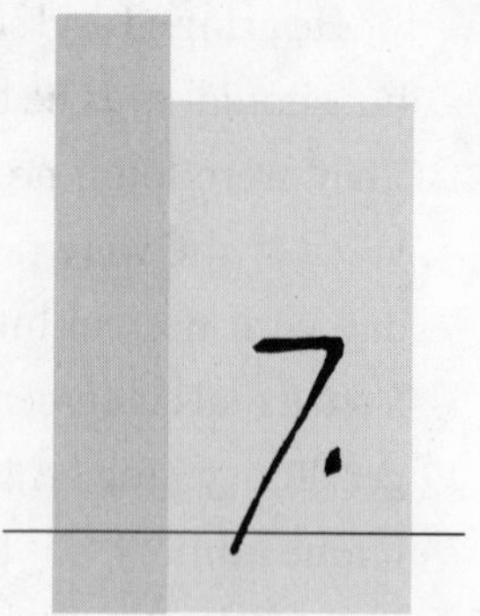

7.

I'm surprised you didn't throw this out before you moved."

Edgar held up the first wedding gift Helen had ever received, a gift worlds removed from Pratesi sheets and heirloom silver. He teased her by pretending to pour from the turquoise pitcher, lifting the handle with a monumental effort, using both hands, then feigning a spill that landed all over the front of her shirt.

"Look what a big, fat bottom it has."

"Edgar, you're making this worse. Go home."

"I can't. This is like one of those horrible car accidents you can't take your eyes off of."

Edgar wore swimming trunks and a T-shirt from Club Med. There was a sunset on his back and a river raging over his chest. He stroked the top of the shirt as he worked with Helen under the trees. They bickered over prices because he thought Helen asked too much for every little thing.

"Trust me."

"I do trust you."

He held up a Lladró figurine. Helen had two, for the aunts had not consulted with each other. Why either of them assumed she would like the thin, sorrowful porcelain girl with a bird trapped in her hand remained a mystery to Helen.

"If you sell things like this for ninety-nine cents, people will swarm all over this sale. Some of the things you have to let them steal. You just have to, Helen. Please believe me. I went through this when Teddy left."

Edgar, a private man, had never given his departed lover a name. Helen shook out a velvet coat she kept thinking would come back into fashion.

"At first I kept his things marked high. Let's say excessively high. Well, by noon I certainly had the picture. Nothing was moving, least of all me." Edgar nearly knocked an ashtray from the table Helen had loaded with chipped or scratched things. "You do know that's what this sale is about, don't you?"

"I'm not going anywhere."

"Not with all this stuff you're not. You'll never move on unless you get rid of all this."

Edgar was using his ominous tone. He was conservative, only falling back on it when absolutely necessary. He decisively wrote "99¢" on the bottom of the little Lladró girl.

"There. I believe we have our first customer."

He turned to a young woman in overalls and a black beret. She stood in a shady diamond that had fallen across a section of sidewalk before she moved toward the first table. She seemed to draw others. A couple of cars approached Helen's house slowly, as if headed into a foggy, mountainous stretch of road. One of the cars parked two doors down, its driver smoking for a while inside before getting out and locking all the doors. The other driver used Edgar's driveway, smiling and apologizing as he got out of the bucket seat.

"I never park the old gal on the street anymore. Brings me bad luck."

The man continued his story of bad luck as he handled Helen's things. Edgar took over. Even though the man's hands rummaged through the shoddiest things, watching him touch them was unpleasant. Edgar understood. He understood most things connected with unpleasantness. Helen busied herself with a new customer, a small girl who wanted a present for her mother.

The first two hours passed. There was a lull just before lunch, and Helen thought of sandwiches and drinks. But suddenly people needed hair dryers tested and old lights plugged in. She snaked an orange extension cord out of the back bedroom window. Her stomach growled and Edgar laughed.

"My. Someone's hungry. Go pick us up something to eat."

She went into the house to search for her keys and came out to find Lang sitting in her chair. Boyd was in the Volvo, its bad side parked at the fire hydrant.

"Who gave you the right to sell my stuff, Mom?" He held a cardboard box full of discarded playing cards and ink stamps. He eyed an old baseball bat that stood in a tall electric-blue trash can he had spray-painted himself.

"I gave you a deadline. You were supposed to go through the things in your closet and you didn't."

"That's not fair!"

"He's right, Helen." Boyd had gotten out of the car. Helen set a cracked soup tureen in the center of the tablecloth she spread on the lawn.

Boyd picked up a leather briefcase. Edgar and she had agreed on this, at least. It was one of the few high-ticket items in Helen's sale. Boyd's old briefcase was priced at forty dollars. They had labeled it MUST SACRIFICE the night before, deciding it probably wouldn't sell at that but why not try? It had somehow gotten thrown into a box packed together in that one crazy week it had taken to sort her things from his.

"This date has been circled on his calender forever."

"Still. Isn't this all pretty hasty?" He held the briefcase in his hand and Helen felt sorry for how he looked in his beach thongs. The ragged, gray-white T-shirt meant either infrequent washings or the wrong temperature setting. The wrong everything, she thought as the broken lock on the briefcase sprung open. "And anyhow, isn't this mine?"

"Take it."

Boyd banged on the lock a couple of times. "Doesn't work. The damn thing doesn't even work. It did back then, Helen. Hey, there's still some of my stuff in here. You couldn't clean it out before selling it?"

Lang took his bat out of the trash can and headed into the house, letting it drag behind him and bounce up the front-porch steps.

"Instant party!"

Edgar clicked a couple of Helen's mismatched wine glasses together in a toast and two chubby middle-aged twins giggled and hugged their pocketbooks tighter.

"It's too wonderful," Edgar said, looking from one round, identical face to the other. "Have you seen the Lladró figurines?"

Helen walked toward the Volvo, hoping Boyd would follow. He did, leaving the briefcase on top of a footstool.

"Lang's good, Helen. You know that, right?"

"Of course I know that. I go to all those matches, remember?"

"But I mean really good. It was just practice, but the coach is totally focused on him. Digs into him like crazy, but it works. He's faster than anyone else on the team. He makes these dives. It's like watching a little pit bull."

Boyd had a hand on the car door. His fingers tapped against the metal and she thought of Ray Richards with alarm. Nervous tapping was just something men did. Boyd and Ray weren't alike at all.

"I left it damaged on purpose, you realize."

He trailed his hand over the dent, which seemed to look worse than ever. Maybe another driver had hit the gash a second time, figuring what the hell.

"Help me, Helen." Boyd's eyes softened and as they did, Helen took a step back. The interior of the car was full of wadded-up papers and empty Sprite cans. A phone book lay open in the backseat, some of its yellow pages torn and lying on the floorboards.

"Aren't you ashamed, Boyd?"

"Yes!"

"How can you take clients around to properties in this car?"

"I'm in luck there. Most of them are legally blind."

Helen wondered what it would feel like to push him. What it would be like to let her fingers press into his flesh, to feel the initial resistance and the slow stumbling backward. He would catch himself in the middle of the fall because he had balance and instinct after years of surfing. He would grow steady starting with the balls of his feet, the palms of his hands flattening, fingers spreading wide apart. Then he would pop back up, surprised that he hadn't tipped over. Surprised he'd ever been pushed in the first place.

"Please help me."

She began to count, to counsel herself in the split-second exercise she had memorized over the years. He looks like a grown man, but don't be fooled. After repeating it several times in her head, she could calm down. And though kindness was often far off, blinking at her in the green, wooded distance, sometimes she could summon pity. Coax it out of the shadows like a shy animal.

"With what?"

"Help me hate you."

His nails curved over the edges of his toes. She wondered where his clippers were and if his feet ached inside his black Bally loafers, the good ones he had somehow managed to keep out of harm's way.

"All right."

Edgar's voice rose in laughter. One of the twins was trying on Helen's velvet coat while her sister twirled and spun in a long raincoat that had never known a single downpour. Helen felt lighter, happier just watching them. Two less things crushed inside her cramped closet. She beamed at the twins, who looked to her for a signal. Yes or no? Buy or leave behind?

"Here's what you do, Boyd. It's an exercise that will work. I promise you. Lie down at night like usual."

She thought of Dead Woman, the smile he always wore as he started the game.

"Close your eyes and think of me."

"I said hate." He drummed his fingers on the car door, then gave it a sharp bang.

"Think of my eyes. Think of hating my eyes. You can do it. Hate the way they look in the morning. The way they squint and have sand in the corners."

The twins thought the prices were too high. What if Edgar nipped five dollars off the coat? Well, what about two?

"Go to my nose, Boyd. Imagine I've got a cold. The worst cold I've contracted in my life and it's red and I'm mean because of sneezing and coughing."

"It won't work, Helen."

"Go to my mouth. Think of it shouting the worst things possible. If you haven't heard me say those things and you don't believe I can, then remember something rotten I have said. You taught me this, Boyd. Actor's Workshop for Little Psychos, remember?"

He had captured the hearts of television viewers with his wide-eyed, little-boy charm. At a certain point his agent had suggested an acting school that taught him to "upchuck anger," or fear, or love—any one of the big feelings that made Boy tremble and suck his thumb in public.

"I've got to go." Helen was really hungry and wanting egg salad, of all things.

"That wasn't helpful." He looked pathetic, like one big tear starting its lonesome dribble down.

"You just want to make me feel sorry for you."

"Then why don't you?"

"We're not married, Boyd. I keep telling you that. Feeling sorry for you isn't my job anymore."

She hoped there would be lots of egg salad at the deli, so much egg salad heaped in a pallid yellow mound that seeing it would change her mind. She'd choose something healthy and sensible, something to see her through the long afternoon ahead.

Lang looked out at the table in the front yard. It was almost bare. A few shabby bath towels were left. Weird, unmatched junk that his mom and Edgar would stuff into a grab bag at the end of the day. The only two things that did match were those sculptures, what did she call them? The Lladró figurines were gone, the ones her aunts had given her. His favorite belt was probably sold, the brown braided belt that fit any waist. Unless, of course, you weighed five hundred pounds and were one of those people who went on *Jerry Springer* to cry about how hard it was to get up and down stairs, in and out of bed. There were five of them on television now. Five huge fatties with their bellies sitting on top of their knees. It didn't even matter if they wore belts. The fat hid everything.

"Did you sleep at your father's house, Lang?"

"Where do you think I was?" His eyes moved reluctantly from the television screen. She made him feel late for an appointment he didn't want to go to in the first place. She could do it by putting her hands on her hips. It made her look different, like a dental assistant or the lady who weighed you in at the doctor's office. She didn't look like a mom at all.

"I didn't mean that. I meant did you get any rest? You seem tired."

"I'm always tired. So what? I can't find my good belt."

"Did you look?"

"Yeah. Did you sell it? Maybe you did. You're selling everything today."

He turned his attention back to the television fatties. They probably had belts and moms who knew exactly where they were. Maybe their fat looked worse in real life. Probably. He hadn't slept, but that was his business. He'd listened to his dad all night on the phone, hearing the way he was scared and mad at the same time. After that, after Boyd had hung up the phone, Lang carried the conversations way into the night. In his mind, Lang made it madder than it had been. He had to go outside and stand on the stupid deck because of how mad the conversation got in his head. Looking out to the water, Lang missed drunks on the beach, people doing it off in the dark. If his dad would only move away from Mission Bay, the stupid little kid beach, there would be something to see. But his dad never moved; he just talked about it. Stayed there in the same house where Lang had been five and seven and even twelve. But not thirteen. Lang hadn't lived there starting when he turned thirteen.

"Here. Half of what we have so far."

Helen handed him money. She handed him one hundred fifty-four dollars. Lang counted out the money and looked at her, waiting for the punch line.

"I just want my belt."

"That should buy a belt."

"I've got money from work. It's okay, Mom. Keep it."

He felt his flesh creep over his middle, the way it would if he let himself eat everything he really wanted to eat. He was always tired, but mostly he was hungry. He could think about food, a table full of food. Nothing sweet, not junk food, just good, cooked things. If he thought about them long enough, thought about exactly how each thing tasted in his mouth, he could stand not actually eating it. Sometimes he thought about food in class and then . . . She was frowning. She was looking at him hard and frowning.

"I've been wanting to talk to you about that, honey."

"About what?"

"Your work. How's it going?"

"The same." He was afraid he would catch their aches and pains, the ones old people talked about so much. Sometimes he imagined they were trying to suck all the strength out of him for themselves. And that it would work. That he would go to practice one day and get slammed on the mat and cry just like they did about their bodies.

"The same good or bad?"

"I show up, Mom. That's all your friend wants." His mother straightened up. She never called Robin or saw her at night the way she had when they first moved to Feldspar. Maybe they weren't friends anymore.

"Robin wants much more than that and you know it. She hired you because you're a cheerful, hardworking boy."

"She hired me because of you."

Robin Baker watched him all the time. There was probably not one minute of the day when she wasn't watching him, except for when he was with the Captain. The Captain wouldn't let her in his room. Lang started separating bills, the fives from the ones. Putting the change into the right piles. He slid his tongue quickly over his chipped tooth, which reminded him of how his mom kept talking about how a crown was all he needed. She liked to pretend he didn't look like a beaver. She didn't like hearing how everybody was getting braces off before he'd even managed to get them on.

"I'm getting rid of this stuff for both of us. Treat yourself, Lang. I'll find the belt. Go buy something you don't need. Out. Go."

When she walked to the television, he didn't get all mad, the way he usually did when she turned off a favorite program or told him to go to his room like it was his destiny to just go. Instead, he was glad to see the fatties flicker and disappear. He was glad to have a hundred fifty-four dollars to put toward the crown that still wouldn't make him king. It wasn't that great when he spent money from work because each time he did, he thought of Sunrise Home and the Captain, who would never escape even though he'd escaped plenty of other things in his life. It was like the money from work smelled the same way the old people did. This money was different, though. His mother was smiling and all of a sudden, he did, too.

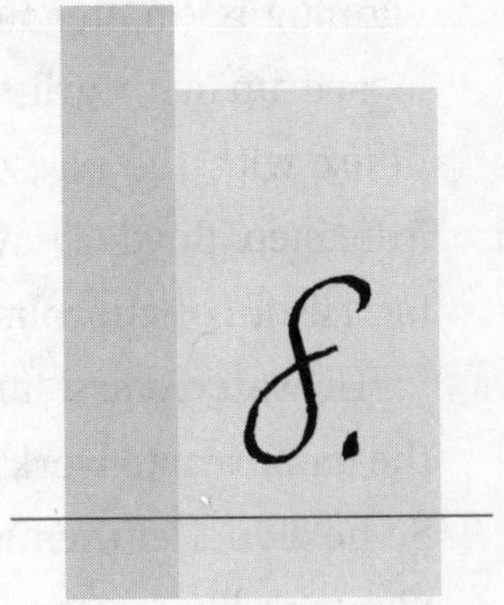

Zanzibar Court, Verona Court, Toulon Court. They made Boyd feel like a king, Helen's accusation was true. Why was that bad? He still didn't understand. He did feel good living out here on the skinny finger of land pointing south. As he squeezed his car into the traffic that narrowed into the corridor that threaded through Mission Beach, Boyd felt better and better. Someone waved from Brighton Court, one of the last stumpy, residential alleys he passed before turning left and heading underground to the parking spot he rented from his neighbors. Space was hard to come by on the narrow peninsula, but people were friendly out here and devoted to keeping it that way. There were no fights over parking spots. You'd never see a fist raised, watch a face turn purple just because someone had gotten somewhere first. Even that had bothered Helen toward the end. Friendliness, Boyd shook his head. Making a good thing like friendliness bad. It still puzzled him.

The kids were out, like always. They were swinging on swings, turning sidewalks into game boards with bright yellow chalk. He slowed down to watch a couple of boys send toy trucks down a long road to home. Home was the sandy beach at the end of the sidewalk. Home meant both boys won the race, their trucks landing on headlights and hoods. That was what home should mean, Boyd thought. Everybody winning no matter how you landed. He jiggled his keys and both boys looked up with grins. They knew he had the Halloween House, the house with the nice orange door and the cat that lay winking on the front step. Boyd always had candy on hand. All a kid would have to do for a fistful of chocolate was knock.

He watered first, an old habit. Once he got inside, on the phone or in the basement to work on some project, he would let the plants go to hell. So he didn't let them go to hell. He watered all of them out of pity. The plants he liked best needed lots of attention and, if he were being truthful, shouldn't even have been on this hot terrace in the first place. He chose them on days when he felt most contrary, most at odds with the world, and the fragile pink blossoms drooping at the end of the day reminded him of that. He stood slumped with the silver can in his hand, the phone just beginning to ring. He stood longer, waiting for the answering machine to click on. It didn't. Lang must have shut it off last night.

"Boyd, that you?"

Wrong call to ignore. It was Steve, and Steve Mason was impatient to begin with.

"You're fucking, right?"

Boyd looked at the front door. Still ajar, it creaked open a bit further with the breeze.

"What is she? Blonde or redhead?"

Why not brunette? Boyd thought of Helen's brown hair in a distant way. It was a thought that took place way outside his body.

"Matter of fact, Steve, I was watering my plants."

"You son of a gun. As hard as you work and there you go taking on plants."

Boyd stiffened and he thought of a longboard against his body. How the wood felt welded to your gut on good days. Like you were carved out of the exact same thing. Steve's voice swirled the way it did, going one way at first and then shifting directions. It was a tricky voice because he was a tricky man—and a tricky boss. Boyd had hated to call Steve two years ago, hated to call an old friend, but Helen and Lang were gone and he'd been in a jam.

"Something came across my desk today."

Boyd thought of the blonde or the redhead Steve had mentioned. How the women would look on Steve's desk, the way their bodies would hide all the papers and the pencils, the desk accessories Steve liked one day and hated the next, pitching them into trash cans with so much force they often hit the wall instead.

"Something you must have mentioned to me a long time ago, but with all that's going on around here, I must have forgotten. I plain forgot, Boyd. So imagine what it was like suddenly seeing your head in a box. Not that I don't like that, but it came as a surprise."

The cat pushed the door open the rest of the way. She never let a door stop her. *Door stopper.* Boyd thought of a cast-iron, cross-eyed cat like her and almost laughed. Then he thought of his head in a box and didn't.

"I don't know what you're talking about, Steve."

"I know. Just wait."

Steve was getting old in a good way, a way that pulled in both men and women. He wasn't handsome, particularly. In fact, Boyd had examined his own features in the mirror, taken them apart one by one, as if Steve and he stood side by side. Boyd had come out way, way ahead. Steve certainly wasn't kind, so that wasn't it.

"'Boyd Patterson Prescribes.' Great stuff. You wormed your way into their hearts with this, didn't you?"

Relief washed over him. Boyd pictured the sheet again, happy he could help himself and help others at the same time. He had put together twenty-five household tips from what he knew. What he knew because of Helen leaving and old people hung out to dry by their very own children. All the sadness that washed over him when he saw the leaves of a rose bush blacken or an old man struggle with a zipper on his windbreaker. He'd tried to fix everything he could and had only come up with twenty-five things. He felt pride for his photograph, his head in a box, and the words Steve Mason Real Estate with the phone number at the top of the sheet.

"I've got a hunch, Boyd." Steve paused a moment. "Something tells me I'm wasting my best resource here."

"You know when I dreamed that up—"

"I said they were great, didn't I?"

"Yes, but—"

"Don't 'yes but' me. Never 'yes but' me."

Boyd held his stomach. It hurt now. It had peeled off the wooden board like a layer of laminate. He took a deep breath.

"You've responded to the market, Boyd. We got five calls on that house you got marked down, and the last call tells me it's practically sold. You know how to do what you do."

He felt better. A child stood outside on the deck.

"I'm thinking it's time to do what you don't know how to do. The Majestic, Boyd. Like to take over the Majestic?"

A sour taste came into his mouth at the mention of the condominium building. Its elegant marble entry was the butt of many jokes at Windandsea Beach. He'd made more than a few of them himself as he plugged a nick on his board or slid into the crusty seat of the Volvo he parked across from the building. His car had always annoyed Walt Wilson, leasing agent on the property.

"What about Walt?"

"Fifty-eight visits to the penthouse. His time was up, that's what about Walt. Next week I'll walk you through it myself. All that good work has paid off, Boyd. I want to take you on board, buddy."

Hadn't he been on board all this time? What ship was Steve talking about?

"Boyd?"

"Yes?"

"Buy a couple new suits." Steve hung up.

Outside the cat purred under the child's hand. Boyd gave the boy some chocolates, then went back inside to lie down. Before he did, he hit the candy bowl in a big way. In a ritual of loathing and leaving, he ate the rest of the chocolate himself. He wouldn't be needing candy once he was inside the Majestic—he would need something else. Just what it was he didn't know.

Boyd had barely touched the button for the thirteenth floor when the woman standing next to him lay her hand on his arm. She was dressed too warmly for California and had been shedding layer after layer of clothing. Her jacket and the raincoat with limp lapels were tossed into the backseat of the Volvo. Nothing seemed to help, though. She kept patting the back of her neck with pink Kleenex. She was finally down to a sheer white blouse and a dark, pleated skirt that didn't make any noise. She crossed her legs, she crossed the room—nothing. Boyd liked the sound of clothing, the slide of silky lining against wool, for example. It was good when you could hear a woman come and go. Boyd had his lips pursed. He was all set to whistle.

"I'm sure I know you."

He released one steady note and shook his head.

"Is that right?" Boyd sounded dull, slow. He watched the numbers increase on the elevator panel, wishing he was wet. God, he would love to be wet right now, standing there dripping, his skin smooth and salty, sun throwing a spotlight on his damp head. Instead, she was the one who was damp, and he could tell by the way she closed her hand over that rubber purse that she wasn't going to buy a thing.

"Didn't I see you on a bus bench? Coming in from the airport, I saw—that's it, isn't it?"

Boyd flinched. He'd had some rough times, but it had never come to advertising on a bus bench. That was for Jonathan Rosen, or the Ellmans, a blond married real estate pair who beamed out at traffic flying past the airport. No, things had never been that bad. Come to think of it, things had never been that good. Rosen's listings had sprouted up all over Pacific Beach. He hated Rosen's teeth. Each time he looked at those teeth he could see them chomping down on more property.

"Here we are. I don't do bus benches, Mrs. Alther. Sorry to disappoint you."

"Marsha. Oh, you don't disappoint me!" She laughed as they stepped off the elevator on the thirteenth floor. "You'd have to work real hard to do that."

She peered out of the elevator before stepping off, reminding him of how she had climbed into his car, taking a good look at the seat as if it might contaminate her, and the gingerly way she took the brochure on the Majestic from his hand . . . this wasn't easy for either of them. Mrs. Alther was researching property for herself and her husband, but now she was Marsha and she'd switched to the word *buying.* Buying property—and hopefully from Boyd Patterson, now that she had said he didn't disappoint her.

Mrs. Alther—Marsha—walked down the hall toward the unit without him. The belt she wore hung around her hips, not her waist, shaped her nicely, and Boyd just bet her husband was a slob. Flabby from booze and then he made her research low-fat menus, since he was so big on research. Why wasn't Alther here with her?

She waited for him with one hand on the belt, but not unkindly. He walked through the next part in his head as he worked the key in the lock. He'd start with security, then move to all the individual features. He'd draw back his hand, she'd draw in her breath, and he'd mention landlocked Dallas, insinuating she couldn't buy this view there.

"I'm never wrong about these things."

Boyd imagined her husband's gut, the one individual feature that was fixed in his mind. They had a Jacuzzi, the pool in the backyard she'd already mentioned. He thought of Alther's heavy sack of skin tumbling over the top of his bathing suit, if he bothered to wear one. Maybe he didn't, since there were no little Althers. How pretty could that view be?

"I know I know you."

She'd probably seen him on *Talktime.* Watched him and four other losers. Going on *Talktime* to describe what it had been like to be a child actor and what it was like now, being neither the child nor the actor, had been the worst move he'd ever made. Baby Overboard! People called him for weeks after that. Maybe he'd start with the view. Maybe he'd walk over to the window, pull back his hand, and move to the finale since the morning was probably over anyhow. You want it or not, Mrs. Alther?

"I'm someone who trust her instincts. Whereas most people don't."

She wasn't looking at the layout or the leap you made from the entry to the quick vertical shift in perspective that was the point of the journey to the thirteenth floor. Boyd was prepared for it and not prepared at all—the heave of sudden space shocked him. She stared at his cheek. Oh, the hell with it.

"Ever watch *The Langleys at Sea* when you were a kid?"

Mrs. Alther began to pant. She began to hop up and down, with squeals interrupting the hops and claps interrupting the squeals. The morning was over. He wondered if he could sue the television host and, if he could, what the charges would be. Loss of faith? Loss of heart? Boyd ran his hand over his hair.

"I wanted to marry you! I wanted to be Mrs. Boy Patterson!"

He didn't react, and that was his problem. He never reacted when he should have. He didn't double over when someone socked him, he just wobbled and straightened back up. He doubled over later, way after the blow, when it was too late. Helen, the real Mrs. Boy Patterson, had walked out before *Talktime* aired, but in his mind she had left him as soon as she saw him on a show with four assholes. He'd been in better shape than any of them, but how good was that? One of them, the one who played the acrobat in a circus-family series, had served time for armed robbery.

"No kidding. Now for the best part."

Boyd felt for the metal lever under the length of linen. The way Marsha Alther sized him up brought back the pain of auditions and the certainty, permanently lodged inside, that he didn't have it. Whatever it was they wanted—his agent, his mother, the director—he didn't have it to give. But terror gave him substance, that was the thing. He was nothing, really, until he was scared shitless, and then, he, Boyd Patterson, ten or forty-nine, at a callback or a meeting with his boss, could materialize. Coalesce into something, for God's sake, come together in a recognizable shape instead of being grimy bits of metal flung all over a blank board. Terror was a magnet. He felt Marsha Alther's bland blue eyes on his face and wished he feared her. He didn't, though. He felt nothing as he released the lever. The window darkened slightly, blotting out the sight of her, blotting out the sight of him to the world below while their view of the beach remained crystal clear.

"My," Mrs. Alther breathed, liking something finally.

My what? Her what, he corrected quickly. She continued to sweat quietly, making big O-rings appear on the sheer white blouse. She didn't smell bad, even though she sweat like a farm wife. The rising screen worked, fixing her attention on something besides him.

"We see and are not seen."

Boyd didn't know if this was too theatrical, too reminiscent of Boy. But it happened to be true, and maybe truth would cause her to buy the unit. Boyd thought of Steve's magic numbers, which was fine because it kept him terrified. He'd seen how the numbers worked for three guys so far. You could show a property without success to fifty-seven people, but if you showed it to fifty-eight and that was Steve's magic number, you were history. Take Walt Wilson. The magic numbers changed for each sales consultant and nobody knew what they were. Women broke down as a rule and it was Boyd's opinion that a man would eventually break down, but in a way that was ugly and final, surprising even Steve Mason.

Marsha Alther seemed to be catching on. Maybe living in Dallas made you smart, alert to the wonders of the world. A three-story slot in the sky where you could see and not be seen simply by pushing a lever was worth a couple million dollars, and here they were at just a million and a half. He thought of kissing Helen because of it. He felt a doubling up, a late doubling up. He thought of leaning into Helen's body, then looking up to see Lang over her shoulder as he came free of her lips and hair, and how seeing his son lengthened the kiss in a funny way.

She was opening her rubber purse and shaking her head.

"I am just never wrong."

She started digging around inside, revealing another side of Marsha Alther, a slightly desperate side. She couldn't find what she was looking for, and it made her mad. It shocked him to hear her say the words he said so easily himself. His heart pounded harder when she got to her checkbook. Her fingers were on the checkbook, and the clear nail polish she wore gleamed inside the handbag. This had never happened to him before, at least not this fast. She took the checkbook out and put it on a table. A table that was faux something. Helen would have known faux what. He was wrong about Marsha not smelling. You couldn't sweat that much and not smell.

"This has been such a treat."

Light did come in through the tinted gray windows, and he could look down on the water, the tiny specks that were birds on the water and the darker specks that were men. The way the wind brushed over the surface of the water made him sleepy. A treat. You didn't pay a million and a half dollars for a treat.

She didn't touch the checkbook. Boyd wondered if Marsha had her own account or shared one with the big guy.

"I trust my instincts. Did I mention that?" She changed the way she looked at him.

She was unbuttoning her blouse. It wasn't as sheer as he thought. It had covered lots of things, all the things he was able to see right now, clear as sunlight falling through dusky glass. Boyd was quiet inside and alert, clear in his mind.

"To think that I'm with the actual Boy Patterson way up on the thirteenth floor."

He got good and scared when she opened her blouse as if it were nothing to her, just the end of the morning in a city she didn't know with a man who could have said anything, been anything, done anything. California was baked on Boyd like a harsh enamel coat; he should have taken it easier. Watching her invite him to scrawl Boy Patterson on her white chest made him want to puke with fear. He didn't, of course.

He smiled a broad Boy smile from bygone days and took the gold pen from her hand. The hand that was free.

"Sign right over my heart."

Marsha Alther squealed as the tip of the pen touched her skin.

"Too bad it's not indelible ink." He signed his name boldly, with a tail on the end of Boy. He didn't like the way the tip of the pen dug into her flesh. She pressed her pink Kleenex over the signature, patting it dry.

"There. I knew I knew you." Her fingers pulled at the buttons of her blouse. Boyd stood blinking in the light as she moved over to the faux table. Marsha Alther tapped her teeth with the checkbook.

"Nobody can be a child forever. Or a star. Can they?"

What had he looked like before *Talktime*? Pleasant features, nice eyes, and a nose that pointed up. Nothing too emphatic. Now he was blending into the other time, that time when stage fright made his eyes twinkle with panic. He was blending back into Boy.

"No."

"You grow up. You learn to accept life on other terms, don't you, Boyd?"

Wasn't that the truth.

"Is it hard?" she asked calmly.

Her eyes were bluer than ever, and he understood that she didn't mean his life. Though it was hard. It was harder than anyone knew. And the blows kept coming.

She held her checkbook between her teeth and he finally heard the sound of clothing, the slow glide of a zipper that didn't stick, the slipping-down sound of satin. He understood that he was supposed to do something. It was hard as hell—she had asked the right question—and he dreamed himself through the next fourteen minutes, traveling through a turquoise pipeline, the speed and undimmed sound sucking him up inside. The shape of the whole world was wrapped inside a wave. The shape of the world was him.

9.

The painting of Gatley Point that hung in Alice Nash Design had been reproduced years before in a book on local history. Boyd maintained that Helen studied the book and its pictures to emphasize his failure, but he'd been wrong. She consumed the facts and the philosophy as if they were an expensive delicacy. Peering at the dim black and white photos both starved and satisfied her.

The cliff houses, viewed from the east, seemed more a cluster of sturdy, round-shouldered women huddled under the Torrey Pines than the clever homes they were. But when observed from the water, each one was more complex than the next, showing off a new Gatley notion about shelter and stewardship. There were the needs of man, yes, but more important, there were the duties of man. These duties included seriousness of purpose and sound mind, attitudes appropriate to residents of an unearthly world. For Elmore Gatley believed his land to be exactly that, a bit of heaven that had wobbled loose and landed in his sturdy lap. Mr. Gatley studied birds and especially admired an African species able to fashion handsome globes out of humble mud and straw. He did the same, keeping building techniques and materials crude and indigenous, as if the cliffs themselves had risen up to become houses. That Elmore Gatley, architect, developer, and God's trustee, wore clerical, white-collared shirts and worked on each house with his very own hands surprised no one. He constructed a miniature birdhouse for every residence; a replication of each completed structure dangled from the twisted pines.

Nineteen twenty-three. The watercolor showed this year and this place ably enough, but it was only half a view and half a truth. The rest was out of sight, hidden below in five caves that dug underneath the houses and eroded more than just the kitchen floorboards. Downstairs bathrooms at Gatley Point often smelled like death and damp, according to the ocean drama spinning along below. Sick animals took shelter inside the caves. Pelicans and gulls sought refuge there, as did sea otters and sharks with their jaws opened in a nasty final yawn. The smell of rot rose as punctually as the sun, and owners had gotten a sort of burial crew together when the homes were first built, rotating week to week, family by family. There were jobs for everyone from the smallest child (in charge of telephoning the Department of Health), to the eldest, who knew how to end an animal's screaming misery if Papa was away and Mama was too fearful to steady the gun.

Some of the caves had names, and Helen thought of them as she looked at the painting. Creeping Cat, Sideways Sarah . . . she couldn't remember any others. She wondered if Ray Richards did. She wondered if he knew of Gatley Point's history and imagined his face turning toward hers as she told him. Gatley's boldness excited her: he had reshaped a piece of the world, made it even more beautiful than it had been before. She scooted deeper into the blue sofa that affably filled the space where the bench had been. The Gatley painting pulled the room's individual pieces together. A pair of rush-bottomed chairs now looked on to a view of heaven casually tossed down to earth.

"Why did you move my painting?"

Alice stood at attention in the doorway. She wore a white blouse, rolled up to the elbows to expose a wide silver bracelet that looked more liquid than metal. She wore slim, cotton "policy pants" in a slate blue. Skinny pants are my policy. Big was bad, baggy horrifying. Alice crouched and bent in the comfort of tight pants.

"Isn't it great?" Helen felt flooded with color. The painting made the blue in the sofa more vivid. The yellow wash that Stan had used for the chairs shone. Who could resist this composition?

"No. It isn't great at all."

Patricia grunted lightly in the background. It sounded as if her thin body struggled with more weight than it could carry.

"I'm surprised at you."

Watching her, Helen fought down admiration. Alice climbed even higher when she was angry. Furious excitement pushed her further and further from the dull, the earthbound. Hadn't Jack said it right out loud? He'd fallen fully in love with Alice the first time he saw her get spitting mad.

"You *disturbed* my favorite view." Alice pointed at the painting with a trembling finger. Her hair was pinned up, but not for long.

Her tirades were short, muscular outbursts that cured something as yet invisible to Helen. But she would eventually see. She would learn the true cause of Alice's tantrums and how to avert them. Alice loved trouble, loved setting it right; the issue was seldom a genuine mistake. It was something more obscure, some intrusion far more troubling to her than a manufacturer's delay, a client's failure to pay on time.

Alice glared at the wall where it had hung before and Poor whined, anticipating a spank. The painting had been lost in a dark corner.

"Alice, you've never had a kind thing to say about Gatley Point."

"Of course not. Outsiders bought up the most beautiful place on this coast." She stuck her chin out. "I can still love that painting, can't I?"

"You're looking at the bad guy."

He stood next to the open window in the bedroom. The sun pressed against his shoulders and hair, and Helen felt as warm as if she were standing next to him. The light was so bright that Helen couldn't read the expression on his face. Alice could.

"You don't look bad to me." Alice kept the same tone, but added injured cheer. "Do you always sneak up?"

"I do when I'm in a hurry to buy something."

WHO IS THAT? Alice mouthed to Helen as she jangled keys, her back to Ray Richards. CUTE. Ray made his way toward them from the window. Helen pushed at her hair and frowned. Elizabeth Adams Perkins's secretary was coming up the walk. Helen looked around for Patricia, who had conveniently fled.

"What's all this about being bad? We don't have any bad clients here."

He was Jack's height. Alice twittered over him, since tall men were another policy. More important, perhaps, than tight pants. He looked over Alice's head to Helen. That look launched a long, slow conversation that Helen hoped would last all day. She sighed and turned to Elizabeth Adams Perkins's secretary, who had climbed the stairs and knocked a book from the ledge.

It wasn't Neddy this time, it was the historical society nibbling at poor Elizabeth's heels. They wanted to tour her home, turn the downstairs over to the curious on Tuesdays and Thursdays. Tours! *This* was the dark underside of marine research, the true belly of the whale. Not only did the public want to review the professional records of Arthur Adams Perkins, famous oceanographer, the public wanted to review the private life. Elizabeth was unhappily compliant, thinking of her dead husband's generosity and the certainty that he would not only have said yes but would have served tea. Scones and that raspberry jam he adored. The secretary's eyes turned to the dining room, the set of Spode. The serving tray with three silver tiers.

"Patricia is just unpacking something you might like. Let me see if she's got it out of the box."

"This ottoman is nice and cushy. I'll just wait here." The secretary didn't look comfortable at all. She sat as if her knees were tied together.

Patricia, a porcelain cup in her hand, stood in a corner of the stockroom studying a mound of packing peanuts that had fallen on the floor. The radio was playing too loudly and Helen turned it down.

"Can you take over for me out there? It's a brand new Perkins drama."

Patricia kicked at a peanut. "Neddy again? I can't stand that twerp."

"Much more urgent. Anyway, could you go help her after you get this cleaned up?"

Patricia put another hand around the cup, as if it truly held something she was about to drink, then set it on a back counter. Helen noticed that her necklace was new. Pearls. Fake pearls, Helen corrected herself. What could a girl like Patricia afford on her salary but fake pearls?

"How do you know Neddy?"

"Oh, him. He's the biggest nerd in town. Everybody who grew up here knows him." Patricia put her hands behind her back and stretched. "Is something wrong, Helen?"

Helen had imagined that such a light, fluffy girl had always been airborne, floating from one place to the next. It was odd to think of Patricia growing up in La Jolla, odder still that she had moved to Pacific Beach. Helen plucked unhappily at the sleeve of her shirt. The cuff was frayed. Why hadn't she noticed that before?

"I had no idea," Alice said.

A new accusation? Helen clenched her teeth and looked at Ray, whose face betrayed nothing.

"I don't mind sacrificing my favorite view to such a lovely cause. Mr. Richards will be taking all of this *and* the things in the small bedroom."

Helen nodded her head slowly, composing her features. Ray grinned from where he sat on the sofa and slid a pillow behind the small of his back. He sat in the same spot that she had minutes earlier.

"I'll let you two work out delivery dates." Alice happily patted Helen's arm. Her petulance over the painting had disappeared. "Tell Stan we're giving Mr. Richards top priority. It's for his little girl's birthday. Ten, did you say?"

"Next week."

Helen felt as if she'd swallowed a rock. The news of a daughter struck with a solid thump.

"Great age. Interested in the stars?" Alice pursed her lips.

"I'm hoping she will be after she looks through that telescope."

Helen looked down at his hand, thought of the way it strained open inside the lamp shade. She tried to picture his wife, even though he didn't wear a ring. She probably had those rumpled good looks, was the kind of woman who rolled out of bed each morning looking pure and lovely. Helen imagined his hand sliding down his wife's back, welcoming her into the world again. She shook her head and spoke in a measured voice.

"I didn't realize you were shopping for a little girl."

"Neither did I. I didn't know I was shopping for a blue sofa, either. You planted all kinds of ideas." He sat still for a moment, then shifted positions. "Does your boss always talk to you like that?"

"Pardon me?"

"When I came in she was all over you for moving a painting."

"Alice is a perfectionist, that's all."

He sat up straighter, his attention on the painting. Then he turned to Helen and rushed at her with words. They came so fast it was difficult for her to understand. He seemed to be singing, composing a quick new melody of words.

"Here's the deal. My little girl lives back in Oklahoma with her mother. She's flying out next weekend and it's her first visit."

Helen's hands relaxed and dropped to her sides. He was divorced.

"Can I get you to do something else for me?"

Anything. She wished she could say it, then remembered Alice.

His voice dropped a bit and he adjusted the pillow. "Would you mind helping me put these things together? I want her to feel at home."

"I'd be happy to help."

"You'll come out to the house then?"

"Whenever you'd like."

He looked so pleased and surprised, just the way Lang did when he received sudden, unexpected praise. Ray Richards patted his sofa and she nearly sat down next to him. She blushed as he stood up. He turned his back on her to study the painting of Gatley Point again.

"Do you have children?"

"I have a son."

He leaned forward and lightly touched the frame. He squinted at the signature.

"My girl's such a tomboy I sometimes feel like I've got one myself. Oh, that reminds me." Ray reached into an inside pocket for his wallet and tossed a credit card on a side table with a sigh.

"I'd better pass on those lace gloves."

The rest of the day was horrid. Minutes and hours scraped by. Helen wanted to sit at her desk and think of Ray, to prolong that imaginary conversation. She licked the tip of her finger and touched the *R* in his signature, thinking it might reappear on her skin. She searched the sofa for some lost item, a comb or a key, something she could tell him about lightly, easily on the phone. *Mr. Richards? Hello, this is Helen Patterson. I was just calling to let you know* . . . her voice would stay on his machine. He would press PLAY, then press it again to hear how her voice sounded in his own home. But she couldn't. Everything intruded on Helen—phone calls, delivery questions, and, especially, Amanda Reston. Amanda was "opening" the house in Las Brisas. Helen almost laughed out loud at the phrase. Everything about Amanda was open. Alice usually received the best details over lunch. How Amanda got her new husband. How Amanda got her new villa. How Amanda wiggled her way into the locker room at a Lakers game and into a membership at the Beach Club in the same week.

"We're hosting my husband's business group in May. I thought your store would be just the place to start."

Your store. Helen didn't correct the mistake. She understood that corporate meant more freedom, not less. Freshening up today would be written off tomorrow. She smiled and reached for Amanda's portfolio. Helen took instruction from Boyd for once, feigning interest in

Amanda's plans. Acting. She opened a folder full of old sketches for the villa and began reworking two or three interiors.

"This could stand a new focal point. If you just heighten the mood here . . ."

They worked over the designs for an hour, adding color details and accessories that would quicken corporate hearts and minds. Amanda clapped her hands together at the end and waved a fabric wing in the air. It was perfect, Helen was perfect, and could she please, please, please have the fabric by next month? "You're right, of course," Amanda said. "It's got fabulous hang!"

She meant the flirtatious English cotton, which would swing and blow before the balcony overlooking Acapulco Bay. Helen slid her fingers down the length of the bright orange pencil. *Was* she right about Ray Richards?

"I want you to keep thinking about the house."

Helen stiffened. That was exactly what she didn't want to do.

"I've got so much to do. Here, take my car phone number. Call me the minute you have an idea." Amanda swung her legs to the side of the chair and Helen thought she would sit on and on. But she'd moved on to another important focal point. Amanda looked at her own legs. Then she looked at Helen.

"Do you wax or shave?"

Helen crossed her legs under her desk. She wondered how Amanda's thoughts connected and glanced at her broad white forehead. Maybe they didn't.

"I shave." When she had time and the energy to fight Lang afterward. He claimed she used too much hot water for showers and baths.

"You should start waxing, Helen. Tell them to use honey. After the first few times you won't even mind the burn." Amanda leaned forward and whispered in a louder voice. "Since I'm always in a bathing suit down there—"

Helen wanted to think about Ray Richards without Amanda's noise, or any other. She wanted to blot out everything else that interfered with him. Then Amanda leaned down and stroked her own leg. As she did, Helen tightened the grip on her pencil.

"I go ahead and have *everything* waxed. It drives my husband crazy."

Helen must have been polite. She must have said good-bye and thanked Amanda for coming in. But she didn't remember any of it later. She went to the cloistered hidden room. For once no one was there and she quickly turned the lock on the door, leaning against it. She sat down on the stiff wooden chair, feeling each and every round spindle press into her back. She squinted and looked at the tub, filled with scented aqua-colored water, and the dainty antique bathing stand that held a water pitcher and a block of olive soap, lotions and potions of every sort. There was magic involved in love, black magic. Helen thought of the short list of tricks she had in her head, the longer one she would have to develop. She felt something pleasantly gnawing away at her. Whatever it was, this sensation would demand all of her energy now and maybe all of her courage. Helen stood in front of the small, uneven window, letting her chin touch the bottom of the sill. The view admitted scruffy clouds and a stretch of blue. Helen couldn't see the water from here. She could only see up, into tree tops and sky. Looking down, she studied an interior view: her dark cotton skirt and flat shoes. She inched her skirt up so that she could see only her legs and her dark socks. She lowered her underpants, pleased at their prettiness. Helen prized them. They didn't look silly around her ankles. They looked beautiful.

She thought the dark triangle of hair away. Thought of having it removed, of how that would burn and leave red marks and then . . . nothing. Nothing but skin as white as the skin on her thighs. Her thighs would simply roll into her hips and her hips would melt into a flat, perfect plain until all her skin finally belonging to one body, one soul. Her skin would be one smooth piece, the way it had been as a girl. Was that what Amanda meant? She felt the gnawing begin all over again. She thought of honey, its hot, sweet bite on the skin. She imagined it spread everywhere with a short wooden plank. There. She touched herself tentatively, imagining the burn. She spread it further and further, even over the voice that was coming upstairs. She heard footsteps approaching and she held on to her raised skirt and the vision of dark hair that would soon disappear into magic and love.

"Helen?" Patricia's voice had that worried ripple at the end.

"I'm in the bathroom." Helen held on. The skirt shook slightly in her hand.

"But we didn't know where you were!"

"What is it?" Helen answered sweetly.

Patricia didn't answer right away.

"Your son's here. You'd better come see him."

"I can't do it."

Helen gave him a quick, angry hug. Books and papers lay in a neat stack. He didn't dare a mess in Alice Nash Design.

"Of course you can. Never say you can't do something, Lang."

She heard Patricia crunching her way over the gravel. She was such a deliberate girl—Helen had to give her that. Lang mournfully peeled the paper from a protein bar.

"I can't make these sounds and this book is stupid. The teacher won't speak to us in English."

Helen looked down at the textbook. Tu, vous. Lang had scrawled Who in the margin. I wish I knew completed his poetry of despair. He was close to tears.

"I'm going to fail, Mom."

"What about the language lab? Remember how you were going to stay a couple of afternoons a week?"

"I did. Didn't help."

He put his pencil down. He watched it roll to the edge of the table and almost drop off. He didn't move to save it and Helen snatched it up in her hand.

"It's all memorization, Lang. Simple memorization."

She made a neat stack of her own, piling up the worries that would otherwise scatter hopelessly beyond her reach. His weight, his grades, his scholarship. She organized all the messy trouble, but looking at it that way only made it worse. What if French was beyond him? What if he really did fail? She tried to remember her last conversation with his teacher. What had she suggested, if anything?

"Hey."

Patricia toyed with something in her pocket, rolled it around with her hand hidden deep inside. Helen looked at her watch. Fifteen minutes until they could close up, go home. Fifteen minutes until Lang's panic would blow up into something completely unrelated. He would scream at her in the car.

"Have you two met?" Helen couldn't remember.

"Just now."

Lang sat back in his chair and flipped the page of his textbook.

"School. Big drag, huh?"

"Yeah, I guess." Lang's voice cracked and he cleared his throat.

"Where do you go?"

"Almont High."

"I knew a bunch of people who went there."

Maybe they would have had much more to say if she weren't there. Helen thought of an order number she needed to look up and decided it could wait.

"Where did you go to school, Patricia?" Helen hadn't asked. It hadn't seemed important.

"Talbott Academy. Where else?" Alice appeared. She was eating a Snickers bar.

Talbott Academy was Trinity's prestigious sister school. The uniforms, the curriculum, the classical buildings . . . the two schools seemed to meet and marry under a wide, prestigious arch. Alice waved her candy at Helen and she shook her head no.

"Lang? A pinch?"

"No, thanks." He still held the uneaten protein bar.

"Of course not. I forgot all about training." Alice wadded her candy paper in a ball and let it drop into a trash can. She moved to the table and frowned at the open textbook, then put one hand on Lang's back. It looked artificial there. "Now, what's all this?"

Patricia and Alice leaned in together, clucking over the textbook which obscured rather than clarified. Lang was right! It was stupid, Patricia declared. They'd packed too much confusing information into one chapter. They gave terrible examples for the written exercises. And the photographs of the French?

"Unbelievable. These photos are a hundred years old."

Alice chimed in, pointing to the skirt length and the idiomatic expressions that were no longer in use. Lang nibbled on his protein bar. He laughed at Patricia, who made a snorting sound and said something in French he understood. He looked up at her and rolled his eyes.

"It's totally not his fault, Helen."

She hadn't said it was. Patricia reminded her of someone. That babysitter with the long brown braids, the one she had finally fired. Boyd had seen something off-kilter in the girl long before she did.

Helen moved closer to the table and put her hand on Lang's back, letting it rest there for a long minute. It didn't look artificial at all. It was a mother's hand, the most natural thing in the world.

10.

The house stood over an unnamed cave. Years before, Boyd had done a title search on the house, discovering that it was owned by somebody in a different state and rarely used. Austere, estranged from the other houses on the point, the house and the imagined owner might just have shared some of the same qualities. Boyd had developed a dignified sales style to go with the house, rehearsing a pitch that went nowhere. Ray Richards had bought the house. Helen wondered who the broker was. She thought of Steve Mason suddenly and flushed. Of course. Steve Mason would succeed where Boyd Patterson had failed.

Helen studied the entrance. An oeil-de-boeuf window loomed above the carved, paneled door. She flinched at the watchful glass eye. Its lewd, leering presence saw not just Helen's exterior outline, the careful, attractive appearance that would have satisfied anyone. This eye peered all the way inside.

She pressed the buzzer, then touched the rough texture of the entrance with her hand. The doorbell left a slight echo; the house sounded empty. She shifted her weight from left to right and winced, getting it out of the way. She would register pain once, then go on to other things. Great legs, bad feet, her mother used to say. Forget Pappagallos, Helen, and get on with it. The prettiest shoes on earth always turned out to be the most painful.

Big mistake, Stan had said after delivering the furniture. He'd been cryptic and brief, punishing her over the phone when she called to check on the delivery he hadn't wanted to make. He didn't like changing schedules once they were set. *What's* a mistake, Stan? But another line was ringing at the warehouse and he had to pick up. He'd get back to her later.

She had drunk coffee in a hurry, spilled some on her blouse, and changed into the flowered dress that forced her to slow down. She had wrapped and tied with the same concentration she brought to design problems, leaving cereal to disintegrate in gray milk. Then she had slipped two small foil packets into a zippered interior pocket, thinking about how ordinary they seemed. She clung to the thought for comfort as she drove. The square packets didn't suggest anything remarkable. They could have held tablets for indigestion or heartburn. The content of the packets could have been confused with a cure for any simple, innocent complaint.

He swung the door open wide, not letting his words register welcome right away. His face did, though. Emotion flitted over his mouth and eyes and Helen knew he was glad to see her at his front door. Helen wished she could kick off her shoes to be barefoot like him. He wore a frayed white shirt he hadn't bothered to tuck into khaki pants. Ray Richards examined every detail: her new haircut, painfully pretty shoes and the bright dress that hugged and held every curve.

"There you are." He pulled his hand from the door frame. He finally stood aside to let her into his home.

She let excitement take over as they roamed through the house, lingering in a guest room, asking any question that came into her head. The house was as eccentric as Gatley himself, enthusiasms spilling over into rooms, ideas connected as crazily as the hallways in the old house. A pinched view of the ocean here, a window that seemed to lurch into the arms of a tree. A straight and narrow bathhouse on the edge of a long garden that looked icy and rigorous as a winter swim, then an enormous fireplace to take away the chill. Ray stood next to a folded iron screen.

"He lined his wife and his daughters up right here." He pointed to a spot in front of the fireplace. "He made it large enough for them to all be warmed at the same time."

Ray shook his head. "He was kind of a nut, I guess."

"Think of what he did for his family." Helen sighed.

Ray was quiet for a minute. "I suppose you're right."

Some rooms were private, roped off with invisible cords. They were meant to enclose and contain, protect what was hidden away. Every space they passed through was empty until they came to the kitchen. The club chair sat in a niche. A circular, hand-painted table sat next to it, ducks breaking through branches of a weeping willow. Helen traced her finger over the lake scene. He moved quickly to her side and wiped the top of the table with the edge of his shirt, even though it was shiny and clean.

"I'm proud of that. I picked it up myself at a yard sale."

"Don't you mean estate sale?"

"In Oklahoma? Oh, no."

Large, dark green-glazed tiles led to an herb garden in a sunny window. Who had planted the sprigs of basil and thyme popping up in terra cotta pots? Big mistake. She thought of Stan's mysterious aesthetic, how he must have worked the club chair into the small space, then caught sight of the offending soup tureen on the counter or the colorful antique baking tins that lined one shelf above the appliances. Cartons were grouped in corners and the sofa, for the moment, was placed in a light yellow living room underneath another watchful eye. Helen looked up to see a larger oval window in an upstairs room.

"That was something else Gatley liked. Bull's eye."

Hearing this calmed Helen and she pulled her shoulders back as she passed the window. She'd been so nervous before. Nervous and silly. The glass oval wasn't meant to indict anyone. She followed Ray upstairs, letting his voice guide her along. She liked the quick, quiet way he moved. She wondered what it would be like to watch him unobserved. How he would enter a room or pass under a low doorway. What he would look like straining for something just beyond his fingertips, some lost item that had rolled under his bed. Then she thought of all the adjustments his big, graceful body would make to conditions and contours not its own. Bolder images fought their way into her mind. She was sure he would detect them, in the empty hallway.

"See? Everything's out of whack." He pointed to his daughter's room and Helen felt her heart speed up. The whirring made her uncomfortable. It felt as if Lang's overwound clock had been jammed inside her chest.

"This won't be so hard. But I have a confession to make before we get started." Helen tried to steady the words. "I've always wanted to get inside this house."

There. Now she could talk Alice up, get down to business. Design services, all that Alice Nash could do for this wonderful, oddball diamond in the rough. Helen saw the room, how a shift could be made here and there to open new space for the girl, but Alice would see the whole house. Size it up in a second.

He worked open a window in his daughter's room. The air was stuffy and closeted, as if wrapped in damp paper. The heel of his hand slammed against wood once and a fresh current of air rushed in.

"And now that you're inside, do you like what you see?"

She liked more than that. She liked this talk that said so many things at the same time. But she was on a job. She worked for Alice, and as long as she did, she didn't do anything else. Her breathing felt light and shallow; it was the kind of panting Poor did when he wanted something he couldn't have.

"Very much. You've got plenty of possibilities here," Helen said.

She walked carefully around the room. Rebecca, shortened to Becca by an adoring father, grinned from a photograph. It was Ray's favorite. Look at my little monkey, he said. In the photograph the monkey dangled from a jungle gym. She clowned on top of iron bars, then frowned in an Oklahoma frock from the center of a second photo. The picture had been torn and the raggedy tear was taped back together. Helen felt a blister begin at her heel. She wished she could walk right out of her pretty, painful shoes.

"She hates these outfits her mom makes her wear. She tried to tear up the picture, but I saved it."

"I had to stop telling my son what to wear a long time ago."

"Is that right?"

"The more I nagged, the worse he looked."

"You were smart."

"I was desperate."

Ray lifted his head slowly. He didn't speak and Helen moved reflexively to her handbag. She opened it, feeling along the bottom for a Kleenex or a pen. It didn't matter what. Desperate. What kind of word was that to use?

The clumsy word must have provoked something in Ray because he began to talk. He told her stories, long, slow tales that had all the time in the world. He spoke without wrath, without the wrath she felt for Boyd. The business sold, the life turned inside out by divorce, and the move west, away from the small Oklahoma town he and his family company dominated. He seemed bemused as they lifted the bed together to a new angle away from the door. They plotted out the narrow vertical space that was left. A tall chest of drawers would be perfect for a tomboy's collection of T-shirts and shorts. Talk of her rugged clothing made him pause.

"I worked crazy hours when Rebecca was little. She could have used a big brother. Somebody to toss her a ball now and then when I wasn't around."

And now that I'm out here . . . Helen filled in the rest for herself. Rebecca needed a brother more than ever. She thought of Lang and long afternoons when he didn't have wrestling practice. She had called her old friend about a part-time job, fearing the stark, empty house and the despair that would sneak up on her son if she didn't act. Helen needed to phone Robin. Catching up would take hours. She would call when things settled down.

"I know what you mean. Only children spend way too much time alone." She looked up at the grandfather clock and remembered the store. She pulled at the tight waist of her dress. "You might think about a narrow chest of drawers going right here."

"I might."

A smile started on his face and his glance ran over her chest, then down to her knees. Helen stopped what she was doing. She remembered Alice's anger exactly. The hardening of her features and her diction. The clickety-click of her fury.

"You shouldn't have worn that dress." He said it matter-of-factly.

"Why not?"

"You'll get it dirty with all this hauling and lifting."

He glanced down and she nearly laughed at his shyness. He was too timid to compliment her dress. Maybe he was thinking of Alice in his own way. Maybe he felt as constrained and frustrated as she did right this minute.

"Helen?"

She liked hearing him isolate her name. *Helen* became something special.

"I have a confession, too."

If she had dreamed the words and dreamed the day, she wouldn't have added one more detail. What would his confession be? Had it begun the first time he had seen her? That was what made him rush from the store. She felt hurried by the thought, as if just thinking it gave her a deadline she couldn't meet. Maybe if she didn't reach out quickly, he would disappear again. Helen let her eyes wander to the lit bateau, the boat bed floating out to sea and away from her, then brought them back to his face.

He looked down at his pant leg, pulled on a loose thread that seemed to have no end. He pulled and pulled, laughing at the damage.

"I'm falling apart here."

Surely that wasn't the confession. She looked at the photograph of Rebecca again. She was so young, so far away. They *had* to share the same sad knowledge. The sturdiest things were always the first to go, the khaki pants you thought were indestructible. The fragile things (silk, satin, antique brocade) continued beyond the occasion, the one fabulous night designed to dissolve into a memory of fine things. And not just things. A cow dog would drop dead before a Siamese cat. Healthy parents would disappear, leaving thin, bloodless aunts who coughed and wheezed through one hard winter after the next. Marriages . . . love affairs . . . but which of these were sturdy, which fragile? Which tripped you up as badly as Poor?

"I thought it would be easy to make a home, that all I had to do was buy the right house and the right things to put in it. I was way off."

She looked at his bare feet. They looked so unlike Boyd's.

"A few weeks ago I bought furniture for this room. It wound up looking even emptier than before and I sent everything back."

Rebecca, Lang, Helen, Ray. Those weren't empty sounds. They rang in her mind. Only children became only adults. Sisterless, brotherless Helen knew this for a fact. But there was surely a cure for every confession. A falling together for every falling apart. A purplish blush began to spread over Ray Richards's face. He patted the bed, fussed with the edge of the blanket. The violent spill of color grew until Helen had to look away.

"I want this place to open up and take me inside. I guess I'm no different than you."

Helen kept her eyes on the bright room that danced with light and lovely things. She held very still and thought of other rooms. Painful, narrow rooms that shut out laughter and light. They were the rooms she inhabited for too many years, the rooms she lived in still. She dreamed of escape in a dream that had grown more and more voracious. It cried for real food and real attention, demanding as an only child. She felt tickling down the back of her neck. She reached under her hair, but there was nothing to wipe away but the faint feeling.

"That's what I'm here for."

She felt the pinch of her shoes, the pinch of the strangling lie. She wasn't really here for that reason. Something much more important pushed her toward Ray Richards.

"I'm sorry. That's just not true," she said.

Ray looked puzzled, but he didn't complain. He listened so carefully that she was encouraged to speak. His silence encouraged her to say more and more. The smooth leather of her handbag was the color of a nut. She imagined splitting it open easily and moved closer to Ray. They both stood still.

"I thought of you after you left the store the first time."

"You did?" He looked at the shoulder of her dress. It looked casually knotted, though Helen had worked and worked to get it right. He cracked the knuckles on his left hand. Was he wishing she would speak more carefully? Or was this fine so far? Good, even?

She put her head down, and bumped her forehead softly against his shoulder. She hoped her touch would inspire his. She wondered if she should say more. What did women say? (A woman like *her.* She corrected the question, eliminating Patricia.) What did women do? The dream had ended now. She was stringing her actions together without its help. She reached out to touch him and watched her hand fall on his chest. She let it rest there for a moment. It drew heat from his body and sent it down a separate path through her body.

His eyes were open wide. They gleamed like one of Gatley's windows.

"What about you?" She asked the question quietly.

"I've done enough talking about me."

She let her other hand circle his waist, drawing her closer to him as if he were pulling her. It continued until she pressed up against him lightly. His body shocked her: she had forgotten the way a man's body felt. She shook her head and frowned. She thought of the elaborate dance she danced with Lang. Their embraces, the only embraces she'd known in the past two years, were measured by distance. Space marked the love of a mother and son.

She could smell the shampoo on his hair. She was close enough to kiss, but Ray watched her instead. His mouth looked separate and mean. She brushed the thought from her mind.

"Helen, there's something I need to tell you." He cleared his throat. "I don't know how to do this."

The color had crept back into his cheek. The skin looked singed, tender. Helen made herself watch the color progress.

"I'm really the new kid on the block. Do you understand what that means?"

Oh, she did. She understood what that color meant now. It was polite and deeply frightened, a blush too deep to disappear right away. Helen looked at her handbag, the secret it held. She knew more than she cared to about the humiliation of desire.

"I took care of everything."

"You did?" His voice had turned mild.

She worked her leg inside his. He let his foot slide to one side and she moved her knee into the open space. She held him tighter and looked down to see how they were shaped. What fine form their bodies created this way.

"I brought something for us to use. Don't worry."

Her hands came around to the front. She flattened them and ran them slowly down his body. He was strong and hard. But his shape insinuated ease, not effort. She kissed the corner of his mouth and closed her eyes.

"Helen, I'm so sorry."

She let her cheek rest against his for a minute. "For what?"

"I can't go through with this. I guess I'm just not ready."

"Oh." The word rattled in her throat. She took a step back and straightened one of the pillows on Rebecca's bed. It suddenly seemed affected there, foreign and outdated as a powder puff.

"Marriage didn't exactly prepare me for the dating scene."

"I am *not* the dating scene." She moved toward the door automatically, her eyes on the empty hallway. Ray stepped to the center of the room, blocking her path.

He reached out as she tried to sidle past him and closed his hand on the back of her neck. She wanted to run away. She would have, too, had it not been for the steady pressure of his hand. There was no warmth coming from him now. She'd once held the loose, floppy skin on Poor's neck in the same dead clamp.

"You misunderstand me, Helen. You're very brave. Much braver than me."

His hand began to knead the back of her neck. She let herself relax the slightest bit.

"This took me off guard, that's all." He stroked the back of her hair several times. She knew he was trying to apologize, but his hand was damp. It fell too heavily, pulling at the crown of her head with each stroke.

"Very pleasantly off guard," he added this as he continued to touch her.

"And where were you all this time?"

The tone was familiar, but it wasn't Alice asking, it was Patricia. She pulled on her fake pearls. She was dressing better and better lately. Surely it was Alice, her good influence. Patricia was in the formal sitting room. She sat at the edge of a day bed, her back erect as the tapestry pillows surrounding her. A tight ball of ivy had been successfully tamed. Its coiffed green head rose from a porcelain planter like an aloof third party. The leaves glistened in the sunlight. Patricia studied Helen's dress. Helen had thought her plain linen jacket toned it down. Maybe she'd been wrong.

"The Richards business took longer than I thought," Helen answered. Why *had* it taken so long to leave that room? She cringed at the question and began to focus on the room she was in now. She straightened a lacquered Chinese box once used to hold fans and thought of the relief a fan would bring right now.

Patricia handed her a sheet of paper with names and numbers, pleas to call back. Her hair wasn't jelled this morning. It was curled and dry, coming to a sweet curve around her jaw line.

"Oh, that cute guy that bought out the whole bedroom." Her smile was sly.

Helen crossed her arms over her chest and squeezed. *Cute.* It was a stubby little word. It made Ray Richards sound ordinary. Alice had called him cute, too.

Patricia punched in a telephone number on a cordless phone and quickly headed into a conversation about sales tax and shipping out of state. She looked so authoritative . . . was it the longer hair? Helen heard Alice's loud cry from downstairs. She couldn't tell if it meant pleasure or pain.

Poor was banished to a corner. He sat shivering, having probably suffered a whack on the bottom. Helen wondered what he had done. It must have been something very wrong. A big mistake . . . Stan's words pressed at her back. She moved quickly across the gravel.

Alice looked up from where she knelt in a corner of the shop.

"Cute dress. You look like you're on your way to a luau." She was hunched over an old book. "Help."

Helen squatted beside her, followed her fingertip over material samples, narrow red and black columns of figures. The pages bulged with stripes and checks, minute flowers and mauve bombazine. Each page was curled and warped. The book seemed to have been dipped in water and left haphazardly in the sun to dry.

"What is this, Alice?"

"It's a cuttings-and-record book. Lyons, fin de siècle. God, look at this. Of course the factory went straight down the tubes. This was much too expensive to produce."

Helen sat close enough to feel heat coming off of Alice's skin. She wore one of Jack's old sweater vests from college and a white oxford-cloth shirt she had custom ordered from England. But Alice's rising temperature had nothing to do with wool.

"Tell me to close this book and never think about this again."

"Where did you get this?"

"A dressmaker in Paris. She had mounds of things and all I bought was a trunk full of old souvenirs. This was buried at the bottom. Feel this! If I were to copy a few . . ."

"Alice."

"A *few* and have them done up as damask. It would ruin me, of course."

"And Jack. Don't forget about ruining Jack."

The sweater vest was a complicated weave and a creamy yarn rippled through the sea green. Alice had stolen it right after they were married and preserved it through thick and thin. She grew indignant whenever Jack suggested wearing it himself.

"I can see a jacquard weave. Six or seven designs."

"And a trip to Paris for more souvenirs."

"Bless your heart. You always see the whole picture."

Helen's laugh was thin. When had she ever seen the whole picture?

"Helen. Since we're speaking of money . . ."

Alice closed the book gently and waved her hand in front of her nose. It had been locked away for years and the scraps of fabric inside smelled mildewed and dank. Two women burst through the door, talking at once. They screeched at a pair of footstools. One of them spotted Alice.

"You mustn't take advantage of me." Alice pinched the end of her nose and sniffed.

"What are you talking about?" Helen asked.

"Don't order any more champagne at the Club. And don't invite other people out to lunch on me. That's not beating the tax man. That's cheating poor Alice."

She turned her attention back to the fabric. "If I can figure the numbers out, this could be very, very interesting. Don't look so cross. When have I ever failed?"

Never. Alice worked hard, and part of that effort was making work appear playful. Frivolous. Nobody ran the risk of being ruined, regardless of how much champagne was consumed. Helen felt the side of her face. It was red-hot.

"You'll rep the line once I get it set up."

Helen let the words swirl around her for a moment, releasing her anger. She liked the look of the reps who came to the store. Their clothing was as extravagant as the fabrics they sold. There were constant references to island escapes and mountain adventures. They assumed Helen had visited the same expensive getaways.

"We'll start slowly, maybe with that dreadful convention business in

Dallas. You'll do the road show for me, Helen. It could mean that fat Christmas bonus will get even fatter."

"What about the store? You're barely here as it is."

Alice lifted her eyebrows.

"Reproach?"

"No. Just a question. Who's going to take care of the shop?"

"Patricia's growing into things nicely."

Helen sat up straighter. She heard paper crackle and turned toward the noise. These weren't ladies who lunched. They were ladies who snacked. One of them had a bag of Chee-tos in her hand. She wiped orange dust from her fingers with a handkerchief and flipped through a book on glassware. The other drank from a liter of water she had hung over her shoulder in a mesh bag. She was headed toward Alice, who hooked her hair behind her ears and began to stand up, unfolding one limb at a time.

"Ouch. Getting old," Alice complained loudly.

"Alice, I don't know about the road show part. I hate leaving Lang alone."

"Don't be silly." Alice's voice was sharp. She beamed at the hungry shoppers and changed her tone to cheer. "Hello, hello!"

Alice kissed the woman with the water on both cheeks, then peeked in the bag.

"A baby!" Alice cried.

A puppy's paw and pink nose appeared from the depths of the bag and Helen's expression relaxed. A baby! Wasn't that just like Alice to confuse one small creature for another?

"I hope Poor doesn't gobble you up." Alice stood poised on the balls of both feet. She continued to peer into the dark pouch. Something else occurred to her, and she glanced accusingly at Helen. Alice's gray eyes were fierce.

"When he's not wrestling or going to that awful job—"

"It's not awful at all."

"He's working with people who are dying. He's touching their bodies." Alice glanced at a chandelier. Light sliced through its glass prisms.

"Anyway, he can always come here after school. Patricia and I would love to look after him."

Patricia was coming down the stairs, but not clomping, not breathless. With her glasses, with her pearls and the simple gray dress, she didn't look like a salesgirl. She looked like a rich young wife with better clothing and better manners than the two women in the store.

"Now, where have you been? I thought we were going to finish that library before it finished you." Alice closed down one discussion and opened another.

The woman looked happy, mock contrite. She had been away.

"Mallorca."

"Oh, the famous finca!" Alice's voice rose, in pitch and volume.

"It's going to finish me, too."

The stonemason, the plumber, the village goat. The woman sucked on her water bottle and collapsed into a dining chair. How could travel be so exhausting? Helen wondered, remembering Amanda Reston's chic weariness. For one quick moment, Alice's proposition seemed simple. Even if her destination would not be a remote island or mountain resort, Helen had earned the chance to escape for a while. She thought of how sleepy and slow Ray's body had seemed, then how his speed had surprised her as he moved to touch her hair. That was it. She'd been caught off guard, too. His agility had kept her in that bedroom too long. Well. She would forget all about that and regroup out on the road, making money as she did.

Helen eyed the back of Patricia's dress, though no dark, wet stain circled her waist. No water dripped from the nape of her neck, for Patricia had sacrificed her midday swim. Helen considered this new set of priorities and rubbed the tops of her arms. She felt chilled to the bone. Maybe Patricia was having a growth spurt, moving from gangly girl to woman in Alice's greenhouse. Helen yanked at a strand of ivy. It had begun to sneak free of its careful route through a trellis along the wall. She pulled hard and forced it back through a neat diamond. She thought of how it twisted and clung. How difficult ivy was to dislodge once it had truly taken root.

Helen picked up the sample book and sank into a squeaky wicker chair. It stood by the staircase, ready to catch travelers exhausted by the journey from one floor to another. Helen watched the four women talk and laugh, tenderly petting the puppy as exiled Poor mourned. She had no business planning an escape. What had she been thinking? Everything she'd always wanted was right here at home.

11.

Alice and Jack's lean white boat was still. The two of them could sail from port to foreign port in this very boat, stepping off the wooden deck to buy whatever they pleased. Everything done with a casual touch, smooth as the motion on the boat, each purchase made on a whim, according to beauty, with no thought to the weight the boat would be forced to carry. Where Alice and Jack sailed, there were no tourists, no bottles of suntan lotion, caps grimy with sand and salt. Jack spoke and punctured her reverie.

"Tell me, Helen—"

Jack was getting plump; his new shape confused him. Sometimes he pushed his pudgy middle down as if to try tucking it into his pants. Helen looked past him toward Coronado Island, the space where the old ferry had run for years. It was her favorite hour, a time to come about without wind, to change direction motionlessly, to watch the sun sink and to dream. Alice clanged pots in the galley below. Talk to Jack, she had said. Alice was having one of her grim, unequivocal nights—maybe cooking would help.

"—how was Bitter Monday?"

Helen chipped away at a broken nail, then collected herself carefully.

She'd first seen Ray Richards on a Monday. He'd come into the store a second time one week later. Mondays *were* bitter, though Helen hadn't known at the time.

Enough. She would keep her mind on business, where it belonged. She thought back to the beginning of the hectic week. Two client appointments had been canceled at the last minute, a color job bungled on a bolt of raw silk, and a container delayed in Marseilles.

"Pretty rough. Why do you ask?"

"Alice said you had lunch at the club. I don't know how you can stand all the pageantry. If the food doesn't kill you, that tradition will. On Mondays the men take off early, then sit there and get snockered in The Grill while the boys blow up on cookies and sugar drinks. It makes them feel they've done their job as fathers."

What was a father's job? Helen heard the old roar inside. She thought of Lang's room with its dim reading light and crooked, curling posters, the collection of things that didn't work, and the greater collection of things that weren't there at all. Boyd and his excuses shouted inside her head. I can never give him what he needs, Helen. Or you. Why didn't Boyd just come out and say it? When she thought of the room waiting for Rebecca Richards, the roaring increased. She tried to push the unpleasantness out of her mind. She tried to tear herself away from that room, make herself scuttle away from the thoughts that pinned her there. She envisioned the silvery pouch she had tucked inside Rebecca's closet as a secret gift to the little girl. She'd done it when Ray's back was turned, before he . . . stop! Now her own voice shouted in her mind. She made herself steal back into the room to retrieve the gift she'd given so innocently. She imagined stuffing the sachet back into the bottom of her purse. There. Helen returned to the flat varnished surfaces of the boat. Everything was shiny and blond. The perfect silence inside permitted her to ask the most obvious question.

"When the boys grow up to be rotters or when they don't grow up at all, everybody's bitter. I was lucky. It was hamburgers and tennis for me."

And golf. Helen liked the way Jack drank. She imagined he played golf the same way. Stroke after even stroke with his goal in sight. Three drinks and a nice, smooth landing. He took his chin in his hand, jerked it left and right. Helen winced at the cracking sound.

"It helps me stay loose in an uptight world."

Helen couldn't help looking at his glass.

"That was unkind." Jack bit his lip and continued. "Has Alice told you our big secret?"

The bowl was empty. There were no more pistachios, nothing else to sop up Jack's liquor.

"I don't like secrets." Helen stomped on a spider that was crossing the deck. She cleaned the bottom of her tennis shoe and the slick wooden surface. She loved this boat. She loved the quiet hour. She wanted to feel lulled and calm inside.

"Hearing them or having them?"

He was probably past par. Helen had once seen him drink too much at a fund-raiser, then blinked it away. Alice had flapped her alpaca cape, matador to bull, to turn Jack's drunkenness into a joke and to turn him to the door to leave. Neither of them had mentioned that: Jack with one drink, Jack with five. Instead they had filled in the uncomfortable blank with mean vignettes. They'd focused on the committee chairman's foolish speech. He forgot he was talking to people who'd been rich for years! People like Alice and Jack.

Jack poured another drink. He had switched to Johnny Walker all of a sudden. Helen tried to think of their ad campaign. Besides golf, Jack's other hobby was advertising. He had a file cabinet full of his favorite print ads. Alice made him keep them at the office. Helen took a sip of her drink. Maybe she should loosen up, too. Take her chin in her hand and pop. Pop. A pot crashed in the galley below and Alice swore.

"What if *I* want to tell secrets? Just one, to see how it feels?" He gave her a sly smile.

"All right. I won't try to stop you." She hoped he didn't expect for her to tell one of her own.

"I'm going to have a baby."

She sighed and heard the faint sound of a radio playing. It was gay. It was mariachi music. People were having a lively time somewhere; it relieved her to think of that. It relieved her to hear Jack joke around. But not for long.

"Alice would like one, you know."

No. She didn't know. Alice (at *her* age) with a baby in her arms? Smelling like vomit and breast milk? Alice cooing? NO. Helen shifted in her seat and pulled on the sweater she'd thrown over her shoulders.

"In fact, that's why Alice is so testy tonight. The lab results came back." Jack looked at the flat water that wouldn't be flat for long. A grand cabin cruiser was coming into the bay. Helen guessed sixty feet, long enough to throw a showy wake. "Let's just say I'm not exactly the great sperm whale. My wife will not be able to accessorize with a brand new baby."

Jack wore a tangerine-colored polo. It would have been the perfect shade for a new kind of candy. A candy that brought a hard, artificial taste of the tropics to the top of the tongue. Helen concentrated on the color of his shirt, the sweetness of that flavor. She didn't want to think of Alice wanting something she couldn't have, the effect her unhappiness would have on all of them. I'll only ruin Jack a tiny bit.

"She called you so we wouldn't have to be alone."

Her drink was strong, and she drank it down quickly. She tried to isolate the crisp flavor of lime and bitter gin, but couldn't. It swelled into a single sharp taste. She wiped at her mouth and looked at the bay. The other boat was smart and stylish. The low chug of its engine was discreet, even if the wake was not. She would think about that boat and the passengers who must have been below in the cabin. The smell of leather. Hearts, winners and losers. Women with long, wild hair trapped any old way. Dinner plans grinding into gear. There, for a moment, Helen could see them all. Not see Jack, unable to give Alice exactly what she wanted, hands folded over an amateur gut. Maybe Jack would grow fatter and fatter until one day nobody would remember him any other way. No.

The galley door swung on its hinge as the boat rolled slowly from side to side. The cabin cruiser battered the sailboat with its wake. Helen rocked with the waves as Alice staggered up the steps carrying plates. Helen's discomfort rose higher and higher.

"Man overboard."

Jack hoisted himself out of the chair and wiggled free of his shirt with a cross-armed struggle. Then he unzipped with his back to Helen and stepped out of his pants quickly. Helen felt his arm brush hers.

"Now you see him . . ." He straddled the guardrail and winked not at Helen, but at Alice, who was setting plates down. Goose bumps stood out on his white skin. He hunched over, made a face, and looked at his wife for a long minute.

"I've ruined the eggs," Alice said.

"Then you won't mind if I skip dinner."

It was a messy dive and Helen felt the shock of cold water on her own skin, watched as he broke the black surface into trembling, fragmenting rings. She thought of the Langleys at sea, their rush to the edge of the boat to find their little boy. Then she reprimanded herself for the association. Jack Nash and Boyd Patterson were nothing alike.

"High drama." Alice had begun to eat and her mouth was full when she spoke.

"He's been drinking."

"We all have, Helen." Alice's voice was tired.

There he was. Helen let herself breathe. He'd already swum a good distance out. He didn't clown or splash. He worked as diligently as Patricia did, maintaining a good clip with sharp, drunken concentration. He stopped swimming and called out to them happily.

"Now you don't!"

He dove down, pressing his feet into a shape that looked to Helen like the flipper of a playful, disappearing fish.

"Now you don't. You *don't* see him, Helen." Alice paused. "Of course, you don't see me either."

"That's not true."

"You've made me up completely. You've invented the person you love. But Jack knows me. Only Jack."

Alice's face hardened. The pout that appeared was so stony and serene, Helen imagined it might last forever. She began to eat the ruined eggs and drink what was left in her glass.

12.

Understanding hadn't come easily. Helen first imagined that what she'd seen on Alice and Jack's boat was something she would have to ignore. But when Alice didn't remark on the evening and when the following week passed briskly, even happily, Helen saw that Jack's shortcomings weren't the end of the world, and neither were Alice's. In fact, Alice and Jack's world began there—in an acknowledgment of human frailty. Helen finally understood. Love didn't prosper because of perfection, it was just the opposite. She smiled, thinking of Jack, and took it one step further. Love could *only* grow from a clear understanding of limitations. Love was fed by compassion and kindness. What had Helen been thinking?

Not of Ray's ordeal. She'd been selfish, thinking only of her needs, her desires. She'd forgotten what it took for life to right itself again after divorce. And it did eventually, like one of the plastic cups she'd bought for Lang when he was little. It rocked and wobbled under his baby grasp, but never tipped over completely. Manufacturer's guarantee.

Helen let the phone ring on and on. She thought again of Ray Richards's garden out on the point. Seen from the ocean, it looked like a bright green toupee set down on a hapless head. The mouth of the cave below opened in protest. She could help Ray. She would tear off the toupee and cover the bald spot with a thick, jumbled crop of brushy plants parted by gravel paths. Yellow-tipped grasses waving in wet wind, a haze of gray-green framing the grizzled face. Lavender . . . the smell would saturate the house. She would haul rocks from the cave to the artist who worked on India Street, see if she could sober him up long enough to chisel them into sculpture. If it were hers to make over, she would—

He answered the phone and she struggled to drop the shovel she'd just plunged into a patch of rich black soil.

"Ray, it's Helen."

"I know who this is."

His voice was hoarse and ragged. She wanted to hang up. She wanted to forget that it was she, not him, making the first call after that disastrous afternoon. But she thought of Alice and Jack's boat pitching violently from side to side. Then she thought of it steady and still long after the cabin cruiser had passed. She thought of the voyages that sturdy boat could make.

"I've been thinking about your daughter."

A machine ran in the background. She couldn't see him. For a moment she couldn't imagine where he stood. She gripped the phone tighter as if he would slip away.

"Hold on a second."

He was just running a load of laundry and hadn't heard the phone ring. He'd probably put all the wrong colors together, like the furniture he'd ordered and had to send back.

"You have?"

"Yes, and I've had a crazy thought. If she's the tomboy you say she is, I've got a suggestion for you. For her."

Helen described the outdoor jungle gym, perfect for a lace-hating ten-year-old. The woodwork, the solid construction, the former gymnast who designed the redwood domes and tunnels. Play Passages. Helen had wanted one for Lang when he was little. She'd spent a tortured afternoon watching him play on several models she and Boyd could never afford, finally prying his fingers from the bars when it was time to go home. Of course, Lang was too old to use a jungle gym now, but he could spot for someone younger. He was gentle with little children. Lang could be trusted to watch them for hours and hours. She slid the palm of her hand down her thigh and spoke. Would Ray Richards like the address and phone number?

"It wouldn't disrupt your garden a bit. They're really beautiful."

The truck, crammed full of things for the empty bedroom, squeezed into the delivery area in back of the store. Helen leaned toward the window as she talked, watching a boy unload the first piece and start up the back stairs. Alice had pulled curious combinations from the warehouse for the next little girl. No telescope this time. The galaxies were to be ignored. Alice had something else in mind now.

Ray didn't answer. Maybe she had suggested the wrong thing. She had intruded on his privacy, that was it. Helen bit the inside of her mouth, thinking of all the ways she'd been wrong. She tried to remember how badly she had felt when she'd left Boyd. But it wasn't leaving Boyd that pained her. It was what had followed. She'd headed toward her bright future in a sheer dress that floated over her body. She'd been dead serious about that dress. It was daring, implying the future that spread out before her. The meal, which she could still taste, and too many drinks after awful news from an awful man. That man was no Jack Nash. He was certainly no Ray Richards . . .

"Is this a bad time for me to call you?" Her voice crumpled a little.

A woman in a knit suit climbed the stairs. Helen could see her from the office. She watched the fabric stretch as the woman tackled the wide steps. Big brass buttons shone on the front of the suit. The woman stopped to blow her nose. She sounded like a lost goose, sounding a lonesome call for her mate.

"Not at all. Let me take that number."

Ray's voice grew enthusiastic and he spoke more quickly. He'd meant to thank her for the flowers, the bright orange ones, what were they called? His mother had grown them down in Oklahoma. They made him sneeze back then.

"But they don't make me sneeze now. That was a nice touch."

Helen's lips were dry. As dry as Ray Richards's hands. She ran her tongue over her lips quickly and spoke. She felt something pushing her, insisting that she hurry. It was important to move ahead, to march quickly. Not to listen to the roaring inside that was just silly, irrational noise. The roaring could shut everything down.

"I hope you'll call me if there's anything else you need. Either that or just drop by. We're always getting in new merchandise."

"Helen, I want to apologize for the other day."

"Oh, don't. I understand."

She felt his hand again at the back of her head. He had pulled and pleaded with that hand. He hadn't understood that the gesture only made things worse. She could help Ray Richards. She could empathize with Ray's experience, no matter what it was.

"Do you?"

"You're rebuilding your life and that's a hard job. Those flowers were my apology."

"For what?"

"For not understanding right away."

"But Alice thought it was terrific."

Helen was ready to close up the shop. But before she did she called Patricia to her desk for a talk. The Montblanc lay in a leather trough narrow as a tight, warm cot. She touched it once and spoke to Patricia in the voice she often used with Lang. But Patricia waved Helen's voice away as if it were a gnat buzzing in her ear.

"She even said that with big sales, we ought to do that automatically. He liked them, didn't he?" Patricia asked.

Helen wasn't thinking about whether Ray liked the cluster of orange and yellow tiger lilies, the bear grass that would bend into a graceful bow after several days. She was watching Patricia's face, the way it shone at the end of a long day. Patricia was the sort of girl who loved going to Peaches just to say no. She would laugh at the older women who drifted toward the men she so casually rejected. Maybe she would begin at Peaches, then head to one of the bars in her own neighborhood. Long, sloppy margaritas with a friend and a bowl of chips that would be filled and refilled as the night spun along. Yes. Would she leave the bar with the same friend? Or someone new. Someone cute.

"Helen? I was asking if he liked them."

"Oh, yes."

"So why are you pissed?"

Pissed? She got up from her chair and Patricia did the same. They moved toward the stairs together, but then Patricia skipped past her, driven by something outside the store and the flowers and the possible infraction. She waited at the bottom of the stairs and Helen slowed her step even more. Patricia put her hand on her hip and swiveled from side to side.

"I'm not sure pissed is the right word."

"I am. You look mad."

"I think you might have mentioned it. That's all," Helen said.

"You know what else, though?"

She didn't know. She had no idea what would follow as she watched Patricia throw her shoulders forward, working the straps of the backpack into place.

"Alice thought it was such a good idea, she wants to use those Portuguese vases we have at the warehouse with every arrangement we send out, the ones with the store initials painted on them, and that way . . ."

Helen tuned out the rest as she pictured the initials on the vase, rendered in the same tangled, lovely script that marked the entrance to the warehouse.

Patricia ran her hand over her shoulder and rubbed. "I'm not trying to steal your customer, Helen. I know he belongs to you."

Patricia pulled at the ends of her hair. Bits and pieces were getting longer, long enough to twist behind her ears. She grinned at Helen. The shape of her little white teeth made Helen want to shake her and shake her.

"Patricia, I'm going to be real honest with you."

"OK."

"There's one thing you ought to know about working for Alice. She insists on being very professional. She discourages personal relationships with customers." Helen wished she had a peppermint. Her mouth tasted dusty.

"Uh-huh."

Helen looked at Patricia's book bag and thought about the white columns of Talbott Academy. What would it be like to have something firm and solid to lean against, not just at fifteen and sixteen and seventeen, but always?

"Do you understand what I'm saying, Patricia?"

She giggled. "Uh-huh. You're saying I shouldn't sleep with that guy."

Helen took a deep breath and opened the door. They both stepped outside. A car filled with boys drove unevenly down the street. The car swerved to avoid a door that opened suddenly on the passenger's side. Helen shivered, thinking of the damage. She was glad to let Boyd take over, give him that teaching task. Her driving with Lang hadn't been successful. She shrieked and clutched the dashboard at the first sign of a brake light. One more gash in any car would cost Helen more than she cared to think about.

"Just think about what I've said." Helen felt so tired. She sounded like someone who had given up completely.

"I have been thinking." Patricia pitched her body forward. The angle was strange and uncharacteristic. "But about something else."

She looked awkward. Helen wondered if she had a mother who studied how she moved and thought and felt. Helen thought she didn't and shifted her keys to the other hand.

"I feel bad for Lang. About how he's struggling with his French? Maybe I could be his tutor."

She backed away and waved. The gesture looked as if she was grabbing at something flying by.

"Anyway. You can think about it."

Helen stood outside for a long time after Patricia left. Lang wouldn't be home for another hour. She leaned back against the front wall, thinking the store was steadier than the Talbott Academy columns could ever hope to be. She felt stronger as she watched the pretty coast town loosen its stays, shake free of the tiresome day. The bank across the street emptied from the bottom up. Helen watched as the lights went out, darkness creeping higher and higher until at last even the corner suites went black. Two girls staggered past with packages and promises to never, ever shop together again because just look what happened! A man and woman coming toward each other from opposite ends of the sidewalk collided. The woman cried out and covered her mouth with her hand. The two dark figures moved closer and closer, then embraced without a word.

The motor of the Escort snapped on. It always surprised her when it started without a hitch, even though it was a well-mannered little car that demanded nothing much beyond gas and oil. A Mercedes rolled out of a space beside her in the parking structure, and she waved the driver on, letting him go, letting her thoughts shift to the other Mercedes from before. That car had ignited in its own way, producing sparks between Boyd and Helen. She hadn't wanted to let it go. She loved the red leather seats, all its clocks and dials, its smooth ride. She even liked the dip in the roof, something she resisted in the beginning. Even now, spooning a neat dip of trembling custard from a bowl, she would think of the pretty depression in the center and the jiggling bellies of the repo boys who took it away.

Helen turned out of the lot and took the drive that curved over the top of the town, passing schools and tract homes and empty sun-scorched lots. Alice must have ridden these roads when they were dirt paths. She would probably stop to let her horse graze, slipping the bit out of its mouth, listening to the rip of grass and the steady, mechanical chomping that followed. Did she let the occasional brush of its tail and the heat lull her into the only rest she knew then? Helen slowed down. She was getting too far from home. This wasn't even the long way back. It was no way back. She signaled on the empty road and turned right at the next street.

Fortuna curved left and ran under the freeway. Another car pulled in front of her abruptly, making her bring her speed way down. Helen put her hand on the horn and stopped, thinking of the tinky sound it made. She flashed her brights on and off several times and turned the radio on, searching for some good music. She stabbed at the button, annoyed by all the talk. She didn't know where she was, AM or FM.

The car ahead drifted to the right, then pulled too close to the center lane. Helen slowed down further, then squinted at the license plate. Lang was driving Boyd's car. She would have taken her son for a drunk driver.

They took the same streets she would have taken, Fortuna to Belvedere, then over to Chasm. He drove better once they got into heavy traffic. She wouldn't have thought so, but maybe the stream of cars comforted him with their headlights guiding the way. Or maybe they terrified him into performance. Like father like son.

He was Boyd's boy. But he was hers, too. Helen's hands tightened on the wheel as Lang came to a sudden stop before a pedestrian crosswalk. There was no pedestrian that she could see. Wait, there was someone. A man with a white, moony face glared at Lang, then crossed in front of him. He raised one fist and yanked on his dog's collar with the other. Lang hadn't given him enough space. She wanted to honk. She wanted to divert this man whose face was too wide, too pasty.

The man moved on, glancing back only once after he crossed the street, and Helen continued to follow her son. She thought Boyd would turn in her direction. She felt the pull of her own thoughts. How could he not know she was right in back of them? But he didn't.

Lang was immobile, fixed on the road, while Boyd turned his head every now and then. Chatting? Instructing? Helen fed him the words in her mind. You can speed up a bit, Lang. Your blinker's still on. You're doing fine now. You're doing a hell of a job.

The old Volvo chugged along evenly behind the other cars. The driver was indistinguishable from any other. It was as if Lang had driven for years. Maybe he'd been daydreaming up in the hills, letting the car swing out while thinking of a girl, back in as he remembered a forgotten homework assignment. It must not have mattered to Boyd. Boyd, who had a much higher tolerance for dreaming than she did.

The Volvo screeched to a stop and she jammed on her brakes, feeling her chest contract as she did. A banged-up Chevy had pulled into his lane without signaling, cutting him off more violently than he had done to her. Lang hit the horn hard, she could see his whole arm rise and fall. He didn't let up, he just pressed and pressed. The blare sounded hopeless, a car overturned, bellied up on a slick highway. The brake lights on the Volvo shimmied and Lang leaned out his window, taking the car too far left as he did.

"Fuck you, asshole!"

But that wasn't enough. Lang put his arm out the window and flicked off the man driving the Chevy. It wasn't silly. It wasn't a boy's voice cracking apart in the middle of an angry argument. It was a man's strong arm and stiff finger. Helen felt that arm close down over her chest. She took sips of air, barely swallowed bits of cool wind just to keep going. She turned off at the next intersection.

She waited for them in the driveway. Her legs were still shaking as they turned down the street, Lang cruising right down the middle. Maybe he didn't lack confidence at all. Maybe he had too much. Fuck you! Fuck me!

"Hey, Mom. Why are you just sitting here?"

He needed to brush his teeth. His mouth was a stale hole. He leaned way into the car, not giving her room. She had to scoot over in the seat just to talk to him.

"That was some performance."

The sharp smell of perspiration began to fill her car. She breathed it in deeply, grateful he'd been to practice.

"Which one?"

"The one on Sapphire." The list of gems glinted in her mind. Diamond, Emerald, Garnet. That she lived on a street named Feldspar when there were so many gems to choose from seemed like a bad joke. "Were there others?"

"Did you see what he did to me?"

"It doesn't matter. Suppose he was carrying a gun. Suppose you could have really gotten hurt."

Boyd was hanging back, waiting in his car with the interior light on. She felt hot, liquid anger just about to spill over. She held herself as still as she could.

"It sounds like you were following me, Mom."

"Why don't you go turn on the oven for me? We'll talk about it over dinner."

Dinner would be desultory. There would be grunts and hunched shoulders, monosyllabic answers to Helen's questions. Lang took a long time finding his key. When he finally did, he kicked the door open and walked to his bedroom, not the kitchen. Helen opened the door of her car.

"You look great, Helen."

Maybe if she held herself exactly like this, rigid and sharp, she could have a clean conversation with a beginning, middle, and end. No dripping over the edges. No mess to worry about the next day. It was Boyd who looked great. Boyd who had a brand new suit, an expensive one with details she could admire thanks to the light inside his car. He was in the spotlight again, seeking applause. He'd cleaned the interior. There were no dirty papers, all the sand had been swept out. An orange wooden tree hung from his rearview mirror. Someone had made a fortune from such a stupid idea. Who would have dreamed that people wanted their cars to smell like phony orange groves?

"Thanks. I hope you called him on that temper tantrum."

"Oh, that."

The phrase put another scratch on an old, old record. Oh, that. A second notice, then a third. The lights were shut off, then the gas in one remarkable week. It had been a dress rehearsal for the final departure, with Helen scooping Lang up into her arms, throwing things in a bag helter-skelter, with no thought to what they would really need. She had driven to a section of Imperial Beach, the one town where Boyd would never go, then returned, terrified, the following morning. She opened a separate checking account in her own name. The initial deposit was twenty dollars.

"He'll learn, Helen."

"Not if someone doesn't teach him."

He adjusted his tie, tightening the knot. It was a dark, nubby fabric, not at all what Boyd usually wore. The lights in the car seemed exaggerated by the dim street. Helen was practically standing in the dark. Why were street lamps so few and far between here? She wondered whether Boyd's clients ever thought about this before snapping up one of *his* jewels, whether a city's investment in street lamps was something they considered.

"Is that new?" Her eyes moved over his shoulders. The suit could have been custom-made, the way it fit him.

"A lot is new, Helen." Boyd jiggled the tree with his finger. "I sold a penthouse at the Majestic."

"I didn't know you had the listing."

"I didn't until Steve handed it to me. He's really taken me on board."

"He's quite a friend, isn't he?"

Helen was hungry. She thought about an elegant dinner, not the one that she would prepare tonight, but the one she had eaten two years ago. There were several courses, enormous decisions to make about flavors and textures. Crisp, tangy skin stretched over a miracle of moist game. Creamy green puree that didn't contain a drop of cream, another miracle. The dinner grew more and more precise in Helen's mind.

"Well, congratulations," she said.

Boyd sat looking straight ahead, as if he saw something directly in front of his car. His lousy, beat-up car. Here it was, the mess, the misdemeanor, words splashing over the sides.

"Now maybe you can stop being such a martyr and get your car fixed."

Boyd shifted suddenly in the seat and she ducked out of the way, though there was nothing to dodge but Boyd's quivering voice. He grinned and she stared at his lips. They looked so moist and soft. She wondered for a terrible minute if Boyd wore pink lip gloss. She didn't remember that rosy shine.

"This woman was my wife."

He said it cheerfully to the center seat in an empty front row somewhere off in the dark.

"This woman stands here and has the balls to call me a martyr. To refer to the scene of the crime that she committed as if *I* did it. You left me, Helen."

He turned his head from the vacant theater to her. Color flooded his cheeks. He shut off the light in the car.

"You left me and then you acted as if it were the other way around. You've turned your crime into mine."

He reached for her, and this time Helen didn't duck. She let his hand close over her forearm. She let him peel back her fingers one by one, forcing the fist open. She gasped as he moved her hand over the crushed left side of the car. He put the gash there himself, cracking up the surfboard and the car as Helen cringed in the driveway where she waited for a cab. She had been prepared for a final departure, but not one like this. Boyd's expression on the day she left had broken apart like the wood and the metal.

"Did he buy you lots of pretty things? Did he write you pretty letters?"

Her hand lay on the side of the car.

"What was his name, Helen?"

If she relaxed the palm of her hand, didn't flatten it, she could touch the sharp, jagged metal without hurting herself.

"You never told me his name."

Her hand was still relaxed as Boyd began to pull her arm inside the car. His profile cut through the darkness. She kept her hand soft, even as it closed over his crotch. He rubbed himself hard against the inside of her wrist.

"This is my crime, Helen. I still love you. I still want to be inside you."

Helen's head hung down. She was glad to live on a dim street, with lights that were too far away to matter.

13.

I'm surprised you're home on a Saturday night."

Helen stood shivering, wrapped in a bathrobe. Bubbles still clinging to the back of her neck. Her toes curled on the kitchen linoleum.

"I've got a problem," Ray said.

She thought of Play Passages, the wide spaces between the climbing bars, the number of steps it took to get to the top tunnel. She imagined Rebecca lying inert, one arm cocked behind her back, blood on the steps, blood on metal rings, blood marking the long fall down. Stupid. She'd ruined a future before it had begun.

"Is it about your daughter?"

Ray cleared his throat and hesitated. "Listen, do you think we could meet for drinks somewhere? It's difficult to talk about this over the phone."

"Sure. Give me half an hour."

Boyd was coming over for some mail that had been mistakenly sent to her. She didn't need to stay home for that.

The bar he named was jammed during the day. How did a newcomer to town know about this place? Right across the street from a Catholic church, the bar had gotten lots of attention when it first opened because of the couples who were collared there by Father Andrew, a plump, aggressive priest who usually dressed in full habit and stained Converse high-tops. Father Andrew often waltzed in at noon to convert secretaries and salesmen as they wolfed down a hot lunch special and a glass of house red. He had even performed marriages in the bar. The photographs made the society page, sharing space with debutantes and Junior Leaguers. Helen hurried into a pair of jeans and a cotton-knit shirt. She pulled on a jacket and tried to imagine who would fill the funny little bar at night.

She parked her car in the church lot and checked her watch. She had just washed her jeans and they were tight, cutting into her as she walked across the street. The soft knit shirt was a comfortable contrast, even more so since she wasn't wearing a bra. Wet and still dripping, they hung over faucets and shower heads in her bathroom. She thought of Lang finding them there and walked faster.

"Thank you for coming."

Ray was already in a booth near the back of the room. A pianist was rubbing his hands together, warming them up for his first number. Helen frowned as she sat down. She wanted to keep her mind on Ray's little girl without interference from second-rate show tunes.

He motioned to the waiter and asked for a French wine, not one she recognized.

"I hope you haven't eaten," he said.

"No."

"I have their special every time. I've never been disappointed."

He squinted slightly at Helen, as if he had trouble bringing her into focus. Dark smudges, like thumb prints, colored the skin under his eyes and his hair needed washing. His nails were as cleanly clipped as ever, though. If she found them washed up on the beach, pretty and perfect as shells, she would save every one.

"I'm a terrible liar," he said.

No one had ever come out and admitted it to her. Helen, I've been lying to you again! She heard Boyd's voice rise to a playful pitch. Then a lower voice, a serious voice cut in deeper. Helen, all those things I promised? All the things I've told you? Lies! No, the true liars never came out and admitted it. Her hands continued to tremble and she hid them under the tablecloth. The waiter cradled the wine for both of them to see and admire. Helen wouldn't remember its name the next day. The pianist had slipped into his song and the piano whispered a slow, sad melody.

Ray covered the top of his wine glass with his hand when the waiter returned.

"I'll let my friend do the tasting."

Helen breathed in the scent of the wine. She sipped, not knowing it would wander everywhere, discover its own corridors of taste and sensation. She smiled and nodded to the waiter.

"Most people don't consider this a good year," Ray said, after the waiter had gone.

"So this will be our secret." She looked at his empty glass. "Aren't you having any?"

"I wish I could. The truth is drinking any kind of liquor knocks me out."

Helen drank again and took a deep breath. "So what have you lied about?"

Ray Richards carried light with him, it lay behind his eyes. It didn't matter that they were tired or marred by dirty prints.

"My daughter disappeared over a year ago."

Her hands stopped shaking. Helen transposed the child's happy face to a milk carton, watched it shift to the pink and white descriptions of low fat, vitamins, proteins, and missing children. As she did, she added another image. Posted Lang's picture next to his father's, idly wondering where they would run. How low Lang's weight would read on the side of a carton of milk, as if he were a neglected and underfed child. People wouldn't understand that his weight gave him champion status. What would people misunderstand about Ray's ex-wife? Would she be blamed for her daughter's disappearance?

"I have to tell you that I'm completely overwhelmed right now. That's why, the other day I just—"

"Don't think about it." Helen meant it. That day was finished and done.

Ray started to speak and stopped. He took an aspirin out of a pocket and swallowed it down with water.

"How awful for you. For both of you. Your ex-wife must be going out of her mind."

Ray's eyes drifted to the center of the table and Helen felt her breasts tighten, the pleasant tweak of a nursing baby. He dragged his eyes away from whatever he saw there, something beyond cheap silk flowers and salt that would stick despite bits of yellowed rice in the shaker.

"When we divorced, the court awarded me full custody of Rebecca. A year later my ex-wife vanished along with my daughter. Yes, I would say she is out of her mind."

Ray looked at her for a long moment. The amber lights in his eyes reported a theft she could barely imagine. Relief washed over her, then shame. She had no business thinking about herself. She tried to remember Rebecca's face, the face in the torn photograph, and failed. She couldn't remember a single feature. The other day *hadn't* been her fault. She hadn't behaved crudely or precipitously. She hadn't know enough about this man, that was all. Surely that wasn't a crime. She lifted her head.

"I'm getting close. I was so sure I would have her here with me on her birthday that I lied to you and to myself."

"You didn't lie."

"What do you call it?" Ray drank water dully, without pleasure. Helen leaned closer to him in the booth and she could smell his hair, the oil from his scalp mixed with her own perfume.

"Hope." She almost shouted it. A woman turned to look at her from a center table. "Didn't you believe your daughter would actually be lying in that bed? And couldn't you picture yourself beside her, peering through a telescope? You hoped so much it felt real. And that's *not* lying."

"All right, Helen. Since you insist." Ray smiled briefly, then looked down at the tablecloth. "I'm not lying. I'm just looking for my little girl."

He excused himself and slid out of the booth, forgetting to take the napkin from his lap. It dropped to the floor and Helen picked it up just as the waiter brought deep bowls of gumbo. Crab and shrimp floated next to an island of white rice. The chef hadn't spared the hot peppers, and the steam stung her eyes, making them bleary and wet. When Ray returned, she could barely see him through her teary vision. He had combed his hair, put himself back together in the men's room.

"My job for a long time was looking after a family business. My only job now is finding Becca." He knocked at the rice a couple of times with the back of his spoon. "Being crazy has its advantages. Sometimes it's all I can do not to give in to it myself."

"What do you mean?"

"She's completely at peace. She managed to hook up with a whole network of women who keep her locked into the same self-righteous mindset she always had. The people hiding her believe I turned a whole town against her. That I had that much money and influence."

"What's the real story?"

"That I could certainly have done that. But I didn't need to."

He struck the bottom of the salt shaker hard, then harder. Again and again until salt finally fell.

"People back home didn't need to be convinced that she was an unfit mother. They watched the scenes themselves. But that's not what bothers me the most."

Helen wanted to touch him. But she couldn't move fast, she didn't want to startle Ray again. She wasn't suffering anymore, but he was. She would wait until he was ready. Something in him was so private, roped off like the rooms in his house. She would honor that reticence.

"Elizabeth is exactly the same woman I knew then. This crazy, vicious woman is the woman I chose to marry. What does that say about me?"

What did her choosing to marry Boyd say about her?

"It says you were young and in love. Don't turn her crime into yours." The words flew away too quickly. They floated on the air, flew over her head. Helen took another sip of wine and demolished the rice island, spooning seafood into its center.

"You say that with a lot of authority."

Helen didn't answer. She turned her head to the piano player, who sang the first few notes of a new song. His voice was thick, as if he needed to clear his throat.

"I've got experience. And an ex-husband whose name for years was Boy Patterson."

"Boy Patterson is your ex?" Ray smiled again. "Holy shit."

Helen frowned.

"Sorry. He sure was a cute little kid." He shook a few drops of hot sauce on the tip of his fork and speared a shrimp. "Must have been pretty wild being married to him."

"I never felt I had an adult partner. He was a child actor who never grew up. But this isn't interesting. It's not even worth talking about." Helen leaned back in the booth. Her jeans were too tight to let her eat any more.

"It's interesting to me. I could use a little distraction."

Helen repeated the one Boy Patterson line she remembered. The flabby line had done more for the show's ratings than throwing Boy overboard each week. Pass the peas, pweeze. Pass the peas, pweeze. Pass the peas, PWEEZE! She didn't like saying it, but as Ray laughed, some part of her warmed and softened. She nearly forgave Boyd for the sailor suit that still hung beside a ruined rented tux that had become Patterson property. Ray's face relaxed and he poured more wine for Helen.

The singer sang louder as the scorn in the bar increased. Someone sent him a drink, not a martini, but something more colorful with crushed ice rammed into a tall glass. The drink didn't stop him completely, but he did take a short break to suck on the straw.

"What are you doing to find your daughter?"

"I fly all over the country when they contact me," Ray said. "Sometimes I'll get a call in the middle of the night. Elizabeth will agree to meet me in Iowa or Nebraska, places like that. This last time I thought I had her was down in Mississippi."

"What happened?"

"What always happens. She disappears. She keeps running, with the help of the good Mrs. Lowell."

"Who is she?"

"Mrs. Lowell runs the show. She intercepts my messages to Elizabeth, tells her how to think, when to move. Mrs. Lowell's mission is protection. It's also lying and manipulation."

"Why don't you go to the police?"

"I don't need to. She never wanted to be a mother in the first place. A year at a job she despises is already too long." He tapped on the table with his fork. "I'll outlast her."

"Of course you will."

He stopped tapping.

"There's something you can do for me in the meantime."

Helen waited.

"You can make a home for Becca and me."

"Alice—"

"Your loyalty to that woman is stupid."

Helen pulled herself up, stung by the word. Ray sprinkled more hot sauce on his food. A little splattered on his shirt and he grabbed the dirty napkin. "Goddamn it."

"Ray?"

His anger was messier than the spill. He rubbed too hard and a button popped free. "Look at that. Talking about Alice Nash really gets me going. She's got you trapped inside that beautiful shop."

Helen thought of Elizabeth Adams Perkins's aviary, all the exotic birds hanging upside down from the top of the dome. The picture blurred, then went away.

"Anyway, I don't want Alice. I want you."

He rested his chin in the palm of his hand.

"What do *you* want, Helen?"

Ray Richards didn't move. She had seen his home, heard his private sorrows. He had exposed himself to her, while she still remained hidden. She imagined his immaculate nails on her skin, felt his fingers gently depress the flesh on the soft inside of her arm. Her mind rocked gently at first, then faster and faster, back and forth like an angry cradle. How could she even begin to tell him what she wanted?

"I want to raise my son."

"You're doing that now."

"I want to get further along in my work."

"By becoming the manager?"

"I am the manager."

What do *you* want, Helen? Alice had never asked. In fact, no one had. Assumptions had been made over the years, but no one had cared enough to be that direct. Helen's eyes burned slightly and she felt as if she might cry. Ray's expression softened.

"Then come to work for me. I can adjust to your schedule, Helen. I'm not a difficult man."

She thought of the beach club and Mrs. Tally's motto. *I simply dabble until I get to the voilà moment.* Could she do the same, dabble and dress Ray's home—not to Alice's code, but to her own? To his?

"I need help, Helen."

She put both hands around her water glass and tipped it slightly. "I'd lose my job if Alice found out."

"I'm not asking you to lie. I'm asking you to fit this job in around the edges of your life."

The edges of her life had already begun to expand. Helen thought of the French sample book and Alice's oblique announcement. Alice Nash Textiles—nice ring, don't you think? The accountants had capitulated to Alice's business strategy and Jack's shameful infertility. Jack could and would deliver this particular baby.

"I trust you to put together a good home for my daughter and me. I trust you entirely."

What sort of trust did he mean? Did he mean he would trust her not to steal from him, not to inflate a bill, not to thwart him the way she would be thwarting Alice if she said yes to what he offered? Maybe she didn't understand what he offered. Did he mean another kind of trust? A deeper tie? Helen held on to the edge of the chair and tried to think clearly.

"I'd like some time to think this over."

"You've got it." Ray rubbed the corner of his eye. "Just remember, I chose you. Not Alice. Not that young girl in the store. What's her name?"

There was barely any water left in her glass. Helen looked around for the waiter.

"Patricia." Helen slipped her hands under her legs.

"Right." He shook his head. "I'm sure she's a great shop girl, but I doubt she would have handpicked the first comfortable sofa I've ever owned or a painting I can't stop looking at. If I were to give her carte blanche to furnish an empty house, who knows what would happen?"

Their waiter had his back turned to their table. He was standing near the bar.

"Something wrong, Helen?"

"It's warm in here. I'd like some more water."

Ray motioned to another server.

"There's a story about Gatley, about what he risked for his houses. Have you heard it?" Ray asked.

Helen shook her head no, though she knew the story well. She rolled one shoulder forward and pulled on a sleeve. Ray's hand had brushed the back of her neck as he helped her ease out of the jacket. This time his touch was light, accidental. This time his hand brushed by her too quickly.

"He took a boat out all by himself. He spent five days and five nights on the water taking photographs, making notes on the shadows that fell on the cliff, the tides he observed. He wanted those houses perfectly positioned."

Helen leaned forward and felt the loose weight of her breasts against her own arms. Ray rubbed his hand over the tablecloth as he spoke.

"He didn't know how to swim. He'd never even been out in a boat before. Imagine wanting something that much."

"I don't need to. I know all about wanting something badly."

Helen didn't blush or stammer. She lay her desire in his hands like a gift. She gave Ray Richards knowledge so personal, so private that it guaranteed her safety. He would never use it against her.

Dessert arrived unannounced. It was dark chocolate cake flavored with jasmine tea. The first trace of chocolate perfume lingered on Helen's tongue. Her pants could pop; she didn't care.

He ate slowly, thoughtfully. Was chocolate cake his little girl's favorite? Helen touched the top of his arm and didn't pat. She let it rest there until she had his attention again.

"Can you give me five days to decide?" If Gatley could consider things for five days, so could she.

"Helen, I'll give you whatever you want."

She laughed for no reason and ate more cake, unashamed that Ray Richards had stopped well before she did.

"You shouldn't leave this window open without a screen." It frightened Boyd to watch his son jump at the sound of his voice. But it frightened him more to watch him doing push-ups all alone in an empty room, with the wind blowing papers off the table (Boyd's papers, probably) and the lights turned down the way they were.

Lang brought himself to his feet in a split second. God, the boy was light, fast. And thin, too, now that he saw him without a shirt. He looked thinner up close than he did on the mat.

"Which one? You mean the screen that's all twisted up?" Lang's voice mocked him. Boyd would let that pass.

Lang pulled a shirt over his head and stomped toward the door. The door stuck. Boyd pushed while Lang pulled.

"Mom's not home."

"Out, huh? Well, it's Saturday night."

He was taller than Boyd by an inch. But Lang didn't use his height in the way some boys his age did.

"So I shouldn't come in?"

"I'm just saying . . ."

"I need something, Lang. I won't be long."

He turned his body at an angle and Lang took a step back to let him in the house. The boy worked all right. A dark yoke of sweat stained the front and back of the shirt. Boyd wondered why his son was almost always by himself. When he'd been Lang's age, my God, the things he'd done with his friends. He dragged those memories into the house, which would have been empty if his son hadn't occupied most of the living room. His weights in the corner, the mat, the jump rope. Boyd wondered if he would ever get down to 168, his ideal weight, according to the coach. What was Lang's ideal? He touched his son's face gently.

"I just came by to pick up some mail. Helen probably left it right over there."

He made it to the table. There, a bill addressed to a Boyd Patterson on Feldspar. That wasn't a mistaken address. He should have lived right here with his wife and his son. Boyd thought of truly mistaken mail, a letter that had come to Helen when it shouldn't have. He worked his shoulder until he heard it pop.

"I need something in your mom's room."

"Dad, please."

"It's between me and your mother, Lang. This has nothing to do with you."

He moved beyond the hurt he saw on Lang's face. Paper crackled under his shoe. As long as Boyd could keep moving, the wind wouldn't blow *him* off course. It was warm, coming in from the desert, but that was all right. He was airtight, sealed up inside, intent on a different sort of paper he would find in her room.

"You go on back to your workout, Lang."

He opened her drawers and pushed his hands through satin, cursing her softly under his breath. At the end of the marriage she'd worn cotton. Those thick cotton underpants with a crotch like a Kotex pad. She'd said they were cheaper. These weren't cheap. He felt his way to the back of the drawer, looking straight ahead at the wall. He was here on business, not pleasure. He pulled on elastic and let it snap back into place. He wouldn't think about her skin, where that snap would land if she were wearing these.

His hands were smart gloves (smarter than he was, ha!), spliced to his body. They knew what they were doing. They let things drop to the floor that shouldn't have been important to Helen. She was a mother and so much of this was wrong. He felt the outline of something hard, not soft, with stiff cups for her breasts and straps that dangled down over her thighs. He felt for the exit or the entrance, anything that would explain this puzzle. It fell harder than the nightgowns. The noise it made as it hit the floor told him of its importance to Helen. More important to her than Lang, certainly more important than Boyd.

He felt under her bed, but his hand came up clean and empty. He checked her bedside table, behind it, not in the drawer. Anyone would look there. Any fool. He wasn't a fool. He imagined the letter he wanted, written by a lefty, he just bet. I love you. I love everything about you. Then Boyd would read the signature of the man who had stolen his wife.

Small, hard fists pounded at his body, urging him to move more quickly. Time! He saw the five-minute timer all over again, the red plastic, the grainy spill that taught him to compress emotion, control behavior, and then let it rip for one fast performance. This is all that counts for you, Boyd. And his acting coach had been right. That summer and the summer that followed, a flip of the timer was all that mattered to Boy Patterson. He'd found he could be funny, fearful, or fearless in five minutes' time. Five minutes was all he needed.

"Dad?"

Lang's face twisted into a smile and a smirk. It was a good expression, tough to read. An opponent would probably see it and shrink with confusion.

"Why are you doing this?"

And then, in one awful moment, Boyd saw Boyd, not Boy. He saw a middle-aged man with his hand inside his ex-wife's pillowcase. Only it wasn't really inside the pillowcase, it had somehow slipped into the pillow itself, splitting it open so that when it withdrew, feathers coated the arm that now hung at his side. He saw someone who could twist a window screen into a mangled piece of performance art, shouting Let me in, Helen! For God's sake, let me inside!

"Boy Overboard." Someone laughed in a dim room. Someone enjoyed the performance, found humor in it, as well as sadness. The person who laughed could enjoy the show, even when it slipped into excess. Boyd was sorry that person was not his son.

Did he hurt you?" Helen asked.

Lang thought about deafness for a moment. He wondered whether you could hear some words and not others or if all words were muffled. That would be partial deafness, though. Not the deafness he was thinking about, the kind with no sound at all.

"He's my *dad.* Why would he hurt me? What's the matter with your eyes?"

He'd seen her cry a few times, so he could be fairly sure it wasn't that. Lang leaned over the sink for a minute. He felt sick sometimes. The feeling stalked him, sneaking up when he didn't know it was coming. It was like that now, when he remembered he couldn't be sure of anything anymore. Being sure was how you felt when you were a little kid.

She didn't ask if he was all right. She didn't do anything besides stand in her room and shake her head. She didn't even touch the stuff on the floor. He leaned further over her sink and thought about everything swirling down into her drain—the little dots of powder she put on her face, all the loose hairs. It was a good thing his dad hadn't gotten this far. He hadn't seen the wet bras hanging over the faucets of the tub or opened her jars and her creams. His dad would have had a field day in here. Lang looked over at the toilet and pictured a cigarette floating there, just the butt, the way it would spin around forever before disappearing. The toilet would back up, refuse to take it, spurt water all over the place. But in the end the butt would disappear. Go into the pipes or the sewers. There. Finally.

"Lang! Oh, honey. Oh, Lang."

She rubbed his back as he vomited all over her sink and her shiny tiled wall. Like rubbing his back would help. Why was that always the first thing she did? Why didn't she rub his arm or his neck? Or his heart? Hey! Why didn't she think of that, for a change?

Lang straightened slowly and importantly. He was through being sick and weak, a stupid little baby who threw up everything he ate. He was finished being someone who couldn't take it anymore. He could take it, that was what he knew. His mother couldn't hurt him or help him anymore and neither could his father. Only the Captain fought against sickness and death. He whispered in a voice only Lang could hear. Listen to me, boy. Lang's heart floated under his chest. It turned corners under his skin, shifted positions, evaded both friend and enemy. Hide this away, Lang. Hide it! The Captain had handed Lang the map to his own heart. Now nobody knew the way there but him.

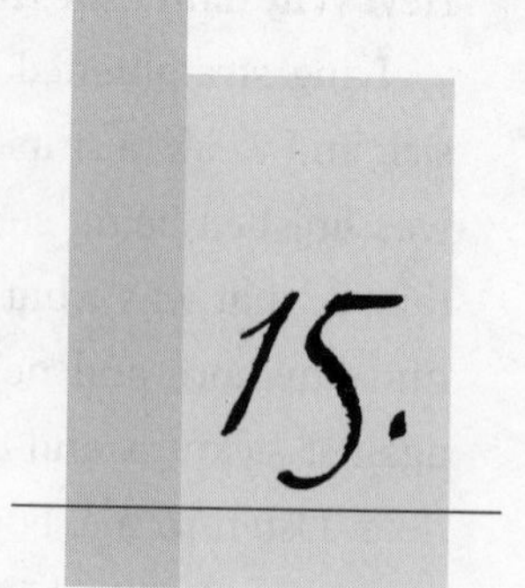

Circumstances this morning have forced me to capitulate," the Captain shouted from his bed. "Shut the goddamned door."

Lang held his breath as he pushed inside. The sweet smell of sickness emphasized the neatness of the shiny room. The sickness was bottomless, without particular origin, as the Captain had often explained. It roamed the rest home floor by floor, selecting only the finest victims. What good would it do to fell the sickly and the weak? No, its function lay in attacking the real enemy, those with sound body and soul.

"It's hit me in the bowels today, son."

Lang heard balls, and thought of his own with dread. There was a match in two weeks and he thought of the ultimate violation, the blow below, that could knock him out of competition forever. That story the coach told at the beginning of every season. How to see it coming. Some kid called Sisley, bent double just last year, with a torsion and further complications that meant hospitalization and rumors. Hydraulic rumors generated by Nick, the fireman's kid. He hosed Sisley completely, whispered "one nut" so many times that it was finally believed, especially when Sisley's girlfriend dropped him for no apparent reason, well after he had returned from the hospital.

"This isn't to say I don't welcome your visit," the Captain fingered the thin blanket on his bed and smiled for the first time.

The hazing was almost over and Lang could breathe again, even though it took some concentration. He beat back the smell by thinking it wasn't a smell, but a cobweb. A thing that hung over the gray plastic chair in the corner, down in a droopy beard from the television pressed into a high corner. Lang could clean it off the slick surfaces of the room and off his own body whenever he chose.

"You're a good boy."

"Thank you, sir."

"Your mother and father must be proud of you."

Lang hid his face from the Captain. He set his athletic bag on top of the old dresser where the Captain had the pictures of all the ships he had ever built for the United States Navy, some of them with his buddies standing in a tight little clot near the rail like they were scared of being washed away. He thought of his father and the two or three surfing friends he had. They never looked scared. Just dumb, with their Birdwell Beach Britches and bald spots.

"They are proud, sir," he said it the way the Captain said it, launching each word from his body. If he didn't, the Captain got mad and he wouldn't be able to stand that today. Poor little words spoken poorly, the Captain would say during hazing, create poor little souls. Work on your body is complete. Now mind your soul, Lang.

"What are your instructions today?"

They were the same as they always were.

"I'm supposed to read to you," Lang was starting to itch. It wasn't dry skin, it came from inside him somewhere. It was the itch that always told him something was about to happen.

"I suppose the book is in that bag of yours." The Captain's lips barely existed. His mouth sliced open and shut when he spoke. Lang thought of his own fleshy lips, too generous. He could have been a lip donor for the captain. "Anything else?"

Lang had once been afraid of the Captain, afraid of losing his job because of the old man he could never please, who punished him with fancy words. At first the old man had been bitter and powdery as the aspirin his daughter smuggled in. But now he wasn't afraid anymore. He had something in the bag that pleased the Captain much more than crumbly white pills.

"I found the size nines."

The Captain chuckled. The haze of fine words would disappear, be swept from the room like the bad smell. Now they could talk.

"And the wool?"

"Got it, Captain. I think you're going to like this color I found."

The Captain dropped the thin blanket to begin warming up his fists and fingers. He opened and shut them slowly in the beginning, squinting a little at the pain. For his passion had a price tag that wasn't included in the money he slipped Lang to buy knitting supplies. His passion brought him pain. The clickety-click, the uncertain taps of the metal needles didn't mean the Captain was unskilled. It meant his small muscles burned and his eyes watered at the effort overcoming pain demanded. It meant he gobbled up the aspirin his daughter brought, even licking what was left from the palm of his hand.

Lang locked the door and dug in his bag for the mohair. It scratched his skin. How did the Captain stand it? Maybe you didn't feel any itch once you were seventy-nine. Seven, nine, seven, nine. That was Lang's calisthenic on bad days, days when the Captain wasn't knitting, wasn't shouting words at him he couldn't understand, but dribbling like an old faucet and asking for old buddies who called to him from photographs on his dresser.

"Those biddies."

"Yeah."

They could talk now, oh they could. They could talk about the women downstairs and the way they knit each other up in dropped stitches and mean stories, exchanging sorry purple lap robes every Christmas. Every damn one of them chose purple. The women didn't like how the Captain watched when they knit. They complained to the nurses. He was in the wrong home and his daughter knew it, but she and her husband couldn't afford the other homes that lined the coves and sandy beaches, the homes with tennis courts and golf pros who dropped over for putting practice. Men were prizes in those fancy homes. Teeth didn't matter or sickness or dance steps. You don't even have to walk to their beds, the Captain would shout. Hell, they'll run to yours. Not like here, son. No! Speaking of which, I know of one old guy at Elysian Fields who makes them take out his teeth first.

"Feel this, son."

Lang did, then sneezed. The Captain was making a blanket that would outweigh anything in this sorry old home. He had him shop for the dull gray of the old merchant vessel, the gunmetal finish in the photo where he, the Captain, stood with his hand on the hull he had built himself. He understood pressure under fire and for that reason had given Lang thirty extra dollars to stand in a shop filled with chattering women who would automatically misunderstand Lang's mission, would look at him sideways, assuming pink. Lang sneezed again.

"We'll show 'em."

The happy tap of needles began, an easy rhythm Lang could follow from anywhere in the room. The Captain hunched under his light, burping every now and then, sending a sometimes sweet, sometimes sour smell burning a path to Lang. He stood by the window. There was little to report. Croquet, toppled wickets and legs so knobby it seemed the hard wooden balls had multiplied and slipped under the skins of several players. The same three brothers who visited their grandfather every Tuesday were standing under the same tree, armed with reefers. Lang watched for a while and wondered if their mom knew how nicely they shared.

"I wouldn't mind a little deodorizing in here," the Captain muttered.

He must have been something when he was younger. Lang liked his face in the pictures, the way it dared you to say anything, just anything. He had one wife, now dead, and one daughter, still living. The greatest wealth is always found in the number one, the Captain said. Lang was one. He fingered the money he had in his pocket one more time, the money his mother gave him as well as the Captain's, and saw how this was true. Most of the things the Captain said were true.

"Would you like one, sir?" Lang pulled out a wrinkled package of clove cigarettes and held it up so the Captain could see.

"Busy at the moment. But go right on. Mind where you stand."

And how you blow. Lang had some expertise there. He had learned to smoke alongside all kinds of open windows, letting the smoke drift gently through the opening, never forcing it. He smelled the box of Djarum, tried to remember where Indonesia was on the map and couldn't. The nut-colored cigarettes burned bad breath out of his lungs and his mouth, replacing it with the taste of cloves.

"Zero shine in this gray. You did well, son. Experience has taught you a thing or two."

"Yes, Captain."

"If something isn't right . . ."

"Correct it."

"And why is that, son?"

"Because otherwise you'll have to live with it at sea."

The Captain bared his teeth over a dropped stitch. Experience had taught Lang more than that. It had taught him the length of a single mistake. The Captain had knit Lang's punishment together over months as he watched. Damned if this isn't the wrong shade. No plank owner would ever mistake this for regulation gray. Goddamn this red. He awarded the flawed lap robe to Lang, who hadn't noticed the scarlet strand of wool snaking its way through the yarn when he purchased it for the Captain. Burn this, boy. And Lang had, but not before hiding his head inside the malodorous folds that captured all the sickness and death roaming the corridors of Sunrise Home.

"We did everything right or we did it over. The cutting and scraping, every bit of it was critical. We welded those bunks into the wall. Stacked 'em four deep."

The boys below staggered across the lawn to greet their grandfather. Lang wished one of them would look up and see him in his white orderly coat. He could beat the crap out of any one of the three.

"Is your bunk at home nailed down, Lang?"

"I don't think so."

"Ought to be. The land here rolls just like the sea."

The Captain was tricky. Even though he'd never seen action, just sat out the last part of World War II on a research ship he and his buddies built, he knew how to fight his way into your mind. He was just like those cryptographers he talked about, guys who spent their whole lives decoding secret messages, messing with machines that told them the truth about lies. The Captain knew his mind like no one else did and even though he hid his concentration, pretended it fell upon a row of neat gray loops that would keep out the cold forever and ever, it was pointed on Lang's mind exactly like the needle of one of those secret machines.

"I believe you said your parents are in the same business."

The Captain kept wanting them to be. He mixed it up on purpose, even giving them the same office space sometimes. Lang tried imagining it for a moment, even though it was impossible now. He put his mother and father in the same office, watching them answer phones at exactly the same time. He thought of his mother laughing at his dad's jokes the way she always had when Lang was little. She would turn so red and laugh so hard his father would put his arms around her to calm her down. Lang could still remember what that looked like.

"No, sir. My father sells real estate and my mother sells things for the home."

The skin on the Captain's forehead puckered. He put down his knitting and scratched one eyebrow until flakes flew.

"But isn't that the *same?*"

It was here that Lang needed to count. To realize that being old made things simple, not complicated. And at seventy-nine, things were very, very simple to the Captain.

"It could be the same business, sir. Or almost." Lang thought it had been, once. "My father could sell someone a house and my mother could furnish it."

"That's just it!" The Captain screeched and hit the iron guardrail that ran along his bed. "I am no different from the Captain of the ship for that very reason. We are both members of the United States Navy. A drink, please."

Lang poured out a ginger ale from one of the bottles in his refrigerator. No ice. No foam. He poured carefully, down the side, under the Captain's watch.

"Good. Good boy."

He shouldn't have been pleased. Good boy, a dog's endearment. Lang, the pup longing for a pat. But hearing those words made him happy. And imagining the Captain's frail hand on his head made him happier still.

"What about your kitchen, son?"

The Captain sipped.

"Safety hinges on the cupboards? All heavy objects strapped to the wall? Wax bottoms on vases and miscellaneous glassware?"

The Captain rested watery eyes on the television screen suspended in the corner and waited for a response.

Lang had been named for a captain he'd never met, a captain of the Saturday morning airwaves. Now that a real captain had finally appeared, one he could see and hear and smell, Lang couldn't even answer his questions.

The watery eyes closed shut for a moment. First they pierced the Captain's discolored, lashless lids. Then they pierced Lang's mind, scoured it as he had scoured his own face, examining every impurity.

"Your house is unsafe, son. Why don't your parents protect you?"

Lang jumped at the question. He touched his face, surprised at the smoothness that met his fingertips. There were no painful bumps, no cysts hidden under the skin. For once, Lang had nothing to hide.

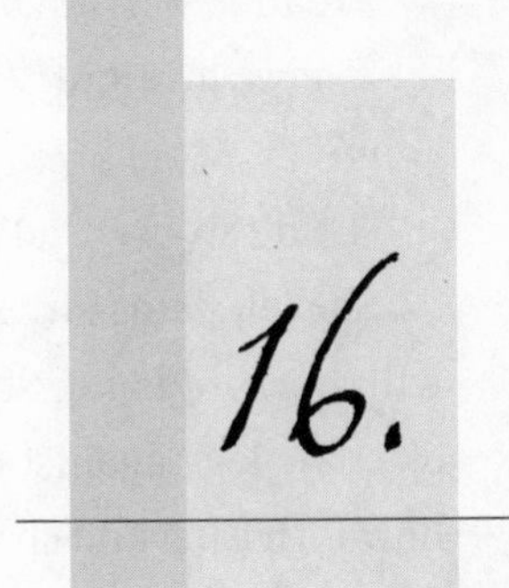

16.

The light in the architect's office dimmed briefly. Helen held the phone with both hands. She could hear the peep of the microwave setting and the low drone as it began to reheat Lang's dinner.

"My meeting went way over, honey. I'm so sorry."

The architect's office was full of hard right angles. The chair she sat in was comfortless, and she wondered why Elizabeth Adams Perkins had chosen such an ascetic for the job ahead. She rubbed the small of her back and almost laughed at her sudden understanding. The wily old widow was satisfying her dead husband *her* way. She was reclaiming her own home, throwing the public out of her private life and building them an uncomfortable annex on her property. They could look at the dead oceanographer's records there, in rigid, dispassionate rooms. If only she had understood that sooner . . . the clock in the office read 7:30. She thought of the clock she'd bought for Lang, how dependable it was. She should have thrown it into a grab bag at the garage sale. But she hadn't, and it kept ticking on and on, reminding her of a silly, irresponsible impulse.

"Anyone call?"

"Some guy, but it was a wrong number. He said, 'Put your mom on, Thomas.'"

"'Thomas'?"

"Yeah. I told him being Lang was bad enough."

"Never give out your name to strangers. Are you listening to me, Lang?"

"Don't worry. Dad's coming over later."

She felt panic sweep over her, then pushed it away. Boyd was furious with her, not Lang. She heard the microwave door slam and the scrape of chair legs against the kitchen floor. She could see the phone cord, how it twisted and strained from the wall. No phone conversations during dinner hour. She was making him break the rules she had set.

"Miss me?"

His mouth was full. She didn't ask what he was eating.

"You're just late for dinner. It's not like that other time."

"Your dad was supposed to—"

"It was long. You were gone a long time."

She had only been gone a few days that time, and Boyd had covered for her. Hadn't he? Lang had behaved so strangely when she returned. She didn't like to dwell on it, but unwelcome thoughts tripped her up anyway, clumsy and unannounced as wretched old Poor. Lang acted so jittery once she got home. Helen scooted back quickly in the chair. The bushy-haired architect poked his head in the door, then disappeared down the hall.

"Did you get that essay done?"

"Not yet. But it's OK. Patricia's here."

Helen didn't move. Instead she watched movement in her mind, heard the *swish swish* of Patricia's cotton swing coat. Helen had never heard of that kind of coat before, until Patricia wore it to work one day. It did just what its name implied, too; it swung right and left, back and forth, bumping just below Patricia's bottom as she walked.

"I didn't know that was on your schedule this week."

"I didn't, either. She said you can pay her when you want."

Helen sat for a long time after hanging up. She tried hard to see Patricia at the dining table, or even Lang as he must have looked slamming the microwave door and sliding into a seat across from her. But she couldn't. She couldn't see her son at all. Unpleasant images assaulted her one by one, images without clear shapes or sense. Vague worries brushed past her consciousness, matted and rough as Poor's gnarled coat. Helen rocked slowly in the chair and tried to push the ugly pictures out of her mind.

"Who was that?"

"My mom," Lang said.

"She's just great," Patricia said. "You're lucky to have a mom like that."

Lang lowered his head and sat down, wishing she hadn't already eaten dinner. He sliced the tail from a piece of tortelloni, then began to eat one small piece at a time to fool his body into thinking it was much more. He liked having Patricia in the house. The house felt more filled up. Lang watched himself chew in the mirror over the cupboard.

She'd brought her old textbooks over to help him out. She reached into her backpack, spread the French stuff all over the table and then waved a plastic sack in front of his nose. It was full of fat-free cookies. He looked at the straps of her backpack, the way they were almost worn out. He thought of the hard work the straps had to do, how they struggled and strained—

"OK, Lang. Let's both concentrate." She covered a yawn, but not before he saw the whole inside of her mouth. It didn't look like she had one cavity. "Do you smoke?"

"No."

"Come on. You can tell me." She stuck something in her hair, way at the back where he couldn't see it.

"Well, sometimes."

"It better not be Marlboro."

"Djarum. Just once in a while."

She sighed and he could smell Binaca on her breath. She pulled off her jacket and rolled up the sleeves of her shirt. She had on a flowery bra. Lang could make out pink and yellow flowers. He wished he could think about that instead of French.

"Do you need one to work?"

He shook his head no. He hadn't put any butter on the tortelloni. They were cooked in a pouch full of fat-free vegetable broth. There were three left and when he was finished he would be hungrier than ever.

"I have to do something."

Patricia shrugged and he could see the flowers move under her shirt. He got up to brush his teeth. In the bathroom he opened his mouth and decided he'd rather watch himself brush than eat. Anyone would. He was happy she'd watched his flabby jaw move up and down those few times without running off screaming. His face went red with gratitude and surprise. He worked at the chipped tooth with his brush and smeared toothpaste on the mirror, staring at it with disgust. It looked like it got there accidentally.

Lang stopped brushing and listened to a sound on the other side of the wall. Probably just a tree. Or just gay Edgar coming home to his dog. Lang thought of its tube-shaped body, the sound of its sharp, frantic claws as it raced to greet Edgar after a long, hard day.

Patricia's eyes were the thing. They were so calm. Even when she was saying that about the cigarettes, her eyes held him steady. All at once they appeared in the mirror and he jumped, cracking his head on his own reflection.

"I didn't mean to scare you. This your bathroom?"

"My mom's."

Her eyes narrowed as she looked at the tiles above the faucet in his mother's tub. The tub was long enough to allow a full stretch, curving in back to smooth out a nice space for your neck. Patricia traced a straight line down one of the tiles. She did it slowly, maybe pretending her finger was a paintbrush.

"Come on, lazybones. The clock's ticking."

"OK."

"Let's do drills."

He did them, as many as he could, trying to make sense of the exercise. Certain words stopped sentences before they started. *Tu* and *vous*, for example. If he just met Patricia, would he go with formal or informal?

"*Vous* at first. Then we'd slip into *tu* if we got to know each other better." Her face looked round and slick as a baby seal, her eyes expecting something from him. "Now do *aller.*"

He did it without stumbling, moving through all the traps she set up. He watched as she moved her head from side to side, then shook the plastic sack.

"You deserve this."

She broke one of the cookies in half and handed it to him. He swallowed it hoping he wouldn't choke or cough. Something stupid like that.

"*Être.* You have to know *être* like the back of your hand. Or mine."

She lay her hand on the table, sliding her fingers so they fit inside his. He looked down and saw how different the two of them were shaped. How different a girl's hand was. He felt himself get hard under the table and knew he couldn't stand up. Shit. Stupid. Even if someone broke in he couldn't. He didn't know whether or not to move his hand. He waited until she moved, then took his hand off the table fast. He only missed once on the next drill.

"Wrongola. But you did pretty well, so I'll partially reward you. Open wide."

It nearly killed him. She saw the hole at the back of his mouth where they'd had the rotten tooth pulled. All the cavities and the whole crooked jawline was right there on display. He covered the chipped tooth with his lip and she pitched the first half of a cookie, then another. He snapped at them halfheartedly. At least she laughed.

He'd been stupid, eating all the damn tortellonis. Even if his mouth had looked decent, he was too full to even try to catch the cookies. He wondered what it would be like to feed her instead, like he did the baby seals, even though it would cost him a huge fine if anyone caught him. He knew just when he could wade into their midst as they sunned in the center of the moon-shaped beach. They just lay there, beached and believing. They trusted everything, rolling over on their bellies and blinking their huge baby eyes. He sliced up pieces of fish like he did the tortelloni, bit by bit, then carted it over in sacks small enough to slide into a pocket. He fed them carefully, his back facing the road on days too bitter for tourists or patrol cars. He imagined the tickle of their whiskers as he watched Patricia lay her cheek against the tabletop.

"I'm exhausted."

It was OK to move now. Lang reached down and tied his shoe. Looking at it made him sad even though it was just an old shoelace, worn and gray in places.

"Wake me when it's over."

He heard a brushing sound in the back and tried to remember the tree that stood outside the window, the way it flipped from side to side in a storm. But would a tree make that sound? Hey.

"Hey!"

She stood up, bringing him him back to the moment, away from the sound of that tree. His eyes, it was their turn to remain calm. They rested on her breasts, moving underneath a whole flower garden. Lang felt sleepy and secure.

"Let's make up our own exercises. Let's say you're a guy—"

"I *am* a guy."

She moved her foot and everything jiggled. "You know what I mean. An *older* guy. Somebody my age. Say you're trying to come on to me."

"What about my essay?"

"We'll do that next. We've got lots of time." She fanned herself. "Oh, this is so much fun. Go on. Try to pick me up."

Lang rolled his eyes and wished he was at his locker. He wouldn't care if his lock was stuck and he was twirling the numbers around and around. It would be a lot better than being here, even though she was nice. And pretty.

"Hi." What an idiot. Only an idiot would do that with his voice. She looked down at his crappy shoelaces. He was pathetic.

"In French, Lang! Otherwise I'm not doing my job."

"Bonjour."

She sat down again and put her cheek back on the table. She started doing fake snoring.

"Vous êtes très jolie."

It woke her up. She put her chin on her hands and stared at him. She was about to say something, but she didn't get that far. Neither of them did.

"It's dawn. The old cock's crowing."

He forgot to shut it off. The clock was set for his seven-o'clock workout. The language got worse the longer the clock continued, and that was the trick. Lang ran to shut it off before things got way worse.

"It's all right. It's my alarm."

"*That's* how you wake up every day?"

She looked at him so long he began to squirm. Maybe listening to that every day made you mentally ill. Maybe he shouldn't even try to go to college. Finally she smiled and he thought he had a chance of getting there after all. Patricia would help him. She looked so happy.

"I had no idea you were that kind of boy."

"You two working hard?"

Boyd ruffled the back of his son's head, pleased to feel it was still the same texture as his. Sometimes hair just changed, got brushy, and fifteen was about the time. But Lang's hair was still boyish and smooth. Hey, his too!

"Trying."

The girl beamed and said her name. It sounded familiar.

"I work with Lang's mom. And now I'm working with your son."

"Whoa. Pretty soon you'll be working with me."

"Only if you want to learn French."

"Oh, French! Now there's a language for you."

Lang glowered at him. Boyd was still in the doghouse with Helen and Lang. He would have to work harder than ever. Demonstrate restraint, for a change.

"You two want some hot chocolate?"

"That would be great, Mr. Patterson. I've got to go pretty soon, though."

"Helen's got some instant out there. Right?"

What did it take to say something right these days? Boyd sighed and moved to the kitchen to find Swiss Miss or whatever she bought now. It used to be Swiss Miss, the kind with tiny marshmallows. Come to think of it, those marshmallows were the point. He'd bring two cups out on the cafeteria trays they used to have, the stuff steaming, and watch her spoon off most of his marshmallows into her own cup. You don't care, do you, honey? He *had* cared. He should have said so.

He went carefully through the first cupboard. That didn't take long, since it was nearly empty. Some unmarked grains and flour in sealed jars. Bugs, he remembered how angry she got when she found a bug anywhere near the food. He continued, opening the second and third cupboard doors. Four sealed boxes of dried fruit, six packages of soup mix. It was like an outdoor adventure–supply store. He had more food in his kitchen than Helen. He shivered and looked through the dark window. She'd fixed that leak. It was done well. He could barely see the putty.

"Hey, where does your mom hide the good stuff?"

"There isn't any good stuff, Dad. I'm trying to make weight."

"Shoot, who isn't?"

Boyd went to the doorway to watch them laugh at that one, but they didn't. Patricia looked at his son. Even though Boyd was cold, his armpits felt hot and sticky. He felt for a lump. That guy who worked for Steve: riddled with cancer. Some riddle. How did it quietly spread to the lymph glands in under a month? Boyd thought of Steve Mason's hand on the widow's back at the funeral, remembering how his wedding ring stood out against all the black and the way his hand really seemed to touch her through the heavy coat. He was so kind to her after the death, even though her husband's magic number had been about to appear. Before cancer and death, he'd listed a great little golf property out in Bonita and hadn't done a thing with it. His professional failings didn't matter to Steve, though. He kept paying visits to the widow for a long, long time after the funeral.

Patricia slapped his son's arm. A play slap, he knew all about that. In fact, Helen used to do that all the time. The play slaps had often turned into kisses then. He looked harder at Patricia. Something about the way she sat made him think of Marsha Alther. He shook off the queer sensation that started at his throat.

"*Vouloir,* not *pouvoir!*"

She turned her head toward Boyd and gave him the biggest, sweetest grin he'd seen in this house for a long time. Something squeezed him deep inside. He wished he could see that grin when Lang looked at him. Or Helen. There he went, spinning off into stupid dreams.

"Helen brings this terrific herb tea in to work sometimes. I wouldn't mind a cup of that, Mr. Patterson."

"Coming up."

Boyd stayed in the kitchen until the water boiled, keeping one hand on Helen's teapot the whole time. Then he found a package of thick, fat-free biscuits. He smelled one and frowned, thought of his moist underarm. He looked down at the ground as he served them cookies and tea. Broken biscuits lay around the bottom of Lang's chair.

"You two have a food fight or something?" They were a little old for that. Boyd corrected himself. *She* was a little old.

"Oh, that." She didn't blush. She didn't apologize.

He knew her. Now that was something new and different. But how? Where had he seen Patricia?

"Sugar?"

His son rolled his eyes.

"Hey. Aren't you carrying this a bit too far?"

"The first match is almost here!"

"*Gagner!*" Patricia cried, reaching for a cookie. She took an enormous bite and crumbs fell all over a colorful section of Versailles.

She drank her tea happily as Lang worked on his verbs, trying to ease them into an essay on kings and rogues, maps and charts, who was related to whom. Wonderful excess. Boyd leaned forward, eager to think about that. He had always wanted to see the Hall of Mirrors as a little kid. He snapped his fingers hard.

"I've got it!" He *hadn't* gotten the listing on her mother's estate near Mount Soledad. It had gone for five million five. "You're Elaine Sorenson's daughter."

It was a palace in the hills. He had called on Patricia's mother poolside. He remembered the length of her body, the implicit understanding that it was built to admire, like a slick coupe or sedan. She hadn't even stood up to greet him. A butler showed him in, a butler showed him out. Patricia's mother took the entire meeting lying down.

"Were you an actor ever?"

Her mother had never let on she knew he'd been Boy Patterson. Never said a word. He watched the way her daughter moved in the chair. What the hell did she have on under that shirt?

"That's right."

"I know all about you. Me and about a million other people." She blew on her tea, sending little waves across the cup. "Mmmm. This is yummy."

He had some cash. He would pay her whatever she wanted and then she would go. But what did she want? Cold shot through his gut. Boyd sat down at the table and patted his son's wide shoulders.

"So. French, eh?" He drank his tea a little too eagerly and made a slurping noise through the gap in his teeth. The gap he had given his boy.

Lang growled.

"Sorry, sorry." Always sorry, it seemed. Lang's work was almost done and he hadn't taken a sip of his tea. It was probably cold now. Boyd lifted the empty teapot and shook.

"Is this tutoring a one-shot deal?"

"No, no. We want to make sure Lang gets on his feet."

Who wanted to make sure?

"If Lang falls behind now, it will only get worse."

"Gee." The word felt sticky in his mouth. "But aren't you awfully busy with the store and all?"

"Oh, I take on all kinds of odd jobs." Her cheeks shone. They were bright as lamps. "You've got to these days, just to make ends meet."

He thought of Marsha Alther again, her pen tapping the checkbook. Boyd's insides coiled into a snake's tight tail. He reached out fast to touch his son, but Lang pulled away before he could. He was agile, no doubt about that. Boyd was suddenly gratefully for his coach. Lang was ready for just about anything.

"Want to know who's going to win the match?"

"Dad!"

Patricia looked like the eager student now.

"Who's going to win?" she asked.

"Let's find out, shall we?"

Boyd ate the last cookie himself, sucking the pasty remains off the roof of his mouth, and took the lid off the teapot. He peered inside with a frown on his face, then flipped the pot upside down. The tea leaves landed on the table with a splat.

"You're a clairvoyant! Lang," that little slap again, this time to his son's shoulder, "why didn't you *say?* It's not enough that your dad is famous?"

Boyd wished he'd been to more matches, knew more official terms. The only ones he knew floated through his mind without sticking to the soggy mess below. But there was one thing, inside that crooked X. The way it thickened just after the cross.

"That's a scissor grip, Lang."

His son pulled his shoulders back slowly.

"And that's a head between someone else's legs."

Lang didn't smile, not quite that, but something different moved across his face.

"Foul," Boyd offered. He leaned way back in his chair.

"Whose foul?" Patricia's cheeks burned with excitement.

"Can't say."

Boyd had once seen that same red color spread out over a whole field. He'd had Helen beside him in a beautiful car and nobody, for once, in pursuit. They'd pulled over, because they were like that then, and both of them waved hello at the field of poppies. It wouldn't even occur to him to wave at a flower now. Would Helen still think of it? What did Helen think of? He pictured her face when she saw her bedroom that night and winced. Patricia stood up and began to gather her things. She looked efficient and hurried. She glanced at her watch.

"I don't get it. Is Lang the winner or loser?"

She waited at the door. Boyd thought of the wood-burning set Lang used to have, the way they had burned his initials into everything, with Boyd's big hand closed over Lang's. That hand had been so small then, tender as a puppy's paw. Boyd squirmed, thinking of another set of initials. He saw blue ink on Marsha Alther's white skin. His son's eyes were scorching the surface of his skin now and Boyd had to tell the truth.

"I don't know. But we'll find out when he wrestles Larchmont."

Bye. Bye. The front door banged and the bedroom door banged and Boyd sat alone at the table, easing the scissors apart with his spoon, breaking the wet, brown hold.

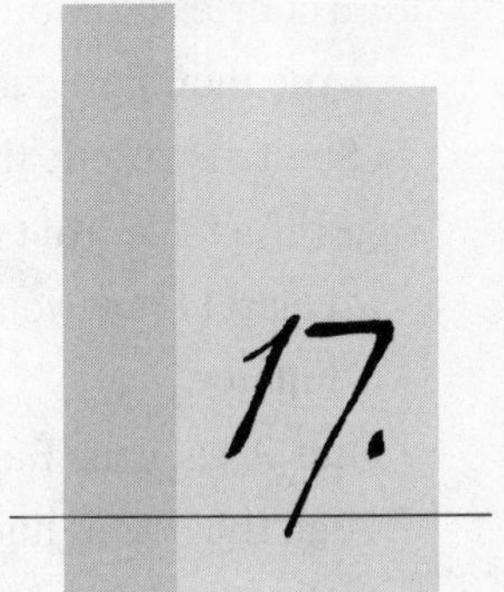

17.

Ray sat in the middle of the crowded patio at the Ramone Ranch. If he hadn't stood up when she crossed the polished tiles, Helen would never have recognized him. Dressed in light wool slacks and a dark jacket, he looked comfortably enclosed in someone else's life. He took off his sunglasses and laughed. The end of his nose was raw.

"You've forgotten me already?"

"You're sick," Helen said. Five days had passed. She'd done nothing *but* think of him.

"I'm not contagious." Ray poured some coffee into a cup for her, closing his hand firmly on the handle of the silver pot. The smile remained on his face. "You didn't answer my question. But that's OK."

Helen pulled her eyes away from his face and looked around the terrace. She hadn't been here in years. The commercial center was several miles inland from the center of San Diego. Interior designers and their clients filled the stores during the week; a very different clientele arrived Saturday morning. Young, ambitious wives armed with resale numbers, measuring tapes, and grease pencils vied for precious spots in the dusty parking lot. Free of husbands and children, jobs (when they occurred), these women circled the former stable singly or in pairs. They unrolled blueprints, punched figures into pocket calculators, and phoned home from courtesy stations located in the patio area.

"You didn't prepare me for this," Ray said.

She tensed, but then saw he was being playful. He plucked at the edges of a folder that lay on the table. She hadn't noticed it before.

"I didn't know you were so fond of horses," Ray said.

"I'm not."

But Alice was. Ray had zeroed in on Alice's bitter complaint. Even though the horses had disappeared along with most of the wealth, Alice resented the shrewd reconstruction of the Ramone Ranch. Leasing the stable to the city insured historic preservation and a respite from taxes. Filling the empty stalls with precious antiques had been as dramatic as building a pretty French château in the middle of a California beach town.

"I hear there's a Mrs. Ramone behind all this," Ray said.

All the Ramone men were dead now, and Leone Ramone rarely left her terraced gardens to see what had become of her property, ravaged as it was by furniture wholesalers and antique dealers. Opinion on Mrs. Ramone varied. Some thought her senile, others considered her just plain mean. On mornings when the sun shone enough to warm her thin blood, she could be seen in her orange grove, guiding a young boy up a tree with her cane. The cane was used for more than pointing to juicy oranges or supporting her great weight. Witnesses were too fearful of her wrath to suggest that Leone Ramone rattle her own tree for fruit and leave the boy alone.

A woman and her young daughter sat down at the table next to theirs. The woman stared at Ray, as if her daughter wasn't there at all. Helen took a quick sip of coffee.

"I bet she gives your boss a run for her money."

"Not at all. We serve a completely different kind of client." Helen looked at the woman from the corner of her eye.

"Hey, calm down. I'm not attacking Alice. I just meant they have some pretty things out here."

Many years before, Mrs. Ramone had been offered a free space in the converted stable, a place to sell her lovely lace, a family piece or two that she could bear to part with. If not, then perhaps the hospitality courtyard would interest her. Mrs. Ramone represented *living* history. Her family, the missionaries! With her bright cotton skirts and the open fan she kept mounted in her hair, her very presence was a bit of spun sugar for the tourists. She was offered a modest salary. Mrs. Ramone had signed her name in the presence of a public notary, spit into the piece of paper, and mailed her response back to the Director of State Parks. Alice loved the story. It was the only thing thing she loved about Ramone Ranch. The design center was the one place in town that presented any real threat to her store.

The woman at the next table stood up, gave some of her packages to her daughter, and began dusting off crumbs. Most of her croissant seemed to have wound up on her chest, and she was making the most of it. She was shameless. The word stuck in Helen's mind. It gathered strength, bullying other words out of the way. She was just the kind of woman who would strike up a conversation with a stranger, who would imply anything and everything in a girlish, breathy comment on the lovely weather or a question about how to get back on the freeway. I always wind up getting lost! Helen could almost hear the lie.

Ray's eyes flitted to the other table and back. He sneezed and grabbed a handkerchief, then slipped his sunglasses back on and began pulling from his folder magazine articles and odd scraps of paper. The woman dipped a napkin into a water glass and cleaned her daughter's mouth, then both turned to go. She only looked back once, as she was about to turn down a corridor. Ray's face was flushed and Helen wanted to cool it with her hand. She wished she could comfort him. She wanted to chase away all the damage in his life. Was that how his ex-wife had behaved with their little girl? Was that the way she was behaving with Rebecca right now?

"Look, I don't know how to go about this."

"I'm not sure I do, either," Helen said, and lowered her gaze to the table and the mess of papers. On the pictures, arrows pointed at a table lamp here, a big bronze kettle under a rugged kitchen table there.

"That's what I'm counting on."

"My inexperience?"

"Your instincts. They're much stronger than you think."

She could see his eyes through the dark lenses, and knew that he wasn't thinking about his daughter. The pit of her stomach felt unsettled and she added milk to her coffee. Slow down, Helen. She had to remind herself of Ray's fragility.

"So."

So he had spent the past week going through old design magazines, picking out things he liked as well as what he didn't like. He tried to say why on a separate sheet of paper. Helen held it in her hands. It would be more valuable than pictures of a glossy enfilade of rooms, each one opening into the next. One view contained all views.

"You're concerned about security," Helen said, thinking of her own home.

"This has nothing to do with strangers. It's about the people who already live there."

Helen liked the easy space in the photograph. She could feel a current of air brush over her bare feet, the slow introduction of warm color that ended in a winey splash at the end of the hall. A library that was home to a region of the mind.

"There's no place to hide. Everybody's under scrutiny," Ray said, shuffling papers. He looked embarrassed. A different blush rose on his cheeks, one that didn't invite the cool touch of a hand.

"Well, you certainly bought the house that suits you. It's extremely closed off."

"You know, we've never discussed money, Helen."

She cleared her throat. I'll give you whatever you want, Helen. He was getting cold feet, that was probably it. He'd had time to reconsider and now that he had . . . She covered her disappointment with laughter.

"Yes, we did. And I understood it was just talk, so don't worry."

"I'm not worried. But I've been thinking."

She looked at the vines tangled over her head. They sat in a sheltered section of the patio. A fountain gurgled at its center and children would gather later to toss in coins and marbles, anything that would clog the filter. No children played there now. No security guard hovered. No one sat at the edge of the clear pool.

"I'll match your salary for as long as it takes to make over the house. I figure that makes me at least as important as Alice Nash."

You can work me in around the edges of your life. Helen looked at a small gray bird pecking at crumbs. Sensations rolled over her as she watched it.

"Look, I know I'm a one-shot deal. I've got to do something to hold your attention."

Helen kept her expression calm. Once the fabric line was up and running . . . there was a calculator in her briefcase. She was no different from the women in the courtyard in that regard. But seeing the cars in the parking lot revealed how different, in fact, these women were.

"I've done some figuring—," Helen started.

"I know she pays you well."

Helen's eyes widened. She couldn't hide her surprise.

"Doesn't she?" Ray asked.

"It's not a terrific salary, but she makes up for it with all kinds of benefits."

"Like what?"

As she recited them, Ray rolled his eyes. Helen's voice dropped lower and lower. "What's the matter?"

"I get the picture, Helen." He touched the top of her hand. "You might want thirty percent of whatever I spend instead of a flat fee. That's what most good designers think their services are worth."

She felt cold. They should have been sitting in the sunlight. How did he know that? Was he shopping around for someone else? Maybe he'd driven to Los Angeles and combed the area around the Pacific Design Center, finally finding someone who would be all too happy to take on this job. Someone for whom discretion wasn't an issue. She imagined someone like Patricia, someone with cold white lights in her eyes. She pressed her heels together.

His voice shifted as he leaned forward over the table. "What do you think you're worth, Helen?"

"A lot." It came out fast, but she liked the way she felt after the words tumbled out.

"Now you're talking." Ray folded his arms over his chest and the sleeve of his jacket slid up his arm. She looked at the exposed skin on his wrist. She wanted to bend his hand back gently and lay her lips there. Discover his pulse for herself, in her own way. Discover all of him.

"So your answer is yes?"

She thought about the strength of a dream. How it could survive for long, difficult years without ever seeming to come any closer. Then all at once the dream was everywhere she looked, on every side, at every angle. A dream this strong was impossible to escape. She blinked at the odd logic. Why would she want to escape?

"I think my answer has been yes all along."

The view from where they sat seemed to swing back and forth as easily as the Dutch doors. Such a stall might have held a dapple-gray mare long ago, but the whitewashed room was now overflowing with wonderful things.

"It would certainly be easy to overpower your home."

He rubbed his shoulder with one hand. "I get it. You brought me all the way out to a stable so you can rein me in."

She laughed.

"Don't worry. All I need is good furniture and good fabric."

He began going through his folder again.

"But I don't just want a shopper. And I don't really want an interior designer. I need somebody to translate my ideas."

Ray found what he was looking for. He held a crumpled piece of red flannel in his hand for Helen to see. Fire trucks and wagons, old Santa himself. It was the color of childhood.

"Can we do something with this color?"

"That bathhouse is pretty bleak. It might work there."

He stood up and slid his folder into a leather envelope as he did. Yellow-eyed birds had begun to squabble over a piece of croissant that lay on the ground.

"Where did that swatch come from?"

He slid his hand in a pocket and she heard loose change jingle.

"Her favorite pajamas." He moved quickly as one of the birds flew past him into the vine overhead. "I figure this will bring her home sooner."

She wished she could slip her hand into his as they walked to the west side of the plaza. She wished they could stroll away from his misery and her fear. This was enemy territory and Helen knew it. A woman approached them and Helen looked away, thinking she was Alice's customer. The woman was no one she knew, but she imagined the look of Alice's jaw as it slammed down on the information. *What* were you doing there?

Helen leaned on an open door and tried to relax. She chatted with the shopkeeper, a girl who gurgled with pleasure as they discussed the room. Then the girl looked past Helen and broke free of her conversation almost at once. Someone else had captured her attention.

"Come on. I've seen enough for today," Ray said.

He touched her neck and guided her away from the room and the view. Other shops waited at the end of the esplanade.

18.

Over the next few weeks, Helen and Ray returned to Ramone Ranch four more times. And each time, Helen's shortcuts backfired. She took the freeway. She took chances, shooting past a car too suddenly or carelessly switching lanes on a crowded interchange. She took turns excusing herself to Alice for long lunch hours or to Lang for starting dinner so late. She accounted for her time by blending tasks for the store into shopping trips with Ray. By blending lies into truth.

"Helen, it didn't take you all this time to drop off the china."

"I didn't just drop off the china. I stopped to buy cord for the Salzberg order. They were out of stock at Lehman's and since Stan needs it by the fifteenth, I—"

Helen imagined telephone lines crackling at first, then bursting into flames. Alice's voice when she was angry . . .

"You should have sent Patricia on all these expeditions. Is this because of a man?"

Helen hunched over the telephone, wishing she was further from the noise of the waterfall. Ray stood in the shade watching her.

"Yes." Helen fished for forgotten money in the coin return. She cleared her throat.

"I'm not running a dating service, Helen."

"Of course not."

"You *work* for me."

"I know that."

"I hate to be tacky, but can't you take care of your needs at night?"

Helen wondered what they were as Alice's anger sharpened. She could hear her heel scuffing over the floor where she sat upstairs. There would be black marks under her desk, and gold Godiva papers all over the floor for Helen to pick up because Patricia certainly wouldn't.

"I could. But I need to keep this part of my life private."

Helen listened to the long, anguished sigh and turned her back to Ray. She felt crowded and pushed. There was no air inside the phone booth.

"When are you going to stop overprotecting your son? He needs to see his mother happy, for heaven's sake. Seeing you with someone great would probably—"

"Alice, he's married."

Ooooooh, the long spear of sound gave Helen time to think. It probably did the same for Alice.

"Look, I'm not your mother, but . . ." The edge in Alice's voice created a sudden edge in Helen.

"No, you're not. My mother's dead."

Sorry, sorry, sorry. Helen's shame spread. She touched her cheeks, her chin, finding her mother everywhere. Today she was usefully dead, creating guilt in exactly the spot where it was needed. And where it wasn't. Why did Helen feel guilty? Wasn't it finally her turn to be happy? She yanked on the telephone line, thinking of Alice and Jack.

"Helen, forgive me. Are you still there?"

Married—God, the complications. Did he love her? Did she love him?

"I'll tell you something. He may love you. He may promise you . . ." The scuffing had stopped. "What do married men promise, anyway?"

"That I can have whatever I want."

"Hmmm. Any children?"

"A daughter."

Alice was standing up now. Helen could tell.

"Helen, you're my closest friend, not counting Jack."

"I am?"

"Yes." Alice waited a long moment before continuing. "Saying this makes me very sad. Your story is going to end badly."

Alice hung up abruptly and Helen stayed on the line a few seconds, startled by the confession. Alice's closest friend—Helen repeated it again and again until it blotted out the bad ending Alice predicted.

like this," Ray said.

They sat in a soot-colored love seat. Rounded, joined arms curved like an S. The faded brocade fabric had ripped on Ray's side and he explored the tear with his little finger. A short, sallow-skinned man watched him from an armchair. The other man leaned down and toyed with the cushion of the chair.

"You know where it would work best?" Helen flipped through photographs of Ray's rooms she had piled on her lap. She had borrowed Lang's Polaroid last Sunday afternoon and the color was already starting to fade.

"I have no idea."

"Here. In this funny little corner."

The space winked at the gardens and ocean view from the back of the house. Gatley must have built it to trace the progress of an olive tree that fanned the side of the house. Gray-green leaves trembled at the base of the two high windows that pointed at each other in a sharp angle.

"If we put the seat here," Helen's finger touched the tight wedge, "two people could share the great view."

"Which one?" Ray crossed his legs and slid down a bit lower on his side. The sallow man across from them studied Ray a bit longer, then hurried to his feet. He clapped the owner of the store on the back as he left and called him by his first name.

"There are lots of things to watch from here," he said.

His eyes wandered over Helen's face, pausing to see the sights as they never had before. He lingered over the cleft in her chin as he fingered the damaged fabric. Her skin warmed. Helen felt as if he were actually stroking her there. The owner was on his way over for the final sales pitch. He'd circled the store with them until Ray suggested otherwise.

"You two certainly look at home."

Helen recognized the scent the man wore. It was a hybrid cologne, acceptable for a man or a woman. It leaped over age as well as gender, was presented to grandmothers and teenage boys in a gilded bronze gift box. Helen smiled at the owner. She wanted him to go away.

"You've found the perfect spot for it, I see. May I?"

He started to reach for the photograph Helen held in her hand. As he did, Ray racked up the pictures from her lap as if they were poker chips. Her jaw tightened. His hand slid over her so quickly.

"Your sofa's falling apart," Ray said.

"It's called shabby chic. Some of our customers are wild about this look."

"You're conning your customers. You should donate this thing to Goodwill."

The other man took a couple of steps back and Helen swung her head around to stare at Ray's tranquil profile, then recovered. She folded her hands over her knee. "Since the fabric is damaged, could you take something off the price?"

She wished the scent would disappear. The air felt sticky with it. It was making her sick. Looking away, she could see the top half of a UPS man standing at the Dutch door, awaiting a signature. Reaching inside his jacket for a pen the owner of the shop excused himself.

"Sorry I was rude. That guy's giving me a headache." Ray pressed hard on his temple and frowned.

"It's the awful cologne. Let me measure this and we'll go. If you decide you want it, I'll come back and take care of things."

She could see Leone Ramone and the boy up above the parking lot. They lowered the Mexican flag together. He ran the flag down the pole. Helen watched it flip from side to side in the wind; the abdication that seemed to end the day saddened her. Mrs. Ramone's lime-green skirts flapped more wildly than the flag.

"Maybe we could cover the seat with that. I've got nothing against Mexico." Ray shaded his eyes with his hand. He kept it there as he continued talking, as if he were telling his story to Mrs. Ramone instead of Helen. The woman at the top of the hill held her back straight, but leaned to one side with the effort it must have required. The boy worked the pulley faster and faster.

"I have to go to Michigan in about two weeks. God knows what I'll find there."

So that was it. That was what had him so edgy. Helen felt the relief of understanding.

"You'll find Rebecca." She began to look for her key as she spoke. She would still have time to fix baked chicken if she hurried.

Mrs. Ramone sprung into action all at once, grasping at the flag as it bucked into her range. The boy stood aside and bent for her cane. He mocked her behind her back, turning his thin body into a pained, bent crook above the wooden shaft. She lay the flag out on a cherry red picnic table, folding it into sections with exaggerated care. Mrs. Ramone was oblivious to the charade taking place behind her. Ray kept on watching them as he spoke.

"What if I don't? What if I never find my daughter?"

"You *will.*" Helen was suddenly tired of words. Talk wasn't bringing them any closer together. "You've got to believe in what you're doing, Ray. If you don't, that Mrs. whatever her name is—"

"Mrs. Lowell."

"Mrs. Lowell will just keep you running around the country for nothing. And what is she getting out of this?"

"Money."

"It's blackmail?" She shivered as she asked the question.

"She doesn't present it that way. She makes it look as if it all goes to them."

Helen's key entered the lock part of the way and jammed. It wouldn't slide in or out. Panic gnawed at her. The sensation was too sharp, too real for this scene. She would make the key work. She would get home and make her son a hot meal. Alice would never find out about Ray. What did she imagine would happen?

"Here." He knelt beside the lock, his shoulder grazing her leg. He worked with it for a few seconds, his movements so subtle it didn't seem he was doing anything at all. The key finally slid out.

"This must be your house key."

He had driven her to the edge of the lot where her car was parked. The sound of his engine running so flawlessly calmed her. A car like that would never break down, never swerve, never do anything but run perfectly until the end of time. Ray was a man who took care of the things he owned and the people he loved. She could see all the sacks and packages lined up in the backseat like obedient children. She wanted to ride proudly in the front seat of that car. She thought of Alice with real anger.

"Cars. Houses. Sometimes it's hard to keep it all straight," he said.

The orchard was blanketed with early-evening fog. Anyone could have slipped up the side of the green hill that fell into as many folds as Mrs. Ramone's voluminous skirt. Anyone could have reached up into the branches of a tree to steal a sweet ripe orange.

"Ray?"

He turned his head toward her and, as he did, she watched the reconstruction of the world she knew. Ray Richards meant more of what was already good in that world. She was adding an important new dimension to her life, not tearing it apart. Her emotions were so clever. They were always trying to trip her up and turn her away from the very best things. What she felt was excitement, not fear. Ray Richards was what she had wanted from the very beginning.

"When are you going to kiss me?"

"Right now."

He lifted her face and looked soberly at everything he found there. His hands were warm and dry. She expected his lips to feel the same way, scratchy and pleasant and plain. They weren't. They were as smooth as the inside of her own mouth.

19.

The flowers were out of control. They had no smell. They weren't the kind of flowers you could cut and put in a vase. If you looked at them up close, as he had done, you saw they were nothing but colored leaves. Light, papery things if you plucked them off one at a time. Together, though, they massed like an orange army over your head. Lang looked up at the roof as he let himself into the empty house. It seemed to him the heaviest part of the vine was centered over his room, so that when it crashed . . . what were they called? Boo something. Boo hoo, poor Lang.

The flowers didn't smell, but he did. He smelled like the bus and work, the old people (excepting the Captain) he tried not to touch except when he had to lift them in and out of their wheelchairs. He cupped his hand over his nose and breathed, then tiptoed through the house, the way he would have if he'd wanted to steal something. In his dreams, Lang was always running or lunging at a stranger to grab something out of dark, gloved hands. In his dreams he won, but not without a struggle. He always got the package marked with their address. He always stole what was supposed to come to them anyway. He went into the bathroom just as the alarm clock sounded. As if he were likely to forget what he had to cock-a-doodle-do.

Lang began the ritual of forgetting old people and the way they looked when he left Sunrise Home. He had to get the smell off before he could start on other things. He picked up some soap and tried to unwrap it using a fingernail, then tore at it with his teeth until he could taste soap on his tongue. With his free hand, he turned on the faucet.

He rubbed the thick bar back and forth over his forearms, then worked it between his hands, then again, only harder. It was the clear kind his mother said was especially for his skin type, pretending he had a skin type. One that didn't make you puke. Some days, the sides of his nose looked as if they were coated with his mother's cooking oil and other days his whole face peeled and flaked like his head had gotten caught in a snowstorm. He had asked her for an acne scrub, and she'd brought this home instead. He stopped rubbing the palms of his hands together and smelled them, thinking of his face once it was coated with this, whether it would smell good or bad. It would smell neutral, like the orange flowers over his head, like nothing. Good. Unscented Lang.

He dug his fingers into one side of the amber bar and began again. How could he get his face clean if there was no lather? It had foamed up that one time before when he used it. Lang took a deep breath, then released the air in a puff. No foam. He rinsed his hands, then shut off the faucet. The water dribbled to a stop after he left the bathroom.

Lang wheeled into his mother's bathroom. She had the tub, of course. She had everything. She had the big bathroom, the big bed with four pillows. He watched what she did with them, sleeping on one for awhile, then switching the order, the way he watched everything in the house.

He didn't look into the mirror on purpose. What he would see there was all memorized, horribly in place. The only way he'd look in the mirror today would be if he sensed a change. Eyelashes that were regular, for example. He was taking care of that, though. He pulled out one or two every week, so they would grow in straight instead of curled. He would look in the mirror if he thought his chipped tooth was suddenly capped or his flabby pink mouth had become thin and normal overnight, the way his father's mouth was. He was a genetic joke, with his mother showing up where his father should have been and vice versa. Lang got her medicine cabinet open without seeing himself. He didn't have to look at the pimple between his eyebrows and the way his chin was red and just beginning to swell into some new and ugly life form.

Vitamins, vitamins, prescription. He took the green-capped bottle down and studied it for a minute, then put it back in exactly the same spot, prescription number to the front. She'd notice if anything looked different. She got ideas like that from stupid magazines printed on paper that left her hands gray when she finally put them down. "RAISING HIM RIGHT." "THE TRUTH ABOUT RITALIN." He reached for her perfume, but carefully this time. That time she left on the bad trip he had let it drop out of his hands and, though it cured him, it killed her because it was expensive. She'd been on a business trip that went on too long and he'd gone into her bathroom when he couldn't sleep. He had felt for the perfume, his eyes sore and tired, to smell for just a second. Then the bottle had slipped through his fingers like it was a strand of spaghetti, and he wound up holding just the red top, shaped like a misshapen heart, with the smell she always wore spreading all over the room. He stood for a long time like that, leaving the glass on the floor for his father to clean when he finally showed up the way he was supposed to. He fell asleep right after that, with his mother's smell all over him, and didn't dream anything. His dad had come over late, or else not at all, when she was on that trip. She would have killed him if Lang had let on. So he didn't.

Liquid Cleansing Solution. Was that what she used instead of soap? He unscrewed the cap and sniffed, then started to cough as he looked through the bathroom window into Edgar's garden next door. The window was wide enough to see the whole thing, to see Edgar in the middle of his flowers with a trowel in one hand and an apron in the other. Edgar wasn't looking at him then, but he probably had been with his scrunchy green eyes. Lang grunted and put the cap back on, not too tight, not too loose.

He liked his mother's towels. That was one good thing about living here. They just had one set of everything now, not like before when his parents were together. She didn't get embarrassed or mad when company came and saw the wrong set of something. Lang, you set the table with the wrong plates. He'd never understood how a plate could be wrong. Lang ran his finger down the side of the yellow hand towel. Guess what I spent on these towels, honey. She said it like spending lots of money was a victory or something.

Lang made his way down the narrow hall to the living room and kitchen the way he always did, pinball style. He threw his weight against one side, then the other, pretending that when he wound up at the end of the short hall, he'd be the winner, the high scorer who brought everybody to their feet in a cheer.

He glanced around the living room, putting Patricia in it, the way he'd like to see her now. Stomping one foot and saying Lang. Doing that made her seem closer to his age, even though he knew she wasn't.

He wished she were sitting on the campaign chair right now. No, the chair wouldn't be good because he was too ugly and there was the swelling on his chin that wouldn't go away on its own. But Patricia could be in his mother's bedroom while he stood out here, doing conjugation drills loud enough for her to hear. That way she'd be in the house without having to look at his ruined face. It was good he'd figured out how to make it disappear.

He pushed the campaign chair with his leg. No eating and drinking in the living room was the rule, but he and Patricia had broken it last week, then spilled Gatorade all over the area rug. Patricia had put some blue stuff in a bowl and mixed it with water, then rubbed the spot out with a rag. That was Patricia, someone who knew exactly what to do when stuff spilled. His mother hadn't found out. Ajax. He went to look for some under the sink.

He lifted the can and frowned. It was light, and he shook it next to his ear to make sure there was still a little something left in the can. It'd be nice if his mother shopped for a change. It'd be nice if she'd forget about antique paisley and Tuscan red and think about Lang for a change.

He opened one drawer, rooting through all the metal, then a second drawer that held wooden utensils. This was his mother's idea of organization. He found a basting bulb and held it up high, pretending it was a syringe, and jabbed it into his arm. Too bad Edgar couldn't see into the kitchen. A crow was the only witness, squawking and shitting on a high wire behind their house. Lang closed the last drawer and looked around the tight kitchen. It'll be a tight fit for awhile, won't it, Lang? She said that when they first moved in. What did that mean? That the house would stretch out to give them more space? Or that they would leave the tight fit for another house that wouldn't give them blisters, bad dreams, bad breath? His breath smelled rotten almost all the time, and if he didn't keep spraying it with mint or cinnamon, the smell got worse and worse. Even Patricia knew about it. She would start talking about being a vegan and how pure it made your body. Bad breath had started when they moved from the other house. It had started when his parents split up, when his father ruined everything. Nobody had to tell him that, it was just something he knew. Your mom and I have hit a pretty bad patch, Lang. We've decided it might be best if . . . Blah, blah, blah. Was bad breath part of the bad patch? The patch meant soap wouldn't lather in his hands, dogs wouldn't come when he whistled, and the thoughts he didn't want to think were harder and harder to uproot. They were like weeds in the piece of hard-packed earth where he stood.

He opened the door to the narrow closet where she kept the broom and the thing she used for windows and looked on the shelf above. Lang laughed and reached for what he wanted: a sponge. He had his choice because she had . . . how many did she have exactly? He shoved one package to the side and found more in back. Jesus. Forty sponges, wrapped in packages of five. He could choose from a rainbow of colors. Lang sucked his lower lip for a minute and chose yellow.

He tore the package open, thinking of his T-shirts, purchased in shit-brand bulk. He had T-shirts still unwrapped from last year. Never shop poor, Lang. She would get that expression on her face and he knew she was thinking about the aunts. She shopped poor, too, except when it came to her. She gave herself little "treats" when she wouldn't get him acne scrub. He found them on his searches and would bring them out of the back of her closet and line them up on her bed when he needed to make her feel guilty. What had it been the last time? A nightgown. She had forgotten and left the price tag on. His face started to throb as he remembered. The cyst was getting worse. He didn't even mention the material, how she might as well have worn *nothing,* it was so stupid and cheesy. Instead, he made a big deal about how small it was, how they were cheating her by getting her to buy something that was about the size of a T-shirt, like the shitbrand ones she bought for him. He made her cry over it but she didn't take it back. Finding out everything used up most of his time. The time when he wasn't wrestling or listening to the Captain. Information is capital, Son. Information is true wealth. Lang was getting rich all right, only the currency didn't come from his mom or his dad. It came from an old man who knit better than a woman.

He let the water run for a while, until it finally got hot. Then he wet the sponge and squeezed most of the water out, wincing because it scalded his hand. He sprinkled a layer of Ajax on top and thought of sugar on butter, the sandwiches he used to eat when he was little. He wouldn't eat this, though. No way would he eat this.

He started scrubbing his face slowly, beginning with a cheekbone. Slowly, so he could get the feel of how well it would work. How clean his face would be and how free. Free of spots and trouble and swelling. It felt good, like planing that surface once. His dad's surfboard, that time when they'd bought a blank board. Lang had been little. Eight, maybe? So it was a big fucking deal back then. Lang looked out the window, rubbing the sponge down now, the way they'd taken down the wood, planed it smooth and clean. His dad had walked into the store, asked for a six-foot-four blank and then touched the top of Lang's head.

"Stupid."

He had been, back then. Lang had been little and stupid and just as religious about the waves as his father still was. He would practice looking, the way his father did. Be still, he used to say. Be . . . still. And in between the words he'd packed silence as usual, pretending it meant something. What it meant was his father didn't know how to talk. Lang knew that now, like he knew most everything. He was doing circles with the sponge and realized it didn't feel grainy anymore. He sprinkled more powder on top and continued, this time scrubbing harder. It was a real acne scrub and Patricia wouldn't have to look at his face and ever see anything but clean living. He'd be able to look in mirrors, too, because the change he was waiting for was finally here.

He fingered the back of the sponge, thinking that was nice, too. Smooth and rough at the same time. You got rid of the top layer of skin every time you scratched yourself. He'd read that, or something like that. This side would top it off. He ran cold water over the sponge now. Cold after hot, that would be good. Shit, he was going to franchise this thing. He'd have people lay back in chairs, their necks cushioned on something puffy and he'd hire high school kids and buy a bunch of sponges, no, he had enough sponges right here. He'd open up a cash register and let it roll. Mexicans. He'd hire Mexicans. They'd scrub harder than white kids. Lang would make them rich. Make this tight fit of a house nice and loose, the way it should have been from the beginning.

The sting was good. He saw the crow again. It had sidled down to a different spot on the wire, and every once in a while it would flop around, like it was losing its balance. Only it wouldn't. It stayed put. Maybe if he whistled the crow would come to him and change his luck. Make the bad patch fertile and green. Not quite Edgar's yard—he wouldn't want to get near Edgar's pansies, but some grass would be nice. His mother didn't have time to plant. Or that's what she said, so there was a lot of creative cement. Bright, colored surfaces that led to a great big pot of succulents. Except he couldn't see anything succulent about the plants his mother preferred. Nothing there he would bite into. He ran a little water over the sponge, his eyes still hooked on the bird, and thought of what he would like to eat right then. It sure wasn't a plant.

He put his head inside the freezer to cool the sting, which was mounting. He didn't want to rinse his face yet, to rid it of the scrub. Those spinach triangles, what did she think? That he would eat those? No poverty buying here, of course, where he might have appreciated it. He thought of a case of ice-cream sandwiches. Twenty boxes of Trix or Frosted Flakes. Ice cubes, vegetable turnovers. He snapped the freezer door shut and practiced leaning on the counter top. He would get good at leaning until his face let up.

He heard a car fart up the street, the way his dad's sometimes did. He usually welcomed the sound, the way he didn't really mind hearing his mother sometimes in the bathroom. It reminded him he still had a family, even though it almost never felt that way.

If his mother didn't bring milk, he'd do something. He didn't know what. Sometimes, even when he phoned her at work and she said yes, yes, alright, love you honey, she'd still manage to forget milk. He'd look at the billboard on the corner that asked GOT MILK? and feel bad. That made him feel really bad sometimes.

He had left the door unlocked and she thought her key was unlocking when it wasn't, so he passed through the arch that took him from the tight kitchen to the tight dining room and living room combo and straight up to the front door. He didn't need mirrors because of his mother. He saw himself reflected in her face. Of course she was surprised. No more Blotch Face. No more Mr. Mound's Bar. He pulled open the front door for his mother, scrubbed and shining, his neck wet, he guessed because of the water from the sponge.

"My God, Lang."

She said it so loud, he was convinced for the first time ever that God actually heard.

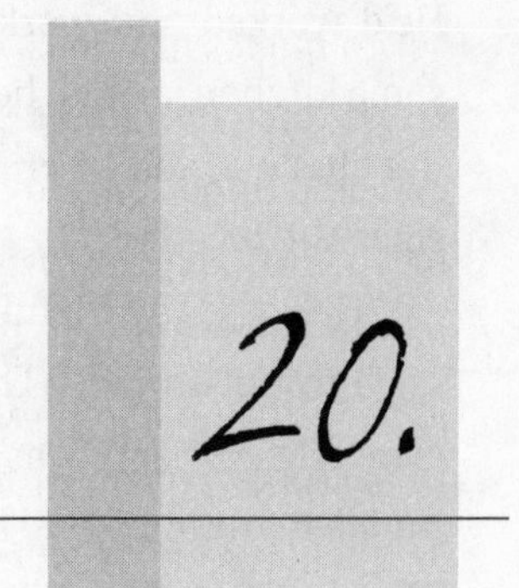

Lang looked out the bottom half of the bathroom window. Edgar was having a party, and people had been streaming in for the last half hour. For once, he wished he could go to Edgar's house.

"I don't see what this has to do with me."

"Ray is proud of the work I've done on his house so far. So am I."

"Great. You're proud and I'm what?"

"You're invited to dinner," Helen said.

He snorted and turned around. "What makes you think I can actually eat?"

"You've got to eat *something*, Lang."

"And why did he call me? I don't even know him."

"I think it's nice that he asked you directly." Helen experimented with the part in her hair, placing it below where it usually ran. "He's being respectful of your feelings."

"Your hair looked better the old way," he said. He jiggled the blinds with the plastic wand.

"Cut that out." Helen readjusted her part and shook out a few drops of perfume. She rubbed her wrists together and the scent began to spread through the small space. "Lang, I have to tell you something. He's not just a customer."

He wore a polo shirt with a yellow stain just under the last button. He'd worked and worked to get it out, scrubbing at it with the exact same kitchen sponge he'd used on his face. Ruining his face and then going after the shirt were just part of the accidents that had ruled his life since the divorce.

"He's also my friend."

"I'm not stupid." The blinds opened and closed like slowly blinking eyes. Edgar's party was taking shape. People stood outside in his garden, huddled around pitted statues and tight pink roses. The pits came from a BB gun. Edgar had talked to the kid who did it, a scrawny little boy at the end of the block who was finally graduating from middle school. Something was wrong with the kid, and Edgar hadn't gone to the parents about the statues. Edgar had been very cool, Lang had to say that. He could see the first puff of smoke from Edgar's chimney, the signal for the party to move back indoors. Edgar cooked for a long time before his parties, stirring and chopping at his kitchen window. Sometimes he drank so much champagne when he cooked Lang was afraid he would fall into his big black pot. Hey. Ray. Maybe she and Ray had parties, too. Pajama parties where everyone ran around in cheesy nightgowns eating Gouda and Laughing Cow. That would be pretty funny, except thinking about it didn't even make him smile. He looked through the blinds one last time.

"What kind of friend?"

"I don't know yet." Helen ran her hand down over her hip. She would have preferred a man's flat shape for the black velvet pants: her hips were too conspicuous. She thought of Ray touching her there with his fine long fingers and took her hand away.

"Come on. We're going to be late."

"Ray. What kind of dumb name is that?"

"Listen, I want you to call me Ray. Anything else makes me feel like an old man."

Helen held her breath, watching the two of them shake hands. Ray stood taller and had a bulkier frame, but Lang's body made a deeper impression in the room. Her son's presence felt hard and rigid. He'd never stood up quite so straight, held himself at such attention.

"Pleased to meet you, sir."

"Let me get you something to drink."

"I'll have some water, please."

"You sure? I've got all kinds of soda and fruit juice."

"Water would be fine."

Ray nodded and went into a storage area behind the kitchen. The cramped space looked like a frontier larder. Ray emphasized the effect with bottled water, dried fruits and meats, a larder for the long haul. Helen and Lang sat down across from each other in the kitchen. Iron garden chairs, stripped of color, circled the round table. Lang looked down through the glass top and peered into the enormous terra-cotta urn that supported the fragile surface.

"Any more rude behavior from you—"

"What's all that stuff inside?" He traced over the top of the table with his thumb, as if he was trying to rub away whatever he saw.

Ray returned with Lang's water.

"I hope you don't mind simple cooking, Lang." His voice was glittery and bright.

"That's the only kind he knows," Helen said.

"I put together a shepherd's pie. With kind of an Oklahoma twist." Ray looked across the table at Helen. "Wine?"

Helen held out her glass. She wanted a lot of wine.

"Can I use your bathroom?" Lang asked.

"Sure. It's just to the right of the entrance."

Lang wandered out to find it, guessing it was the smallest door he could see. It was a weird house, he could tell that much, the kind little kids threw rocks at. He heard the sound of those BBs again, the way they ricocheted from Edgar's statues to the driveway. That kid would have a great time with Ray's house. Ray, Ray. What did he know about that word? Lang pressed down too hard on the handle to the bathroom and slipped inside, felt for the light. The first thing he saw were his mother's candles, the ones from the store that had stuff crawling up the side. He pulled open a drawer to look for matches. There weren't any, just a lot of folded towels. If you used one to dry your hands, somebody would have to iron it right away. He thought of their own yellow towels and brightened. These two sets of towels had nothing to do with each other when you thought of it. He thought of it hard and stood over the toilet.

He couldn't go. He thought of Patricia, who knew what went in houses. He thought of what she would say about this place. She wouldn't say anything. She would be polite (he seems like a nice friend for your mom) and he would know exactly what was in her mind by the way she looked at him. One look would promise him that this thing wouldn't last. That soon this guy would stop calling his mother because nothing in this house went with their stuff. The two houses, if you pushed them together, would blow up on contact.

He still couldn't go. He sat down on the toilet quickly and leaned back, folding his arms over his chest. The seat was warm. The goddamn seat was warm. The freak! He had heated toilets. Lang would have hopped off and run away, except that it felt good. Not too hot, not too cold. It was just right. As soon as he thought of Papa Bear, Mama Bear, and Baby Bear he started to go. The sound of it probably carried into the kitchen. He would probably flood the bathroom, he'd held it in for so long.

He bent over his knees and touched the top of his shoes. "Shepherd's pie with an Oklahoma twist." What the hell did that mean? Ray. It was a hick name. He'd thought Lang was bad, that Boyd was worse. He hadn't understood just how lucky he was. He shook himself dry and got up to wash his hands.

The faucets had an H and a C printed on the top. Next to the fixtures for retards was his mother's favorite soap. Some Swiss stuff, he'd given it to her for Christmas one year. One bar, because he couldn't afford more. Lang had never seen her actually use the soap. She said she was saving it. Saving it for for what? For Ray? Alright then. He wouldn't wash his hands since the fancy soap belonged to Ray now. Lang squashed a towel to make it look used. He kneeled down and opened a door under the sink, then moved aside jars of cleansers and brass polish. He found a set of rags and different jars full of colored grainy stuff. Behind all of that was some medicine with a funny name. Lang frowned and studied the label. Information is capital, Son. The Captain's words followed him around all the time. Ray must have been pretty sick since there were just a few pills left. Lang put everything back. Then he opened the door quietly and tiptoed up the stairs. The moonlight falling through the weird window above him followed every move he made, but he didn't care. He wanted to find out what else his mother had given Ray.

Lang sat down. He took a big piece of bread and tore it in half. He put the smallest piece on the table next to his plate and left the other one in the basket.

"Just in time," Ray said.

Every word came out right. The words were like his weather-man hair that never got out of line. His dad's hair was stupid, too, but in the right way. He actually forgot to get haircuts was the thing. Sometimes he struggled to see, peering through long strands of hair, and Lang would have to tell him to get it trimmed.

Ray was putting something on the table that looked like a pie, one of those pies with puffed tops Lang remembered from fairy tales. Blackbirds would fly out with the first cut. His dad had always added flapping when he read the story out loud, pretending his arms were wings. He held his breath to watch *that* and saw the same expression on his mother's face. She was watching and waiting too.

"Say when," Ray said as he cut.

"Too much for me."

"I'll take it," Helen held out her plate and breathed. It looked simple and delicious to her. She couldn't see the Oklahoma twist yet.

"Is that hamburger meat?" Lang asked, scooting down lower in his chair.

"Yep. Some meat, some potatoes, and spices. Cornmeal crust," Ray smiled as he looked at Lang. "Big, small, or in between?"

"The smallest. I guess my mom didn't tell you." Lang worried about what was under the lid on the other pan. Nobody was talking about what was in that pan. He saw bottles of salad dressing on the counter and a big bowl.

"Tell me what?" Ray's knife slipped into the hot crust one more time.

"About my match Tuesday afternoon. I've gotta make weight."

"No, she didn't mention that." Ray stopped cutting and looked at his mom. Then the knife tap, tap, tapped its way to the edge, making a neat cut. "Helen, I guess you'll need to cancel that appointment we had for the floors."

His mother's napkin went up to her mouth and Lang saw her eyes shoot wide open. What were they going to do with the floors? This guy was a freak. He'd never seen such a freak in his life, not even at the beach with that friend of his dad's who collected old boards and stood them in the sand as if they were girls. He still remembered the names . . . Lis Fish, Brewer Gun, Pintail, and Wafered Flip-Tip. Old guys would pass by and swat the backs of the boards as if they were butts. What was his mom going to do with the floors? Was this guy going to make her wash floors? His face hurt. He wished she could make a compress for him.

"Oh, Ray, I'm so sorry. I completely forgot."

"You can't miss Lang's first match." He moved to rescue that saucepan on the stove and turned to grin at Lang. "You hurt your face at practice, son?"

"It's a zit." Lang pressed hard on the word. As hard as he had pressed on the cyst.

"Oh, man. Those can kill. Now let's eat while it's hot."

Lang watched how his mother ate her food. He could tell how bad she was feeling. Lang could always make his mother feel bad, he knew just how to do it. He looked at Ray's back, the way it was. It was a dad's back, bent and doing things in that way they always did them. How did Ray know so much about his mother? How did he already know exactly how to make her feel bad?

"You can eat this, Lang. No problem here," Ray looked at *him,* not his plate, as he spooned beans in the middle where the pie should have gone. That was how he did it. He looked right into her, the way he was looking right into Lang. He did it to make sure things went his way.

Lang held his hand up.

"That's fine, sir."

Ray sat down and slapped the napkin in the air once to straighten it out.

"You've got great manners, Lang. Girls eat that up. Pretty soon they'll be crawling all over you."

"Ray!"

The hell. They started to talk and he started to listen, thinking of the Captain. What the Captain would do now. He would call in a cryptographer, that's what he would do, who would tell him exactly what all the words meant. How they fell into shapes that really meant other shapes, that lay outside or underneath or above this weird house. They forgot he was there and that was good. He could do his work. His work of seeing and understanding what he had discovered tonight. In the meantime, there was other business to attend to. He stuck a green bean into the gap in his front teeth. The Gap. His favorite, favorite store in all of America. He could still chew on other stuff, even with the green bean sticking out. It was going along quite nicely.

"Lang, take that out of your mouth."

"What, Mother?" It wasn't as if he hadn't practiced. He'd done it with Red Vines and Patricia, who'd thought it was funny. Once she fished the candy out of his teeth with chopsticks.

"The bean, son. You have a green bean stuck in your tooth."

Son. That freak. He sucked the bean out and down, not using his napkin. Not giving them that pleasure. Ray waited for Lang to strike next. He knew how to wait for things. Lang wondered what the Captain would say about that.

He moved his glass to the edge of the table and chewed some more. Right on the edge where it could fall with one false move. It was good practice and he always did that when he ate alone. She wasn't going to see this, though. His mom had decided to pretend he wasn't there.

They talked about house stuff, using design code words and he got more interested in other things. The chair he saw in the corner, just one. If he wanted anyone else around, he would have bought two. Two that were exactly alike. There was more stuff in the kitchen than anywhere else, he thought. Cooking things except that they were about cooking. They weren't for cooking. At least Lang didn't think you'd use those rusty pots that were on the top of the fireplace. It was nice he had a fireplace in here. It was the only thing that wasn't weird. He lost track of the thoughts he wanted to keep in his mind. He drifted out on one wave, then one more before he came back in and peered through the glass top on the table.

"Your mom had a great idea with those dried flowers. She thought we'd bring the outside right on inside."

"Why would you want to switch them around?" Lang sucked at the water in the glass. Helen thought of the juice cup he'd had as a baby, the fierce way he used to swallow every last bit of apricot nectar.

Ray smiled and folded his arms over his chest.

"Good question." Ray didn't answer it. Maybe he thought that shit-eating grin would shut him up. Lang's jaw was clenched. He didn't make his face grin back.

Lang leaned forward and turned his head toward Ray as if he were ready to listen for the first time that evening. "Where'd you get all these flowers?"

"I really don't know. You'll need to ask your mother."

"Where'd you get them, Mother?"

She thought of pinching his leg under the table, then felt the glass surface under her forearms where nothing escaped notice. He'd never called her mother. She remembered Mrs. Ramone and the boy's mocking dance behind her, then shook her head.

"I bought them at a dried-flower wholesaler."

"Oh. Then where did he get them?"

"She. Del Mar, I think."

"From peoples' gardens?" His dad had a whole garden growing on his terrace. Those pink flowers, the little ones growing in pots . . . what if someone stole all the flowers his dad worked so hard to keep alive? He suddenly wished his dad was here. He wished his dad would come charging through the door right now, even though it would be really embarrassing. He wished his dad would stop everything. *Stop!*

"From cultivated fields, Lang. What are you fishing for?"

Ray folded his napkin neatly in half. He lay it above his plate and listened to Lang.

"Me? Personally? Nothing. I just think that it would be wrong to destroy a whole garden if all you want is to pretend outdoors is indoors. If you're just trying to fake everybody out."

"Lang, you're being very rude."

Ray scooched his hand over the bread crumbs and the salt that had fallen on the table. It opened and closed over his mother's wrist like it was just one more thing in its path.

"Let him be, Helen."

She did, for a change. Ray's face registered nothing and Lang wondered what else he could get his mother to do. He stopped eating and pushed his plate to the center of the table.

21.

That was one hell of a match, Lang." Ray's voice was soft. Lang had to listen hard to get every word.

"Thanks." He held the phone with the tips of his fingers. His mother was always griping about finding dirty fingerprints on stuff.

"Good escape there at the end. Your mom must have been proud."

Even though she'd gone out and bought a rule book, she was always mixing up terms. Calling a reverse an escape when it wasn't. Lang scratched his head and brought the phone a little closer to his ear. This time she hadn't.

"Do you want to speak to my mom?"

"Sure. In a minute."

He was so serious about everything. Lang thought of what it would be like to have his dad in the same room with Ray. Probably awful. Probably one of the worst things in the world.

"You sure know how to go after what you want."

Lang put his little finger in the dial. They were the last family in America to have a rotary phone. He wondered if Ray would still want to talk to his mother when he found out about the dumb phone or the bugs in the kitchen.

"You work hard. You get results. That's good stuff, Lang."

He knew that already. So why did he want to hear him say it again? He thought of Ray's hair and his weird house. Sick. He moved his little finger from 6 to 7 and back.

"You there?"

"Yes, sir. I hear you."

There was nothing on the phone for a second and he thought Ray was gone. Then he heard some music barely turn on.

"Too bad your father couldn't make it to the match."

Did she have to tell him everything? He'd looked up at the space she saved in the bleachers until he couldn't stand it anymore. The next time he glanced up, after he won, some girl he didn't know had taken the space.

"You talk like you were there or something."

"I was."

The space between his shoulders felt like it was shrinking. If it got any smaller his shoulder blades would touch. Then he wouldn't be able to wrestle or even move. He would turn into a human cylinder with his arms pinned behind his back. He would have been scared, except he knew all about this feeling. He got it right before a match. He got it right before he had to go into school. It usually happened on the sidewalk before he went inside, and then it passed, leaving him perfectly normal.

"I didn't stay long. I was afraid I might screw up your concentration. Anyhow, good job. I'll talk to your mom now if she's there."

She was feeding the plants in the backyard. She looked too skinny in those shorts. Her legs were whiter outdoors than he'd ever seen them. Somebody should be feeding *her.* The window made it seem like she was standing in a picture, like what he saw was barely real. Maybe it wasn't real. She was saying stuff to Edgar, who was working outside too. But then, how did he know since he couldn't hear the words come out of her mouth? Lang set the phone down with the receiver on its side and shouted once from where he stood.

"MOM! PHONE!"

She turned her head once, as if she heard him, then bent down over the pot again.

"Mom. Phone." He said it another time, making his voice almost as soft as Ray's, then turned to go out the front door. He didn't want to be late for work. That was funny. It was his mom who didn't want him to be late for work.

Helen stepped out of her sandals and padded across the living-room floor. The wood was warm where the sun fell, and she thought of curling up inside a gold patch of light. Poor's life wasn't so bad. If he would just follow the sun through the store, instead of desperately clinging to clients, he would be a happy dog. She looked out at the neat row of plants and the crooked walkway, now free of weeds sneaking up through the bricks. The hard, physical work felt good. She slid the cushions from the chairs into the center of the floor and swept out the chair frames. She began to polish and dust, humming strands of songs that floated through her mind. She talked to herself every once in awhile, lecturing Lang when she found a food wrapper, lecturing herself as she thought about the week that was coming up. She needed to get Alice focused on backing for the new fabric. Alice was bored by details like durability and shape retention. But Helen wasn't.

"That's why we're a good team."

Alice didn't answer, of course, since she wasn't in the room. Helen continued in a circle, pounding away at dust and dirt.

"What is this . . . ?"

But she knew what it was. Patricia's headband lay hidden under the pile of cushions. It must have slid out from under one of the chairs. Or maybe it had been under the rug all along. Helen held it gingerly in her hands. Velvet on one side, plastic on the other, it had sharp little teeth to hold it in place. She tossed it into a plastic garbage sack and began to clean faster.

She wished Ray were on his way over. She wished for a nasty moment that he didn't have a lost girl that took him out of town and away from her. She wished suddenly that she could make him forget Rebecca. Helen rubbed and rubbed at her furniture. Her forearms were beginning to ache. But then, how could a parent forget his own child?

"Oh, Lang!"

The phone was off the hook again. Where was his mind? She looked at her watch, wondering how many calls she'd missed. Impossible to know. She got a fresh rag from the pail and sprayed it with household disinfectant.

"Helen? Are you there?"

The phone dropped from her hand. She heard Ray's voice repeat her name again, but she didn't believe it. Why would he be on the line? It wasn't Ray at all. It was her own madness, her crazy longing to see him even though he was away. She smirked and picked up the phone again, expecting a dial tone.

"It's me."

His voice tightened around her. She felt as if it were pressing her down to the ground, his voice a body forcing its hot weight upon hers. She lifted her chin and closed her eyes.

"Ray. How long have you been waiting?" When did Lang leave? She couldn't make any sense of time. "I'm so sorry."

"Don't be. It was nice."

She looked around the gleaming room. He'd been listening to her as she worked. He had heard all her silly outbursts, the way she talked to herself.

"I like listening to you."

All that time sounds had replaced the sight of her. All that time he had just sat listening to her move around the room. The banal domestic scene suddenly felt charmed. It was as if Ray had actually been here, buried behind the newspaper while she cleaned over and around him. They were exactly like any other ordinary couple on a Saturday afternoon, except that there was nothing ordinary about their kind of happiness. This happiness was supercharged. It tore through her, stirring up all her emotions.

"What a funny thing for you to do." She put her other hand around the receiver. "Are you all right?"

"I'm back from Michigan. Let's leave it at that."

Helen stretched one leg out in front of her. She liked looking at its good, strong shape. She liked the strangeness of its exposure. Her own and Ray's. Her restraint was paying off.

"I'm coming over," Helen said.

He stood at the top of the stairs. A window or a back door had been left open and her skirt beat gently against her calves. She climbed one step at a time, keeping her eyes on his all the time. The trip seemed to have left him wary and alert.

"Tell me about it."

"There's nothing to tell. I gave Mrs. Lowell a check for six thousand dollars and got on the next plane out of there."

"But you must have discussed things."

"Yeah, we did. She showed me a fake stack of doctor's bills."

"How do you know they're fake?"

He turned away from her and headed down the hall. Helen hurried to keep up.

"I called the AMA. There's no Dr. Rudolph Lutz in Birmingham. No Rebecca Richards either."

Rebecca's bedroom had been disassembled. All the work they'd done together had been torn down. Drawers were emptied and clocks stopped. Accessories (the ones she could see) were heaped in a cardboard box. The linens had been stripped and neatly folded. They were stacked at the foot of the mattress.

"What does all this mean?"

"It means I'm not chasing Elizabeth down anymore. It means the next move is up to her."

He sank down on the bed and finally faced Helen.

"I can't do this anymore."

Helen sat beside him and took his hand between hers. It was clammy and cold.

"Then don't."

His leg shifted against hers.

"You're telling me to quit?"

"Not at all. I'm telling you to turn this over to people who can get your daughter back."

"So Rebecca visits her mother in jail, is that it?"

"She's a sick woman, Ray. They won't put her in jail. She'll get treatment and your daughter will get a healthy, loving father back."

He looked exhausted and sad. Helen put pillows at the head of the bed and pressed lightly on his chest, pushing him down.

"You're going through hell."

"My daughter's going through worse."

He closed his eyes, then pulled his forearm over his face to block out the sight of Mrs. Lowell. Or Elizabeth. But surely not Helen. Surely he wanted to see her.

"You've got to let other people help you." She lifted his elbow, peeked at him under the crook of his arm. "Other people can help, you know."

She moved his arm away from his face and placed it carefully by his side. Then she leaned down to kiss him. His face was closed and calm, his eyes shut. She brushed over his features with the back of her hand, kissing every shadow, every line. She would lift and lighten the dark, serious contours with her lips.

"Helen."

He lay so still. She wished her body was larger, stronger. She would cover him completely, protect his cool length. Sorrow held him trapped for now, but Helen would win. She would free him.

"I don't think . . ."

"Sssh. Don't talk."

No words. They were finished with words. They would find a new language. His eyes were still closed. Good. She wanted to look first. She wanted to help herself to everything first. She wanted to be rude and gluttonous, but she held herself in check. But his hunger would rise to follow hers if she was careful. She would be tender and slow. She wouldn't frighten him away again.

She unbuttoned his shirt, spread it open to stare at a body that seemed blameless and young. His chest was square and smooth. She didn't want to touch the skin there. Ray lay dormant under her eyes. She wanted to remember his colors, his steady breathing that would soon quicken.

She straddled his body on the bed, careful not to jar him. Not yet. She placed her knees inside the upturned palms of his hands, smiling at his closed eyes, and continued to undress him. Buttons slid free easily; no resistance, no movement. She lifted her blouse over her head and watched her breasts slip over the edges of her bra as she leaned toward Ray. She smelled her own perfume as her clothing fell to the floor.

His eyes opened, but he didn't speak as she slid her finger into his mouth. She fished for his tongue, brought it forward to meet hers. She licked his face and his eyes solemnly, as if she were cleaning a baby kitten, marking it with her own saliva and making it her own.

"Don't." She didn't want him to move. She wanted to take his whole body with her wiggling tongue. She would claim him first with her lips and fingers, leaving a fierce trail that no one else would follow.

She slipped out of her skirt and tossed it over the side of the bed as he watched. He frowned at the space between her legs, and she thought of Amanda Reston's bare skin. She quickly struggled free of transparent underwear.

"Helen, I'm going to disappoint you."

"Never."

She swiveled and switched positions, her head facing his feet. Her knees continued to keep the palms of his hands pinned in place. Helen was careful to keep herself poised above him, out of his reach. She bent down to part his legs; this dark region was for her. She nuzzled and explored, claiming all of him, while he lay quiet and composed. He rested in the beginning, shrinking a bit at the light touch of her tongue. She kissed him tenderly, telling him in their new language that she was unafraid. Then Helen felt him quiver slightly; sensations shifted under soft, loose skin. She took him in her mouth, her hand, her mind . . . she stretched and shaped him until he pleased her. She dropped down on top of him to move fast, then faster until she was lost and furiously alive. He slipped shyly out of her body once and she had to hold him in place with her two wet hands. Neither of them cried out in the end.

22.

"You mind if we play the radio upstairs, Mrs. Richards?" The burly young man was coated with a film of fine dust. Sanding wooden floors had turned his long blond hair ashy and dull.

"Go right ahead." Helen didn't bother to correct the mistake. She'd driven over to let him and his boss into the house at seven, before Ray was even up. It was natural to think she was Ray's wife. An easy mistake.

Refinishing, plastering, measuring for curtains, and laying new tiles. They would complete the dirty work before Ray's furniture arrived, and today was the beginning. Helen would be at the house all day to answer questions, to synchronize schedules for the following week, to see that all the workers got along. She thought of how quiet Mondays were with the shop closed. She liked Mondays this way, filled with noisy activity and closely timed appointments.

She let her hands slide over the corners of the battered carton. Ray had several of them left to unpack, and he had brightened at her offer to help.

"Really? You wouldn't mind?"

"Comes with the job." She'd moved toward him as she said it, happy at the long, warm kiss she received. He was getting better, quickly receiving the messages she sent and sending out clear signals of his own. Helen thought of the breakfast waiting for him upstairs. It was perfect, intimacy without intrusion on the privacy he needed right now.

She looked down at the return address on the carton. He must have been in a big hurry, nearly crazy with loss and worry for Rebecca. The box read from Richards in Oklahoma to Richards in La Jolla. He'd left off the city in one case, the state in another. The scrawl was barely legible. She ran her hand down one side of the box, wondering what she would do with the contents. Just stuff, he'd said. She remembered sorting out Mrs. Sadler's things. It had been difficult, at first, to see the pattern in personal objects, but she had learned. She'd even proven herself to be a "quick study," as Alice called her the day the article appeared. Helen ducked her head, thinking of the praise, and ran her hands down the side of the box.

She thought of the cave that lay below the library where she stood as she began to open the box. Damp or just cold? She couldn't tell. She lowered her head to see if it smelled of mildew.

She drew her head back in surprise. She knew the oily, rich smell from her walks, the close walks she took when she didn't mind getting wet. Each time foam spilled over her bare feet, she heard the sea sigh and smelled the odor it released as one more wave died on the shore. Recognizing it here felt exciting, something that she now shared with Ray.

"Hey."

His face looked open and clear after a good night's rest. He was happy to see her, though not smiling quite yet. He held several manila envelopes in his hand. They were already stamped and addressed. She squinted at them and he shifted them under his arm.

"Good morning. I think." She teased him, checking her watch. "What have you been doing up there?"

"Paperwork. Can I leave you to take care of things here for a while?"

"Sure."

He looked down at her other hand, the hand that still rested on the box, and lightly tossed her his pocketknife.

"I should be back in a couple of hours."

Helen followed him as he left the library, his envelopes still clutched under his arm. Light spilled through the oval windows in the living room, and he seemed to pass through a series of golden eggs.

"Excuse me, Mr. Richards."

Ray stepped out of the way of a painter, frowning at the man's speckled work boots as he passed and headed upstairs.

"Oh, I almost forgot." Ray turned around and cut back through the room. Helen wished she could make the movement last. His body often seemed vacant, in just the way Lang's was when he was still. They were both full of grace and speed. They shared a natural agility that seemed to dissolve when their bodies were motionless.

He put both hands on the back of her head. He lowered her chin gently toward her chest and kissed the top of her head with a loud, smacking sound.

"I had a great breakfast. Thanks for leaving me that tray."

She lifted her head and felt his hands drop to her shoulders.

"I missed you this morning." She wouldn't always miss him. She would wriggle into his bed the next time. No knock. No warning. She would just slide in beside him and feel him recover slowly from dreams and sleep, uncurling next to her.

"Mrs. Richards?" the floor man bellowed from the stairway. "Looks like we might have a termite problem here."

Ray's hands tightened on her shoulders. Helen looked at his face for a long moment, then slipped her hands over the tops of his, securing his touch. He ran one thumb along the side of her face, stopping at the cleft in her chin. He pressed his thumb into the space there and Helen imagined he might deepen the depression, encourage the flaw.

"Introducing yourself as Mrs. Richards these days?" It was a father's teasing voice, probably one he had used dozens of times to extract confessions from Rebecca.

"I—"

He kissed her before she could answer. It was a hard, rushed kiss with many messages curled inside. She waited until Ray closed the heavy front door, then ran her fingers over her lips, wishing his embrace hadn't been so brusque. Then she laughed. Ray felt as hurried as she did. He was eager to break through emotional barriers that kept them apart. Mrs. Richards? He had touched her face so thoroughly. Maybe he was memorizing feature after feature with the tips of his fingers, making sure Helen's face would never be confused with Elizabeth's. Ray's quick kiss was a deliberate, frightened verdict in her favor.

Helen went to the guest bathroom by the front door and squeezed one neat dollop of moisturizing lotion into the palm of her hand. She rubbed and rubbed until it disappeared, then headed toward the music pounding away upstairs.

The top and dominant layer of Ray's childhood was Oklahoma. In the old box there was a lariat, stiff and unused, and several gray-green saddle blankets folded precisely under the rope. They seemed brand new. Helen took them outside and forced them to unfold as she slapped them against the side of her leg. Ray must have been a reluctant cowboy at best. Under the blankets there were books on horse handling and roping. When she opened the first brittle treatise, *Caring for Your Pony*, it was so stiff that the binding snapped. Helen swiped at each book with a cloth and left them stacked in one corner of the library.

She dug deeper, through wadded paper stained watery brown in places. She smoothed out each sheet, examining back and front. There was no message in the design, no missive written in a little boy's hand. She straightened the last sheet and lifted a flat red cushion from the box. It had been well used. Six black buttons wobbled on single strand thread and the fabric was rubbed thin in the center.

"Helen, we've got another problem." The floor man looked penitent this time, his hands clasped in front of him and eyes cast down.

She'd corrected the mistake, become Helen again.

"Don't tell me."

"Cat. Or something. Some kinda animal."

She followed him to the second floor. Benny, was that his name? Music wasn't the only noise up here. A talk-show host was insulting a female guest who had fallen in love with a dead man. Where'd you meet a dead guy? the host screamed. How do you two have sex? Helen stopped to gather the coffee cups and crumpled napkins, then went on to examine the stained wood.

"See? Years of it."

A coved ceiling rose to a single point, pinching the top of the bedroom. Two sets of small-paned windows opened over the ocean and lights from the water skipped over the white walls. Stains appeared on the floor next to the baseboard. The room had been playfully carpeted with wheat-colored sisal. It had been Helen's idea to unveil the wooden floors upstairs.

"How could an animal do that?"

"Lifts a leg." Benny grinned. "Fires away."

Helen walked around the room slowly, bending every once in a while to examine the damage. "So systematically I mean."

"You'll have to replace all the boards in here. Mr. Richards will, I mean."

"Why not just the damaged boards?"

"This wood's older than old." He unwrapped a piece of gum and offered it to Helen, careful to keep the bottom protected by foil. She shook her head no. "This wood can't be replaced by anybody."

Maps, many of them the same, were rolled up inside the carton. They were maps made for a child with boats skimming the oceans, railroad cars chugging from one major city to the next. Ray had made his way to the water early. Shells and stones were wrapped in plaid flannel. A starfish was enclosed in a bubble of glass, along with unidentifiable sticks and stones from the sea. Every discovery delighted her more, as if she were the child who pried the abalone from the rock or scooped up a length of kelp to hang over a nail to dry in the sun. The organization of ocean debris revealed Ray's ordered mind. Sand samples made up one full layer. Ray had been as intent upon proper classification as Arthur Adams Perkins, arranging the sand in glass vials according to color and grain. Helen opened one she recognized, sure she felt Windandsea Beach between her fingertips. The vial dropped out of her hand. She was scooping up dark, quartzy sand with a piece of cardboard when Ray came through the door.

"Any more good news?" He was tucking his shirt in more tightly. His face was red, as if he'd been holding his breath.

"Nothing's broken, Ray. I'm getting it cleaned up."

He looked at the spread of things. It was as if the ocean had risen up from the cave to leave tidings. Glad tidings, Helen had thought. Now she wasn't sure. She swept the rest of the sand into her hand and cupped it over the vial.

"This is the plan?" he asked.

"Phase one is emptying the box." Helen put both hands on his desk and leaned forward. "What's wrong?"

"I thought they were using dustless machines upstairs."

"They turned out to be too pricey. We talked about that."

"Let me get this straight. They leave a layer of dust all over the house and in the end I have to replace the floorboards anyway."

She hadn't heard him come in the house. Helen reached across the desk to close the window.

"That's just one room."

"It'll stick out like a sore thumb."

"We can duplicate the floors exactly. No one will know." She would manage that. She would find a way to get the same wood.

"There was never a cat in this house," Ray said. He blinked his eyes quickly and swiped at his mouth with the back of his hand.

"The previous owners must have had one."

Benny came to the door with his boss Neil at his side. Neil looked like an X ray of Benny. His chest bone seemed sharp enough to tear his T-shirt.

"Like to have a look at what we've done so far?"

Helen trudged up the stairs behind the three men, feeling punished.

They crowded into the small guest room and Neil knelt before the worst of the stains. Ray stood looking out to the ocean, his eyes on a faraway sailboat tiny as a toy. He coughed several times, stopped, and began to cough again.

"Mr. Richards? If I could get you to look at this?"

Ray dropped his hands to his sides. It wasn't a gesture Helen had seen before. His arms dangled at his side, registering a defeat she couldn't understand.

"I don't know if Helen mentioned it, but Benny and me think it was a cat that did all this."

Helen watched Ray more closely, not understanding. She could see his arms change, though they still hadn't moved. The muscles tightened quickly, then relaxed.

"We'd be happy to replace just these particular boards for you except we wouldn't be able to work a complete match."

"No one had cats in this house." Ray's eyes circled the room as he spoke. He was so certain this was true. How how did he know? Helen struggled to keep quiet.

"I've been in this business a long time, sir—"

"Don't give me that bullshit." He rolled out every word exactly. Ray spoke as if he were addressing an uncomprehending child. "Every floor man comes up with the same crap about animals or leaks or children who can't find their way to the bathroom at night. And then it's estimate time. Estimate. Don't you love that word, Helen? Estimate."

He laughed and stared at Benny, who kept his eyes on the damaged wood.

"Since it's only an estimate, you get to gouge the buyer at the end. Helen, handle this one, please."

She struggled to breathe, counting out each breath as if it were a wave that swept in and out of her chest. Benny began to burble as soon as Ray left the room, and she was glad of that time to fill herself up with air.

She found Ray in the garden. Gatley's birdhouse had been furnished with twigs and rubbery bits of sea offal pecked apart and crammed into the miniature series of rooms. Ray peeked through an upstairs window.

"Look at this, Helen."

Something nagged her inside. His voice was too smooth, too detached. Benny and Neil had walked off the job. Neil wrote out a bill for their work, and the two men folded their drop cloths with conspicuous silence, shaking Helen's hand solemnly at the door and wagging their heads with compassion for her plight. What plight? Helen wondered. The plight of the faithful. They thought they were free and she wasn't, though why would they think that? She could walk away if she had to. She could return the money she'd been paid at any time, write out a check to Ray and sign her name neatly with Alice's Montblanc. She could return to her old life, sadder but wiser. She didn't feel like looking inside the birdhouse.

"Come."

He didn't take his eyes away from the window.

"I'm not interested. I'd rather talk about what just happened."

He reached for her without looking and pulled her nearer to share his view.

"I don't like it when you pout." Ray's hand remained closed over her forearm. She thought of Boyd with a flash of emotion. I still love you. I still want to be inside you. She wished irrationally for Boyd. She wished for his wild, transforming anger that was nothing more than fear. As soon as she blinked the wish was gone. Something else had taken its place.

A turquoise egg sat balanced on a fluff of feathers, leaves, twine. She strained to see what else she could recognize in the matted cushion. Something glittered below the perfect egg. A shiny coin completed the cradle. She stared and clasped her hands behind her back. Then she saw Ray's open eye beyond the egg. He wasn't looking at the egg. He was looking at her.

"Better?" he asked.

She twisted her hair into a knot and snapped a barrette in place.

"Let's go for a walk," Ray said.

They took the wooden steps down to the beach. There were ninety-eight, Ray said, and she counted them as she walked. Pale-green succulents accompanied them on their way down. The fat leaves lined the sides of the steps, filling the air with their smell. The wind struck her face softly. If she spoke, Ray wouldn't hear. The wind would carry her words to someone standing above her.

He was rolling his pants legs up. They risked getting wet only if they turned left, so Helen knew they would curve around in front of the cave, see his house on the cliff overhead. She envied Gatley in his boat, the sure perspective. She would only see part of what he had seen in its entirety.

"Have you ever been this close to the cave?" He brushed at something on the sleeve of his shirt.

"Once."

"Did you go up the stairs?"

"I didn't know there were any. I didn't go in that deep."

The mouth of the cave still seemed to shout, even at this close range. They listened for a long moment as the waves rushed over the rocks.

"Where do the steps lead?"

"To a door behind the tapestry in the library."

She felt as if a wave had struck her hard. She held herself tight and still.

"I can't believe you didn't show me."

He moved off before she could continue her questions. His feet curved surely around the rocks. She slipped once and righted herself quickly. She began to think how comfortable he would have been in this part of the world, how stifled he must have been in a barren Oklahoma vista. She thought of the things he had collected and wanted to tug at his sleeve, question him about other things. Which sands, which beaches had he explored as a boy?

He was waiting for her on a rocky ledge that split off into three separate fingers. She knew them well, had sunned herself in one narrow strip of sand below. That day (she'd been so young!) she'd even untied the top of her bikini to lie flat in the sand. Boyd had been surfing and she stood up suddenly, her breasts bared, to send him flying off his board. She smiled, forgetting that Ray watched her.

"What's so funny?"

She huffed a bit, less from the walk, than from his presumption. "I'm not sharing any more of my secrets until you give up some of yours."

"Sit down, Helen."

The surface of the rock was still warm from the sun, but Helen knew its cold center would soon reclaim it. She brushed the sand from her feet and waited for Ray to begin.

"I'm sorry about blowing up. Lots of things have come to a head." He took her hand in his. "I got the final word on my project today. Wined and dined the goddamn mayor, met with him once more this morning and it's still not going to happen."

"Why didn't you tell me?"

He lifted her hand and kissed it softly. "I wanted to surprise you with good news for a change."

The city wouldn't issue the permit, and there was to be no further appeal. As Ray described the failed plans, Helen's body went soft with pleasure. He pointed to his house as he described the look of the scene at night, the way the floor would have looked and felt once they had blasted through the layers of rock that separated Ray from his lifelong dream, a view of the ocean below.

Helen could imagine the thick glass floor, the design in the carpet that covered it all, even watch as Ray rolled it up to reveal the scene below. She could see the dark water rage and swirl at her feet. Lamps built into the solid rocky wall lit the scene. As he spoke, his eyes were on the library. The olive tree that ran along beside the western wall shuddered as the wind blew.

"But what if you'd gotten the permit? We would have had to redo all the work we've begun."

"I knew all along it was a dream. But that didn't stop me from trying." His hand tightened around hers. "So, things have been accumulating and the floor guys were the final straw."

Helen drew both legs up and sat cross-legged facing him. She touched his ear lightly, letting her finger trace its outline.

"How'd you figure out the cat thing?"

He shivered and blew on his hands. "Oh, that. Those guys always come up with the same routine."

She sighed and drew closer to him. Of course, he'd probably had more experience with workers and craftsmen than she had. For a jealous moment, she wished that she'd been in his life forever. She didn't hate Elizabeth for being crazy or vicious. She hated Elizabeth for her long history with Ray. He tucked a piece of hair behind her ear and she scooted closer.

"You staying for supper?"

"I promised Lang we'd eat together. I've worked late every night this week."

"Your son's so lucky. He's got no idea how lucky he is."

His concentration seemed to break into bits. He shaded his eyes and watched gulls squabble over a fish caught in a tangle of kelp. Then his eyes worried the stretch of coastline. He seemed to search for something that would stop him, slow down the words that tumbled out in a rush of memory. They didn't seem to come from the same man who had packed away a childhood with such precision.

"You let him do what he's good at. You encourage him. That's all a kid needs to succeed in life, don't let your divorce fool you. A party of one can be a very fine party. Trust me."

She did as the memories spilled out, messy and impossible to transform into a pretty collection. The warm, supportive family she'd imagined dissolved as he spoke. An exacting father stood out, one who wanted horsemanship and marksmanship and citizenship. A tall, striking mother who truly struck. Helen felt oddly calm as he talked. He was finally moving toward real trust and so was she.

"She'd get home from church and take those damn white gloves off, one finger at a time, and lay them in her drawer. Then she'd slap me for some misdemeanor."

Helen cringed, thinking of the lace gloves at the shop, the gloves Ray had refused to buy. She started to touch him, but he stood up to go.

"I always liked to build things with my hands. So I did that. My bird-houses were nothing like Gatley's, but the birds liked them fine. My dog liked the shelter I built him out in the pasture."

"And?" She stood up, too, her limbs stiff. It was getting cool on the rock.

"They'd always mow them down. The stuff I built messed up their beautiful property."

"How could you stand to be in business with them?"

"I was and I wasn't. I had my own division, like I told you. I didn't ever have to answer to them. That was part of our deal."

His words slowed down to a speed she could understand.

"Elizabeth was part of our deal, too. God, they loved her. They still do."

"After what happened?"

"My old man invited me over for one of his famous fireside chats after she took off with Rebecca. Pulls on his cigar and tells me I was wrong to try separating a mother and her child. He said it was unnatural. That was when I decided to leave Richardson, Oklahoma."

"They named a whole town for your family?"

"Make enough money in a small enough town and it's bound to happen." Ray smirked. "Now you know my sordid past."

Past. Passed. She felt like waving good-bye for both of them. Good-bye to sober aunts and loving parents now dead and gone . . . now these cruel two. Instead of waving, she clung to his arm as they clambered off the rock and headed toward a path to the street. It was too late to walk back over the beach.

"How old were you when they first brought you here?"

He pulled his shoulders back, then rolled his head left and right.

"They never brought me here. Why do you ask?"

"The things from the box. The sand, mainly. It's *this* sand, isn't it?"

"We took trips to the Gulf. Most of those things are from Galveston."

She thought of the sharp row of shark's teeth hanging from a piece of fabric like treacherous fringe. She felt herself relax, realizing what Ray would permit. A few of the brightest shells tipped open on a smoky glass tray. A garland of kelp over a bedroom doorway to welcome Rebecca home. This was a job that she could do, after all.

Ray would want most of his memories closed and stored away. Old assumptions tumbled down around her as she climbed up the dark rocks. Helen's history was nothing to hide. The sadness of her past and his united them. They were guaranteed joy made completely from scratch. The paradox made her want to walk faster toward their future, but she forced herself to slow down. Helen followed Ray's steps closely so she wouldn't slip again.

23.

Though there was no one in the store, the three women hid behind Alice's painted screen. Patricia wore a brocade jacket and tight black pants. Fabric samples surrounded the women. What wasn't contained in a book or pinned upon a board spilled over Alice's crowded desk. They nibbled the sandwiches and cakes arranged on a beaten metal tray. Patricia reached for a piece of crumbling shortbread. She took a quick bite, then read something aloud in French. Unbelievable! Yellowed magazines lay open on Patricia's lap. Helen listened as she turned the brittle pages.

Helen flipped through a series of contemporary textiles. Diamond-shaped flowers split open inside straight lines. She sniffed once. Alice and Patricia dawdled over history while she forged on in the present. They had closed the shop at noon to choose fabrics that would complement Alice's new line. Gossiping over dead courtesans wasn't the goal. Helen put an extra sugar in her tea and spoke.

"These might work."

"They might."

Alice grunted as the phone rang. Helen picked up on the third ring and flipped to the next sample.

"It's me."

Helen pushed the hold button gently and swallowed. Alice came to. She raised an eyebrow.

"I'd better take this call."

She pressed past Alice's desk before there was a question or a flimsy answer. Ray waited on the line, and she put him on hold to take the call downstairs.

He was phoning from an art dealer's offices. The impatience in his voice told her exactly how long he had been there. The Carlsbad gallery was filled with the sort of art Helen didn't understand. The paintings in the window looked drab to her and thick with colorless layers. She couldn't understand their prices or their appeal. She'd been up half the night hunched over one of Lang's textbooks, biting the inside of her thumb to keep awake as she scanned periods, tried to memorize artists and influences until all the words swam into senseless black lines. Lang sat with her at the kitchen table, measuring her agony against his. Patricia had given him a long list of vocabulary words to learn for their next meeting.

"I'm back."

"You should be here, Helen. You could have managed this much for me."

She had almost pleaded with Ray to decide on the purchase alone. She didn't know anything about art as an investment. She only knew what she liked and didn't like. At least he had narrowed his choices down to two paintings before she had dropped by the gallery to see them.

"I don't understand what the rush is."

"The rush? That's pretty funny. I meet you on Mondays and Sundays. Sometimes you give me a precious lunch hour if I plan it just right."

Helen twisted in her chair and listened to Ray. It sounded as if another person was speaking. Someone who had borrowed his voice, but didn't know Ray Richards at all. Even at his angriest, Ray never sounded like this.

"I want to buy a painting and I want to buy it today."

Helen rubbed the inside of her thumb. It was sore from last night's vigil. Some of the studied words returned to her now, unconnected and confusing. Historicist. Realist. Naturalist. The words were as confusing as any foreign language.

"Is Alice there?" She could hear him tapping his fingers on a hard surface. Indignance throbbed inside Helen's chest. He had agreed not to call her at work.

"You're putting me in a bind and you know it."

"So Alice is still more important to you than I am. Thought I had that one licked."

One of the paintings Ray had asked her to study was of a dark staircase, lit by a single lamp. The second painting showed a young girl standing inside a doorway. The room behind her was spare. An old woman sat at a table behind the girl. Ray's passion for the Dutch artist seemed based on obscure technical details. Helen had searched each canvas for something to love, some image that didn't make her feel anxious and afraid.

"I'm kind of partial to the one with the angel. Hanging the angel over the table is pretty funny," Ray said.

She didn't see the humor. She heard the scrape of chair legs above her. Patricia called out her name.

"Give me your opinion." Ray's impatience only made Helen less decisive. Color. She could talk about color.

"I like the one with the girl because of the white. The way the color connects at three points."

Ray's voice sagged a bit and Helen thought he must have been disappointed. Why, she didn't know.

"This book says just about the same thing. 'The white of the young girl's bodice and the whiter light of the old woman's reading lamp produce a condition in the painting which few people seize immediately.' Congratulations, Helen. You nailed it."

Helen listened to the silence above. She tasted something sickly sweet.

"Alice must do lots of art consulting with all those high rollers she services."

Something gathered surely in the cold greenhouse, even though Ray was absent. Something that had kept its presence hidden until now. It moved toward her, then snuffled at her feet and legs while she held herself dead still.

"I mean, those people are spending real money."

Was there any other kind? Helen waited.

"Alice must know what she's doing. Either that or she makes her clients believe she does."

"Buy the painting of the girl." Would it make him more morose? Would this girl become his own daughter, peering out from a barren room?

"Now, what was so hard about that?"

His voice swept over her as she pulled herself up out of the chair. Those weren't Patricia's light steps she heard on the stair. Alice's heavy, deliberate gait beckoned to her like a friend. Helen thought of the word with a twinge. What if she and Alice were lazy, extravagant shoppers with lunch planned afterward. Maybe Alice wouldn't mind the champagne if they drank it together.

"I'll let you in on a secret, Helen."

She stiffened. She wished for secrets, frothy and light as Cristal in the middle of the day. All the intimacies that other women easily exchanged.

"I don't need you to be some big art expert or flashy interior designer. You bring much more to your work than that. You always have."

The words thrilled her. All the work and worry of the past seemed to pile up like brilliantly-colored magic carpets and fly away.

"Old Mrs. Sadler knew what she was getting. So do I."

She struggled with his words, let them expand into the newspaper article about the work she had done so long ago. Helen had the piece at home. How did Ray know what it said? How could he quote from it so precisely when it was folded inside a scrapbook she kept next to her bed?

"You see? I've wanted you to make me a home from the very beginning." Ray's voice was clear and happy. "Hey, you'd better get going. You wouldn't want Alice to find out I've stolen you away from her. Would you?"

The brightness of Ray's voice confused Helen. She felt kissed and slapped and blindfolded by an imaginary friend, then spun around in fast, wild circles. Let's play blindman's bluff! Helen thought she might once have played the game, but that was too long ago to think about now. Alice stood before her and the expression she wore was anything but friendly.

Helen hung up without saying good-bye.

"It's him again, isn't it?" Alice slapped the side of her leg.

"I planned this."

"Alice—."

"Don't speak. I closed the shop and bought us special cakes; I took Patricia off of a big project and while you were down here talking to your paramour, made some very important decisions about the new line.

"All this for a man who cheats on his wife." Alice's eyes blazed brighter than coins.

Poor lay his head on his front paws.

"Is it worth it, Helen? Don't answer. Don't speak."

Alice yanked at a strand of stray hair. She snatched a piece of paper from a dining-table drawer and cupped it in her hand. She wrote herself a note and jammed it into a side pocket of her fitted green pants.

"I've got to make a call myself. Think we can keep at least one line open while I do that?"

Alice marched to the back of the store but her anger didn't last. The Princess had her laughing right away.

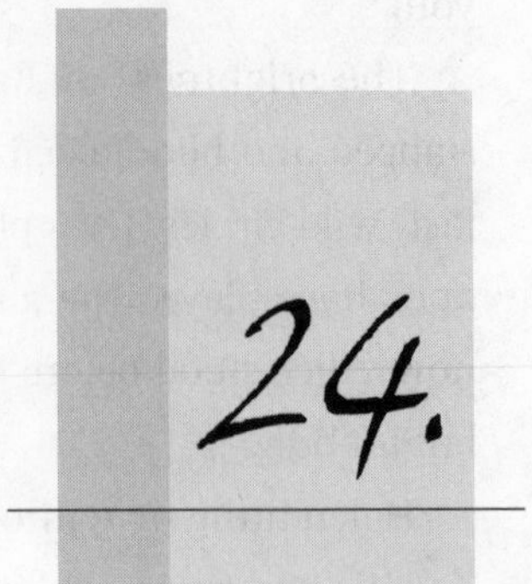

"Quit complaining and swallow this," Edgar said. He handed her a cup of sludgy, black coffee. "You'll have to keep up with the kids."

"Swell."

"Your new friend must be a man of great imagination."

Edgar knelt in front of Helen with a comb in his hand. She wore a tightly belted satin robe. She had napped, then risen to shower and dress for a strangely exclusive benefit ball that began after midnight and ended at sunrise.

Proceeds from the ball's expensive tickets would repair Tiffany windows or restore chips of gold leaf to an eighteenth-century altar in the lobby of a moldy hotel that stood on a crowded and rundown hill above the San Diego harbor. The building was a hodgepodge of architectural excess—Tudor, Moorish, Italian Renaissance, and even Japanese influences fought for dominion. From a distance the old inn looked like a sloppy gray sand castle, and Helen couldn't imagine who would want to stay there. Certainly not people who would pay five hundred dollars for a ticket. She shook her head in wonder at Ray's interest in the Sunrise Ball.

"I'm going to rat it." Edgar didn't look a bit sleepy. He looked as elated as a boy. Helen thought of Lang as Edgar took the first bunch of hair and back-combed it into a thick wad. Lang was so lucky, so free. He was still a child, safe in his bed, while the adults whispered in another part of the house. She touched her soft, bare shoulder inside the robe. She'd used the last of her body milk, pounding the open mouth of the bottle over her arms to smoothe what little was left over her skin.

"I want to look beautiful."

"You will. When do I get to meet this Prince Charming? A person might think you're ashamed of your friends."

Helen grabbed his hand and held it tightly. Edgar, she realized, had become her closest friend. What would she do without him? "Don't say that. He doesn't hang around out of consideration for Lang."

"Is that so."

Edgar bit his lip in concentration and parted clumps of hair. He looked doubtful.

"Fifteen is a sensitive age. As you know," Helen added.

She would drive through the bleary coastal towns to meet him even though it was three in the morning. She always drove to meet him, now that she thought of it, and at this hour that seemed wrong. It was dangerous and deceitful. Well, dangerous for her, but deceitful to whom? She looked at the slim sheet of stationery by the telephone, filled with emergency numbers for Lang. He would know exactly where she was. Helen drank more coffee. She was so sleepy she couldn't even think straight.

"That's better. There's nothing my coffee won't cure. You will be the most beautiful, if not the youngest."

"Why do you keep harping on that?"

"Because it happens to be true." Edgar pounced on the last mound of hair. Then he pounced eagerly on Helen. "Speaking of youth . . . you wouldn't be dating a minor, would you?"

"Edgar!"

"I've guessed it, haven't I? The mystery man is a mystery boy."

Harsh music struck her chest as soon as she entered the baroque terrace. She hadn't seen Ray's car in the crowded lot or on the street outside the hotel. What would she do if he didn't arrive? She looked around at the group and felt wide awake. The ticket, which no one had asked her for so far, was passage to a distant country. The loud sounds and the white, hard faces swept her inside its borders.

"Massive!"

A young man in a top hat said this directly into her ear. He wore purple oval shades exactly the size of his eyes.

"Dance?" he asked. Maybe he could only say one word at a time.

A woman appeared at his side and handed Helen a drink.

"Get off, Harry. She's mine."

Helen caught the glass just in time. It seemed to be headed toward the front of her dress, which wasn't hers at all. It belonged to Edgar, who rented out costumes and couture as a hobby. Tonight Helen borrowed a little of both. The woman eyed the silk flower that opened at her waist.

"Come dance." She lifted her gaze to Helen's face.

"I'm looking for someone," Helen said.

"*Everyone* is." The woman pulled lightly on the tips of her fingers.

The crowd didn't seem to have a center. Helen wore a red charmeuse under a light rayon dress Edgar pulled from a battered trunk. The charmeuse felt slippery and cool as she followed the girl. She laughed at the impossible throb of music and tried to move to its heavy beat.

"My name's Curtsy."

"I'm Helen."

"Who're you waiting for?" Curtsy dipped down slightly, her skirt floating into petals of color.

"A man."

"Shame!"

Curtsy kept on dancing, sometimes turning her back to Helen. Helen looked for Ray, taking in the scene around her. No one seemed interested in eating even though tables heaved with food and flowers. Brass lamps hung in niches along the wall of the hotel. Helen watched as someone stepped out of the shadows and lifted one of the lamps from its hook. The light swung toward her, back and forth, and her heart beat faster. She couldn't see Ray's face, but she could see the side of his body intermittently, as yellow light brushed back and forth.

Ray held the lamp over her head and Curtsy danced away to find another partner. He wore a black jacket, a red silk tie. His head looked polished and damp. He touched the silk flower at her waist and ran his finger over the edge of her dress. It was cut low and a smoky topaz dangled between her breasts on a strand of rose seed pearls. Edgar had slipped the necklace over her head at the last minute. Ray lifted the topaz from her chest and examined it under the lamplight.

"New?"

"Not exactly." They were bartered. Edgar made her promise to bring back stories in return.

Ray bent his head to peer at the necklace, and goose bumps rose on her skin. She looked at his sculpted head. Every hair seemed single and precise. She thought of the neat folds of the old newspaper article, the careful way he must have examined the photograph and the text. The careful way he must have examined her.

"It's not nearly as beautiful as you are."

He raised his head and kissed her, right there on the dance floor. Someone whistled as the kiss went on and on, his tongue flicking once at the roof of her mouth. His hand slid to the bottom of her back and Helen moved nearer, touched and thrilled. He had never seemed this eager.

They walked back to the alcove where Ray had been standing. He hung the lamp up again and leaned against the craggy wall of the building. The inn was even more idiosyncratic than Helen had known. Dark-red stones were set into the wall at intervals, as if the architect had tried to offset the gloom by dressing up the dismal exterior with haphazard jewelry.

"I didn't see your car."

"It's parked underground."

"I thought that was for guests only."

"We are guests." He lifted his head above hers and kissed her again. "I've booked us a room."

The music slurred for a moment as if a hand were turning the dial to a different station. The dancers swayed to silence, then a different sort of music began to play.

"Much better. This is what I came for."

Ray took her up in his arms, firmly guiding her through new, unfamiliar steps. He felt so sure, carrying her past young faces determined to follow the music wherever it led. They seemed indifferent to the slowed beat and the softened sounds, retuning their movements mechanically. One couple broke into a stiff, campy waltz, and others followed, intent as cotillion dancers. Helen let herself be led. Her body felt lighter, more supple as it shifted to match Ray's movements. Edgar's topaz swung between her breasts. The whole evening seemed borrowed, built on the sleek artifice of a dream. Even Ray. She looked up at his face. She didn't seem to be sharing him with anyone tonight. Not Elizabeth or even Rebecca.

Ray had booked a room. Would they go there just to watch the sun rise? Ray slid his hand up and down her back and the charmeuse whispered over her skin. Her steps moved more surely, her own tiredness became a freedom. He leaned down and spoke in a low voice. You look lovely, Helen. The darkness was clearing as they danced. Helen could see a phantom ocean as she turned on the uneven stone floor. And then it wasn't a phantom at all. A blue-black basin of water lay below a high terrace and a hotel that only appeared fierce and foolish at first. On closer inspection it crumbled into grave, aging elegance.

"Hold me," Ray said.

The entreaty jolted Helen from her own dream. She slipped both arms around him and did as he asked. Was he afraid of sunrise? Did he fear that he would be pulled away from her? She held him tighter, pressing her face against the soft black jacket. The sound of his voice and the feel of the velvet drew her closer and closer.

"Unbelievable!"

She pulled away from Ray and turned her head toward the voice. It was Patricia, looking flushed and fresh. It was as if the sunrise had already stained her skin pink. Helen didn't speak. Her throat constricted as Patricia pushed through the crowd with her elbow. Gold and silver bangle bracelets covered the length of her right forearm.

"It's me!" She pulled at her long, black wig until it slid off her head. Still beautiful, even with her hair pressed down under a net, she turned radiant eyes on Ray. "I'm from the store. Remember?"

Ray shook her hand and greeted her friend, a much older man whose own hair was caught at the back of his neck with a bright red bow.

"Lucien, I'd like you to meet my colleague . . ."

Helen's attention wandered to the man's accent. Not French exactly. Of course, how would she know? His speech was halting, not from uncertainty but from pride. He paused over every perfectly chosen word. My colleague, Patricia had bracketed the words, given them more weight than Helen's own name. Helen rolled the words over and over in her mind, watching them squash other words, press them into flat unimportance.

"I dragged Lucien away from the dumb old Jewel Ball."

Ray's face tightened.

"Happily for me. All the jewels are here." Lucien pulled on his red bow and managed a brief smile.

Helen's eyes opened wide. How had Patricia crashed that party? Alice and Jack went to the formal dinner and dance every year. Alice would always read the newspaper account out loud the following week. The guest list (which included names of missing members) appealed to her sense of the macabre. Fact checking was sketchy at the small town newspaper and the missing often turned out to be dead.

Lucien turned from Helen to focus on Ray.

"I know you," Lucien said as he tugged on his red bow.

"You're mistaken." Ray's lips barely moved as he spoke.

"I'm never mistaken. You look exactly like him, you understand."

"Ray?"

Patricia pulled at her arm. She reached for Helen's necklace without asking. She studied the stone and adjusted her voice so that only Helen could hear. "Fuck. You should wear stuff like this to the store."

The music sounded muffled to Helen, as if she were listening from inside the safety of a closed car. The back of Patricia's hand touched Helen's chest as she released the necklace and its solid weight banged heavily against Helen's breastbone. Helen tried to remember if Patricia had ever used that word in front of her and couldn't. The four letters now seemed set into the wall of her mind like one of the red stones in this ugly gray building. Patricia's skin gave off a slightly foul odor. She didn't smell young or particularly clean.

Patricia pointed to the ocean with her long slender arm. Ray and Lucien and Helen all glanced at the water which was turning a sick purplish green. The basin had been fouled; its water now looked like a poisonous drink. Would Patricia tell Alice that Helen had been here? She stared at Patricia's head. Her hair was beginning to spring into hot tendrils near her temples.

"I think the ball is almost over."

Ray said it to all three of them, his eyes gravely fixed on the ledge of light that was rising over the water. Helen slipped her hand into Ray's to wait for the orange cap of rising sun.

"Paging Mrs. Patterson."

Helen's head spun as she heard her name called. Ray put both hands on her hips and moved her in front of him. She faced the horizon.

"Paging Mrs. Helen Patterson."

He stiffened behind her, his legs tight and hard against her bottom. His hands strengthened their hold on her.

"Let that wait. I want you to watch the sun come up, Helen."

"Lang could be in trouble."

She felt a low, dull cramp in her belly that subsided as she pulled free of Ray's hands. The cramps began again as she took the receiver from the concierge's hand at the scarred golden altar in the lobby. She took comfort in the familiar pain and let it bring her back to a world she'd completely abandoned for dreams. I've booked us a room. She hadn't thought to object or even wonder how long he meant to stay. She had forgotten that she was a mother, tethered to this boy whose anger was probably doubling and trebling a misdemeanor until it had become a terrible crime. She had forgotten all about her son.

"You didn't tell me!"

"Tell you what?" She cleared her throat hard. Her voice sounded wet.

"That Edgar was sleeping over!" Lang pounded the phone against the wall twice. She knew where he stood and what the wall would look like when she got home. She would putty over the upside-down crescent marks.

"He wasn't supposed to. He came over to help me get ready."

"He was asleep on our couch and I didn't know it was him."

There was silence on the line. Helen said his name several times. Maybe the phone was broken.

"It wasn't my fault."

"What?" The cramps widened. She bent over slightly and let out a deep breath. Had he turned on Edgar? Not recognizing him at first, scared out of a deep sleep by a sound, a cough. She saw her son's hands on Edgar's back, then his throat. "Lang, what did you do to him?"

"I said some stuff. He'll tell you."

Helen touched her hair, the back of her neck. Some rough words were said, that was all, and she would smooth over them with words of her own. She thought of all that Edgar knew and prophesied about boys becoming men. He volunteered at youth centers. He volunteered at her home at 2 A.M. Maybe her words wouldn't even be necessary. Instead Edgar might apologize for falling into an unscheduled sleep and frightening Lang. She could return to the Sunrise Ball. She could reenter the dream.

Who was that creepy man with Patricia?"

"Some fool who'd had too much to drink."

"Why did he think he knew you?"

"Pull the curtains closed, Helen."

She stood by the window in the hotel room. Ray lay a towel on the white chenille bedspread. He smacked the wrinkles out of the pillows with the side of his hand.

"Come look at the view," Helen said.

The dancers stood in little clots across the terrace, frowning at the sun. Helen couldn't see Patricia from the fourth story. Maybe she was having breakfast with Lucien. She could be poking at soft boiled eggs right now with a toast point, pushing a blob of uncooked egg white to one side of her plate and gritting her teeth in disgust. Lucien would clean his mouth with a napkin, something like that, and try comforting Patricia for the bad meal. Helen shivered and ran her finger along the side of the heavy curtain.

"Too late for the view. You missed the sunrise," Ray said.

"You're not angry, are you?"

"Do I look angry?"

Helen turned around quickly. He was already out of his clothes. He lay in the middle of the terry-cloth towel. His long legs stretched open wide. She remembered to smile.

She undressed slowly, thinking of Lang waking up a second time, slamming his hand down on the clock. Maybe he would knock it off the bedside table and reach for it in a sleepy daze. He hadn't expected her to be home now. They'd talked about the end of the ball, the breakfast she'd have with Ray and the dinner she'd have waiting for Lang tonight when he got home from work. She let one strap of the charmeuse drop from her shoulder, then the other. It fell into a red heap at her feet and she started to gather it up in her hands. A memory bullied its way into the room, swiping at her sides and her back. She could feel its cold presence against her skin. Numb and still, she waited until it passed. Her breasts felt swollen and separate, detached from shame. She thought of Patricia's rude silhouette and moved quickly to the bed, raising her arms as she did.

"Don't. Leave the necklace on."

She did, and as she bent over to kiss him, the topaz knocked against his chin. Dusty sunlight slanted into the room through a space between the curtain and the wall. The gold in his eyes and the gold hanging from her throat warmed the cold region between them. She sat on the side of the bed, twisting the top of her body above his. The nubby bedspread scuffed the back of her legs and she moved to turn down the cover.

"Let's keep it this way."

He tugged at the top of her underwear and she started to object. But something crossed his face, an expression she hadn't seen before, and she didn't speak. He rolled over on his side, then pulled her underwear all the way off. She sat unguarded on the spread as he traced his finger down her center. She thought of others who might have sat here. She closed her eyes for a moment and pictured a man, a woman and their great hurry. They hadn't been able to wait either. They had loved each other that much. Ray's fingers ran over her slowly. He stroked and caressed her in a way he never had before. She made a low sound and his hand crossed her soft middle where the cramp had been. The roughness of his hands chafed her skin.

"Lie down."

She did, taking the center of the towel where he had been. She stared at Ray. He bent over her, studying the angles of her body, drawing invisible laces and stays over her skin with his fingers. He frowned at the hollow fall below her belly button, placing his hands there and pressing to depress the flesh even further. Then he lay his cheek in the soft cavity and squeezed the fleshy sides of her hips toward his face. He wanted to fill her up, fatten her with love.

"You feel wonderful," Ray said.

She smiled and ran her hands over his back to bring him closer. He pressed two fingers together and opened them inside her body. She could hear her own excitement grow as he worked his fingers along inside her, pressing against her to create a wet, warm space. She pushed down against his fingers, against his tongue. She pushed to widen herself and show him more, to reveal everything. She wanted to say the word love. She held it on her tongue as long as she could. Could she say it without frightening him off? Could she slide the word love from her tongue to his? His face came close to hers again. It carried new smells. His mouth opened warmly. The bottom of his face was wet with her as she felt him come inside.

"I can't believe this little body has enough space inside for me."

He pushed deeper and deeper, trespassing to another region. Helen's mouth opened against his shoulder. The bathroom door stood ajar and she could see Ray's back, the blurred white movement he made in the mirror. She thought of Patricia's firm knock at the upstairs bathroom in the store and the news that Lang was downstairs. Lang. She forgot him and forgot him. How could a mother forget her own son?

"And space for someone else."

He pulled out of her body just as she approached the center of her own pleasure. She lay chilled and exposed. She wanted to cover her breasts with her hands. She wanted never to show herself to him again. Helen couldn't stop her short gasping breaths from coming. Her body wouldn't stop its screaming. His head dropped down again and she couldn't see his face, though he still spoke. She reached for his hands and held them tightly.

"Please don't stop." She hated the sound of the word. She could have taken the same babyish word and asked for anything, even things she was entitled to . . . please love me, please care for me. Please, please, please. The sound sickened her. She felt a pinch at the back of her neck, close to the base of her skull, but no one was pinching her. It was pure sensation, disengaged, disinterested. The feeling told her nothing and she pushed it away.

He opened the fingers of her hand and led them down her body.

"This beautiful body. When I think of you carrying a baby and giving birth . . ."

She felt her forefinger sucked into a wet, warm cave that was at first his mouth, then her own body. He led her fingers inside and out, gave them rhythm and motion, speeding them up and suddenly letting them go until she was touching herself without him.

Birth. Lang. The words were separate from her. She closed her eyes tight and climbed inside her own excitement, forgetting shame and patience. The sound of her rattled breathing pushed her forward, toward something that split suddenly into dark and light. She felt a shot of something hard and sharp as stone. She strained to feel more of it.

"Helen?"

She opened her eyes again and lifted her head. Ray sat in a chair at the foot of the bed. He had quietly put his clothing back on, even smoothed his hair back into place. He had crossed his legs at the knee and watched her as she lay on the bed alone. Helen closed her legs. She tore open the bed covers and brought them up to her chin. She thought of the Sadler article, the circle of ink around her name. Ray had been watching her for longer than she knew. She looked away and felt his dry hands against her cheeks. He turned her face toward him.

"You're so lovely. You have no idea how lovely you are."

As Ray admired her body, who was he really admiring? Did he think of Lang's birth or Rebecca's? Would his pleasure always be compounded by sadness?

His hands squeezed her face gently.

"Did Boyd get to watch his son being born?"

She nodded, then felt a wave of unreasonable regret. After all that had happened, why did *this* feel like betrayal?

He lifted one edge of the blanket and settled his hand over hers.

"I want you to come live with me. I need you to make Gatley Point a real home." Ray ran one finger over her closed mouth. "Don't you get it, Helen? I've been watching you for a long time."

Helen lay still. She heard the rattle of dishes beyond the closed door and smelled coffee and bacon. She studied the brightening room, watching its straight wooden furniture and faint pastel paintings.

"What about Lang?" She would never forget Lang again. She would never again let him drift out of her consciousness.

"I want both of you."

Sun striped a section of the wall and Helen moved her hand to the light. The sun quickly warmed her wrists and the tender skin inside her arms. The world had finally merged seamlessly with the dream. Hold me. She threw both arms open wide and lowered Ray's head to her chest, thinking of what he had finally asked her to do.

25.

I sucked."

"What are you talking about?" Boyd reached over Lang's chest and pushed down the lock on the passenger side. The street was so damn dark. "You won."

"Only because the other guy messed up. He was fat. Did you see how fat he was?"

"His flesh was loose. Big difference." Boyd sighed. Maybe it would always be like this. Two different versions of the same story. He handed Lang another sack of french fries and watched his son refuse.

Lang looked at the house. He didn't know if he should let his dad inside. He rattled his cup for something to do. There were still a few ice cubes inside. Shit, it looked like they were on a date, sitting outside his own house in a locked car. He shifted in his seat and cracked the window open.

"Hot?" Boyd asked.

Lang ran his tongue over his chipped tooth and didn't answer. "Snaggletooth," the fat kid had hissed in his ear at the beginning of the match. That was his first mistake, which he followed with five others. The coach had counted them out loud at the end, Lang was the winner, all right. He looked at his father's arm, the way it hung over the back of the seat.

"Schoolwork coming along OK?"

"Yeah."

"Your mom's all right?"

"Yeah."

"She's working hard, I guess."

Boyd watched a dog make its way up the sidewalk. Was the dog fat or firm? If it turned on you, bared its teeth, and made for your arm or your throat, would its strength come from that white barrel chest or those stumpy back legs that were pumping so hard to carry it along?

"When she's at the store."

The dog stopped walking. It must have spotted something off in the dark. It stood and growled at a flat-topped hedge two doors down. The dog didn't have a doubt about its right to stand there growling. It just growled. Boyd could hear the sound rising up out of its tawny throat. He pictured the dog's thick neck as it swung an arm from side to side. Maybe that was where its true strength lay.

"What do you mean, Lang?" He reached out to touch him, but his aim was off. He knocked his hand against the headrest instead.

"She calls it work when she's with her new boyfriend." Lang watched his knees for a moment, then banged them shut. They should have clamped down on the fatso right from the start, but they'd failed him. He thought of the Captain's hairless knees all of a sudden, the way they creaked and cracked when the old man got out of bed.

"Doesn't sound like you like him much." *New* boyfriend? It could have been worse. Boyd's voice had tightened, even though he was doing his breathing exercises already. Just asking about Helen brought it on, the glottal stop that felt like a punch in his throat. Maybe he was like that dog, growling in the dark. Maybe his force was centered there. That would be right. Of course. He thought of his acting coach, the feel of the man's strong hands on his neck. From here, Boy. Let it all out from here.

"I hate him." The words came faster than the thought. Lang hadn't known that before.

"But is your mom happy?" Boyd approved of the smooth sentence. He said it, even though the goodness in the question belonged to somebody else. What he felt wasn't goodness at all. Did Helen's happiness have to come before everything?

Lang shrugged and put his hand on the door.

"Don't go yet."

"I gotta work on French."

Something else shimmied up in Boyd's mind. A picture of Elaine Sorenson. She lay across the dashboard of the Volvo in a long, tanned slant, growling at him just the way she'd done that day when he brought up points. She'd tossed him out of the house and out of the deal because of one lousy point. Only now she was growling at both him and Lang, baring her teeth like that dog. Maybe her daughter was aiming for Lang, getting his hopes up in French when what she really meant to do was toss him out on his ear before an important exam.

"French?"

"Everything, Dad. I gotta go. OK?"

Lang spit out the window and wished his dad would say no. He wished he would tell him to buckle his seat belt and hang on for a long, long ride. Because his dad had decided he was never going back to school again. And never entering a dark house alone or starving because of dumb college, when all the while it was Lang who was dumb enough to believe that he was going to graduate high school and actually go.

"Want me to come inside for awhile? Just until your mom gets home?"

The edges of his dad's mouth had turned white. Lang pulled on his knees and remembered how often his dad's face had looked that way when he was little, right before he and his mom moved out. His lips would get all white and his neck would get stringy, like something was pulling hard on the top of his head. When his face got like that, his dad would go outside and water the plants. Not exactly, Lang corrected himself. He would put the orange attachment on the hose and twist the end of it hard, then fire away at all the bird crap on the sidewalk. Lang thought it would be better if he didn't come inside.

"That's OK."

They both saw the dog coming, how his growl changed into something else friendly and how his walk became a bouncy trot. They both saw him stumble, too. It was a first for Lang, who had never watched a dog fall down without being pushed, but Boyd had seen it happen before.

He reached out to pat Lang on the shoulder as he climbed out of the car. This time he reached his target, feeling bone and muscle, a young man's strength. Nothing was hidden in the young. The thought helped as he turned the engine over and drove away from the house.

"And Bingo was his name. Oh." Lang always sang the dinky song when he came into the house alone. It was the one thing he could remember about being a little kid, and he sang it loud to pretend he was little again, since what he really wanted was an older brother. Somebody already in the house, lying around and listening to music that wasn't dinky.

"B-I-N-G-O." He liked the way the letters sped up at the end, because it meant the song was in a big hurry to finish and so was Lang. It was dumb to sing a little kid song. It was dumb to be scared. He tossed his gym bag into a corner of the dark living room and decided to leave it there.

She should have come to the match. She shouldn't have divided up matches like she'd started doing with his dad. It wouldn't hurt her to keep coming to all of them, waving at him from the bleachers. She always looked better than the other mothers and he liked that. He liked that a lot, especially when the coach's wife made a point of sitting next to her. Lang blew air out of the side of his mouth, the way he did when he smoked with the Captain. He blew the air up out of his chest so hard it made his head spin.

Lang switched on the lamp that stood by the campaign chair and sniffed. The air smelled like cake and ashes. He slurped more of it into his lungs and studied the empty room. Everything the way she liked it, except for his bag on the floor. He untied his shoelaces, swearing when the worst one broke. He stepped out of his shoes and left them together in front of the door. He lay the dead lace on top of one toe.

She should have come to the goddamn match. His feet shuffled slowly across the living room. He scraped them over the floors the way his dad taught him to walk into the ocean. Slide, slide, make them glide, his dad always said when he was little. The shuffle guaranteed him safety since it gave jellyfish and sand crabs the scare.

The smell grew stronger. Maybe she'd baked him something, put something sweet right in the middle of his bed even though it wasn't his birthday. He pictured the little ridges in the icing as he slid toward his room, and tasted the aching sweetness that worked on the chipped tooth even though the cake wasn't in his mouth. It was in his mind, like so many things.

A tiny orange dot glowed in his room, then went away. His body went loose and fat, his flesh melting like sugar on the bone. He waited, his shoulders sagging. Waiting was all his body could do.

"Hey there."

He was glad it was dark because his mouth was already crying. He could feel it twist apart and wobble into position.

"Welcome home, son."

His bedroom light snapped on, and Lang bent his head over. His feet were there. One sock had a big draggy hole that was getting bigger and bigger.

"Hope you don't mind if I let myself in."

"No." He didn't add Sir.

"Your mom's working late. Thought we'd fix ourselves something to eat after the big match."

The package of Djarums lay on top of Ray's stomach. His legs were relaxed and he'd taken the pillows from under the bedspread and put them behind his back.

"I didn't know you smoked. These things are pretty tasty." He took another deep drag and smiled at Lang. His eyes looked funny. Bigger or something. "I bet your mom would kill you if she found out."

Lang kept them at the bottom of his backup gym sack. His body started to hurt as he counted all the things on top of the package of cigarettes. Three towels, always folded and ready, deodorant, two soaps (a special one for his face). The strap, the cup. His back felt like someone was kicking it.

"What'll you give me not to tell?" Ray's voice was kidding, but his face didn't look funny at all.

"Why did you go through my stuff?"

He didn't answer, he just sucked harder on the cigarette and Lang stared at his mouth. It didn't turn white like his dad's did when he got mad, so why was he mixing them up? Ray fizzled the cigarette out in a paper cup filled with water, then handed the dirty cup to Lang.

"Your mom gave me a key to the house."

Lang thought of how he would have looked at the door, pushing the key into the lock and turning it easily. He looked around his bedroom for a briefcase, but didn't see anything different. Nothing was added and nothing was taken away that he could see. Maybe he'd bought the cigarettes himself. Maybe he'd just guessed about that. Lang's eyes blinked fast.

"Guess she means for me to come and go as I please."

He put his hands on his knees and eased himself up, but not all at once. Lang had never seen anyone move that way. He thought of the dog on the sidewalk, the way it looked as it dropped to the ground.

"Hungry?" Ray asked. His voice sounded different, not anything like the voice before.

"I guess."

He felt nauseated, but maybe it would be good to eat. If he had to throw up, at least there would be something to put into the toilet. He looked down at the cup. Here was something to put into the toilet. He went into his mother's bedroom. He emptied the dirty water and the butt into the bowl, then crumpled the cup in his hand. He flushed and watched the water disappear. The toilet didn't overflow. It handled what it had to handle.

Ray's shirt wasn't too wrinkled from sitting down. He rolled up the sleeves and started moving around the kitchen, looking for something. He whistled under his breath, not something Lang would probably listen to but at least it wasn't a dinky song. Lang leaned on the counter the way he knew how to do and felt his body let go of him. He closed his eyes for a minute and listened to sounds, one by one. As they happened, not all at once, and not looking for which one would come next. It might be OK to have someone here until his mom got home. It might be OK to have that person be Ray.

26.

"It wasn't my fault," Lang yanked the handle of the shopping cart and pulled it out of the long row.

"You should have signaled sooner."

Lang had squealed when the car hit them from behind. Then he struck the steering wheel with the heel of his hand and slammed his door as he got out to examine their car. The rear fender on the Escort was crumpled, and its trunk had sprung open and wouldn't close completely. One shattered taillight completed the tableau. The driver of the other car had stayed where she was, making a phone call from her car. She rolled down the window to talk to Lang, slipping her insurance agent's card through the thin opening, then drove away with her car intact. The wide, silver grid pressed unperturbed and proud through the heavy traffic moving toward the center of town

"Whose side are you on, Mom? She hit me!"

People were turning their heads to stare. For once Lang was immune to the attention. His voice sounded broken and teary. He was scared, she realized all at once. He'd looked so confident and firm, taking his insurance papers out of his wallet, calmly exchanging information with the woman in the car while Helen sat in the car and shook with anger, figuring up her deductible. It was the first time they had ever driven together. She'd planned the day so carefully.

"We'll talk about this later. Let's go look for your things."

The plan was to take care of his room and make it a nicer place to live. She wanted to treat him to some new clothing afterwards. Lunch. For once, she was happy to call the automated phone number for her bank balance. It was brimming. She wanted to share much more than good news with her son. She looked at his square shoulders as he pushed the cart down the aisles of the store. She could tell he was toning down his own strength, forcing his body to take it easy, so he could dodge the women and children who drifted through the aisles without direction. They seemed lost in the confusion of tools and equipment.

She followed him as they strolled through regions of the home store. First repair, then repose. She stopped to finger towels and blankets, but they were cheap and unappealing. She passed Lang and turned left at the end of the row. Everything here grew oversized. Exaggerated proportions ruled this section. Helen thought of Ray's storeroom, the space that invited this kind of buying. She tugged on Lang's sleeve and told him to slow down. She liked looking at the outlandish boxes of detergent and barrels of floor wax, the bins of snack food and endless flats of carbonated drinks. She stopped to look at a price.

"I thought we were shopping for me," Lang said.

"We are."

"Then let's go over there."

An electronics grove opened before them. A glass panel in the ceiling opened to the sky and natural light fell in a wide shaft. Industrial fans turned at the end of the row and the smell of eucalyptus oil spread through the aisle. Lang craned his neck, looking left and right at the possibilities. Proportions turned monstrous here, too, with enormous black speakers and television sets that expanded to wide, walleyed screens. Helen thought of Lang sending signals to outer space and receiving them as he slipped on leather headphones. He fiddled with a dial on a radio and grinned, peering at the orange number that appeared on the screen. They wouldn't have to argue about music if he owned this. His pleasure (and hers) could be closed-circuited, contained. She folded her arms over her chest.

"Want it?" Helen tried to make her voice sound offhand.

"Look at the price, Mom."

She had. She pointed her finger at one of the radios, boxed and ready to go.

"Serious?"

"Make sure the headphones are included."

"Thanks!"

"Thank Ray."

"Why should I thank him?"

"The work I've done on his house is paying for all this."

For the moment, the accident was forgotten. She would go over it with him later. Maybe they would go over the DMV booklet again, without blame or anger. He swung the radio down from the shelf lightly and settled it into the enormous cart. Management here thought of everything. Helen smiled and imagined that she had, too.

They made it all fit. The new mirror sloped across the top of the cart. Its narrow, black-edged oval glass swung on hinges, so Lang could review his body from top to bottom. He would be able to move it wherever he wanted in his room. Under it were rectangular wire baskets nested inside one another, for all his odds and ends. Helen also piled on a replacement for his wicker laundry hamper, which had collapsed on one side because of the heavy load it carried. Weights landed there and textbooks, and sometimes, when he got tired of his stiff wooden chair, so did Lang.

"How about paint, Mom? As long as we're here."

Helen looked at the sign that hung from metal chains above them. The sign advertised paint and wall coverings. The air from the fan swirled, making the sign float back and forth. The chains ground together unpleasantly.

"Not today, honey."

"But you said that time that I could repaint my room whatever color I wanted. What about new blinds? They're pretty cheap."

She thought of his curtains, chewed at the ends by some previous renter's animal. Moths and water stains had taken their toll, too. She couldn't stand to think of his curtains.

"Another time."

"Why not now?"

"Stop whining, Lang."

It was their turn. The woman at the check-out stand sullenly punched in the prices and codes. Her red lips look puckered and painful. Helen thought of her comfortable chair at the shop and wondered what it would be like to stand in one spot all day, pushing buttons, cracking open one roll of coins after the next.

"How would you like to pay?"

Helen waved her checkbook in the air and pushed past Lang. His curiosity didn't surprise her. They had come for repairs and replacements, not presents. She looked at the numbers as they flashed on the register. Her chest felt full, as if she would be coming down with something soon.

"Oh, look," Helen said to Lang. A golden arch broke over the left end of the store. Helen was starving all of a sudden. She couldn't think of anything she'd rather eat than a Big Mac. Lang's profile looked irritable and middle-aged. She thought of how she'd trained him to be so fearful of fat.

Surprise swept over his face a second time. Her chest felt squeezed and narrow.

"You've earned it, honey. The season's almost over."

She wrote out the check, watching the white top of her pen move as she hurried over her signature. The check-out woman smirked at the pen, and Helen quickly tucked it back into her purse.

"Get me the one with two meat patties and everything on it. And a large Coke."

"You never eat this stuff, Mom." Lang held out his hand for the money and watched her line the loaded cart up next to their table.

"Maybe it's time to start trying new things."

Helen crossed her legs and swung one leg slowly as he lined up to be served. Their cashier turned her head once to look at them, banging the register drawer closed with her hip. Helen sat straighter on the bench.

He ate tentatively at first, then gave in to ketchup, more salt, and the rest of her hamburger when she couldn't finish it.

"I'm going to puke."

She thought of Patricia, who had called in sick after the Sunrise Ball. It took three days to recover from whatever she'd done that night, and Helen hadn't said a word when she finally returned. They exchanged cool greetings and settled back down to separate work, separate spheres. Patricia hovered near the front of the store more and more, seizing customers the moment they came through the door, while Helen worked upstairs. There were endless details to figure out about the fabric, with Alice snapping all the while. She was in such a hurry lately. Who was *she* to be restless and impatient? Helen sucked harder on her straw. Ray's desire surrounded her now as it had done for days. The longer she waited to respond, to call him with the news that they were on their way with bags and books—all the belongings she could stuff into her car—the more miserable she became. Waiting too long could cost her everything. She lay her hand on Lang's leg briefly, then pulled it away.

"What?"

She hadn't pictured talking to him here, with so many people and so much noise.

"Something so wonderful has happened."

Lang frowned and turned his head away. Wonderful, maybe she hadn't said the word with enough conviction. She tried again.

"Honey?"

"I know! All right? I know you gave him a key."

"What are you talking about?"

"Ray. I didn't let him in the other night. He was already in the house waiting for me."

"Oh." Maybe Boyd had been late dropping Lang off. What was Ray supposed to do? Wait around in the dark? That was the point of the key. Helen hurried on.

"Ray and I have gotten so close recently. I know you're feeling closer to him, too."

Lang stood up quickly, pushing the wheels of the cart with the bottom of his shoe and holding it in place with his hands. His skin was clear. Helen squinted. There was nothing at all to mar his face. It was the first time in . . . how long? Helen couldn't remember.

"What makes you think that?" He picked at his tooth, making that noise.

"Just a feeling I have. Like when I know you're going to win a match and then you do."

"I don't feel good." He looked around for a bathroom and Helen stood up, too. She didn't want him to use the bathroom here. She almost laughed at her own nervousness. He was big enough to take care of himself. Maybe Alice had a point. She did baby him.

"Let's go home."

"I'm fine."

He wouldn't sit next to her. Instead, he opened the window in the living room and popped off the new screen, using the metal tab. He sat there, half-in, half-out of the house. He looked rude, like a boy who would open beer bottles with his teeth or wipe his face with the end of his shirt.

"Get to the point, Mom."

"All right." The point felt just like what Gatley had imagined, a piece of land poised gracefully on the water. Beauty that hinted at divinity.

"Ray wants us to come live with him."

Lang turned and looked out the window. Then he jumped. She heard his feet hit the dirt outside, then the rest of his body. Maybe it hadn't been a jump. Maybe he had lost his balance and fallen on his back. She hurried to the window and leaned outside.

"Honey?"

"Stop calling me that."

His face was cut and bleeding. She watched him get up from the dirt and run his hand over his bloody cheek. A bush had blocked his short fall and he bent a long, damaged branch until it snapped free.

"What was that all about?"

"It was a cry for help."

"That's not funny. Come inside and let me put something on your face."

"You told me what he wants. Does it matter what *I* want?"

"Of course. I want to discuss this with you."

"You mean it's not all decided yet? Like it was the other time with Dad?"

She saw he wouldn't come inside. He intended to stay right there with blood running down his cheek. Lang's silence was precise, his sarcasm calculated. Helen thought of all the things she had urged him to talk about in those days, his feelings about Mom and Dad. But his face had closed shut the minute she suggested talk, and then he had fallen and chipped that tooth without tears, the way he did everything. Blood would run before tears. There was no money for counseling, no time for skilled and sensitive help. So Helen had talked and he had listened, sullen and sucking his broken tooth. But Lang hadn't run aground. He hadn't run period. She watched his shadow, the crooked cast of his body.

"You're lying, Mom. You've already made up your mind. You didn't want to buy paint today because you want to leave. Everything you bought me can move right over. That stuff doesn't even have to come out of the boxes."

Helen followed his gaze down to her shirt. She hadn't noticed the top button had come undone. Her fingers fumbled with the buttonhole.

"I need to tell you something else, Lang."

She climbed onto the window ledge.

"What are you doing? Mom! Don't be stupid."

She wasn't being stupid. She wanted to stand next to her son. Helen wanted to touch him and promise him that everything would be all right if he would just do this one last thing.

"Cut it out. Mom, you're crazy."

She fell through the open space, letting her shoulder lead. The broken branch cut into her side, and she laughed at the familiar pain. How many times had she wormed out of the aunts' upper rooms, snaked along the tar-paper roof above their heads, followed the path of the rain gutters to uncertain freedom?

"You tore your shirt."

"You tore your face."

They didn't laugh or scowl or scream. They sat under the tree in the front yard looking at the hole in the bush.

"I wrecked the bush. Guess I'll have to pay."

He scratched his back up and down against the back of the tree as she watched Edgar's house.

"He's creepy, Mom."

Helen tried to raise his shirt so that she could scratch his back for him, but he dodged her hand.

"I'm sure you feel you're betraying your—"

"It's got nothing to do with Dad. I hate the way he looks."

"Be fair." Helen thought of Ray's even features, how someone younger might see his face as stiff and rigid.

"At you."

Something in his voice made Helen stop talking. Her son's level eyes stopped everything. He hid them, ducking his head down to the top of his knees. He mumbled something she couldn't hear.

"Oh, Lang." She rubbed her hand over his back. "He's got so many problems. Sometimes he's a little distant."

"It's weird having him around."

She felt him tremble slightly as he said it. She stopped moving her hand and watched a bird hop over the grass. It pecked at the earth and swiveled its head to study them.

"It feels strange for a reason," Helen said. She didn't wait for an answer. "There's something I need to tell you about Ray. Something very sad."

Lang rotated his head to look at her.

"He's got a little girl. And she's been kidnapped."

His eyes were glassy, as if they'd been reading long lines of fine print.

"For money?"

"For vengeance." Helen had never *really* tried to crawl into Elizabeth's mind. She hoped Lang wouldn't ask a lot of questions, because she didn't have any answers. "Ray's ex-wife is ill. She ran off with their little girl and she's been hiding ever since."

"What did he do to her?" Lang lifted his face and blinked.

"To the mother or the child?"

"Both."

Helen didn't want to think. She wanted to move, act. The scrape on her side already burned. She didn't feel like talking anymore.

"Ray didn't do anything. He came out here to start a new life and look for his girl. He wants us to be part of that life."

They sat still, watching the cars occasionally turning down Feldspar. Saturday was generally crammed with errands and tasks that couldn't wait, but this Saturday felt lazy and slow.

"Maybe he'll find her on this trip. He's in Seattle right now looking for her."

Helen counted the trips to herself. The endless search had grown pedestrian, like business trips with results too dispiriting to compute. Her voice must have given this away.

"How old is she?" Lang asked the question dully. He didn't seem interested anymore. His body rested in the sun that filtered through the leaves.

"Ten."

"Is that why you gave him that little statue?"

"What little statue are you talking about?"

"The one from your aunt. The one that's part of a pair. The girl with the bird in her hand."

Helen's eyes flickered briefly, then closed. She thought she'd seen a car she knew at the top of the street. She missed Ray so much she dreamed of seeing him stop there, almost turning down Feldspar instead of hurrying off in a different direction like the car she'd just seen. Her head rested on the trunk of the tree. She shivered and pressed her finger on her neck, squashing an ant that crawled there. She rested a little longer until another ant came, then another.

27.

Soft fur landed on Helen's feet. Poor whined and flopped down on the floor underneath her desk. She ran her feet over the top of his coat and patted his head.

A pair of young voices downstairs escalated and Helen stepped back into her shoes. She was entering data on textiles, Alice's as well as the dozen others they would show. A conversation with a manufacturer's rep still troubled her. Tender goods . . . the term sounded ominous.

"Why are you fretting, Helen?" Alice chewed Corn Nuts noisily. She kept snacks in an antique silk pouch that dangled from her belt.

"I wouldn't call it fretting."

"I would." Alice rolled her eyes as Poor banged his head on a desk leg. Helen's pen rolled to the floor. "Nothing can go wrong now. Trust me."

Alice had been mad at her for weeks, first raising her voice and then turning arch. One wouldn't want to become chronically late. One would want to behave professionally, Helen. The vaulted speech felt cold and punitive. But Alice was better now, and so was Helen. Things were really falling into place with Ray.

"Aleeece. You're a mind reader! This table is exactly what my sister has been looking for." They could hear a stream of sounds from a cellular phone downstairs. English strained and broke into bubbles of Arabic.

Helen snatched her pen up from the floor. The Princess had studied at the Sorbonne, Berkeley, Columbia and finally Harvard until she learned to say no to her restless intellect. The first of the boys made his way to the top of the stairs. Couldn't she try saying no to her wild, unruly sons? Helen petted Poor's worried head again.

"I have to go to the bathroom."

"Take thirty-two long steps down, five short steps to the right and turn the door knob quietly so the monster doesn't wake up." Alice said, with a solemn expression on her face.

"What if it *does* wake up?" The boy looked hopeful.

"You'll take one of those rocks you've got in your hands and knock him down."

The boy grinned and made his way down the hall.

"You're asking for it." Helen said.

"I know." Alice brightened. The second boy stomped upstairs, landing hard on each fifth step and shouting Mugh.

"Looking for me?" Alice said.

The boy glared. A string of clear mucous ran from his nose and he swiped it away with his wrist.

"No. I'm looking for Ali."

"Come play with me instead."

Helen typed away. She made entries on prices and availability, stopped to scribble down special notes about crocking and color abrasions, what mill was reputed to do one or the other. Alice and the second boy went into the child's bedroom at the end of the hall. A window creaked open, then a shutter slammed against the back wall of the building. Helen shook her head and typed faster, trying to focus her thoughts on the job. Tender goods, the term kept teasing her, working its way into her consciousness. Nailing down the meaning of the term hadn't helped. *Tender goods refers to fabric that has lost its tensile strength because of heat or chemicals. The condition is rare but dangerous.*

The Princess wore slim white jeans and a T-shirt. She had fine, delicate features and darkly shadowed eyes. A gold watch was the only jewelry she wore today. The diamonds circling the face of the watch were taken from a mine she owned.

"Helen!"

Who else would she be? Helen stood up for a quick embrace. Three kisses, she reminded herself.

"You're looking well."

"Thank you."

The Princess narrowed her eyes and crossed her hands over her chest. "Is it love or money?"

Helen smiled and said nothing.

"Ah, good. Then it's both." She shook her head as glass shattered in the bathroom. She ran both hands through her hair and stretched the skin on her face.

"Mommy, it wasn't me!" The smallest boy shouted triumphantly from the bedroom. He appeared briefly in the hall dressed in red galoshes. "Look. It's raining!"

His pockets bulged. It was understood that he, too, would break something before leaving. They were fundamentally polite, waiting their turn to create havoc. Patricia had written up the last bill, gladly reporting the boys had done $2,700 worth of damage. The Princess always insisted on paying.

"Keep dry like a good boy." She sat in a chair across from Helen and leaned forward as he disappeared back into the room. "I'm not trained in this, you know."

"No one is." Helen said it playfully, trying to be Alice. Alice enjoyed their appearances. She phoned Jack the minute they left and feasted on Princess tales for days afterward.

The Princess leaned forward and looked at the screen. One of her university stints had yielded an MBA. "Are you designing a budget?"

Helen twisted slightly in her chair, scrolled down a bit. These figures were none of her business.

"Not exactly."

"I must think." The Princess leaned back in her chair, licked the tip of one finger and held it to a temple.

Helen studied her round shoulders and small face. Everything was aligned: the face of this princess could have been drawn by any child with the proper stencil. A large oval for the face, smaller ovals for the eyes, a thin oval mouth. Ali poked his head out of the bathroom, one hand in his pocket. He saw his mother's straight back, her finger pressing on one temple, and retreated. Were her sons trained to wait soundlessly for thinking to take place? Did she have that much power? Poor shifted in his sleep and the Princess twitched. Helen held his head down with one foot.

"I'll take the table downstairs, the one nearest the doorway, with all the china and cutlery. I would like it delivered tonight to my sister's home."

Helen looked at her watch just as glass shattered for the second time. The watch face was easy to read, and it was easy to guess Stan's response to the Princess's request with fifteen minutes until closing time. Helen was thinking, too, though not with her eyes closed and not with one finger pressed against her temple.

"Shall we have dinner catered as an extra treat?" Helen remembered the young woman who had dropped by with her card. She had stuttered slightly, and Helen handled her chipper presentation with care.

The Princess clapped her hands with excitement. "We will be ten, counting the children."

"Around eight thirty?" Helen swallowed once and tried to remember where she'd put that card. Beads of sweat had gathered on the woman's lip by the end of the pitch. What was her name? Addie something. A big girl from Arkansas, probably paying back a hefty college loan, who really knew how to cook. She'd brought delicious samples by the store, a whole lunch. Patricia had held her slice of onion tart tenderly in one hand before wolfing it down. *Pissaladiere!* Helen had looked up the spelling for the funny word that night.

Helen started to dial Stan. "You're a wonderful sister."

"And you're a wonderful businesswoman." The Princess looked at the hands on her watch. "You have good instincts, Helen."

It had been said before. Why had the compliment sent chills down her spine both times?

Patricia set down her dustpan and studied the paper on Helen's desk. It listed artichoke canapes, salmon with fava beans, tomatoes and basil.

"You're a real wizard," she said, plunking herself down in a chair. Helen shuffled a stack of papers on her desk.

"Addie Benner is the wizard."

Alice was already on the telephone with Jack. They had all drunk a toast with a glass of his whiskey. To the Princess. To Stan and the caterer. And finally . . . To Helen! She put the papers into a desk drawer and slammed it shut.

"So how's Ray?"

Helen waited until she was sure of her voice. "What are you getting at?"

"Gyah, Helen. I just want to know how he is." Patricia lifted her chin. "If I were you, I'd be delirious. Or at least *happy.*"

Helen thought of Lucien, the red bow at the back of his head.

"You're not me, Patricia. We're very different people."

"You almost act like he's something to hide." Patricia looked down at her blouse, flicked something off the left side. "It's OK to date customers once they stop being customers. Right?"

Alice's voice was winding down. She cooed at something Jack said.

"He doesn't have any kids, does he? Anybody I might know from around?"

They would have to live with a hole in the front of the store until the end of the week. A rectangular table for twelve was coming in from Alabama. Ordinarily Alice didn't like metal for an eating surface, but this metal glinted with gold, flecks of mica. Judicious use of gold appealed to Alice more and more. The new taste puzzled Helen. She watched Patricia closely.

"No."

"Well, shit. Back to the bars." Patricia's shoulders danced slightly, moved back and forth to some tune in her head.

She was hunting down Ray's sexy offspring. Helen felt drowsy and sick. She needed to sleep off Patricia's effect on her. But she couldn't, at least not yet.

"Now just what are you two gossiping about?" Alice walked and talked fast. She tapped things as she strode down the hall, as if she were taking an informal inventory in the long hallway.

"Men," Patricia said, stretching her arms over her head. "Is there any other subject?"

Alice put both hands on Patricia's shoulders and Helen started to look for her keys.

"There certainly is."

Patricia turned in her chair and Helen stopped digging through her handbag. Alice looked down at her expectant face and smiled gently. She touched the top of her nose, as if she were another item to add to her inventory sheet. "I think it's time to share good news with good friends."

A cloud of sour gas rose from beneath Helen's desk and Alice laughed, fanning the air.

"Ms. Riyadh wants to buy my store."

The smell was suffocating. Poor rolled over in his sleep and snapped at the putrid air.

"Anytime I want. Any amount!"

"I don't understand," Helen said dully.

"I can sell her the shop anytime. That's why nothing can go wrong."

Helen cleared her throat. "How long have you known this?"

"Oh, we've been discussing it forever. Jack thinks I'm crazy not to sell this minute."

Jack, too? Helen watched as a corridor buckled and bent in her mind.

A long ridge ran down its center. As it rose, chairs and ottomans, trays and teacups were thrown into the walls. Glass shattered, sending cruel shards into the air.

"What about the fabric line? Why are you planning all this when you're just going to sell the store?" Helen's head felt hot and full.

"That's the best part! She's offered me the start-up money. I finally have a real investor."

"But—"

"There is no but. This just means we all have lots more freedom."

"*You* have all the freedom," Helen said.

Alice lifted an eyebrow. "Meaning?"

"I've been working here for years. And I've been working at slave wages, too."

Alice's eyes flashed. "You're no slave, Helen. You've had the freedom to go anytime."

"I wanted to stay because you and I were building something together. We were doing something really *important*."

"My God. This is a business. You sound like a jealous lover."

The side of Helen's face burned. She wasn't finished.

"You and Jack went behind my back to do this."

Patricia scooted to one side of her chair.

"You're a fine one to talk about duplicity, Helen. If you know what I mean." Alice winked at Patricia and did a slow shoulder shrug. She let her head drop right, then left. "Now, who's on for drinks and who's not?"

Patricia jumped up from the chair.

"I can't," Helen said. "Sorry."

"Party pooper," Alice slipped her arm through Patricia's and squeezed hard.

"What was so urgent?" Helen asked the question dispassionately. Before Alice shared her wonderful news, Helen had agreed to meet Boyd at the park.

"You're already mad at me."

"I'm exhausted, Boyd. I've been at work all day." She looked quietly at his cardigan and loafers.

"Shall we go somewhere to relax?"

Her mind loitered, picked up unimportant bits and pieces—the golf insignia on his sweater, for one thing. Boyd had never touched a club in his life. And he was wearing his hair shorter. It looked professionally trimmed for a change.

"OK, never mind. I want you to do something for me."

She wondered what it would be like to meet Boyd now, knowing nothing of his history. Would she agree to hear what he had to say?

"Get rid of that girl. Patricia. She shouldn't be hanging around Lang."

Her mind ambled around the attractive possibility. "Why? She's moved him from a minus to a plus. He could jump up a full grade."

"Sexwise, she's driving him crazy." Boyd clamped one hand over his knee. "Fire her."

She laughed and Boyd made a funny sound with his mouth. Helen looked up when she heard that sound. She thought of her gutted pillow, the way she'd found feathers everywhere afterward.

"When are you going to take me seriously, Helen? You're forgetting it was me who fired that babysitter Lang had when he was little. The one who was secretly going through all our booze. She could have really hurt him."

"I—"

"I'm tired of being treated like I'm just some guy who wandered into your life for five minutes. You can't do that to me anymore." He paused, then picked at the side of the bench. "Lang says you're seeing someone."

The park was empty. Pigeons flew too close, vying for the two of them. Wings swiped at the back of her head.

"The same guy from before?"

"I don't have to answer that question."

"I'll find out his name. Unless he dumps you and you pretend he never existed."

Why was it always like this? Strength that showed up late and obstreperous? He had never been strong when she needed him to be or strong in the right way. She pulled her jacket tighter.

"His name is Ray Richards."

The pigeons were getting nasty, circling too close again. She dug in her pockets for a piece of forgotten popcorn or candy. Boyd's face contracted to stillness.

"That's my girl. Going right for the jugular."

"What's that supposed to mean?"

"He's the jerk who owns Gatley Point."

She pinched her elbows to her side and waited. She thought of his voice as he dialed numbers, the way she'd sat listening as a young bride. She'd been proud and entertained. When he got bored, he did accents, played with inflection and intonation. Turned business into acting, acting into business. She looked at the insignia on his sweater. It was getting darker and she could see it less well than before. He *did* persist, keeping up with property titles and transfers. Gatley Point was still a possibility since it had changed hands. He would probably cold call Ray after time passed. Cold call her, she added.

"I didn't choose him to offend you."

"Just happened, huh?"

"I haven't known him long." Her voice was flung back to her, like someone stranded at the bottom of a deep well.

"What's long? Is two years long?"

The bench rocked slightly when he stood up. He stood close enough to touch her.

"Was he the one?"

She shook her head no. She didn't look up until she heard his car leave the parking lot. He didn't turn south on Carlton. She didn't know where Boyd was going from here.

Drink?" Steve Mason asked. He looked like hell. One side of his face was puckered and red.

"Sure. What've you got?" Boyd already knew, but asking gave him a minute to think. He'd never had drinks in Steve's office. They usually went to a bar down the street. That was a hell of a thing when you thought of it. He was the only broker in the place who hadn't had a drink in Steve's office. After two years, you would've thought . . . Boyd stopped himself right there. What would you have thought?

"Scotch. Diet Coke. All the water in the world."

Boyd tapped his heels together. "Arrowhead. Straight up."

Steve winked and went back to his office to pour. Was this about the sign? Boyd struggled for a moment with the lock on his filing cabinet and thought about that asshole falling because of his sign. The whole thing was a scam, hollering like that about his back, digging into commercial code to find out Boyd's sign wasn't exactly where it should have been. It was half a yard off (half a yard!) and the guy was screaming lawsuit. He was a broker and he'd wanted Boyd's listing until he found an easier way to make a buck. Boyd pushed harder on the key and it finally turned.

"You're looking good, Boyd." Steve was already rolling ice around in his glass. His office smelled like he'd been at it for hours. "You're killing them out there."

"Thanks."

"Hey. Who's thanking who? You're making the deals for both of us."

His blinds were down. Boyd was sorry about that. He stole a glance at Steve's gold clock—it was late for him to be in the office. The clock was from Tiffany's, and it not only told the hour, it told how much time was left with Steve Mason. But not really. The gift of a gold clock didn't help if your magic number was up. Only last week that guy from El Cajon, the one Steve had lured from a company he'd been with for ten years—there was already talk about how he'd be next. Boyd took the glass Steve offered.

"I never thought you'd be such a hard worker." He didn't? Boyd wondered why you would hire somebody, even a friend, if you didn't think he'd work his ass off. Steve stuck a pen behind his ear. He didn't usually work this late. Maybe he was having problems at home. Boyd drank his water. It was so cold it made his head hurt.

"You're a real performer." Steve smacked his forehead. "*Performer.* I get it now. Everything OK otherwise?"

The time for that question had long passed. Why would he bother with it now?

"The same, I'd say."

"The same as . . . ?"

"Holding pattern, Steve. You know."

"I guess that Richards guy is a real jerk."

Boyd wrapped his other hand around the glass. He set it down inside a silver coaster on Steve's desk. Steve scrawled all over documents; he used them as scratch pads. It drove his secretary nuts. It was a nervous habit he had, like chewing his nails or clearing his throat. Boyd looked at the numbers scrawled all over a leasing agreement that had to be signed the next day.

"You've got that right." Humming started inside Boyd. Not the kind of humming you do in a house where you're happy, either. The kind of humming you do instead of doing something else.

"Yeah?" Steve asked.

"Bastard. I tried to list his property years ago."

"I know." Steve's breathing was heavy. It was like he'd just run a race.

"How'd you know she was seeing him?" Boyd asked.

"Word gets around."

Boyd kept the noise down inside. He did a good job, too. No one could hear it but him. The trouble was, it always got louder fast. It was mounting, coming in on both sides of his head. He would have to struggle hard to hear what Steve Mason had to say next.

"So you nearly listed his place?" Mason asked.

"Yep."

Steve took the leasing agreement off his desk and came around to Boyd. He held the paper carefully, as if it would break. But paper didn't break. Nothing made sense. Steve sat down in the chair next to Boyd and pointed to one of the numbers penciled in next to the buy-lease clause. There was an address scrawled in the margin.

"That's where he lives, huh?"

Boyd could smell butter and booze. The butter seemed to be coming off the top of Steve Mason's skin. Boyd looked at his puffy face, the way it was swollen only on one side. Ha! The humming inside was too loud. It wasn't letting him think.

"How do you know all this?" Boyd tried again.

"I like to keep up with things."

Maybe the butter was a skin treatment, some new bullshit about staying young when you weren't. The smell made him sick. Boyd looked at the blinds. Air fought like hell to get through. The blinds banged every once in awhile and dragged your attention to the noisy suck they made moving in and out. Steve Mason's office was a suffering place to be.

"I see her in town with him." Steve popped an ice cube into his mouth and chomped down. "Rough on the boy, I guess."

Boyd walked around behind Steve's desk and opened the blinds using too much force. One of the slats broke and he tried to push it back into place.

"It's okay, Boyd. Forget it."

Kids ran at the water, daring the waves to come and get them. Boyd watched as the water did that, retreated and advanced, pushed and pulled. Little kids wanted to be caught. They squealed and ran back to their mothers, all gritty and thrilled that they were wet. But not the older kids. They didn't even approach the water unless they were wrapped in black rubber with a longboard under an arm. Smoking, cool. Fuck you. Boyd put his hands on his head and pulled again. Either way, they were going to get it. The waves were coming for all of them.

"That Gatley Point is something else. If Helen and Lang were to end up there one day . . ." Steve Mason cracked a knuckle. "She's quite a hustler, isn't she?"

Boyd held up one hand, stopping Steve's words and the look of concern. He was moving now and the humming had dropped back down to something he could manage. As Boyd passed the chair, the noise inside started up again. He would have kept his mind on the sound inside if he hadn't turned and seen Steve Mason smile behind his back. It was a smile Boyd had never seen in the two years he'd worked for him. It was a smile that didn't belong on his face any more than butter belonged on his skin. The smile told Boyd everything he needed to know. The smile meant Helen had dumped him for Steve two years ago. The smile told Boyd why he'd been hired two years ago. It had been fun, even better than throwing desk accessories at the wall.

The butter and booze melted completely, and in their place was something he smelled and ate and felt as it ran down his skin in a sickening slide. The nausea kept him moving even as the room tilted, broken blinds letting in slants of crazy white light.

Two. Boyd's magic number had finally come up.

28.

"So this is an apology? Because if it is, your son should be making the call." Edgar's dog yipped in the background.

They hadn't spoken since the Sunrise Ball. Edgar was avoiding both Helen and Lang, slipping outdoors to deadhead only when he was sure they were inside their house.

"He treated me like a *pedophile.* He insulted me. I won't even repeat what your son said that night."

Helen watched his house from the kitchen. Flowers threw themselves at Edgar, arching over his patio, bending supple green stalks toward his French windows. The simple house was almost hidden under lush growth.

"He needs to settle this with you," Helen said.

"Exactly."

"But in the meantime, I miss you."

She missed Edgar's banter. She missed traipsing through her backyard with pruning shears and Edgar telling her exactly what to snap off where. The cold shoulder was killing Helen. Especially now.

"Can you come over?"

She held the phone in a crunch between her shoulder and ear. She polished a silver candlestick holder while Edgar made up his mind.

"I can't pretend this didn't happen."

"You shouldn't. Lang's not here, by the way. Ray offered to give him a driving lesson."

"Oh." Edgar couldn't suppress his interest. "Bonding?"

"Ray thought it might be good if they spent the afternoon together. And Lang really wants to pass his driving test."

The candlestick hadn't been polished in ages. Helen chided herself for letting this happen. The silver was actually pitted in places.

"You're breaking down my resolve. And it *is* lunchtime."

She scrubbed harder, making a silver clearing in the tarnished surface. She should have put this out for the garage sale. She tightened her hand around the square base.

"Edgar, I keep forgetting to ask you something. That little sculpture you sold for ninety-nine cents, the girl with the bird in her hand . . . you *did* sell it, didn't you, when I went out to get lunch?"

"I certainly did."

"Who wound up buying that?"

"This always happens. Afterward, you imagine you shouldn't have let certain things go. Let me think. We were mobbed, remember. *I* was mobbed."

She thought of Ray's Jaguar, the controls and the dials that Lang would have to understand. The concentration driving that car would require. It wasn't a new car, but she prayed nothing would happen to it. Edgar laughed bitterly.

"No wonder I've blocked it out. It went to a perfectly awful man."

Her body stopped. Fear offered sudden insulation, blocked sounds and sights. She felt frozen and slow, unable to speak.

"You there? I didn't do anything wrong, but to a homophobe that doesn't mean a thing. Oh, I may have said some little something."

"What?"

"I don't remember. Anything will set those people off. What do you think upset me so about your son? I'm worried about him."

Helen set the candlestick down and stretched one arm over her head. She thought about what she and Edgar might eat for lunch. That Ray got a little too macho from time to time didn't surprise her at all. That was just Oklahoma talking. They could work on that later. But she needed to work on Edgar now, to insure a friendly future. Edgar and Ray would have to make peace for her sake.

"Just because some men aren't comfortable with—"

"With what?" His voice whipped around a new corner.

"Maybe the guy who insulted you was scared."

"Try hateful."

"No." She heard her own voice rise. Ray wasn't hateful. Neither was her son. She thought of Lang's stupid, rude jokes. They didn't make him evil. They made him fifteen.

"You're overdoing it." She softened her voice.

"You're right." Edgar sighed loudly. "I need to be more casual about being called a faggot by your son and some stranger you're working very hard to protect." He stopped talking suddenly. "Maybe he's not a stranger. Maybe I've finally met the mystery man. Helen?"

She didn't answer.

No goodbye. Helen held the candlestick tightly in her hand after he hung up, then wrapped it inside a soft cloth that would protect it from damage. She sniffed hard and dug around the bottom shelf of the refrigerator, the place where she kept tinned delicacies and wines to cheer her. As she ate and drank, Helen started a list of people she ought to call. There was Robin, but that would be too obvious after months of silence. She stared at the white paper, unable to begin with a single name.

Loneliness was stealthy. It had kept pace with Helen as she hacked her way through a bad marriage and romance and hard, hard jobs. It had waited to make its appearance until there was a wide clearing in her life. Helen had finally arrived. She blinked at the blankness that lay before her.

The leather seat on his own side was hot. Ray had parked his side under the shade while they ate. While Ray ate. Lang chewed and swallowed. He only swallowed when the sandwich was ground into a fine paste that coated his tongue. Lang had taken the offensive and told him all about his father's rampage. He told it without flinching or inflection. He told the part about how his father emptied his mother's underwear drawer to see how Ray would react, but nothing crossed his face. He wondered why, but brought himself back to the center. He had to keep his mind on doing everything right so nothing else could go wrong. Respect and detachment, he inserted the words in his brain and put his hands on the steering wheel.

"That must have been pretty rough," Ray said.

"Yeah, kinda."

"Funny your mom never mentioned it to me."

"She never tells anyone about how mad he gets."

"Boy Boyd is still having tantrums, huh?"

"No. Sort of."

It was a nice car. The engine bubbled up like oil. No wonder rich people liked this car so much.

"OK. Just pull out nice and easy. I want you to get used to the way it drives before we hop on the freeway."

Lang didn't turn his head or change the expression on his face. He looked at the nice level green in front of the ocean where you could play some golf if you wanted. The Captain always wanted to. The shitty home should've let him stand out there and swing.

"Where are we going?"

"How does Mexico sound?"

"Good. Great."

Sweating was out. But he wasn't sure he could control that part. Lang did a very nice left-hand turn out of the lot. Ray didn't say where to go. He was off in another world, Lang could tell. Kind of like his dad. Wrong. Ray wasn't anything like his dad. Lang would concentrate on being good, just great—all the way down to Mexico he would be those things.

"Ever go down there with your buddies?"

"No."

"Gee."

Gee? His mouth was going to get him in trouble if he didn't watch it. He knew that. Shut up, Lang.

"If I were your age, you couldn't keep me *out* of Mexico."

He let himself look at Ray and got what was coming to him. The Jag swerved to the left slightly and a guy in a blue Chrysler lay on the horn. For a long time. The noise was bad enough to make his hands shake.

"Easy."

Ray touched his shoulder once and unsnapped his seat belt at the light. He got out of the car fast, so fast Lang almost didn't see it happen. He crossed in back of the Jag, coming up on the guy in the blue car out of nowhere, nowhere! Banged once on the guy's back window to make him turn, and then reached into the side window before the guy had a chance to roll it up. Caught him by the collar. Lang looked around to see if anyone was watching, but they were the only two cars at the light. He saw the guy's head shake back and forth a couple of times, then bounce back up to stare straight ahead. The Chrysler moved slowly when the light turned to green and turned left at the next intersection. Ray slammed his door hard. He was the one who was sweating now.

"Now THAT drives me crazy. Here you are trying your best to become a good driver and somebody acts like a jerk."

Lang tried to feel either good or bad. He thought about being cut off in traffic that time, the way he had to lean out of the car and tell the guy to fuck off himself because his dad was sitting there doing nothing. But thinking about that didn't help. Ray just pointed directions for a while without talking. He offered Lang some candy and Lang just let the sour candy dissolve on his tongue. He put all his energy there and on driving Ray's car.

"You can drive a little faster, son."

They passed on through the beach towns and the further they drove, the better Lang felt. Pacific Beach, Mission Beach. He passed the street where his dad lived and asked if they could turn on the air conditioner.

"You too warm?"

"A little."

Ray fiddled with the temperature control, lowering it and asking him how he felt, was this good? Shall I leave it here? Lang was sorry he said anything at all. He was forgetting all about the game. He had dropped the offensive and the offensive had been one of his principal plans. That was all right, there was another.

"Mind if we drive by the harbor?" Lang asked.

"Fine by me."

Ray sounded like a smoker. His voice was rough and low.

"Mexico. You can do anything you want to the girls down there."

Lang tried to think about tacos and refried beans. He tried to think about all the pictures he had seen of Baja, the ones his dad had shown him from the one time when he had gone surfing there. He tried not to think of anything but those pictures.

"It's unbelievable what some women will let you do."

Lang could see the ships in the harbor. See the long decks, dream of aircraft carriers and all the ships the Captain had built. He could smell metal. He could suck metal into his body, spit it out on the mat or on the road instead of blood. He thought about spitting nails, aiming his mouth at someone's head and pulling off a round of nails just by opening his mouth.

"I went to the submarine base once." They couldn't see it. The base was just on the other side of Coronado Island, but Lang could feel it. He would know exactly when they were within the sights of a sub. His hands were starting to get slippery. He couldn't let that happen.

"You go there with your mom?"

Ray was right, it was stupid. Why did he bring it up at all? He was little, he'd been just a shrimpy kid who got excited by boats hidden under the water. They'd lifted him to see instruments. He remembered officers, brass, the shiny gray metal that pulled him toward the old men who built them. Or bragged they did. Maybe the Captain's past wasn't exactly what he said it was. Why would he think that? Why would Lang doubt the Captain when he needed him most?

National City. He'd never been down here during the day. Only when he was a little kid too little to know they were in National City. Lang thought of Ray's girl and accelerated slightly. She knew where she was now. She was old enough.

"I guess you did stuff with your kid, too."

Something in Lang's gut rolled over with that one. The words had sounded respectful when he said them in his mind. But not now, now that the words were loose, rolling along in the car with them. Fuck his mouth. Fuck his big mouth.

"So your mom told you, huh?"

Lang nodded.

"Let's pop up to the Five, son. You know how to handle yourself now."

He'd driven the freeway with his dad. It wasn't like he didn't know how to do that. They'd crawled all over La Jolla and the beach cities, but somehow they'd never gotten this far. Lang could see the freeway entrance from here. Nothing to it. He could make the turn right after the gas station.

"What all did she tell you?"

"That your ex-wife ran away with your daughter. That's all."

"Pretty sad story, don't you think?"

"Yes."

Sir. The word lay there in wait. He wished he could have said that now. But he'd been a wiseass. Snaggletooth. He remembered the fatso who had said that to him at the last match and gotten his ass kicked. Lang thought about the bean he'd stuck in his teeth at Ray's house and hunched over a little.

"Something troubling you, son?"

Lang ran his tongue over his tooth and looked at the odometer. Too many numbers. He couldn't read the mileage and drive at the same time.

"You can tell me, son."

Switch. His focus was misplaced. It was on the mind, the poor tiny spot in his skull. He'd forgotten his own strength. He'd forgotten what his body knew.

"It's just that every time you call me Son—"

Make him wrestle you, Lang. Get your weight on him, boy.

"What?"

"Well, it makes me feel weird. I'm not your son."

"Oh, that's right. I forgot you've got a father."

Lang waited. Something told him to just drive.

"He's a real champ."

"My dad's okay!" His voice was whiny. Baby voice for a baby boy.

"Playing with your mom's underpants when she's not home. I'd sure be proud to call *him* my dad."

They were behind a Mexican truck. Everything written in Spanish, something about dancing vegetables, not that Lang could understand it. French, what a stupid language. He felt like slapping himself in the face. He should have studied Spanish, been prepared. He wanted to pass the truck, but so did a car in back of him.

"Get around him, son."

Fuck you, Son. Lang pulled down too hard on the turn-signal and it made a cracking sound.

"That's OK. You can make it."

He looked in his rearview mirror and the other car was almost on his ass. Almost. He swung out into the left lane and floored it. The car leaped into a speed and power he'd never felt in the Volvo. Why should he? He thought of that car, the deep cut in the side his dad was too lazy to fix. Why should he feel anything in that car?

"See? Told you you could do it."

The truck driver's smile gleamed gold. Or silver. Some metal that replaced his real teeth. He was lucky. He had money in his mouth and he knew it. Ray waved and then stuck his arm high in the air. Lang opened his mouth at what he saw behind him. He could see the rage in the driver's eyes as clearly as if he sat in their car. The driver was humiliated. His wife had seen everything and so had his kids. Ray's arm was still up in the air, saluting in the breeze. Lang almost smiled.

"See that guy's teeth?"

"Yeah!"

"Pure gold. How'd you like to have teeth like that?"

Lang kept the speed at around seventy, seventy-five. He tried to remember what he'd read about the flow of traffic.

"I don't know."

"Sure you do. Sure you know."

If they took an exit now, they'd be in Chula Vista. Lang racked his brain to find anything about that name. There was something, some talk about letting Chula Vista back into the league. There had been a big violation or something.

"Would you like to have teeth like that or not?"

"Not really. I mean, not all gold like that."

"But different teeth?"

"Well, sure."

"What I don't get is why your dad doesn't help you out on that."

"I never asked him."

"You shouldn't have to ask, son. Your dad oughta come through for you. Is it money?"

"Yeah. I guess."

Ray shook his head. He could see that out of the corner of his eye.

"He should *get* the money. He should look after you and your mom."

Ray leaned his head back against the seat for a minute.

"He's blowing it, losing his temper, not taking care of his responsibilities. Your dad oughta know what I know for about half a minute. He'd change his tune."

"What do you mean?"

"He should know what it feels like to have his kid disappear."

Boom. Gone. No more Lang. But where would he go? Where would his body go if he disappeared? He didn't care about his mind, forget that. What would happen to his arms and legs, where would they wind up?

"Take the next exit, Lang."

No Son. Being someone's son didn't matter now, he didn't care what Ray said. Lang was on his own. He felt his heart beat faster. It was revealing its location, flopping around, failing him. He thought about the map. He thought about burning the map from one corner, watching fire gobble paper in a big hungry flame.

"Talk about a community changing. You're gonna see something down here."

Ray said to take Broadway all the way and to keep his eyes peeled. How about that? Now when I used to come here they were all retirees, ex-military, good solid people. Shit, look at it now. He pointed right and left, talking faster as Lang drove until Lang couldn't remember why they were driving in the first place. He was good, he was expert, and the Jag felt driven by remote control.

"Fun in the sun."

They were stopped at an intersection. More and more the signs were in Spanish, the flow of traffic had changed once again. Ray was pointing and laughing at the same time, so Lang turned his head to see nothing. He saw nothing, just a baby in a plastic pool, and a mother with a hose trying to cool the kid off. Nothing. He couldn't understand.

"Now, she'll figure he's fine. He's got water to splash in, a toy. Watch her put the duck in."

Lang tried to find it remarkable. The duck wobbled its way to the baby.

"She'll go back inside, leave the door ajar so she can hear him. Man, parents like that kill me. They just kill me. All it takes is one teaspoon of water and that kid is gonna drown. Or worse. What if he doesn't die? What if someone stops, needs a baby and sees one sitting right there with a toy in his hand. Now you talk about a sitting duck."

Ray's face was all purple and it was hard to look at him without wanting to run away. But where would he run? To which house? Lang began to think of which house he could go to and what he could say without knowing one fucking word of Spanish. The offensive. That idea had turned watery by now. It floated in a plastic baby pool and would soon be so soaked and heavy it would sink. Lang eased through the intersection and crossed Main.

"You used to come here?" Lang asked.

"What do you mean?"

Wrong. It was wrong to say that. But how could you go wrong with streets like that? Those streets were like old musicals that came on TV late at night, the ones where all of a sudden, just as the story got going, people would start to sing instead of talk. The story was told with songs and they were happy. Women who wore aprons, fathers who smoked pipes and wore slippers after supper.

"You said how there were only retirees here before. I was just wondering—"

"Just wondering, exactly. What good does it do anyone to just wonder? Check out the estates."

The name of the street changed as soon as they crossed Main and became Beyer. Hacienda Mobile Estates. Granada Mobile Estates. Lang felt children's eyes follow their car as he passed. One kid chased another with a stick that held up a pair of pants. Why would a kid run from an empty pair of pants? Rickety homes crawled up the sides of the valley and Lang saw mountains ahead. High hills, something. They were dry and dusty with faded green patches sprouting up every now and then. Lang wondered if that was Mexico and realized Ray was right. It didn't do any good to wonder. The road ended. Lang had to turn left or right. Ray pointed to the right shoulder and Lang pulled over. They got out of the car. Ray motioned for Lang to cross the road.

"Otay Valley. This is where lots of them try to cross at night."

A white four-wheel drive marked BORDER PATROL sped past them, sirens screaming. A helicopter appeared over one hill. It hovered in the air, whipping up dust below.

"They die out there."

"Who?"

Ray laughed and ruffled his hair. Right at the spot Lang always banged on the wall at night when he slept. How did he know exactly where it was tender? Lang's scalp burned when he took his hand away.

"Mexicans. Who else would be stupid enough to cross at a checkpoint?"

"How do they die?

There were so many people here. How could anyone die in these hills? There were telephone poles there, dirt paths that took you straight down to a busy street. Lang could see motel and factory-outlet signs along the commercial strip below. McDonald's. Christ, how could anyone die here? Another Jeep screamed by. The guy driving was young. He would be someone Patricia would like. Thinking of her brought her here, in a way. Lang was instantly sorry. It wouldn't be good to have her in this place.

"You name it. Heat exhaustion. Dehydration, rattlesnakes. Why, just about anything can happen here."

How could he be so cold in the hot sun? His body was soaked and it was like he was standing in a cold rain. Maybe he had the flu. Maybe he was really sick and just didn't know it.

"Something wrong?"

"I don't feel good."

"What, like sick to your stomach?"

"Kind of an all over sick."

All the color went out of Ray's face. He put his hand in his back pocket and looked at Lang hard. Like hearing about it made him feel bad, too.

"It's no big deal."

"See?" He shook his head again, the way he had in the car. "That's what's so terrible. You really don't think it's a big deal to be sick. Or to be sad. Or not to have the smile you deserve. That's what kills me."

"Maybe we'd better drive back home."

"You worry too much, Thomas."

Lang watched the hill change, become a place where you could die at night, between the beams of helicopters and the headlights of cars and the wobble of a flashlight held in someone's hand, someone who was looking for you. He wasn't called Thomas. He didn't even know anyone called Thomas, so why did hearing the name make his heart do that little jump?

"Don't you remember the first phone call?" Ray asked softly. "The one where someone said, 'Put your mom on, Thomas'? That was me, son."

Lang saw gulches and empty canyons, more than he had seen before. He didn't know what lay beyond. Cars continued to pass them, one at a time. Time-released cars, but he didn't know anything about sequence or speed or Spanish. He didn't know anything at all. He remembered the call now and the way he felt afterward.

"And you said something funny. Something I really related to. You said, 'It's hard enough being Lang' and then you hung up. It's hard being Ray, too. It's always been hard."

Lang had the keys in his hand. They felt hot, like maybe they were about to melt.

"I wanted to know your name from the very beginning because I know who's important in your family."

Ray's eyes made him think of beer . . . what a stupid, useless thing to think. It was the bottle it came in. The sun turned them into that exact color. He licked his dry lips.

"You're important to me, Lang. A teenage boy who lives alone with his mother *should* be important to a decent man. I know she counts on you, Lang. I know that's heavy."

"It's not. It's fine."

"She counts on you to help her."

"But—"

"You help her sort things out in her mind. Things she's unsure about. You're helping her now, even though you don't know it."

The heat made his shoulders bend and he felt like dust had gotten inside his body, coating everything inside. How long did it take to dehydrate? Could it happen while you stood on a hillside?

"Right now she doesn't know if she wants to live with me. And every day you don't smile when she talks about me, your mom decides she won't make up her mind that day. She'll just wait until you come around, until you can pick up the phone and tell her it's me without leaving the phone off the hook. Until you can eat a meal I've prepared without clowning around, sticking a bean where it doesn't belong."

"I didn't mean to—"

"Sure you meant to. You've had her all to yourself for years. Why would you want to share your mom with me? See, I know how rough it is to want something you can't ever have. Now between looking at your mother every day and that girl Patricia who comes around sometimes . . . I've watched the two of you together. She's got her eye on you, son."

Ray stood so close to the edge that gravel was starting to slip from under his shoes. He didn't even have on the right shoes. He was going to flip onto his back and fall down the hillside, smash into the jagged rocks that cropped up along the way. His arms started to wave, but not the way they had in the car when he was saying fuck you to the guy behind them. He wasn't saying fuck you to anyone now.

"Hey! Look out!"

Lang's body moved before his mind did and they both slipped a little, but the scramble brought them up, not down. It was his weight that pulled them both back from the edge. Put your weight on him! For once Lang had made the move, not Ray. He let go of him fast and wiped the dust off his own jeans.

"Wow," Ray said. His mouth hung open a little, he was breathing fast. "I feel like a real jerk. Thanks."

He stood there with his legs shaking, the kind of shaking Lang knew about when something really took you by surprise. Then slowly Ray got better, stood up a little straighter. He mopped off his neck with a handkerchief and studied Lang's face. But his eyes didn't stop there. They scanned him all over, as if it had been Lang who'd almost fallen down the side of a hill. Like something in Lang was now hurt or damaged.

"I don't know if either *one* of us is ready for Mexico today."

Ray's hand had gotten around the back of his neck. It just stayed there at first, kind of warm. Then it began to slide up and down on his skin. Lang wobbled inside. He didn't know what the feeling was. Everything inside was choppy and churned up. He couldn't name what the feeling was.

"But speaking as an old fart, I wouldn't mind resting a little before we go home." Ray's eyes wandered to the bright, noisy street below. He laughed again and shook his head back and forth slowly.

"I guess it turns out *I'm* the one who's sick."

Ray whistled a long, tuneless note and crossed the street to the car. Lang watched the Otay Valley for a moment, then let his chin drop to his chest, feeling the ligaments rip at the back of his neck. His body was here, announcing itself in pain. Lang hadn't disappeared after all.

"Thanks for calling, honey. I would have worried if you hadn't."

Lang stood in the doorway for a minute, as if he needed to be invited inside. Ray's car rolled back out of the driveway. He'd suggested picking up dinner for the three of them. She thought of how considerate he was to drop Lang off first.

"How was it?"

"OK."

"Like his car?"

"Yeah."

"Well, so . . . ?"

She closed her magazine and waited for him to complain about Ray. Her mind was still a little fuzzy from the champagne.

"You look *so* handsome. Did you two spend time in the sun?"

His eyes shone. He looked like a rapturous boy of seven or eight, alive and alert from a day of war games on the block. She thought of Lang's little gold shield. He had vanquished everyone on Brighton Court back then.

"A little."

He moved around the room and she didn't bother him with questions. He would open up when he was ready. He'd never spent so much time alone with Ray. She looked at her watch and thought of all the small talk he'd had to make. She hoped he'd made a real effort.

"So you drove. Then what?"

He cracked his knuckles hard and she frowned.

"Do I have a passport?"

"Yes." She thought it was still good.

"So where is it?"

"In a safety-deposit box in the bank. Why? Are you thinking of going somewhere, Lang?"

Lang lifted his head and looked at her. What she saw almost made her turn away. His love shamed her. Helen felt sickened and thrilled by the emotion she saw on his face.

"It's OK if we move in with him, Mom."

"Lang! You're serious?"

He nodded and continued to move around the room.

"What made you change your mind?"

He shrugged and found a paper he was looking for. He flattened it under the palm of his hand.

"Come on. Why do you feel differently about Ray?"

He read quietly and didn't look up when he spoke.

"I'm getting to know him better, I guess."

"Lang, I'm so happy! Thank you, sweetheart. Come give me a kiss."

He folded the paper in two and walked to the end of the captain's chair. He bent over her stiffly and closed his eyes as her lips brushed his cheek.

"You didn't answer my question. Are you thinking of going somewhere?"

"Where would I go, Mom?"

"Mexico, maybe."

Lang stared out the window at the dark street. He was probably hungry. He must have been watching for Ray's headlights.

"I think I've already been."

Helen nodded at the vague response. She'd *never* known where she was before getting her driver's license. Neighborhoods were full of nameless streets, north could have been south and east could have been west. Lang's confusion wouldn't last. He would soon know exactly where he was.

29.

"You sound awfully edgy." Alice's voice on the telephone was firm. "Is Dallas *that* bad?"

Helen raced through a review of the past two days. The Home Fashion Salon featured, among other things, business tips for beginners and seminars like High-Impact Window Displays, In-Store Promotions, and Management Techniques. Alice had politely turned down requests to speak for years. But *someone* had to go this year, and she had handed Helen the invitation as if it were a jury summons.

"Did you tell the story of the fabric?"

"Yes."

Retailers had pored over the sample book after her talk, discovered what fabrics were produced in 1828, how much of each pattern was printed and sold, and how greatly combinations of color and pattern mattered to merchants in Bordeaux, Lyons, and Paris.

"They went crazy over the designs."

"Fabulous!"

"Hang on a second," Helen said.

She raced to the tub to shut off the water. Steam clouded the mirror and the shiny fixtures. She hurried back to the phone.

"I feel like I'm doing all this work prematurely."

Alice broke off to speak to Patricia. Helen strained to hear what she said.

"You're laying the groundwork. You're polishing a story you'll need to tell dozens of times. You're—"

"You're on the verge of selling the store."

"I have a chance to sell. Big difference."

The hotel was ideal for conventions. There was nothing remotely personal in her room. Nothing jarring. She thought of the stone sink where she had washed her face after the Sunrise Ball. She remembered the uneven splash of the water as it fell from a bronze spigot. Helen rubbed the bottom of her stockinged feet against the smooth carpet until they burned.

"They wanted to know about color abrasions and crocking. They wanted to know about sales terms and shipping points on a line we don't have set up yet."

"My goodness. I hope it didn't overwhelm you, Helen. I know you have so much on your mind right now."

Helen held her feet still. Alice's cold war pained her. The arched eyebrows, delicate questions about the hasty packing and the move to Gatley Point, the assurances that Helen and Ray would live happily ever after when Helen hadn't asked for such assurances in the first place. And how is Lang adjusting? Everything happened so quickly! The exquisite care Alice took in avoiding other questions was taking its toll. How long have you resented me, Helen?

"Perhaps I've thrown too much at you."

She spoke to someone softly. Helen thought of Patricia writing a note with her pen, the pen she'd forgotten and left in the leather trough on her desk. Or perhaps Patricia now had a Montblanc of her own.

"Now, where were we?"

"I took orders for an imaginary product." Helen took a deep breath. "And I'm working for an imaginary employer. I don't know whether I should be reporting to you or a Saudi Arabian princess."

"Are you through having a fit? Be reasonable, Helen."

Helen peeled off her stockings. She tried not to make the snag worse.

"All right. We've got decisions to make."

She worked her stockings down to her ankles, switching the phone to her other ear. She glanced at the map she had spread on the floor. A magnifying glass lay over Oklahoma. Her destination was clear, if Alice's wasn't.

"Who's this person you want to meet?"

Helen looked harder at the map. The state seemed unfocused and puny. It must have been the light. She rubbed her eyes and waited for her vision to clear.

"I told you about her a while ago. I showed you her work and then, I don't know. We got busy on other things."

The baby. You learned you couldn't have everything you wanted, Alice. You pouted and punished Jack and punished me. Helen held the stockings up the light.

"I want to run up and see her studio."

"A weaver from Oklahoma? Helen, this is my *fabric* you're talking about."

"Her work is beautiful."

"Oh, fine. Take two more days." Alice laughed gently. "Lang must have had a real growth spurt."

"What do you mean?"

"Apparently you've decided to let your son grow up."

Helen requested a wake-up call after saying good-bye. She approached the map gingerly and kneeled at one edge, moving the magnifying glass closer and closer. When she was finished looking, she undressed and lowered herself into the bathtub. Maybe Lang was swimming laps now. Ray had urged him to use the pool whenever he wanted. He had plunged his hand into the water to test the temperature for Lang's nightly routine. Ray's hand looked unnaturally pale as it slowly stirred back and forth.

The bathwater had turned stone cold, but she made herself bathe in it anyway, shivering as she ran soap over her breasts and underneath her arms. She washed herself between her legs as her teeth chattered, and lifted the bathtub drain with with one toe. She lay rigid while the slow drain sucked and gurgled, only standing up to dry her mottled skin when all the water was gone.

Did you fall into a sinkhole?"

Hollis Ryan was short and wide, with a thick braided coil of gray hair secured at the nape of her neck. She wore Hush Puppies and a white T-shirt with billowing satin pants. Her face was puggish, as if someone larger had placed a firm hand on her features and pressed. She blinked her eyes hard each time she spoke.

"It took me forever to get out of Texas. Dallas was a nightmare," Helen said. Her blouse stuck to her back. The heat seemed to shrink her skin, bringing it closer to the bone.

"It generally is."

It didn't look as if Hollis would budge, so Helen did. She set her briefcase down gently on a white iron chair and took a good look at the chinaberry trees in the hot courtyard. The trunks and branches looked starved. Dessicated leaves fluttered and fell with every breath of wind. Helen peered at a cat's print in the cobalt blue tile that looked every bit like brick until she stood closer. The cat hadn't put full weight on the tile. A strict ironwork "S" was placed left and right of the door.

"It means sinner saved. How did you find me?"

Violated smells floated past Hollis. Solemn wood and beeswax, breached by something sweet and fruity. Hollis held a half-eaten hot dog in one hand. Mustard spotted the corner of her mouth.

"I found your work in a design magazine."

Hollis blinked. "That magazine folded. I was in the very last issue."

"Your work gave them a fine exit."

"Come on in."

Hollis pivoted on the balls of her feet. She moved with the grace of a much lighter woman. The door swung open all the way and Helen forgot about airport traffic and a long drive north through Texas. She had sped past sinkholes, cavern roofs that could collapse into limestone passages underground. She sighed and entered the country chapel. She was safe.

"I pulled out all the pews myself."

Plain, unvarnished pine planks covered the walls of the two-story chapel. The structure itself contained no decoration. There was no statue of Mary and Child, no crucifix. Color seemed more flagrant against the bleak background. Hollis Ryan's fabrics hung down the sides of the upstairs balcony. Their beauty and brilliance brightened the old chapel.

"The preacher's place is up there. His followers called that a 'wineglass pulpit.' Don't ask me why they came to Oklahoma and why they didn't drink once they got here. They were German immigrants and teetotalers through and through."

A polished-oak pulpit hung suspended over the open space. A door with a small window carved inside stood a few steps above it.

"He spied on his congregation like this town spies on me." She tapped Helen's arm once. "The people around here don't trust what I'm doing, even though I saved them the one little bit of history they have. They don't care about my fabrics or my designs or my ideas."

Hollis pointed to a simple desk and table in the front of the church.

"I sit right here while they fire off questions about restoration. They want me to spend big bucks on repair *and* listen to their plans on how to do it. Think they want to know how a loom works?"

Hollis lay one hand across her cheek.

"Think they'd send me a school bus full of kids for a real education?"

"Maybe they're afraid."

"What do you mean?" Hollis narrowed her eyes and pushed her head closer to Helen. "I'd never do anything to those kids."

"Of course not." Helen spoke quickly. "But people might be intimidated by your work." The beauty in this place could be something to fear. A pipe organ loomed before them. Helen imagined its chilly chords as Hollis steered her to the center of the chapel where nine looms stood.

"I could sure teach those kids something," Hollis spoke sadly.

"I agree. These are beautiful pieces," Helen bent down to look at the construction of the table. "English?"

Hollis nodded and bit into her hot dog as she observed Helen.

"Yup. Come see what all's upstairs."

Benches and hat pegs. Lavish, chaotic piles of fabric and shipping material filled box pews. Votive candles were everywhere. A different scent had risen to the top of the building. Animal fur and the stinging smell of urine. Hollis pushed through the door behind the pulpit, into a room that was mostly blue, blowing sky. A wide section of wall was missing. The floor in front of a jagged hole was splattered with bird dung.

"This is what they hate the most."

"Who?"

"People in town. They think I've desecrated the preacher."

Hollis nodded at a severe figure in a gilded portrait. His face was pinched and disapproving, as if he agreed. Hollis moved toward the opening in the wall.

"Oklahoma doesn't deserve me."

She shuffled her feet as she walked, leaned out into the air and whistled sharply. Helen's skin prickled. She heard the catbird before she saw it. The bird lit in Hollis' hair, then took its place on her strong shoulders. Hollis lifted one arm slowly and pointed a straight, hard finger at Helen. The bird sidled down her arm, then lifted its body into the air. When its tiny claws scraped Helen's arm, she didn't flinch. She tried not to breathe, thinking only of Elizabeth Adams Perkins, how she coaxed tricks from her exotic birds with raisins soaked in rum. One by drunken one they slid up and down her fragile arms.

"How did you train a wild bird?"

"It's an orphan. I can get it to do anything I want."

Helen reddened as she felt the bird take a little hop. Orphan. The word still sounded like a mean tin cup. It insinuated thin-soled shoes forever and ever. Hollis sat at a pocked pine table and opened the sample book.

"A storm took out the chimney, and this little thing was hanging upside down in a sweet gum tree."

The bird flew away, and Helen waited for Hollis to speak. She wanted to escape this broken room. She wished for a moment she could follow the catbird wherever it flew. Hollis spread her arms way out. They looked wretched as her chinaberry trees.

"Now, for my next trick."

She stood for a moment, then walked to a cupboard and opened a door. She unfolded yard after yard of her very finest fabrics, full of mosaics and medallions, all forms of pageantry inspired by the short, puggish woman who stood wrapped in golds and turquoise, a crimson plucked from bitter Oklahoma berries. Framed by full sky and hung with glory, Hollis Ryan looked beautiful.

What does she want for the book?"

"It's not for sale."

The blinking had increased. Hollis understood what was under her fingertips. She turned a page with the greatest care.

"You gonna want me to goose these colors a little?"

The shadows in the room had turned hard and sharp, and the ragged view of red sky suggested a campfire. Somewhere, it was time to tell a familiar story. Somewhere a child struggled into a warm lap, seeking comfort and a lullaby. Helen wondered where Lang was, in what room exactly. Ray had shown him the stairs behind the tapestry one day when she was at work, and the creaky wooden stairs and the secrecy had seduced him. Maybe Lang was sitting on a bowed step now, watching the tide rush into the cave. She looked at her watch. It was too early for anyone to go to bed in California.

"Hey." Hollis nudged Helen's foot with her own. "I asked you a question."

"Sorry." Helen set her jaw. But she wasn't sorry. It had been right to move to Gatley Point. Any kind of change was unsettling. "What did you ask me?"

"Honey, you're a million miles away. I want to know if I should punch up these colors."

"No. They're fine."

"I *could* do it on one condition."

"And what is that?" Condition. Helen didn't like the sound of that word, either.

"I choose the converter. Too many of the big outfits have ruined my designs."

"Let's go over the terms of the contract, why don't we?" Helen said.

"I can't sign anything without my lawyer."

"I wouldn't ask you to."

"Listen, things around here can get real busy real fast. I can't promise I'll be available when you make up your mind what weaver you want for the job." Hollis upended a jar full of paper clips and found a pen. She tested it on blank paper. "Damn it. My ink won't flow."

Helen watched as she rummaged through a drawer.

"I've got a fixed price on strike-offs."

"Fine."

Hollis found a pen that worked. She tapped a wide front tooth again and again until blue ink spotted her lips.

"Don't you want to know what it is?" She swung her knees around to face her.

"Oh, of course."

Hollis handed her a price sheet.

"Where do you go from here?"

"I'm going to drive over to Richardson."

Richardson. It was the first time she'd said the name of the town out loud. It sounded innocuous and neutral. Richardson, Oklahoma, sounded as safe as a country chapel.

"So that's what's on your mind. Pretty wild country up there."

A gate was flung open in the courtyard. No footsteps followed, no friends for the long night ahead, just vacant sounds stirred by a hot wind. Helen looked at Hollis Ryan's soiled blue mouth, then stood up to leave.

30.

He just came in," Ray said. "I think he's in the shower."

She thought of how tall Lang stood, how he would always clobber himself on the nozzle in the old house. The shower in Ray's house was spacious and clean. There was a blue-tiled seat and a shelf where Lang could stack all his skin products and special soaps; an adjustable magnifying mirror reached out to him with a crooked silver arm. Lang wouldn't hurt himself in that shower.

"We're getting along great, Helen. You go on and take the time you need."

"Hollis Ryan doesn't have a phone." The lie didn't even sting. She pushed her hip against the edge of the scrawny phone book. Richardson, Oklahoma. Population 9,000.

Ray laughed. "She's got the right idea."

She thought of her old black phone, packed away now in Ray's closet. The telephones barely rang and when they did, all three of them startled. The house absorbed human sound. Their voices didn't fill it up the way she had imagined. They were an echo produced in a beautiful void, a house forced open only at night when the waves rocked and shook the rooms. There was only one caller persistent enough to break open the silence at Gatley Point.

"Is Boyd calling the house?" Helen asked.

"Hey. Stop worrying."

"All right. Tell me about Medford." Her voice sounded cheerful and empty. A heavy truck lumbered past.

"Mrs. Lowell raised her rates again. They needed ten thousand this time."

Helen didn't answer. She watched a squad car that passed the cafe where she stood. It cruised slowly, amiably through the small town, where Richardson Hardware and the Okie Dokie Dry Cleaner faced off at the intersection. A bus bench sparkled in the sun. Helen looked at the metal and thought of the scorch to the back of the legs. She braced herself for the cordial, careful tea with Ray's mother and father. She ran through Ray's defense: the long, stoic hunts, the money, the unflinching pursuit. They would see things differently. They would see *him* differently, as she had learned to do.

"You with me, Helen?"

"Yes." She really was with Ray. There was just this unfinished business. Her parents were dead, but his weren't. If she was right, she could change history. She could erase sadness, reverse regret. She let her eyes follow the slow turn of the patrol car. The officer pulled into a vacant space and got out of the car. He looked at something on the curb and hiked up his pants.

"I've had it, Helen."

"What do you mean?"

Helen shook her head no and didn't speak.

"I'm going to stop looking for Rebecca."

"You're giving up." Emotion stopped pushing her words forward. It was so hot. Table fans whirred along, but they didn't seem to help.

"I'm just changing my tactic. And Elizabeth will, too."

The squad car was covered with dust. The officer slapped something from his shoulder and moved along the sidewalk.

"I'll always give her money." Ray's voice turned musical. It softened and relaxed. "But if she wants me to be part of Rebecca's life, she'll have to make the next move. Now, what's so radical about that?"

Helen didn't answer. She tried to straighten the twisted phone cord with her thumb and forefinger.

"The truth is, I've got you and Lang to think about now. And that's plenty."

Helen stood still, feeling the words. Something rattled in the background. She heard coughing. Then more coughing, each hard, raspy spasm triggering another.

"Put Lang on the phone."

"Easy, Helen. Something went down the wrong way, for God's sake."

"I want to talk to my son."

He snorted and handed Lang the phone. There was a rush of tap water.

"Lang?"

He cleared his throat and said hello.

"What's wrong?"

"I choked. Big deal." His voice was lifeless and dull. It sank lower the longer they talked.

"You sound so far away, honey."

"You're the one who's far away."

They were quiet for a few seconds, then Ray's voice slit open the silence.

"Worrywart." Ray laughed softly. "Your son's in excellent hands."

He'd been listening all along. Her head hurt as she hung up the phone. The pounding continued, like a visitor at the door who refused to go away. She flipped through the pages of the Richardson telephone directory. She ran her finger down the short list in the small town and found one listing for Richards, street and phone number. Nothing was hidden. The print was large and easy to read.

The officer was helpful. She could hear him over the knocking in her head as he described how to get to the Richards place and even offered to drive out himself so she could follow him. The heat pounded, too, creating another pulse outside her body. She was being pummeled into strength, almost held in place by discomfort.

She could have pushed harder on the gas pedal, or she could have slowed down and planned words. But her thoughts spread out like cards. She selected one and then another in a calm way that helped her gather a full hand. Not necessarily a hand that would win, but she neatly grouped together spades and clubs, thoughts and questions marked with the same strange symbols. If she was right, if this was the town where Ray had grown up and if she was about to meet his mother and father, what would she say to them now that Ray had given up the search? What lie could she concoct that would explain her visit?

The road out of town passed through a long tunnel, though nothing surrounded it but gaping space. Helen hadn't seen so much open land since leaving the aunts. She had run away to people, populations, life! She remembered that. This was the same, but instead of hot, chafed air, this air was blistered and moist. She would be damp when she held out her hand to meet Ray's father. She would be so wet she couldn't crumble and fall. Questions would pucker and fill automatically in this wet, warm place.

The gray tunnel cut through flat land. No hills, no freeways. It was simply a long, cooling passage. Was that it? Respite from the heat and cold, since one extreme required another. Helen shaded her eyes with one hand as she left the tunnel. She saw a sign that read Richards Pipe. She pulled over and sat blinking at the factory that seemed to gobble up land and space, then fill it with hot metal.

The entrance was locked and guarded, but behind it she saw pipes in orderly stacks. They rose to form pyramids in one section, in another they formed simple, rectangular boxes of metal. Smoke poured from a stack. Even though it was Sunday, there must have been a shift at work. She started her car again. It coughed and complained, then finally rolled over.

The road lengthened to an empty black strip. It shimmered and ran in places as if the asphalt had melted. No cars passed or pursued. She had five more miles of this. Where did this pipeline lead? The road split wide sections of pasture and prairie, with hills squeezed to the edge of endless green flats. Trees congregated as cattle did, bunching together in the lush, lonely grassland. Sandstone and sprigs of yarrow drifted into view. Clouds had begun to churn up one dark corner of the sky. Helen watched lightning dip down and lick the earth with a thin white tongue. She pushed harder on the accelerator. She had no plan now. She erased words. She thought of Boyd sharply, with deep regret. He knew things she didn't. How to delay, how to deflect distrust with a joke or a smile. He could have told her exactly how to make this cold call in the middle of heat that would soon jackknife into thunder and rain.

The road began a slow rise and Helen looked at the odometer. A rabbit quivered at the edge of the road and darted into a gully. The grassland took on a tame look as she pulled around a bend in the road. Trees leaned overhead in a sudden canopy, converting the stretch of asphalt to a shadowed hall. Helen could smell rain in the air. Her hair slithered down the back of her neck and stuck.

Sun slapped the front of the rented car again. She didn't need to be told this was where Ray had grown up. The hills were trim and terraced. Helen squinted at what she saw. Stark fencing stilled miles of grassland. It looked like sections of pipeline. A long ranch house lay draped at the top of one of the hills. Thick, oppressive air continued to press through the car's open windows.

There was no buzzer, no formal entrance, just fencing that broke open suddenly and a wide driveway leading up to the house. Geraniums spilled from brick planters at each side of the opening. Helen hesitated for a moment, then drove through the space. Irish setters ran at her car from the top of the hill. The dogs feinted, darting at the front tires, then dropped back to lunge at the front door. She thought of the grassy makeshift shelter Ray had built for his old dog. A power mower appeared from behind the house. Helen could hear the roar of the engine toiling away in the miserable sun. That kind of machine could flatten a little boy's love and labor.

A fat, shirtless gardener straddled the mower. The mower moved back and forth as the old man under the baseball hat continued to sculpt rows of thick green grass. Every now and then the sun would strike the metal rims of his sunglasses. He raced the mass of gray clouds that gobbled more and more blue from the sky.

A willow bent over a dark pond beneath the house and a single lily floated on black water. Several cars were parked in a wide paved circle. Helen pulled in behind a Range Rover and tried to quiet her mind. A single spot on a map had grown cancerous, spreading into her mind overnight. What did Ray have to do with any of this? She thought of his hands traveling over fine fabrics and his eyes as he scrutinized paintings he loved. None of it made sense. She lay her head on the steering wheel for a moment and cursed her own confusion. She wanted to leave and she wanted to stay.

The mower was silent. She looked up to find the gardener at the crest of the hill. He ignored the stone path and worked his way down one side of the slope as if he were sliding on snow. She opened the car door and one of the setters licked her on the mouth before she could escape. They turned around and around her calves in a chestnut swirl.

"They'll love you to death if you let 'em."

The old man panted as he spoke. Though he was wet with perspiration, Helen smelled a heavy sweetness on his skin.

"Down!"

The word pressed on the pack of dogs. They flattened in a single motion. One thirsty dog lowered his haunches as he lapped at the top of the pond.

"Help ya?"

"Yes." Helen smiled firmly as the man came closer. He had a thick patch of zinc oxide on his nose. "I'm looking for Mr. Richards."

"You got him right here."

She let surprise rush over her once, then shooed it away. Helen took off her sunglasses and folded them.

Fat suited him. His strength thickened into greater power still. He rubbed wide, workingman's hands up and down over the sides of his belly. White hair spread over his broad chest and back like sea foam.

"Just who would you be?" He opened his mouth in a grin.

"My name is Helen Patterson."

One of the dogs began a low growl. He turned his head toward the sound and it rolled into an ingratiating whine. Helen dusted a paw print from her blouse and spoke again.

"Mr. Richards, I'm here on a crazy impulse."

He pulled the brim of his baseball cap lower and laughed. "That could get you in a lot of trouble."

His nails were square and neat. She made herself stop looking at them.

"Are you related to someone named Ray Richards?"

He scratched the side of his neck, then took a handkerchief from a back pocket and began to remove zinc oxide little by little.

"It's fixin' to pour. Come on up to the house before we really get wet."

He mopped at his face and motioned to the path. She walked carefully, watching the crooked steps and the view below. Shadows spread over the land like a stain. She could watch the storm from above and below. She stumbled once at the top and felt his quick response, how close he must have been to her all along.

"Careful where you walk, Helen."

His strong hand on her waist, the slow drag of his words at her back . . . it all felt choreographed. He seemed unsurprised that she was here and, suddenly, so was she. She stared at the front of the ranch house and locked out her mind. She entered a region of the senses. Thoughts didn't matter here. Her stories didn't count. What mattered were the feelings that rushed over her as she saw the terrace where Ray had grown up. She thought of a surly boy Lang's age, tipping back in one of the dozen wicker chairs neatly arranged on the long wooden porch. Tipping, tipping against orders, against reason. Chair legs tipping back and then the fast slide and the crash backwards, the slight brush of blood on the wood. Ray hated this place. He tracked in mud and manure, defied and defiled in gestures that Helen understood in one swift glance. Home sweet home was bitter and that wasn't a thought in her mind. It was pain that spliced several things together at once. She watched Ray's father scrape the dirt from his boot.

"It's sure on its way now."

Thunder seemed to break directly over their heads. The sharpness of sunlight had fled, but Helen didn't feel protected by the porch. She peered through a wide window.

"We'll have ourselves a nice drink. I believe my wife squeezed up a fresh batch of lemonade before she left this morning."

He opened the front door and waited for Helen to move inside. Her senses forked into recognition and resolution. She knew the enfilade of reception rooms stretched before her. She had already run her finger over their glossy picture and unknowingly passed through rooms where every movement was observed and recorded. A father had watched a boy here and the boy watched back. Helen touched the back of a Chippendale chair. This was what Ray longed to escape. He had even brought the design magazine to the Ramone Ranch to enlist Helen's help. Why hadn't he told her it featured the home where he had grown up?

"Sit down here while I get us those drinks."

He set his baseball cap down and the sunglasses, then stroked the side of his face once. Clear amber eyes set inside leathery skin made her lean away.

"I guess I don't need to tell you Ray's my son." He turned to walk out of the room.

Her eyes wandered over the wallpaper, painted panoramic scenes she had seen only dimly in the pages of a magazine. She didn't dare wander through the rooms she could see, but she counted them (three) and glimpsed at what they suggested: foreign lands, adventures and vistas that opened like illustrated travel books. She was in a tropical Oklahoma with fruit trees and waterfalls, jungles that flushed monkeys and zebras from the brush instead of cattle.

"Is Ray Junior a friend of yours?"

Helen spun around at the voice that stroked her from behind. Richards appeared at a small side door hidden under a panel of lush flowers. He balanced a silver tray in his hands. Two blue glass goblets and a full pitcher of lemonade rested on its monogrammed surface. Helen strained to read the insignia, but he moved the tray to a low ebony table before she could make sense of the ornate letters. He opened french doors just in time to watch drops of rain speckle the porch.

"Ray Junior?"

"Big Ray and Little Ray. We share a lot more than a name. That's the way it's always been." He took a gulp of lemonade. "What's he want now?"

She looked down into her glass. Sugar had settled to the bottom. She took a tentative sip.

"Ray doesn't want anything."

"I don't believe that for a minute. My son's always after something." He stretched out his legs and fingered the side of the cold glass. "He's just like his daddy."

Helen didn't look away. This Ray demanded his place at the center of things.

"He still mewling about that damn daydream?"

"Which daydream?"

"Little Ray wants to tear down his own house. Not that it surprises me."

He poured himself another glass of lemonade. Drops of water dribbled down his sides.

"You know what I'm talking about, Helen. That is, if you're my son's new friend."

Boyd. Why did she keep thinking about him here? He didn't belong in Oklahoma. He had nothing to do with this mixture of laughter and anger. She tried to think of what Boyd would do now. New friend. How many friends had Ray had? And how many did he have now?

"Ray's had this in his mind for years. Keeps wanting to blast through the floor of the house so he can watch the ocean. Last time we went through this he kept yapping about a special Plexiglas material he found out in Seattle."

Helen was wrong. She had to cut off her feelings now and think. The lemonade was bitter. It only made her more thirsty.

"Mr. Richards—"

"Ray."

It was the voice he used to command the dogs. They lay on the porch in a sleek red mound.

"Ray." She squeezed past the word. "How could he want this for years? He hasn't even owned the house for that long."

The old man pulled at the filmy white curtain and ran it over his knee. He didn't ask her to follow when he stood up, but she did. He sniffed loudly and swiped at his nose with the back of his hand.

They walked through a second room, identical in dimension to the first. The wallpaper told an epic story. Helen studied a long journey through plains and grasslands similar to the country surrounding Richardson. She held her glass tightly and stared at bison and deer, bright birds and plants that lifted the earth into a rich interior landscape. The room honored a history she knew nothing about. Short-legged Portuguese chairs were interspersed with classical pieces. The rooms seemed arranged for ghosts. Invisible seatings and dinner announcements filled the air, bidding them to come to the table.

"This is how it all started. Indians ran the country in the beginning. Ran it the right way, too. Then the oil people came in. He tell you all about how his grandpa went and named a whole town after himself?"

A formal dining table stood in the center of the last room Helen could see. An enormous basket of citrus fruits took up one end of the table. Open wine bottles and half-filled glasses littered the other. The tablecloth was sprinkled in places with crumbs and bread crusts. A rail curled like a serpent above the windows, supporting heavy floral curtains.

"Got all the history a family could want right here in this room."

Photos lined the walls, and the story of oil was written in the contorted faces and lean, muscled arms of working men. Helen's own body strained as she toured the walls of the dining room, reading deeply what she had only glanced over in textbooks. She let her eyes wander to an elaborate sideboard on the opposite wall. Hand-painted plates stood on shelves above photographs trapped in bright silver frames.

Ray Richards picked an orange from the basket. Helen watched his fingers dig into the thick skin.

"Pretty dirty business, as you can see. Like to join me, Helen?"

He held out a section of orange and smiled.

"No, thank you."

"Sure?" He held the orange crescent in the palm of his hand. Her fingers touched his as she accepted the fruit. She lifted it slowly to her mouth and let it rest on the top of her tongue. Richards watched quietly.

"I don't know what my son's been telling you. But he doesn't own a thing I don't choose to give him."

Sweet juice spread through her mouth. She chewed carefully. Her expression was unchanged.

"Part of me almost wants to give him the go-ahead on the damn house. The boy's a driller. Just like his daddy." He sucked on one end of the orange and juice dribbled down one side of his mouth. He grabbed a napkin from the table and laughed. "He's just got to dig his way down to something."

Helen moved to the sideboard. She could hear the rain now, listen to it gust and blow through open windows of the house. The storm would take on more force, she knew. This was just the beginning.

"Then *you* actually own the house in La Jolla."

"I own the house. I own the view."

Helen shuddered. Alice's strained voice had worked its way into the room. You've disturbed my favorite view. Was this what made Ray so furious? A wrongful sense of ownership that extended beyond any ocean view?

"But I haven't visited that snooty little town in years. Had a real estate fella call me years ago. Persistent man. Hard worker, too. I was awful tempted to sell."

She thought of the wild side of the coast that Boyd loved to surf. She had never been able to judge the size of the waves there. But Boyd could. She would stand too long, waiting until the wave was already running to her calves, splashing up the backs of her thighs. She would wait so long, in fact, there was never any use running.

"So he never purchased the house."

"The family bought it from a fella called Gatley back in—hell, guess it was the late twenties when my dad first found it. I decided to keep it in the family even though the thing's a curse. It tends to really heat up here in Oklahoma. I figured this family would always need a place to run to, even if it meant putting up with a few snobs."

He put his hands behind his back and walked to Helen's side. They looked at the photographs for a moment together. There were cattle ranchers and oil people, all sternly facing the turn of the century. Every face was stiff and unforgiving.

"You can see crude's a big part of our heritage." He hiked up his shorts and sniffed. "He get you knocked up, honey?"

Helen's mind floated high and free. She thought of air pressure and sudden changes in electricity, flashes of zigzagging light that cut through leaden clouds. She continued down the line of photographs, breathing steadily as she endured the progress to modern times. The faces began to smile. They invited her to step inside, and she wanted to say yes to the deception. The scenery in the photos began to change, too. There was a migration to kinder climates, finer times.

"No."

"There's a load off my mind. One kid's plenty for an old man like me."

Was his only son such a burden? She turned to face him and felt the silky lining of her skirt brush against fine, strong legs. She felt Ray's eyes travel over her as this Mr. Richards took a slow assessment of her bare neck, her breasts, the thin leather belt that circled her waist. Had Ray lied to spare her this man? Or had he just lied? And to whom? This old man had destroyed one reason for coming here, and Helen needed another to replace it, if only for a moment. She needed to topple Elizabeth. She needed to break the hold that the woman still exerted over both of these men. That was reason enough to come here. She was almost at the end. The plates poised over her head showed charming domestic scenes, men and women working and playing. One of the plates was cracked. Harmony and goodwill had been artfully restored with the break barely visible.

"I'd love to meet Ray's mother." She would ogle photographs and then open the discussion. She could reverse their bizarre support for Elizabeth.

"Is that so? Then you'll have to buy yourself a ticket to Mexico."

Big Ray and Little Ray. That's the way it's always been. Two voices wrapped together over her head, merging in angry dissonance. Ray had sounded just like this with the workmen that day, accusing them with just the same voice. Helen leaned into the sideboard. She let her head fall forward slowly, though Ray Richards didn't seem to notice.

"Guess he didn't mention that. Seems like he never does. We like to joke about that."

"Joke about what, Mr. Richards?"

"Call me Ray. Oh, about how she ran off with the Mexican consul when he was just a kid." He stopped talking for a moment. Helen couldn't brighten or bluff. The dark, heavy furniture continued to support her. "You live in La Jolla?"

She nodded. The room seemed to tip and sway.

"You probably noticed he stays as far away from that beach club as he can get. Poor Ray. He can't even stand to play tennis anymore because of the memories. Don't ever mention the Jewel Ball. He's liable to go off like a firecracker."

Helen stared at his profile, peeling back the years as she did. Ray Richards Sr., tennis champ. It was him in the photo. He was her favorite player, the one in the old photo she'd seen in Alice's apartment at the Beach Club.

"Hell, he still remembers how his mama got all dressed up for the ball and never came back. We like to kid about that now. She's living down there eatin' beans, living at some damn Embassy Suites. Can you beat that?"

She had come to the end. There was only one picture she wanted to see now. She held the frame in her hands. A beautiful woman looked back at her. She wasn't a brassy blond, as Helen had hoped. She didn't wear spaghetti straps or gingham, and when the photographer urged her to smile, her face broke open with real joy. She stood beside her replica, a girl Lang's age, dressed simply with obvious taste. Helen didn't drop the picture when the front door opened with a rush and a bang.

"Hey, ladies!'" Ray Richards shouted. "Helen, I think you're ready to meet my wife and her little girl. Hell, I oughta say Ray Junior's ex-wife and ex-little girl. Becca's so grown up he probably wouldn't even know her now."

Footsteps rang through one reception room after another. He lowered his voice to a whisper the ladies wouldn't detect.

"I had to work real hard to get them to love me as much as they loved him. But by God, I did it. And when I did, Ray Junior lit out of Oklahoma for good."

Helen straightened her head and her hair just in time. Even though she was drenched, Elizabeth Richards looked radiant. So did the teenage girl at her side.

31.

"Ready for a surprise?"

Lang sat in the back seat of Ray's car. Packages and sacks surrounded him. Helen's legs were still unsteady. She had bounced all the way to the Dallas airport in a single-engine propeller plane. The connecting flight home had been almost as rough.

"We did a little shopping but that's not the surprise. Smile, Lang."

Helen's body ached as her son grinned. His chipped tooth had been repaired—but the perfect cap made the rest of his mouth look worse. Ray moved her bag from the curb to the back of his car.

"Isn't it great? We've had it set up for weeks. Haven't we, son?"

Helen leaned forward to kiss her son. His breath smelled like maple syrup. She looked down and saw an open bag of chocolate cookies in his lap. There were only a few left in the crumpled sack.

"We had him fitted for a crown a couple of weeks ago. Damn thing only cost a couple hundred bucks."

Ray opened the door for Helen and let her slide in.

"I don't know why the poor kid had to wait so long."

The door slammed shut.

"Hi, baby." Helen didn't turn around. She didn't want to look at her son. She didn't want to risk a jagged tear in her voice or his. "How'd it go?"

"Fine."

"School's almost out, Lang."

"Duh."

"Summer's almost here."

She smiled as Ray dropped into the driver's seat and eased the car into the lane exiting the airport. He was wearing cologne. The scent was rich and fecund and strangely close to his own odor. Ray's new cologne was an accumulation of him. His thick smell was all around her now.

That's not all. We're moving ahead on the rest of his mouth next week. I booked the first consultation for Monday."

"What do you mean?" Helen saw the table she had filled with dried flowers. She saw place settings that she had selected and accessories that revealed her taste and talent. Not Alice's. The work here couldn't be mistaken for anyone else's. A cold meal waited. Prosciutto and melon rested on a fat bed of tender young greens. In the center of the table, an enormous white bowl was unpleasantly packed with pasta salad. The bowl was too full, the pasta looked rammed into place. Ray reached for a bottle of red wine. Lang watched him ease the cork out of the long glass neck.

"No boy Lang's age should have to face two years with braces. Am I right, son?"

Lang shrugged and brushed the hair out of his face. He reached for the bread basket and put five fat dinner rolls in front of his plate. He tore the first one apart and smeared it with butter.

"Come on. Tell your mom what you told me."

Helen settled her face into her hands. She forced herself to observe this picture of a man and a boy. She stood outside the picture and held it at arm's length. She would be as exacting as Ray had been at the Croft Gallery, reading a picture like a book, going over and over the shadows and light. What produced the condition she saw in the painting before her?

"Honey?" Ray cocked his head suddenly and narrowed his eyes at her. "Feeling OK?"

"Great." She watched as her son separated fat from slice after slice of prosciutto. He piled all the discarded fat into a greasy mound, then pushed it into his mouth using his fingers. He slowly skinned a melon crescent and wrapped a transparent sliver of ham around the ripe orange flesh. Helen bit into an olive and swallowed more wine. It had a sharp edge, and she frowned at the label.

"Go ahead," Ray said.

"It's no big deal." Lang shook his head, as if he disagreed with his own words and rushed on. "Just that it'd be hard to start wearing braces now. Everybody's getting them off and stuff. It would look dumb."

"I looked into it. Surgery cuts the time he'd have to wear braces in half." Ray talked between eager bites of lettuce. "They're not going to call him metal mouth for long."

Ray reached out to Lang and touched him. His hand landed gently on the top of his head. Lang didn't cringe or twist his features in disgust. He didn't even jump away. It was as if he knew exactly where the hand would fall.

"Hey. More good news. I finally got your kid to eat right."

Lang filled his dirty plate with pasta salad. He spooned food into the center until the pile crashed and fell. He lowered his head and ate with horrible concentration. He reached for more bread without looking at his mother.

Helen looked down through the glass table top and saw colors rise and swirl, float round and round as if they were caught in a furious funnel of air. She watched as they settled back down into recognizable forms. When she could make out the shape of a flower again, its petals and pistils, she raised her head.

"Turns out there's a procedure for straightening out his mouth. Takes a couple of days and a couple of bucks, but this boy's worth it. He'll be back in shape in no time. Hell, with a driver's license in his back pocket, something fast and pretty sitting in the driveway and a straight white smile, this boy's gonna lay some serious pipe."

"Don't speak like that," Helen said.

Ray reached across the table and smiled. He placed a finger on her chin and rubbed it back and forth slowly, feeling along the inside of the cleft. Helen pulled away and Ray's face reddened. His voice grew softer and softer as color inflamed his cheeks and neck.

"Come on now, Helen. Lang's gonna be on the lookout for ladies before you know it. It's normal because *he's* normal." He laughed suddenly and began to clear the table. "Listen to you. Who was it got me thinking about Lang's mouth in the first place?"

I did, Helen thought as she cleared the table. I talked about Lang's mouth and Lang's wrestling scholarship. I put everything in motion. But the motion now had begun to throw her off balance. She felt loose inside, every part of her at odds with something else. Her heart ticked along at the wrong rhythm and her breaths came at odd intervals. She looked at all her son had eaten: there was not a bit of food left on the table. He had taken the side of his finger when there was nothing more to eat and wiped it across the top of his plate. He kept his finger inside his mouth for a long time, nodding his head slowly when Ray suggested a swim.

She loaded the dishwasher and turned off the kitchen light. The sound of splashing drew her outside. She watched the clear blue lozenge of water from the terrace. The water in the pool seemed to rise, flooding her chest and lungs so that she could barely breathe. Lang swam alone in the pool. He used angry, messy strokes that barely carried his body along. One arm slapped hard, then the other. His kicks were bent-kneed and feeble, those of a baby in a wading pool. He pulled himself along heavily, then clung to the edge of the pool. Ray appeared from the bathhouse. He had a snorkel in his hand and a mask.

Without speaking, Ray slid into the water and fitted the rubber tube into his mouth. Helen moved closer to the edge of the terrace and saw Lang slowly lift both arms high up over his head. He dropped to the bottom of the pool and stayed underwater, one arm wrapped over the lowest step. Ray floated face down above him with mask and snorkel. His body drifted on top of the water and Helen felt the crawl of seaweed along her own arms. A cloud of bubbles rose from the bottom of the pool, but Lang wouldn't let go of the bottom step. She began to move toward the stairs just as Ray reached down to touch her son. Ray's legs floated open as he pulled on Lang, forcing him to the surface of the water. Ray brought him up from the bottom. Helen gulped air fast and hard. She had been holding her breath along with Lang, but taking in air didn't bring relief. It brought sudden, stabbing pain. The phone shook her. But not as much as the sight of her son in Ray's arms. The embrace was punitive and loving. Lang didn't draw back.

"What the hell is going on over there?"

Boyd's voice got her breathing on track. She had to breathe right to speak.

"That bastard wouldn't let me talk to Lang while you were out of town. Every time I called he just let the phone ring on and on. I drove over once."

"What happened?"

"Gates were locked. Nobody was home. Helen?"

"Something's wrong. I want you to take Lang away from here."

"And you? What about you, Helen?"

She saw her own face in the window. The woman she saw was in terrible trouble. But she believed in the stranger she saw.

"Give me about an hour. Then come and get our son."

"You haven't told me a thing about your trip."

Ray sat in an armchair by the bed. She could see him from the mirror in the bathroom. He flipped through one of her design magazines, licking his finger and setting it down on the top of each page. He wore a dark-blue robe with the belt loosely knotted. She raised the mirror a bit and stared. The skin on his chest was tanned too dark.

"Productive. Long. I missed you guys," she said.

"Missed you, too, honey."

He didn't look up from the magazine, but continued to scan pages. He dropped the magazine to the floor and picked up another from a stack on the floor.

"Got a surprise for you," Helen said.

"Great. I've got one for you, too."

She put a drop of perfume behind her ear and combed her hair, taking deep breaths with every conscientious stroke. She watched her body with curiosity, as if she'd never seen herself brush her hair or bend over the sink to cup water with her hands. Two flute glasses stood side by side on a gilded tray. The glasses were tinged with pinks and purples. Pastels seemed to ripple through at intervals, sometimes coloring the clear glass, sometimes disappearing altogether. She poured champagne carefully, then carried the tray into the bedroom. The solid weight calmed her.

"Wow. I'll have to get you to leave us more often."

"You're forgetting one thing. I left on my own."

"Guess I've got more in common with Boyd than I thought."

She felt his eyes settle on her breasts as she crossed the room. She bent to set the tray on her desk.

"Now it's you who's forgetting something. You know I can't drink."

"And what if I don't believe you? What if I think it's all in your head?"

He reached for her as she leaned forward, pinching her nipple between his thumb and forefinger.

"Not so fast," Helen laughed. A little of the champagne spilled and she frowned.

"Fast." Ray came around behind her before she had time to turn. He pulled her legs apart and pushed inside quickly, then put his hands on top of hers. Notes from work, notes about school lay under Helen's hands. All the mundane details that moved life forward. Helen watched her breasts and the tops of the glasses. She moved her legs farther back and farther apart, forcing their bodies away from the tray. Ray's breathing was private and harsh. His motions, not hers, had taken him far away. Helen closed her eyes and waited. Then she felt herself respond to him and prayed, despising herself for the late hour. What sort of god would listen now? She bent her head and invoked a dead preacher instead. She prayed to him and saw his pitiless face glare from a wine-glass pulpit. She was filled with shame as she passed through this last wicked crack in the world. She prayed first for Lang and then for herself as pleasure became pain. Was it too late to save her son? Was it too late to save the sinner?

He breathed hard and squeezed the tops of her hands. She had pursued Ray Richards. She had wanted him long before he wanted her. Details of her own desire careened. Then they exploded in her mind.

"You're wild, Helen. You are so fucking wild."

They straightened together. Helen felt the strange unity and squirmed.

"Cold? Here, you go, baby."

He wrapped her inside his robe, dirtying her happily. Her thighs, her small, round belly. He rubbed himself contentedly against Helen. Ray Richards loved her for the first time. His passion felt simple and young. His body was boyish and alert, crazily attuned to Helen's shifts and sighs.

"Come on, Ray. Have some of this Cristal with me. It cost a fortune."

"Did it?" He closed his eyes and breathed. "Did it feel good to splurge?"

"Yes." Helen's eyes were open.

"Tell me first what you did. How was this Hollis?"

"Very strange. Too talented to be in Oklahoma."

"What'd you say?"

"I said she's strange."

"No, Helen. You said she was too talented to be in Oklahoma."

"Well, I meant Texas." Helen saw the two of them as they must have seemed. Wrapped in blue, tousled and pink skinned. Lovers. She went on carefully. "Ray, I was *so* close. It was all I could do not to have you fly over and meet me. But I didn't know if Richardson was near an airport. I got a little crazy. I decided I didn't even know the man I was living with."

Ray pressed the back of her head with one hand.

"Now you know that's not right. Don't you?"

His hand rubbed her skull as she nodded. She pulled away for a moment and handed him his glass, and they drank a toast to their new life. He drank the whole glass down and she kissed his chest. He reached behind her for another glass and burped politely over her head.

"Damn. This is like sody-pop." He drank the rest of his champagne. Then he held Helen's glass to her lips and tilted it, laughing as a few drops splashed on her breasts. He continued to tilt the glass and her throat rushed to do its work, opening wider and wider.

"That's my girl."

Ray moved nervously under the robe. He lifted her breast and examined it. Then he let it fall lifelessly from his hand. The robe slipped from his shoulders. He turned the desk light up to the maximum setting.

"Stay put."

Helen looked at herself under the light. She saw everything. Here were all the flaws she hadn't wanted him to see, illuminated as the light shone matter-of-factly. Ray squatted down on all fours. She watched him and as she did, his house opened up into another house filled with a progression of painted scenes. Dark fruit dangled from strange trees. Animals spread out in ambiguous formations. He reached for something underneath his bed.

"Little something for my little girl." He held a box in his hand.

Helen came forward on bare feet, legs trembling slightly. It was as pretty as anything Patricia had ever wrapped with her clever hands. Ray's eyes began to relax along with his mouth. He sat down suddenly on the bed and touched his forehead.

"For you," he said. He looked at the room and the lamps and the precious paintings filling one wall. "It's all for you."

As she opened the box he lay back on down pillows. She lifted her arms and let the nightgown drop over her head. "Man, you really knocked me out. Do you like it, Helen?"

"Mmmm."

His eyes closed for a split-second, then opened again with difficulty. "What is it you want to know?"

She stood still as his hand moved over the frilly pink nightgown. He ran his hand down her bottom, then scraped the tender skin between her legs. Helen held herself steady. Ray extinguished the last of his desire by touching her.

"I want to know who you are."

"I'm Ray Richards from Richardson, Oklahoma. It's named after my grandfather. He made a fortune in the oil business selling pipe. Damn, you look sweet."

Helen lay beside him, pushing at the ruffles that choked her. Did he buy you lots of pretty things? Boyd's question seemed to throw a shadow over her body. Steve Mason had bought her lovely things. Things she had hidden and coveted and stupidly treasured. Helen pushed away memory and shivered in the bed. The material was scratchy. It chafed her breasts and hips.

"Why didn't you tell me about your father, Ray?" She slipped her hand under his neck, tried to tip the words out faster.

"Why would I? I've got you and Lang now. I took back what was taken from me."

Helen's hand tightened on his neck. "You should have told me all the horrible things that happened to you."

He turned his head on the pillow. His eyelids drooped, but before they closed completely, Helen caught one last real glimpse of Ray, the man she'd pursued from the beginning.

"You never really wanted to hear all those details." His eyes clouded over. He stopped struggling as darkness screened out amber light. "Quit lying, Helen. You've known who I am all along."

32.

Helen dressed quickly as Ray's snoring deepened. She moved down the hall, pausing at the door to Rebecca's room. Moonlight glazed the walls and ceiling of the frozen and featureless room. No one slept in the bed or peered through the telescope at a starry sky. Helen stepped lightly, feeling her way across the wooden floor. She touched the bed-spread and the grandfather clock. She ran her hand over the sharp edge of a dresser.

She moved toward a detail she didn't recognize. Something new stood on Rebecca's desk and it drew her along, urging her to touch and recognize with the skin on her hands.

Helen held the Lladró figurine. She touched the tiny nose of the porcelain girl and the thin ribbon in her hair. She stroked the back of the minute bird she held in her hands. He had added this to the room while she was away, dragging it out of the back of a closet or drawer. Ray was finished hiding things. She took a deep breath and set it back where it had been. She hurried down the dark hall toward Lang's room.

Helen's arms and legs went so soft she thought she might fall. A tan-gle of sheets and blankets lay beside his empty bed. He had plugged in an old night light. Mickey Mouse grinned from a socket in the corner of the disheveled room. All that Lang owned carpeted the room. Helen moved toward his closet through piles of clothing and empty sacks. She tripped over the things Ray had bought him. Mounds of shirts and slacks, white socks and white polos lay in a messy line. Helen followed this path to his closet door. It hung open and she ordered her body to breathe as she walked.

Hangers marched along the double rod in straight, empty formation. Lang lay curled up in a corner of the empty closet. He slept without pillow or blanket. His thin, muscled body was bare except for tight Jockey shorts sized for a much younger boy. The shorts should have been thrown out years before. Why hadn't *she* thrown them out? Helen's heart beat dutifully. She could feel its sullen work inside her chest. She knelt beside her son and placed one hand firmly over his mouth. His eyes flashed open. His head struck the back of the closet wall and he struggled wide-eyed out of sleep and dreams.

"Be real quiet, honey. Put some clothes on." Her throat was sore even though she whispered. It felt like she'd been screaming for hours.

"What about Ray?"

"He's asleep. He won't bother you anymore, honey."

He let her hold his hand as he rose from the closet floor. He stepped on the back of her heels as she closed the door, and he lurched as the wooden floors squeaked under his feet.

"It's OK, Lang. Don't be afraid."

He made a sound she'd never heard before. It was a cough and a cry that twisted free of his body, then broke away from both of them. She could see his body shaking by the light of a bright moon.

"Dad's coming over."

"How come?"

"I need his help. He's coming to take you away."

Helen heard the ocean lash at the shoreline under the cover of darkness. Lang slumped against the window with a blanket pulled up to his chin, his head sinking lower into its soft, protective folds. He tiptoed across the room and his hand reached out from under the blanket to punch in the lock on the door.

"Why am I running away now?" *Now.* He looked out the window as a car passed. He evenly beat the back of his hand against the window as if he were ticking away the seconds.

"I found out all about Ray on my trip. I saw where he grew up and I met his father. I found out he's been lying."

"Lying about what?"

"Rebecca's not ten. She's about your age. I saw her for myself."

He beat his hand harder against the glass.

"So she didn't get kidnapped?"

"It was all a lie. She lives with her mother." Helen thought of saying more and didn't. She blinked at a car that was moving too slowly. Was it Boyd? What was the driver doing?

"So nothing happened to her. Right?" He struck the glass again.

"Right."

She thought of Ray's car and the safety it insinuated, then pressed on Lang's arm.

"Dad's probably going to crash the car." He didn't say it with sadness or alarm. His voice was stripped of emotion. "Dad will probably never get here."

Lang shuffled to his desk and turned on the radio with a blast.

"Lang!"

He kept his hand on the knob. The volume stayed at the same level. Loud noise shook the bedroom walls.

"You're going to wake him," Helen had to shout. He snapped the knob hard to the left. It came off in his hand.

"It doesn't matter if he wakes up or if Dad crashes the car. It's too late."

The silence inside his room sounded like a scream. She reached out to touch him and he lunged away from her, hitting his head on the window.

"How come it's OK for you to lie, Mom?"

"Stop doing that, Lang."

One strike triggered others. He hit his head again, this time harder. He banged his head the way he banged his hand, every rough blow equaled another moment gone.

"Then tell me how come."

"What are you talking about?"

Another car rolled past. She could see the black, sleeping heads through the windows of the car. Where were they being carried? And by whom? She wished she could close her eyes and be driven away from the sound of Lang's voice and the sound of dull thud after thud. She blinked away a quick vision of blood on glass.

"You never told me we left Dad because of some guy. I thought it was Dad's fault! I *made* everything his fault after that."

"How do you know about that?"

"Ray said. He told me I was lucky to be here because if I wasn't, I might be living with a real creep. Like that guy from before."

"I'm so sorry, Lang."

"You lied to me. You lied to everyone. You still do."

He dove deeper inside the blanket and lay down on the floor.

"Talk, Mom. Say something."

Helen shivered and knelt beside him. She looked down at her son and peeled herself away from him and what she was feeling inside. She began to talk, resting one hand on the warm heap beside her. She could feel his shoulder under the blanket. He moved now and then as she told harmless stories, old stories gathered from the time when he was small and happy, just a little boy steering toward her with his hands wide open.

"I've got to use the bathroom."

He had taken all the posters off the wall. All the things she had bought him were hidden from view. Lang's room was as featureless as a motel room. There could have been a coffee machine on his chest of drawers and plastic curtains and broken tiles. The room had an exhausted air. Families on their way to vacations and reunions would never pull over here for a night. This room could never be a planned stop, a good night's sleep before a rowdy gathering of people connected by blood and by marriage, happiness and love.

She stroked the edge of his pillow and opened the drawer of his nightstand. There was a red Gideon's Bible in one corner of the drawer.

There were pencils and paper, a guide to attractions and events. Lang had been to Mexico. She lay the tourist brochure on his pillow.

"You want to tell me about this?"

"I was never there."

He grabbed the brochure and turned to face the wall. He slowly ripped the paper apart, faster as the pieces floated down around him. Mexico lay on the floor in shreds. Helen scooped the bits and pieces up in the palm of her hand and wrapped them in a Kleenex. She squeezed them into a hard ball and threw them away. Obeying instinct now, Helen tore back the sheets on Lang's bed and stared. Blood spotted the white surface. She covered her face with her hands for a moment, then let them drop to her sides.

"Lang! My God, what's wrong?"

She saw his body as if for the first time. His neck looked so white, so vulnerable. It worked hard, holding his heavy head high on the first day of classes. It sprung free of a pair of grappling, sweaty hands during a match or strained high and hard to let Lang peer above the heads of taller boys. How easy it would be to damage the source of so much strength. Helen stroked the base of his hairline with one finger and he jumped away. She'd never seen his power and fragility before now.

"I'm not who you think. I'm not Lang anymore."

All at once Lang turned and took hold of her waist. His head struggled into her lap, pushing and pressing into her belly so hard it felt like a blow. He dragged her down in the darkness with cries and moans, hot hands that wouldn't let her go.

"Mommy!"

She lay beside her son as tears wet the front of her clothing. She blew her own warm breath into his neck as he wept and cursed. She felt what Ray had done to her son as his body lay stretched alongside her own. She tried to cover him with her arms and legs, to protect him from all that had happened, every blow that he had suffered because of her lies and her longing. She spoke true words near the open lips of her damaged son until his cries softened to gasps. She held him in her arms as his gasps narrowed to silence. In the quiet that followed, an assortment of fragmented words arranged themselves in Helen's mind. They appeared as chipped, misshapen beads, and she watched as they squeezed together to form a question. The hideous necklace of sound and shape and meaning tightened around Helen's throat. She couldn't say another word. She couldn't ask another question.

33.

Boyd kicked his way toward the sidewalk. He walked faster, his eye on the left wing. He knew the layout of the rooms. He knew where Lang slept, which rooms were reserved for the children and which one had the master bath with the side porch. He remembered the old conversation like it was this afternoon. I intend to keep the property in the family, Mr. Patterson. What else had he heard in Richards's voice that day?

Boyd heard music swell inside the house. The music decomposed structure and form. Instruments turned out harsh, separate sounds. He started to walk around to the side door, sure he wouldn't be heard there because of the noise.

"Looking for someone?"

Boyd closed his eyes at the sharp poke in his back. He kept his hands at his sides.

"My son."

"You're trespassing, Boyd. Guess we've got a few choices here."

The music was louder than before.

"I could shoot you."

Something hard nudged Boyd's spine.

"Or I could invite you in for a drink. What should I do, Boyd?"

"Depends." Boyd styled his voice, put a playful flip at the end. He could hear the man behind him breathing. He listened to the breeze work his shirt like a sail.

"No kidding. On what?"

"On what you've got to drink."

Ray Richards laughed. "Go on inside."

It was a shotgun. Boyd was surprised he hadn't figured it out sooner. There was so much he hadn't figured out. That girl, the tutor. He had thought that she was the problem. He reddened suddenly. The gun was still pushing him along, though not in the spine now. He still hadn't seen Ray Richards's face. He didn't know what he would do when he did.

"Door's unlocked."

They faced the kitchen. Helen was everywhere. Her taste had finally been satisfied by real things, not just pictures in magazines or the hasty sketches he'd found all through their marriage. He'd find sketches everywhere, in drawers where he was only looking for a restaurant guide or a phone book. She'd put everything she'd yearned for into the house at Gatley Point. He could tell just from what he saw through the kitchen window.

"Some place."

"Helen knows her business. I have to say that much for her."

"Where's my boy?"

"Push."

The gun pushed against his back and he pushed against the door. Before he hadn't thought it was loaded. No way it was full of bullets. Richards was too careless. He handled it like it was a toy. But now that changed. Boyd's body took the cue and he felt the top of his skin change. Fear began to crawl toward him on all fours. It was easy, recognizable. He begged it to come near and work its old magic on him.

Metal banged down on glass.

"So. We meet."

Boyd began to turn around slowly. His face didn't match the voice he remembered. The *voice* didn't match the voice. "We've already met."

Ray Richards held his hands out and examined them front and back. "We may have met. But we didn't shake." He reached out to Boyd with his right hand. "I'd know it if we ever did."

Richards's hand was like the wrong side of a sponge. Boyd thought of the way this hand might have reached out to Lang in an angry slap. He imagined it scraping over Helen's skin.

"We had a telephone conversation years ago. I wanted to sell your house for you."

Ray Richards hadn't let go of his hand. He was a big son of a bitch, but his body was slack and easy. He wouldn't last long on the water, Boyd knew.

"You sound different than you did seven years ago."

He poured whiskey into one glass. Boyd studied the kitchen, wondering what Lang did here when he was hungry. He thought of his son's thin torso, the intricate puzzle of bones and skin. The gun was really a length of pipe. It lay across a table topped with glass. Boyd moved closer.

"Don't touch it. That belongs to me." Ray handed him a whiskey. "To friends."

He watched Boyd take a long drink.

"Come on inside," Ray said.

"Thought I already was."

"This is nothing."

Boyd passed through the open door of the kitchen and tried to remember where he was. He didn't want to get lost now. He heard movement in another room. The scurry of someone running past them.

"Lang?"

He heard Helen call out. Her voice was far away, yet it felt suspended in the space where he stood.

"Helen blew it, you know."

It was pretty here, comfortable. Boyd thought of Helen wrapped inside the satin comforter he saw thrown over the arm of a chair. Blasts of music beat back the sound of the waves. Ray pointed to a window, a funny-shaped upstairs window.

"I watch her from up there. When she's cleaning up or reading. Or working on homework with your son. She really had me going tonight."

They went into the library and Boyd took a deep breath of whiskey. He didn't drink anymore, just invited a little into his lungs. He heard a quick series of steps over his head, then the sound of something heavy being moved. Lang must have been right above him. He could see the old blueprint of the house in his brain. Boyd took a chair across from Ray.

"Helen got me to drink some of her sweet champagne. I guess she figured it'd be like putting a baby down for a nap. Except the baby woke up."

Why had Helen waited so long? She should have run the minute this guy had her in his sights. He wondered where he had kept the pipe hidden all this time. Ray tipped his head and studied him with a changing face. Boyd slowed down inside. Ray's eyes switched to sugar eyes, burning down into gold caramel. Everything counted now that they had turned that color.

"Hey," Ray rubbed his hands together. "Helen's really something in bed. You teach her all that stuff?"

Slow. Slow down. Boyd could feel the coach's hands on his shoulders, the imperative in his fingertips. Get rid of it, Boy! Slowly. Not all at once. And it worked, too. The release of hatred, anger. Joy! Performing was gradual and alert. Performing wasn't acting at all. It was a true accretion of movement and speech. He thought of Steve Mason, who was so far away now. Mason didn't matter. Mason was a dry, dull dress rehearsal.

"You bet." Boyd held his glass up in the air and turned his hand so the light shone on his ring. It displayed the profile of a phony king and it made Boyd look like a pimp if he had on the right suit, or a stamp collector if he didn't. The king was fake but the stones were real. He kept it in the glove compartment of the Volvo.

"What's that?"

"Ah, some old ring my dad gave me. Sentimental."

Ray blinked hard. "Refresh my memory. What exactly did we talk about?"

"Price. The market out here was hot. But I couldn't budge you."

"I'll tell you a little secret, Boyd." Ray liked secrets. He patted the top of his leg. "You talked to my father in ninety-two."

"There are two of you?"

Ray shifted in his seat. He wouldn't stay there long. Boyd set his drink to one side.

"No. And there never were. It's just a name we have in common. I'm nothing like him."

"Your dad sure treated me like dirt," Boyd said.

"Oklahoma dirt sticks to your boots. It won't ever come off."

Ray got up and pushed a painting to one side. There was a panel on the wall and he pressed a button. The music stopped. The noise was over for the evening. Ray opened the window and lowered his voice. "This place was always hell on earth. Even when I was a little kid. Especially when I was a little kid."

Boyd waited, his eyes on the tapestry along the wall.

"I got him back, though. I always get my father back."

Boyd could see the silky shine and the way it was worn in spots. It was probably worth hundreds of thousands. Ray dragged his hand hard over the surface. The clasp of his watch tore the fragile golden threads.

"He'd make me mad and I'd make him sick."

Boyd's job now was to listen.

"I figured if he treated me like an animal, I'd act like one. I'd piss all over my bedroom upstairs. Corners, sideboards." Ray grinned. "Helen almost found out when she redid the floors. That was a close call."

Footsteps pounded upstairs and a door slammed shut. Ray's eyes lost their focus. They roamed the room, trailing over beautiful details.

"I had to trap your wife, you know. I had to put all the things she loves outside in a big basket. Then I pulled it in closer and closer. I spent a lot of money on Helen."

Nothing moved on Boyd's face.

"That's not all I spent." Ray looked grim. His happiness passed as resentments were remembered and relived. "I talked to her. They love that, you know. Most of them love it more than fucking."

Boyd watched the tapestry, the man in the trees.

"And then she does this to me. Knocks me out on purpose." Ray's laugh sounded like a dry cough. "I invested in him, too."

Boyd kept everything down low. His weight was dropping fast, falling into his fists and the back of his legs.

"Yeah, I spent all this time with Lang. I taught him to drive. I listened to him and I'll tell you, it wasn't *real* fascinating."

Boyd stood slowly. He was thinking of a blueprint now. It was taking shape in his mind. He remembered something important. Something that lay in the wall of the room. He'd found out, too. It hadn't come out in the blueprint. It had come out in the conversation with the other Ray Richards. The old man had told him about a secret in the room, just before he pulled out of the game altogether. That was the basket he'd laid out for Boyd. One yank and it was gone. There was a door in the room that led to the ocean. Gatley loved tricks. So does the Richards family. That's why my old man bought the damn place.

"Your boy's fine, he's not a retard or anything. But after hours of listening to him whine, your eyes kind of glaze over."

"Lang's young."

"Yeah, but I'm not telling you things you don't know. It's boring, right? I mean, how much talking have you done to him lately?"

A boat was out there on a night sail. They could both see its lights from the window as it bobbed on the water. On another night, the light of that boat would have truly shone. But now it looked dim and lost, floating and unmoored forever. Boyd's arm bumped against Ray.

"Not much."

"Of course not. How do you think a guy like me got inside in the first place?"

"What do you mean by that?"

"I mean I gave your wife and your boy exactly what they wanted. It sure wasn't coming from you." Ray paused. "This is pretty basic stuff."

Helen stood at the entrance to the library. She wore an old shirt. Her legs were bare and strong beneath it. Boyd could just see the top of her breasts. She wasn't afraid.

"What the hell did you do to Lang?" she shouted. "I'm calling the police."

"You're so stupid, Helen. That's not how these things work."

"Where is he? He's hiding somewhere and you know where he is."

Boyd listened to Helen. Her breathing competed with the sound of the waves. Someone barbecued on the beach. Boyd could smell cooked meat, hear the pops of laughter that meant there was a clown in the group, a guy like him, a crowd pleaser. He hung on to that laughter in his mind.

"Show me that staircase. You've got some kind of secret staircase here," Boyd said.

"It's not secret. It's hidden." Ray put his palm on the windowpane and rubbed over it in slow circles. "They're not the same."

Ray's gaze made Boyd's body want to lunge forward. He had to control that, push it back down.

"It's right behind the tapestry." Ray took his shirt out of his pants. He flopped the shirttail back and forth several times and whistled. "It's heating up in here. Or is it me?"

The tapestry was mounted on a recessed track. Helen jerked one edge of the hanging and it moved along the wall, exposing a wide double door. The plaster around the door looked damp and soft. The water below refused containment. Slow ruin climbed higher and higher. How had she failed to see this? Helen yanked the cane bolt that secured the door. The metal handle complained and she ground her teeth together.

"Hurry up, Helen. I hate that noise," Ray said.

The bolt slipped free of the latch. Helen fell back a step and stared down at the long metal rod. She tightened her grip, then turned to look at Ray.

The three of them stood together at the top of the stairs. Helen peered down into darkness and forced her eyes to see. Her vision cleared with aching slowness. She could see steps that began wide, then narrowed with the hard curves, as cunning as the tight passage from land to water. Spongy yellow growth coated the inside of the cave. Helen thought of the rooms behind her. All delicacy and delight stopped here.

She opened her hand and dropped the bolt. Ray flinched at the racket it made.

The smell struck Boyd squarely in the face. It was immediate, rank. It was a smell saved up for years and years. The richness of rot cleared Boyd's head. He savored it, breathed it in like good whiskey, then took the first step. Each wooden plank groaned. They were old cries, accustomed to painful weight.

"Your boy liked this place. We came down here sometimes."

Ray moved past him and Boyd held on to the rail, then reached for the rocky wall. Lamps lit the way. They sputtered and burned, converting darkness to shadow.

"You're disappointing, Boyd. You're not as fun as I thought you'd be."

Boyd kept his hands moving along the slick wall. Helen stayed close behind him.

"I'm the one who feels like crap," Ray continued. He didn't take another step. Ray turned all the way around to look at Boyd. There were so many steps to the bottom. "Unbelievable. She fucked me and made me drink when she knows I can't. Ray Richards could never hold his liquor."

"What?" Boyd didn't disguise the dumb syllable. He thought of the old man, his voice on the phone. Something moved along the wall at the bottom of the stairs. He saw a shadow bend and burrow deeper into darkness. He felt Helen's hand on his back. She steadied him now.

"I was out for a little while. How do you think he got away?"

Boyd shook his head. He heard something inside his skull, something hard and rocky sang to him. The harsh music struck again and again inside his head.

"Helen's so stupid. She probably thought I'd sleep forever."

"Why did you hurt him?" Helen's voice blasted through the cave. The mad sounds seemed to have no source. Her fury filled every inch of the damp hole. Boyd's chest moved up and down. The shadow at the bottom of the cave tightened, then disappeared.

"I didn't hurt Lang. You did, Helen." Ray shook his head.

Her teeth felt soft, as if she had received a slap so hard they had all come loose. She felt the side of her jaw with her hand, surprised at how cool it was. The dampness seeped into her skin. This cold would coat her face and her bare legs for a long, long time. Helen spoke softly now.

"You're crazy and cruel, but you're right. I did hurt my own son. And I'm sorry. God, I'm sorry." The new words had a hard, clean sound as she said them. She felt amazed at being able to speak at all.

"Full confession." Ray laughed hard and wiped his eyes with his shirt sleeve. "You're the best, Helen."

Ray faced Boyd again. He took his hand off the rail and rubbed it up and down his leg, wiping the palm wildly, as if the dirt would never come off.

"You want to go farther?" Ray asked.

"Yeah. Yeah, I do." Boyd took another step down, came closer. He stood directly above him, at a height Ray Richards permitted. Boyd forced himself to take small, steady breaths.

"Your turn to confess, Ray." He squeezed sounds into the small space between them.

"Confess what?" Ray had burned right down to the bottom of the pan. Blackened, burned sugar filled his eyes.

"That you raped our son."

Helen flinched and touched stone with the flat of her hand. The words were finally released. They flew through the cave, black as bats. She leaned against the rocky wall as they rushed toward her. She felt them settle on her shoulders. She felt them inside her hair, trapped and twisting their caped wings.

Boyd's words had scattered all the layers of stale odors to reveal their dead source. The smell of bile rose from Ray. He spat, then his tongue passed over his lips.

"Let's get something real straight. I took care of Lang. I gave your son exactly what he needed." His mouth twisted as he spoke.

Lang crept out from behind a jagged stone curtain. A wave struck his body as his screams ricocheted. They struck Boyd's head and heart from all sides. Fear had finally given way to rage. It gave him solid weight. It held him firmly on the steps, steady and strong. As he reached for Ray

Richards, Boyd embraced memory. A fierce hug, one last hard knock that signaled affection. He remembered the strangeness of Lang's chest against his, a match between a mismatched father and son. He had never hugged him like that again. Shyness? Fear again, a different kind? Boyd felt for the air and the answer, then struck hard. He pushed the white shirt with strength and watched Ray's head snap back. Ray's falling was final. A full, thick sound, solid weight on swaybacked steps. His arms flailed in a bright white shirt, then stopped. A rock below turned radiant and red. Ray's mouth fell open slowly to receive the dark water.

34.

"It might turn out okay," Patricia said.

Helen watched silently as the team of workers moved through the garden. The roses had already been uprooted. A long trench marked the edge of the lawn. Landscaping work pressed most heavily on the pair of Japanese maples. Their heavy trunks seemed to bend lower than ever in the raw, open space. Stan had driven a delivery out to see the demolition for himself. He unloaded a few pieces, then ate lunch standing up. His weightlifter's belt lay on the grass beside him. Even though he was in the way, not one of the workers asked him to move.

"I mean, even though she's a complete princess, she does have pretty good taste."

Helen didn't bother to turn her head. Fatigue was her constant companion now. She was exhausted even if she happened to sleep. She took some comfort from the cloud that had settled over everything. It was weather that wouldn't change any time soon.

"It might even be like the Louvre." Patricia had spent her last week practicing patience. She said she would need it in New York City. You couldn't afford to snap in a city like that. You had to train yourself to repeat slowly, to explain things in simple terms. Like if a cabdriver didn't hear you, say. You would just give him the address all over again. "They threw that awful pyramid up in front of an ancient building. At first everybody was horrified. Then they just got used to it."

The Princess had purchased both Alice Nash Design and the property next door. There was breathy talk of building a petite maison there, a secret house for secret love affairs. Clients would pass from a public garden to something more discreet. A leafy green passage would lure clients to a *very* different shopping experience. Patricia and Alice laughed when the Princess had said that, but Helen hadn't. What was funny about that? Everything seemed distant and incomprehensible now. But Patricia seemed content to repeat sentences, messages, jokes that Helen could no longer hear.

Helen left the view from the bedroom and returned to the stack of press kits on her desk. It was easy to admire them and easier still to assemble each packet. Alice's statement about her new textile line had a happy lilt. A writer had captured the exact sound of Alice's speech, the emphasis on certain words that Helen knew by heart. Reading the words on the page before night fell almost became a private conversation. Almost. Helen drank tea and sipped milk, reading Alice on Lyons, Alice on pleasure. Alice on the history of the fabric and the shape of the future of furnishings. Helen would think about the shape of her future and lay the paper aside.

"I'll help." Patricia settled in next to her. She wore White Shoulders cologne. The cheap scent made her giggle. She even used it as air freshener in the upstairs bathroom. She squirted it into the air and rattled on about Neddy. How Neddy would follow her to New York if he could. It had taken him forever to grow up, she sighed.

"These fabrics are super. Don't you think, Helen?"

Helen turned to her with a smile. Patricia had become a comfort, too. She was precisely who she was, without shadow or nuance. She understood a clear victory. She had won and she could afford kindness. Patricia would study design at Parsons. She would work in the city for the years it took to build a reputation, then return to La Jolla once the rite of passage was complete. It would be fun to compete with the Princess. She would pop out a few babies with Neddy when it came time. Patricia. Patrician. Helen remembered an old coin she'd been given by the aunts along with a long, precise definition of the term.

"So do you feel just awful?" Patricia's voice quivered. "I mean, you were living there with your son and all. And then the accident."

"Yes." Helen knew how to respond without answering. She had learned to satisfy appetites she understood.

"How is Lang?" Patricia made a mistake, sliding two photos inside a shiny white packet instead of one. Helen reached inside and took one of them out.

"Holding up."

She remembered Patricia's backpack and her aversion to meat. She wondered if Neddy would join her in New York. What school would have him? As she considered Neddy's possibilities, her thoughts glided away from her son. She let them wander a bit. They didn't roam far now.

"I could maybe suggest someone for him."

"He's fine."

"His French next year—"

"He's dropping it."

They stuffed packets for a while. She wasn't nearly as fast as Patricia. Voices drifted in through the open windows and Helen could smell the earth being turned outside. Alice was struggling up the steps, helping Poor as he heaved himself along.

"There!" She made it to the top of the steps. The dog looked less pitiful than before. Helen didn't know why, but seeing bandaged, bleak Poor in a corner no longer made sad wings beat against her chest. He had a broken paw, that was all. Nothing less, nothing more.

"I say we put him on an immediate diet."

"Moved and seconded!" Patricia cried. "I don't like fat things."

"Good progress, you two," Alice said, turning to Helen's desk.

She came near Helen and peered at a sample packet, stopping to frown at her photograph.

"Good God. I've completely lost my looks."

Helen looked up from the work and studied the face of the woman she had once loved. She still saw bold, careless beauty. She must once have thought it was a wonderful thing to possess. But it was as if Helen had been away on a long trip and the strangeness of return still lingered. She couldn't understand the words she heard now. Her stillness inside, her failure to properly hear made her wonder if it wasn't really Helen who had lost Alice's looks. Lost them mindlessly, as a careless traveler would.

"Helen?"

She had turned her head once, in a moment that now seemed as long as an entire lifetime. She had let go of a small boy's trusting hand and looked away. When she returned her gaze to where it should have been all along, the most precious thing she possessed was gone.

About the Author

Linda Phillips Ashour, author of *Speaking in Tongues, Joy Baby,* and *Sweet Remedy,* has been published in *The Paris Review, North American Review,* and *The New York Times Book Review.* She teaches writing at UCLA Extension and has been a fellow at Yaddo. She lives in Los Angeles, California.